#6

MY BOYFRIEND IS A MONSTER

Wrapped Up in You

OR

MUMMY CAN'T BUY ME LOVE

OR

MUMMY DEAREST

OR

TRUE LOVE WAITS FIVE HUNDRED YEARS

OR

A RUN FOR HER MUMMY

OR

LOVE INCAN-TATION

OR

HOW TO PRESERVE A RELATIONSHIP

DAN JOLLEY

Illustrated by NATALIE NOURIGAT

GRAPHIC UNIVERSE™ · MINNEAPOLIS · NEW YORK

STORY BY
DAN JOLLEY

ILLUSTRATIONS BY
NATALIE NOURIGAT

LETTERING BY
GRACE LU

COVER COLORING BY
JENN MANLEY LEE

Copyright © 2012 by Lerner Publishing Group, Inc.

Graphic Universe™ is a trademark of Lerner Publishing Group, Inc.

Graphic Universe™
A division of Lerner Publishing Group, Inc.
241 First Avenue North
Minneapolis, MN 55401 U.S.A.

Website address: www.lernerbooks.com

Main body text set in CCWildwords. Typeface provided by Comicraft Design.

Library of Congress Cataloging-in-Publication Data

Jolley, Dan.
    Wrapped up in you / by Dan Jolley ; illustrated by Natalie Nourigat.
        p.   cm. — (My boyfriend is a monster; #6)
    Summary: North Carolina eighteen-year-old Staci tries to keep her friend Faith safe from a group of witches but winds up helping the Incan mummy the group has reanimated, who also happens to be very attractive and charming.
    ISBN: 978–0–7613–6856–4 (lib. bdg. : alk. paper)
    1. Graphic novels. [1. Graphic novels. 2. Horror stories. 3. Mummies—Fiction. 4. Witches—Fiction. 5. North Carolina—Fiction.] I. Nourigat, Natalie, ill. II. Title.
PZ7.7.J65Wr 2012
741.5'973—dc23   2011044655

Manufactured in the United States of America
1 – PP – 7/15/12

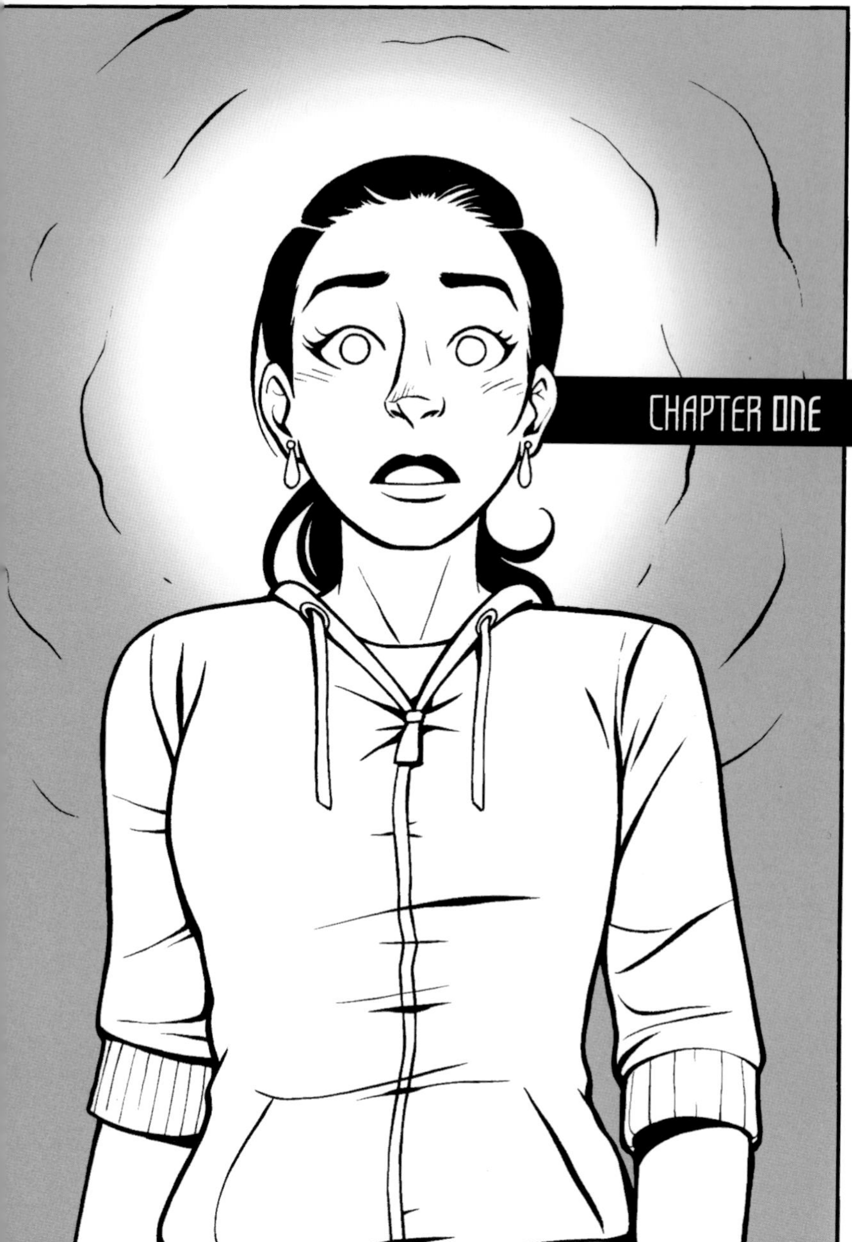

CHAPTER ONE

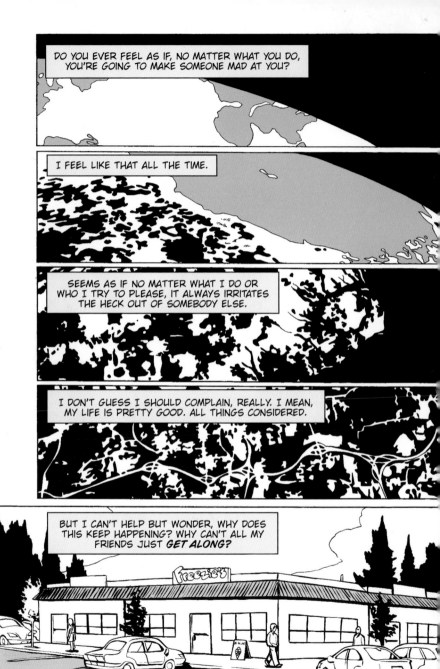

DO YOU EVER FEEL AS IF, NO MATTER WHAT YOU DO, YOU'RE GOING TO MAKE SOMEONE MAD AT YOU?

I FEEL LIKE THAT ALL THE TIME.

SEEMS AS IF NO MATTER WHAT I DO OR WHO I TRY TO PLEASE, IT ALWAYS IRRITATES THE HECK OUT OF SOMEBODY ELSE.

I DON'T GUESS I SHOULD COMPLAIN, REALLY. I MEAN, MY LIFE IS PRETTY GOOD. ALL THINGS CONSIDERED.

BUT I CAN'T HELP BUT WONDER, WHY DOES THIS KEEP HAPPENING? WHY CAN'T ALL MY FRIENDS JUST *GET ALONG?*

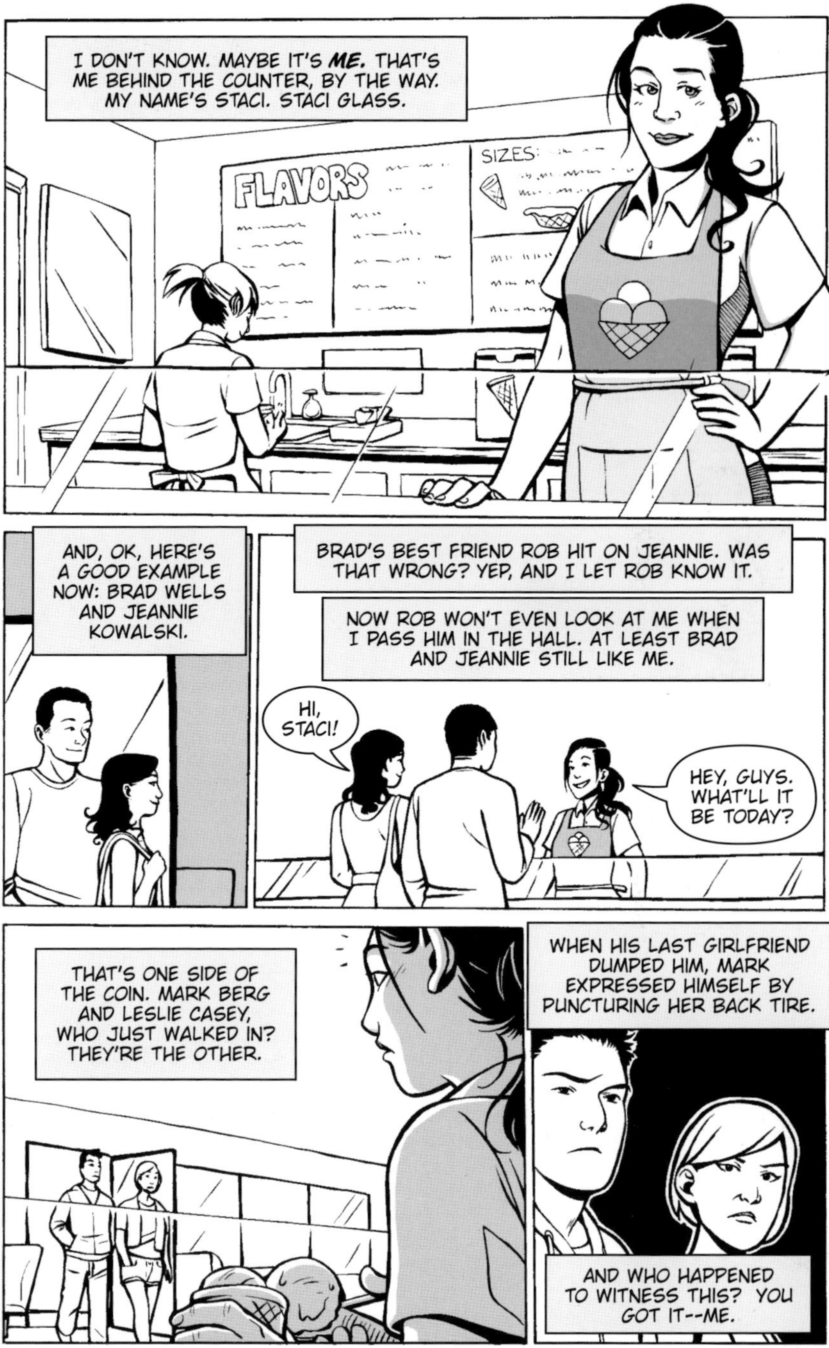

I DON'T KNOW. MAYBE IT'S ME. THAT'S ME BEHIND THE COUNTER, BY THE WAY. MY NAME'S STACI. STACI GLASS.
FLAVORS
SIZES:
AND, OK, HERE'S A GOOD EXAMPLE NOW: BRAD WELLS AND JEANNIE KOWALSKI.
BRAD'S BEST FRIEND ROB HIT ON JEANNIE. WAS THAT WRONG? YEP, AND I LET ROB KNOW IT.
NOW ROB WON'T EVEN LOOK AT ME WHEN I PASS HIM IN THE HALL. AT LEAST BRAD AND JEANNIE STILL LIKE ME.
HI, STACI!
HEY, GUYS. WHAT'LL IT BE TODAY?
THAT'S ONE SIDE OF THE COIN. MARK BERG AND LESLIE CASEY, WHO JUST WALKED IN? THEY'RE THE OTHER.
WHEN HIS LAST GIRLFRIEND DUMPED HIM, MARK EXPRESSED HIMSELF BY PUNCTURING HER BACK TIRE.
AND WHO HAPPENED TO WITNESS THIS? YOU GOT IT--ME.

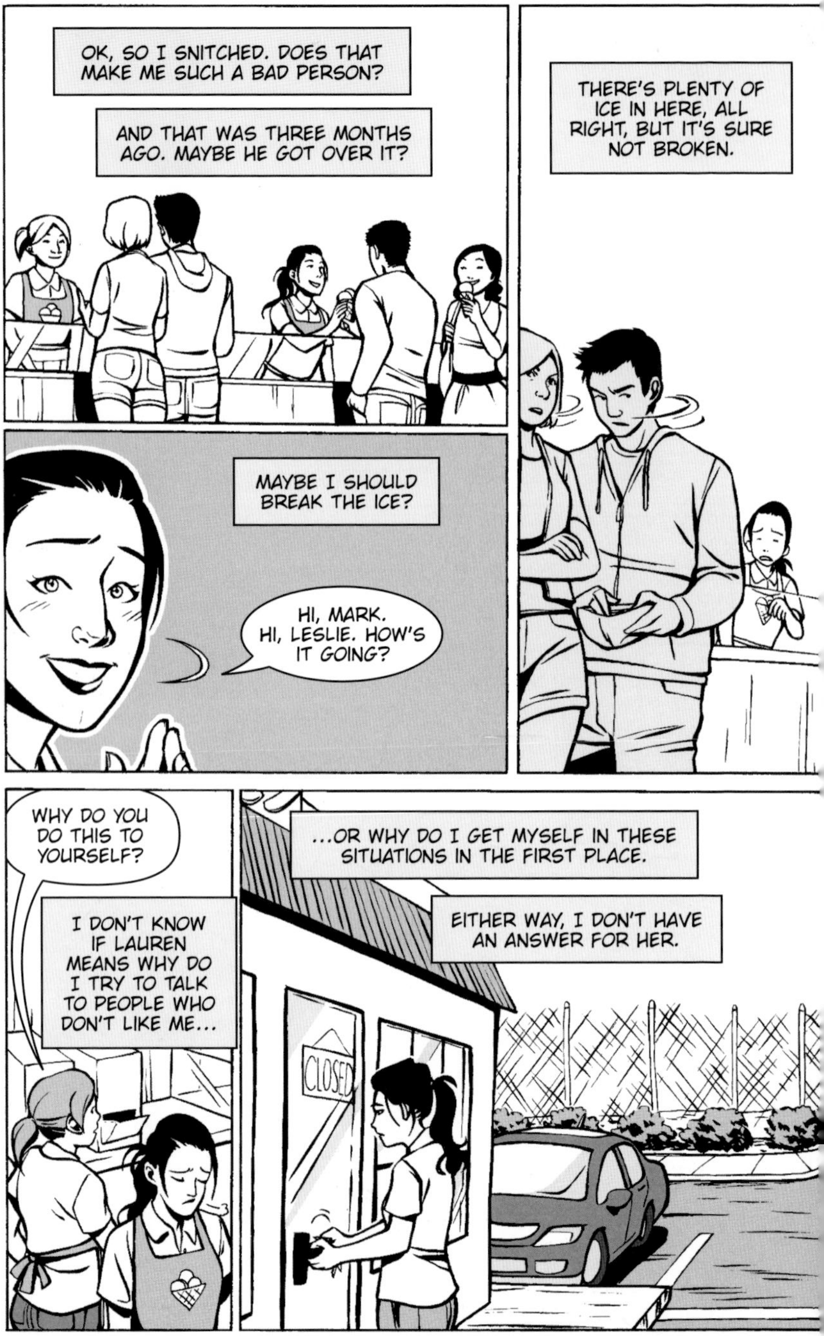
OK, SO I SNITCHED. DOES THAT MAKE ME SUCH A BAD PERSON?
AND THAT WAS THREE MONTHS AGO. MAYBE HE GOT OVER IT?
THERE'S PLENTY OF ICE IN HERE, ALL RIGHT, BUT IT'S SURE NOT BROKEN.
MAYBE I SHOULD BREAK THE ICE?
HI, MARK. HI, LESLIE. HOW'S IT GOING?
WHY DO YOU DO THIS TO YOURSELF?
I DON'T KNOW IF LAUREN MEANS WHY DO I TRY TO TALK TO PEOPLE WHO DON'T LIKE ME...
...OR WHY DO I GET MYSELF IN THESE SITUATIONS IN THE FIRST PLACE.
EITHER WAY, I DON'T HAVE AN ANSWER FOR HER.
CLOSED

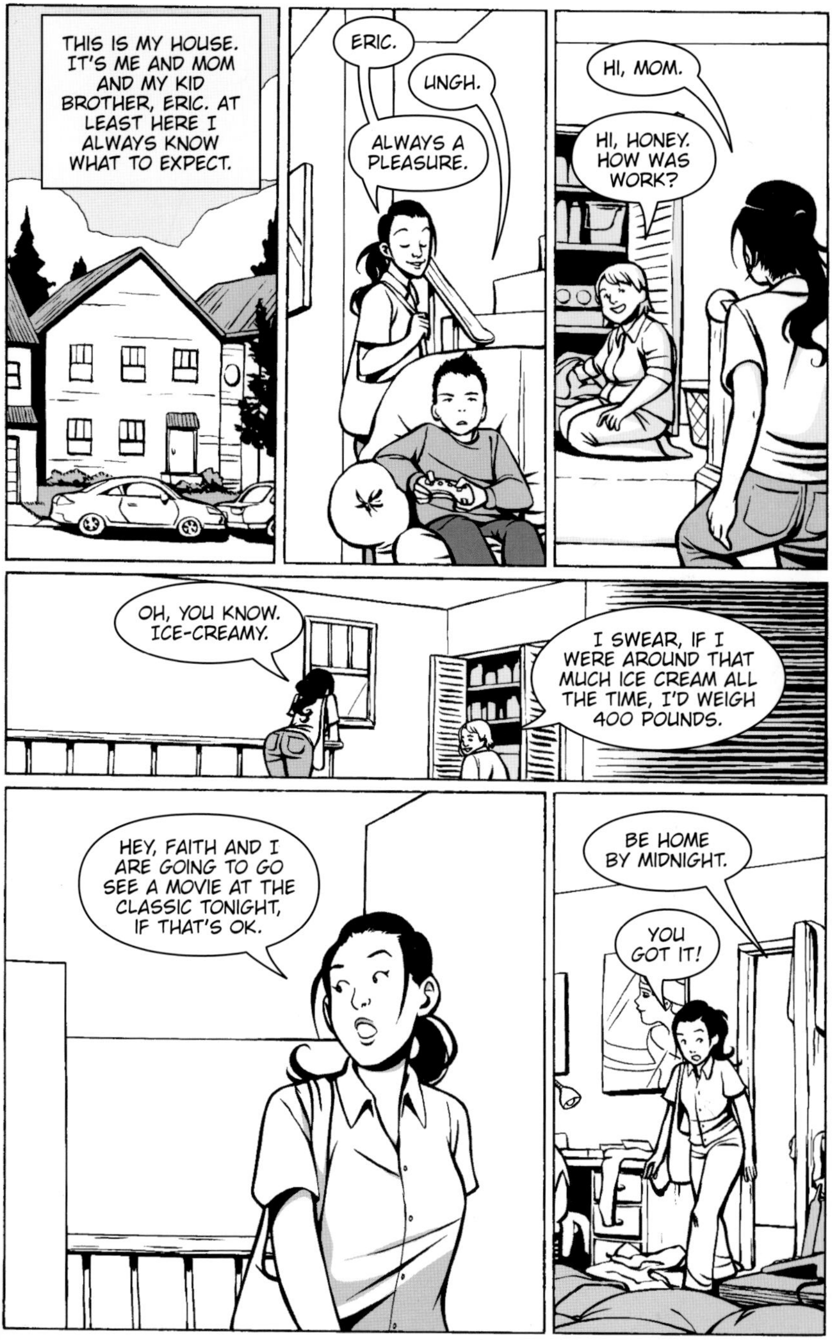
THIS IS MY HOUSE. IT'S ME AND MOM AND MY KID BROTHER, ERIC. AT LEAST HERE I ALWAYS KNOW WHAT TO EXPECT.
ERIC.
UNGH.
ALWAYS A PLEASURE.
HI, MOM.
HI, HONEY. HOW WAS WORK?
OH, YOU KNOW. ICE-CREAMY.
I SWEAR, IF I WERE AROUND THAT MUCH ICE CREAM ALL THE TIME, I'D WEIGH 400 POUNDS.
HEY, FAITH AND I ARE GOING TO GO SEE A MOVIE AT THE CLASSIC TONIGHT, IF THAT'S OK.
BE HOME BY MIDNIGHT.
YOU GOT IT!

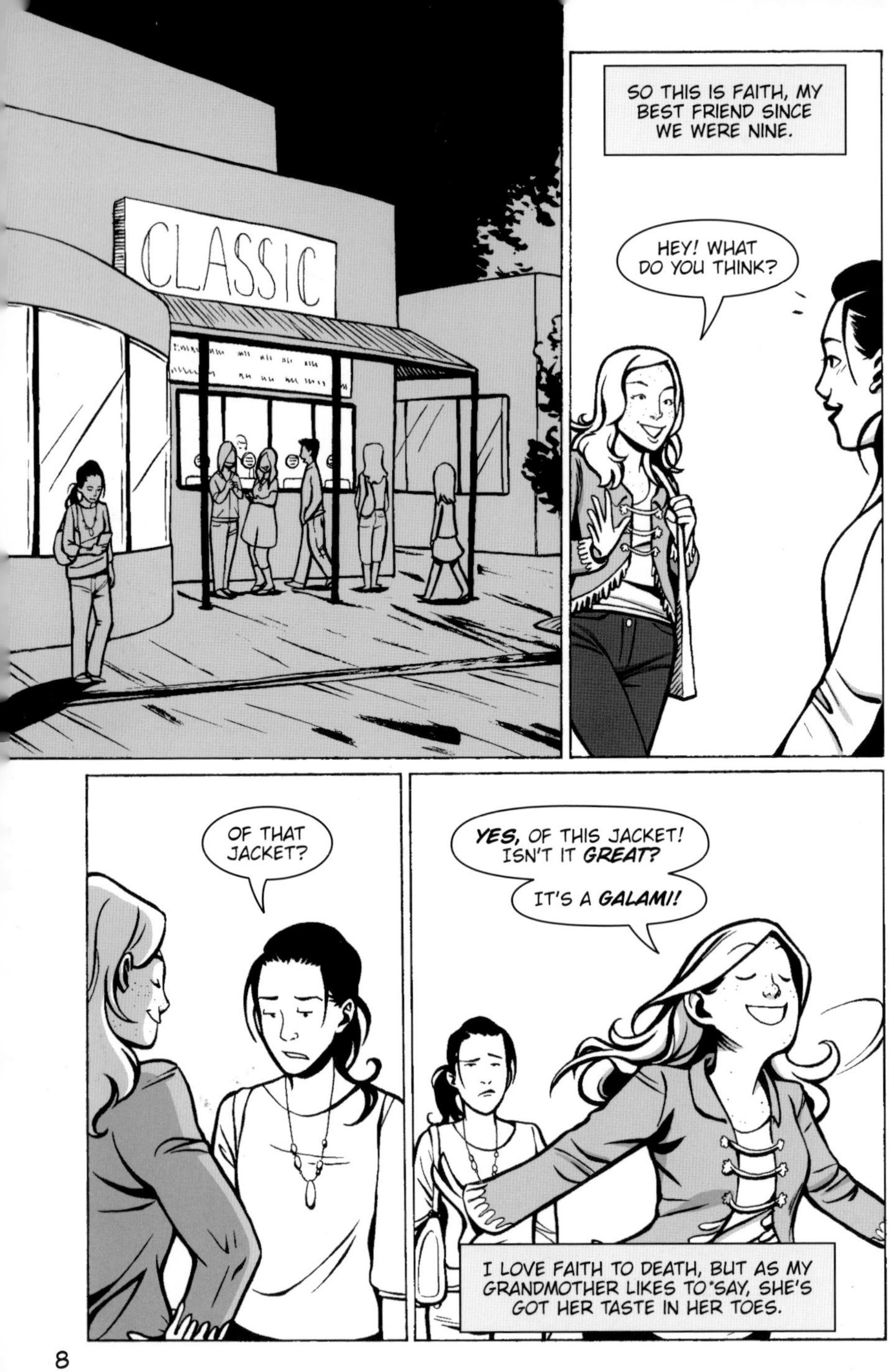
CLASSIC
SO THIS IS FAITH, MY BEST FRIEND SINCE WE WERE NINE.
HEY! WHAT DO YOU THINK?
OF THAT JACKET?
YES, OF THIS JACKET! ISN'T IT GREAT?
IT'S A GALAMI!
I LOVE FAITH TO DEATH, BUT AS MY GRANDMOTHER LIKES TO SAY, SHE'S GOT HER TASTE IN HER TOES.

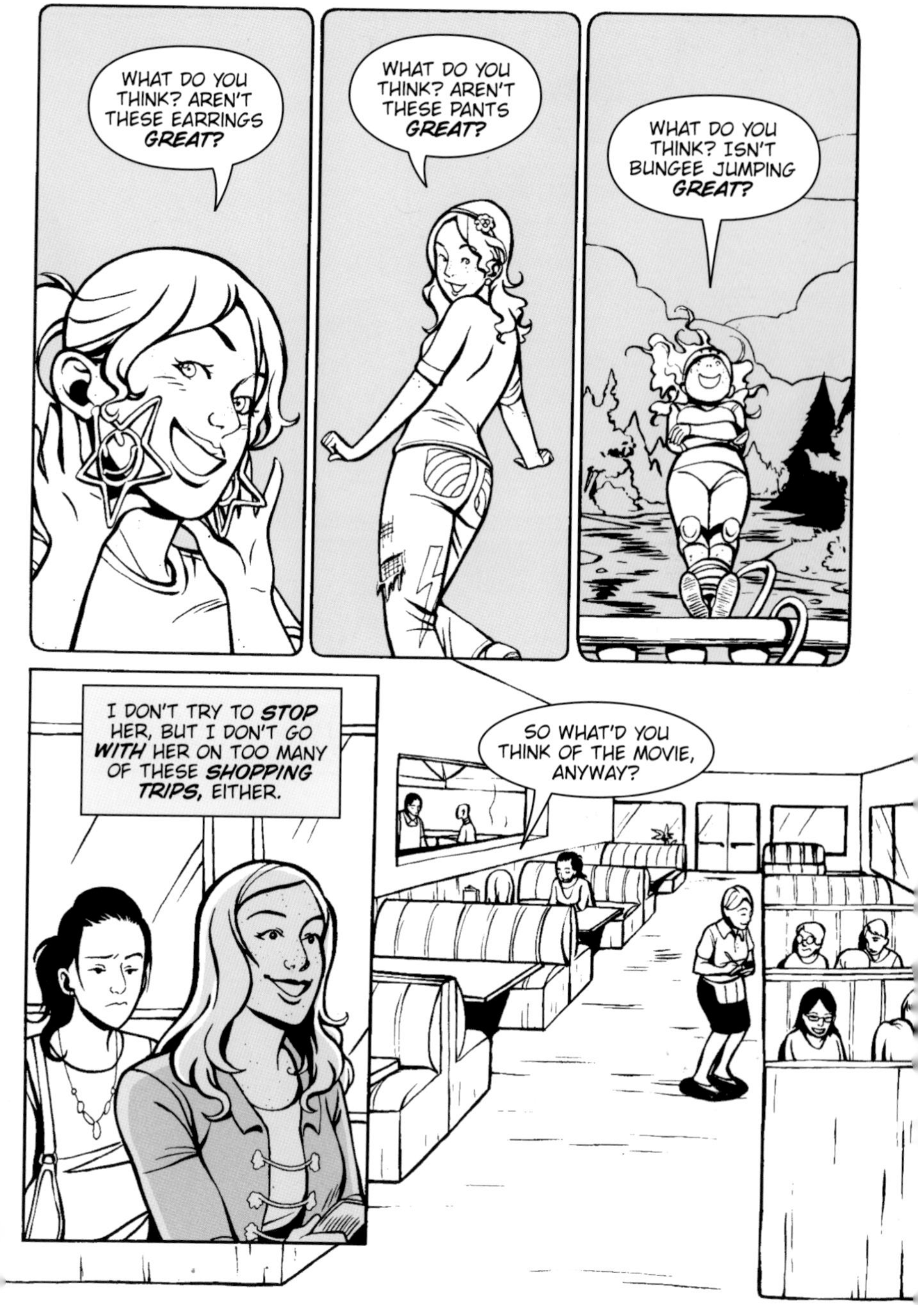
WHAT DO YOU THINK? AREN'T THESE EARRINGS *GREAT?*
WHAT DO YOU THINK? AREN'T THESE PANTS *GREAT?*
WHAT DO YOU THINK? ISN'T BUNGEE JUMPING *GREAT?*
I DON'T TRY TO *STOP* HER, BUT I DON'T GO *WITH* HER ON TOO MANY OF THESE *SHOPPING TRIPS,* EITHER.
SO WHAT'D YOU THINK OF THE MOVIE, ANYWAY?

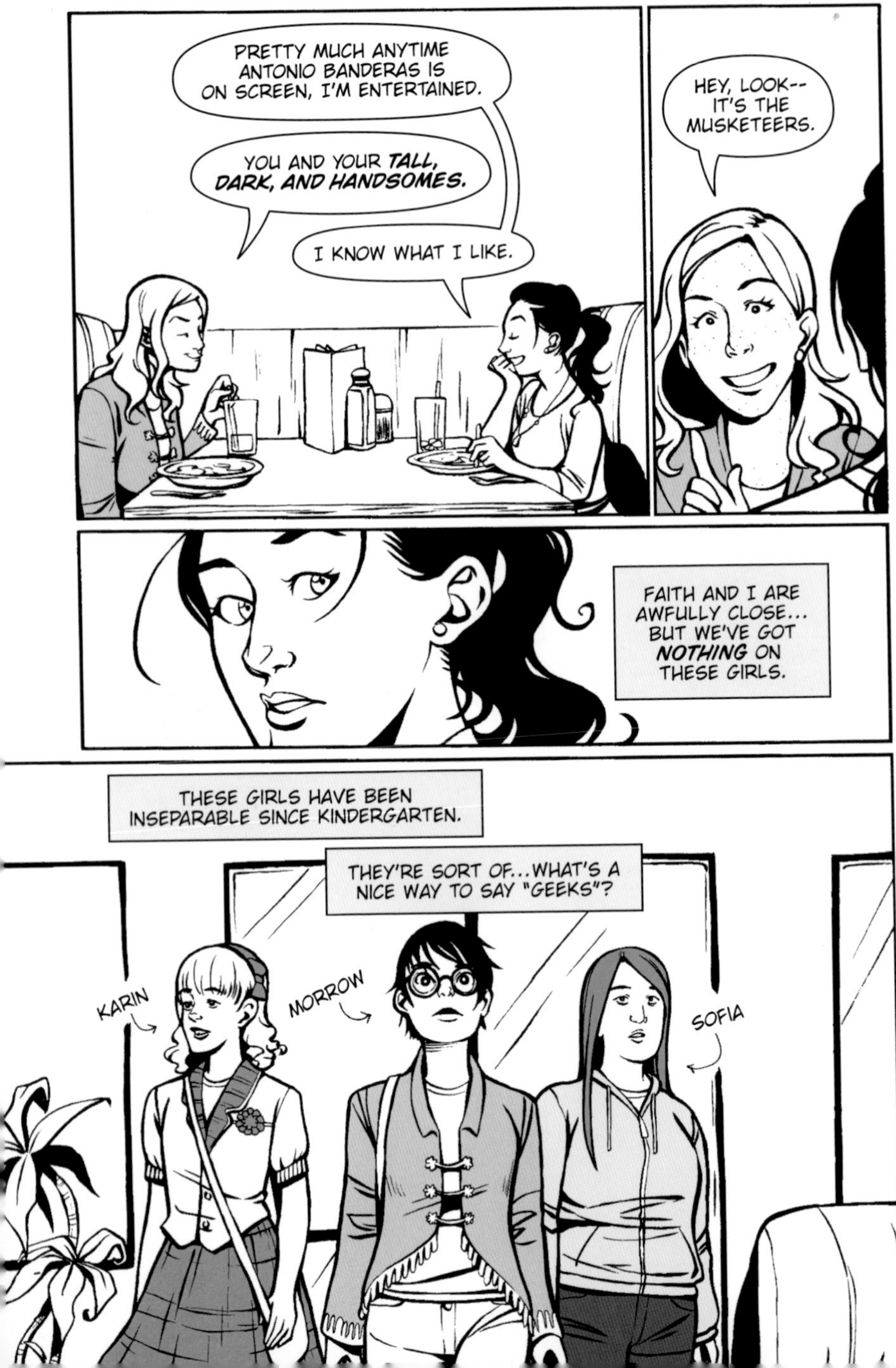
PRETTY MUCH ANYTIME ANTONIO BANDERAS IS ON SCREEN, I'M ENTERTAINED.
YOU AND YOUR TALL, DARK, AND HANDSOMES.
I KNOW WHAT I LIKE.
HEY, LOOK-- IT'S THE MUSKETEERS.
FAITH AND I ARE AWFULLY CLOSE... BUT WE'VE GOT NOTHING ON THESE GIRLS.
THESE GIRLS HAVE BEEN INSEPARABLE SINCE KINDERGARTEN.
THEY'RE SORT OF...WHAT'S A NICE WAY TO SAY "GEEKS"?
KARIN
MORROW
SOFIA

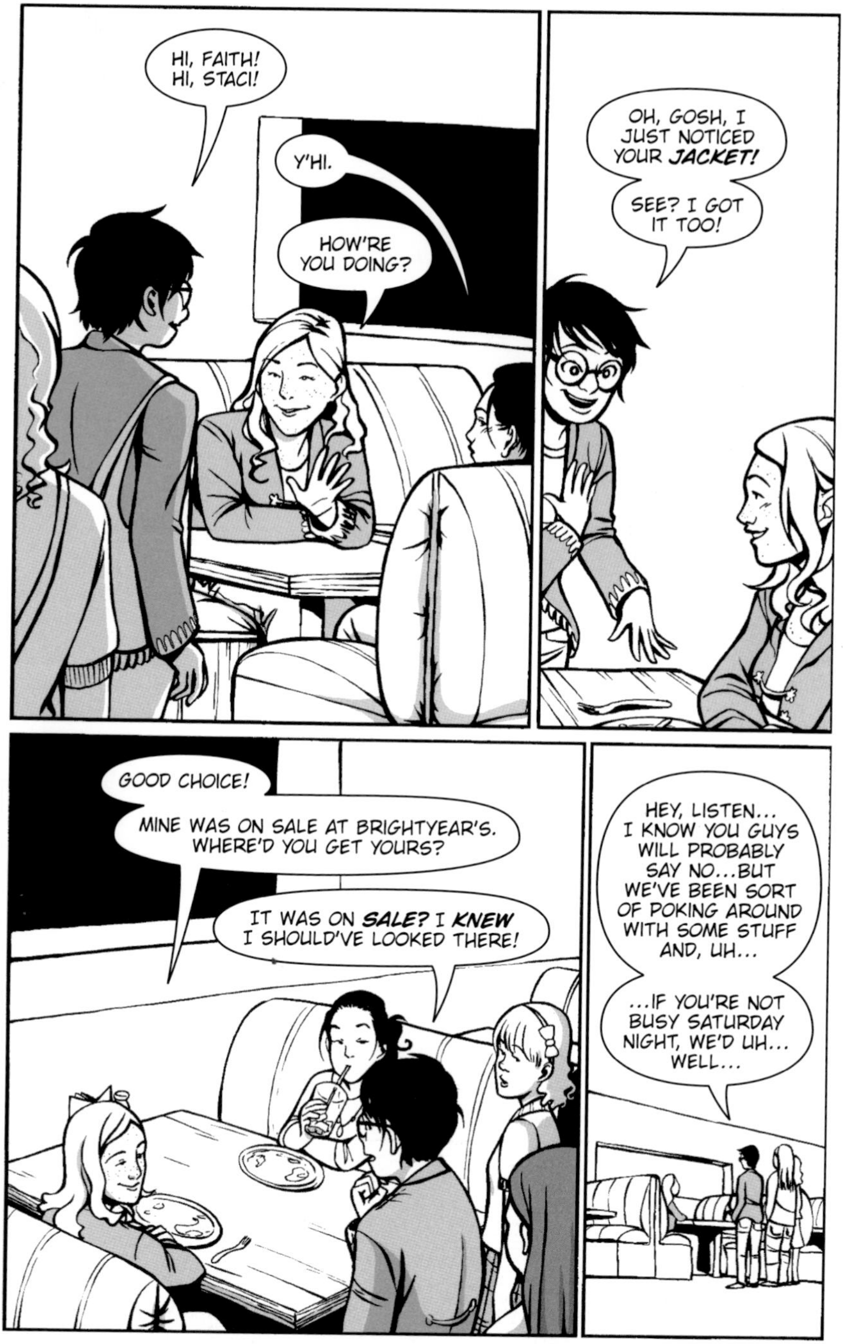
HI, FAITH! HI, STACI!
Y'HI.
HOW'RE YOU DOING?
OH, GOSH, I JUST NOTICED YOUR **JACKET!**
SEE? I GOT IT TOO!
GOOD CHOICE!
MINE WAS ON SALE AT BRIGHTYEAR'S. WHERE'D YOU GET YOURS?
IT WAS ON **SALE?** I **KNEW** I SHOULD'VE LOOKED THERE!
HEY, LISTEN... I KNOW YOU GUYS WILL PROBABLY SAY NO...BUT WE'VE BEEN SORT OF POKING AROUND WITH SOME STUFF AND, UH...
...IF YOU'RE NOT BUSY SATURDAY NIGHT, WE'D UH... WELL...

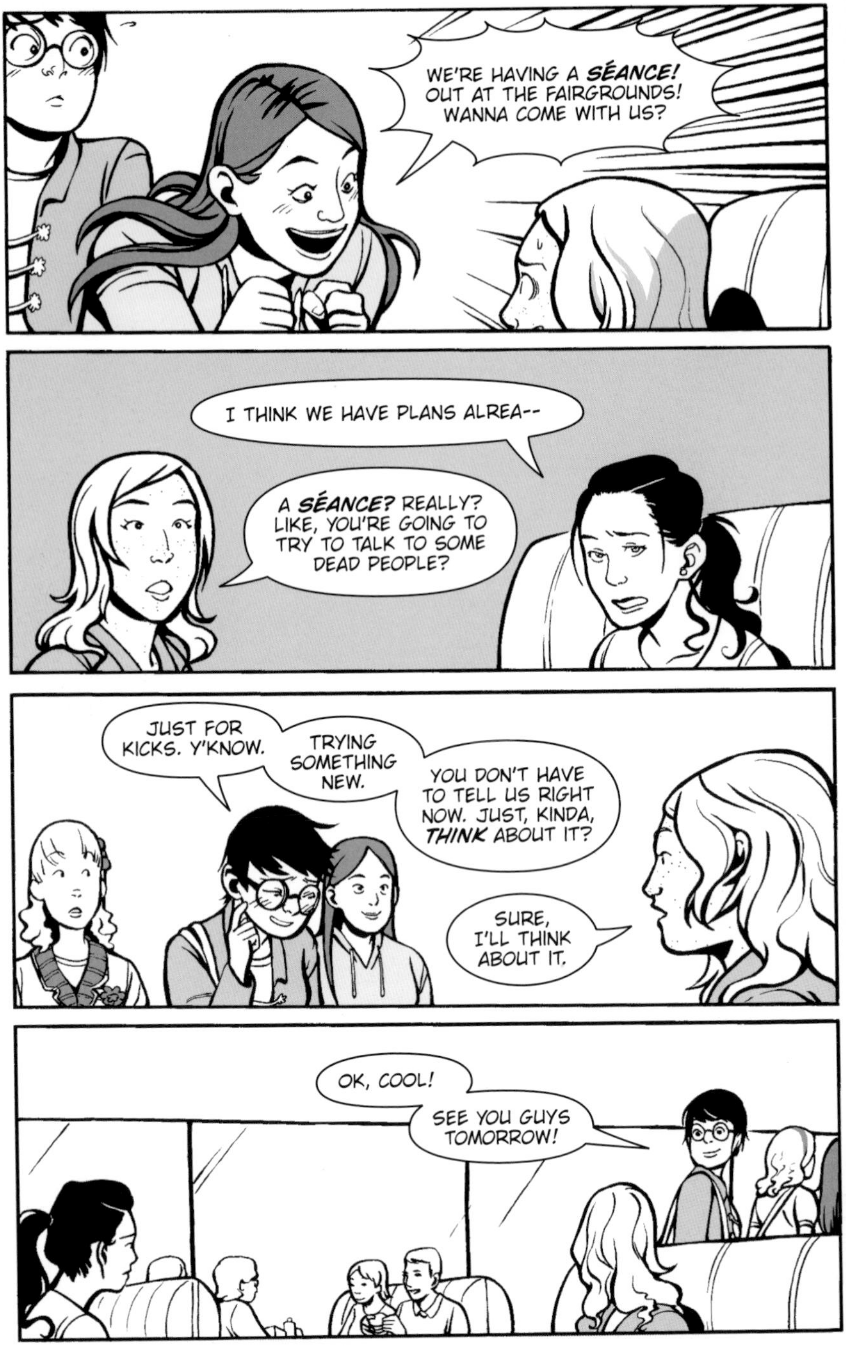
WE'RE HAVING A **SÉANCE!** OUT AT THE FAIRGROUNDS! WANNA COME WITH US?
I THINK WE HAVE PLANS ALREA--
A **SÉANCE?** REALLY? LIKE, YOU'RE GOING TO TRY TO TALK TO SOME DEAD PEOPLE?
JUST FOR KICKS. Y'KNOW.
TRYING SOMETHING NEW.
YOU DON'T HAVE TO TELL US RIGHT NOW. JUST, KINDA, ***THINK*** ABOUT IT?
SURE, I'LL THINK ABOUT IT.
OK, COOL!
SEE YOU GUYS TOMORROW!

SO ALL OF A SUDDEN I'M HAVING PRETTY MUCH THE LAST CONVERSATION I EVER EXPECTED TO HAVE.

WELL?

WELL WHAT?

WHAT DO YOU *THINK*, STACI? DON'T YOU THINK A SÉANCE'D BE *EXCITING*?

SERIOUSLY, FAITH? YOU CAN'T BE SERIOUS.

WHY NOT? WHAT'S THE HARM?

LET'S LOOK AT IT THIS WAY: ONE, THEY ACTUALLY KNOW WHAT THEY'RE DOING...

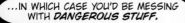

...IN WHICH CASE YOU'D BE MESSING WITH *DANGEROUS STUFF.*

TWO, THEY *DON'T* KNOW WHAT THEY'RE DOING...

...IN WHICH CASE YOU WASTE AN ENTIRE SATURDAY EVENING SITTING AROUND IN THE DARK LIKE AN IDIOT.

BUT DOES FAITH LISTEN TO ME?...OF COURSE NOT.

13

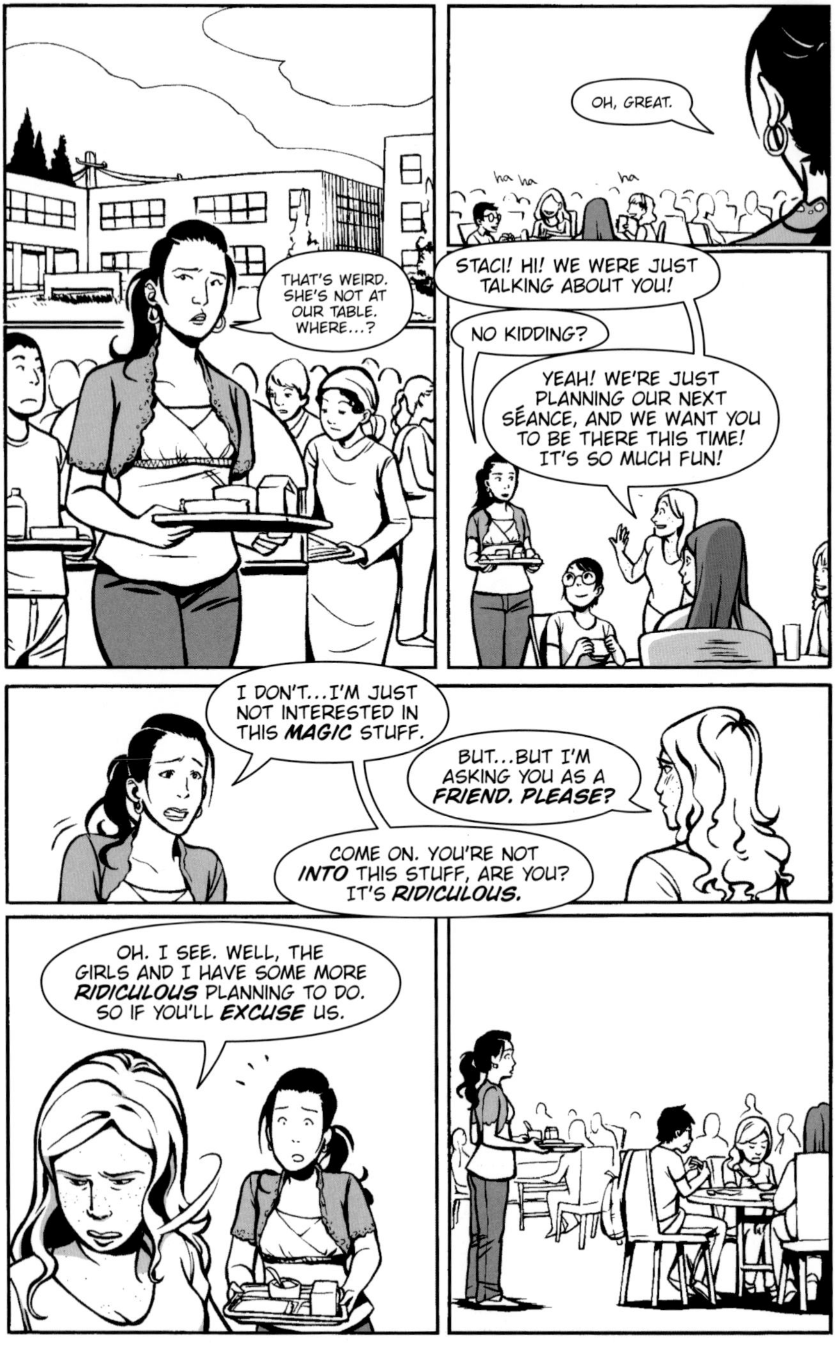
THAT'S WEIRD. SHE'S NOT AT OUR TABLE. WHERE...?
OH, GREAT.
ha ha
ha
STACI! HI! WE WERE JUST TALKING ABOUT YOU!
NO KIDDING?
YEAH! WE'RE JUST PLANNING OUR NEXT SÉANCE, AND WE WANT YOU TO BE THERE THIS TIME! IT'S SO MUCH FUN!
I DON'T...I'M JUST NOT INTERESTED IN THIS MAGIC STUFF.
BUT...BUT I'M ASKING YOU AS A FRIEND. PLEASE?
COME ON. YOU'RE NOT INTO THIS STUFF, ARE YOU? IT'S RIDICULOUS.
OH. I SEE. WELL, THE GIRLS AND I HAVE SOME MORE RIDICULOUS PLANNING TO DO. SO IF YOU'LL EXCUSE US.

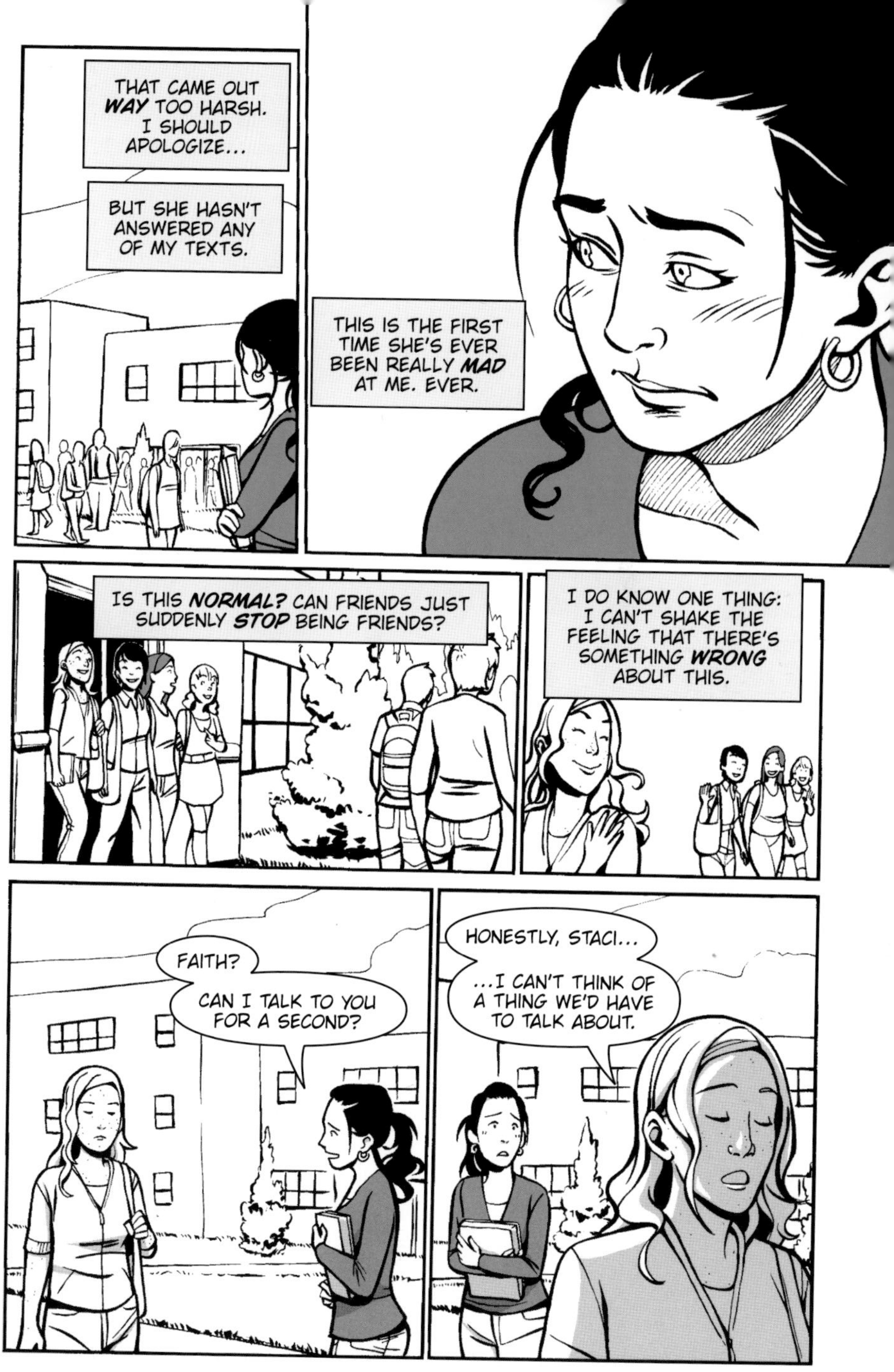
THAT CAME OUT WAY TOO HARSH. I SHOULD APOLOGIZE...
BUT SHE HASN'T ANSWERED ANY OF MY TEXTS.
THIS IS THE FIRST TIME SHE'S EVER BEEN REALLY MAD AT ME. EVER.
IS THIS NORMAL? CAN FRIENDS JUST SUDDENLY STOP BEING FRIENDS?
I DO KNOW ONE THING: I CAN'T SHAKE THE FEELING THAT THERE'S SOMETHING WRONG ABOUT THIS.
FAITH?
CAN I TALK TO YOU FOR A SECOND?
HONESTLY, STACI...
...I CAN'T THINK OF A THING WE'D HAVE TO TALK ABOUT.

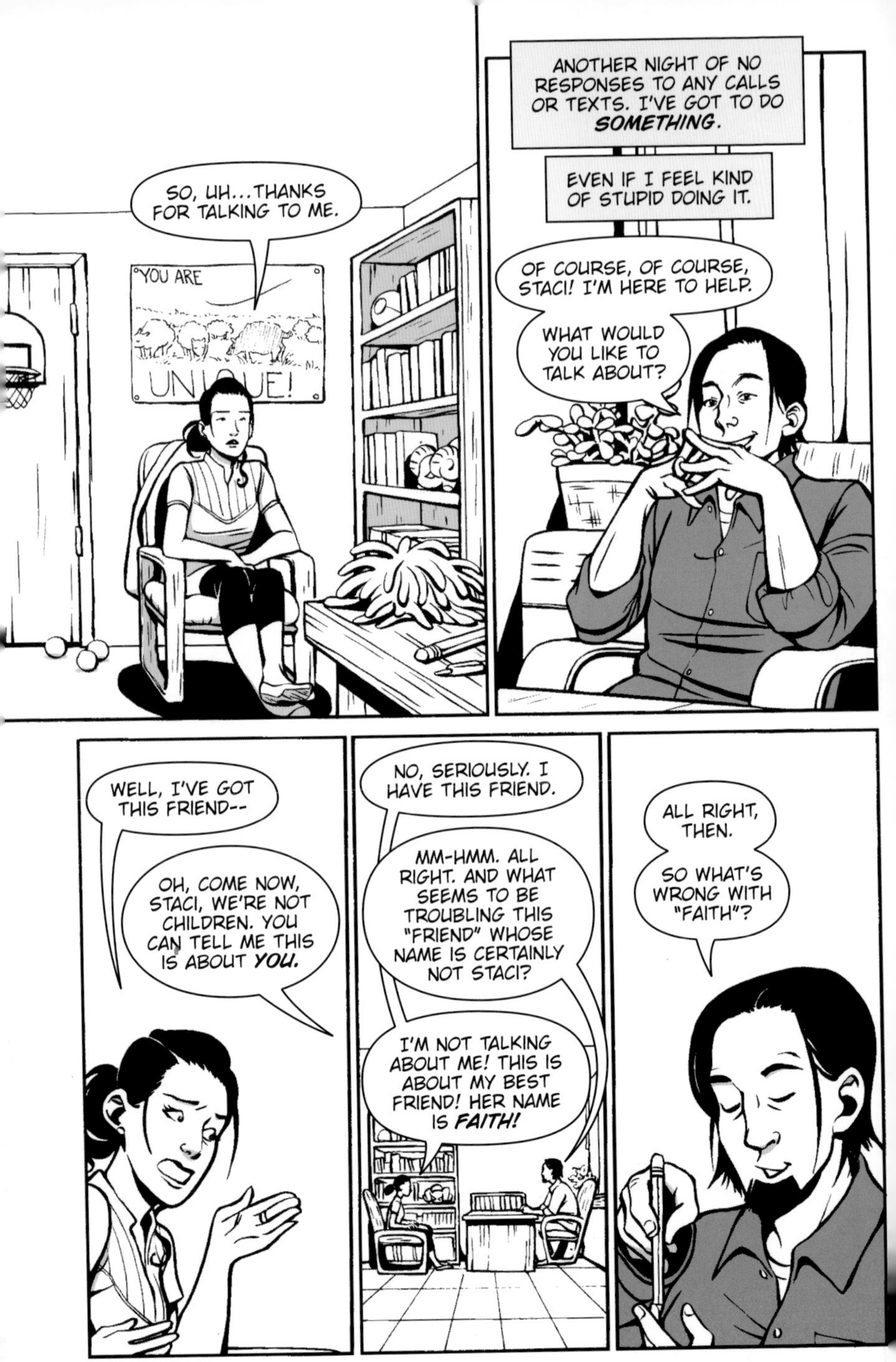
SO, UH...THANKS FOR TALKING TO ME.
YOU ARE UNIQUE!
ANOTHER NIGHT OF NO RESPONSES TO ANY CALLS OR TEXTS. I'VE GOT TO DO *SOMETHING*.
EVEN IF I FEEL KIND OF STUPID DOING IT.
OF COURSE, OF COURSE, STACI! I'M HERE TO HELP.
WHAT WOULD YOU LIKE TO TALK ABOUT?
WELL, I'VE GOT THIS FRIEND--
OH, COME NOW, STACI, WE'RE NOT CHILDREN. YOU CAN TELL ME THIS IS ABOUT *YOU.*
NO, SERIOUSLY. I HAVE THIS FRIEND.
MM-HMM. ALL RIGHT. AND WHAT SEEMS TO BE TROUBLING THIS "FRIEND" WHOSE NAME IS CERTAINLY NOT STACI?
I'M NOT TALKING ABOUT ME! THIS IS ABOUT MY BEST FRIEND! HER NAME IS *FAITH!*
ALL RIGHT, THEN.
SO WHAT'S WRONG WITH "FAITH"?

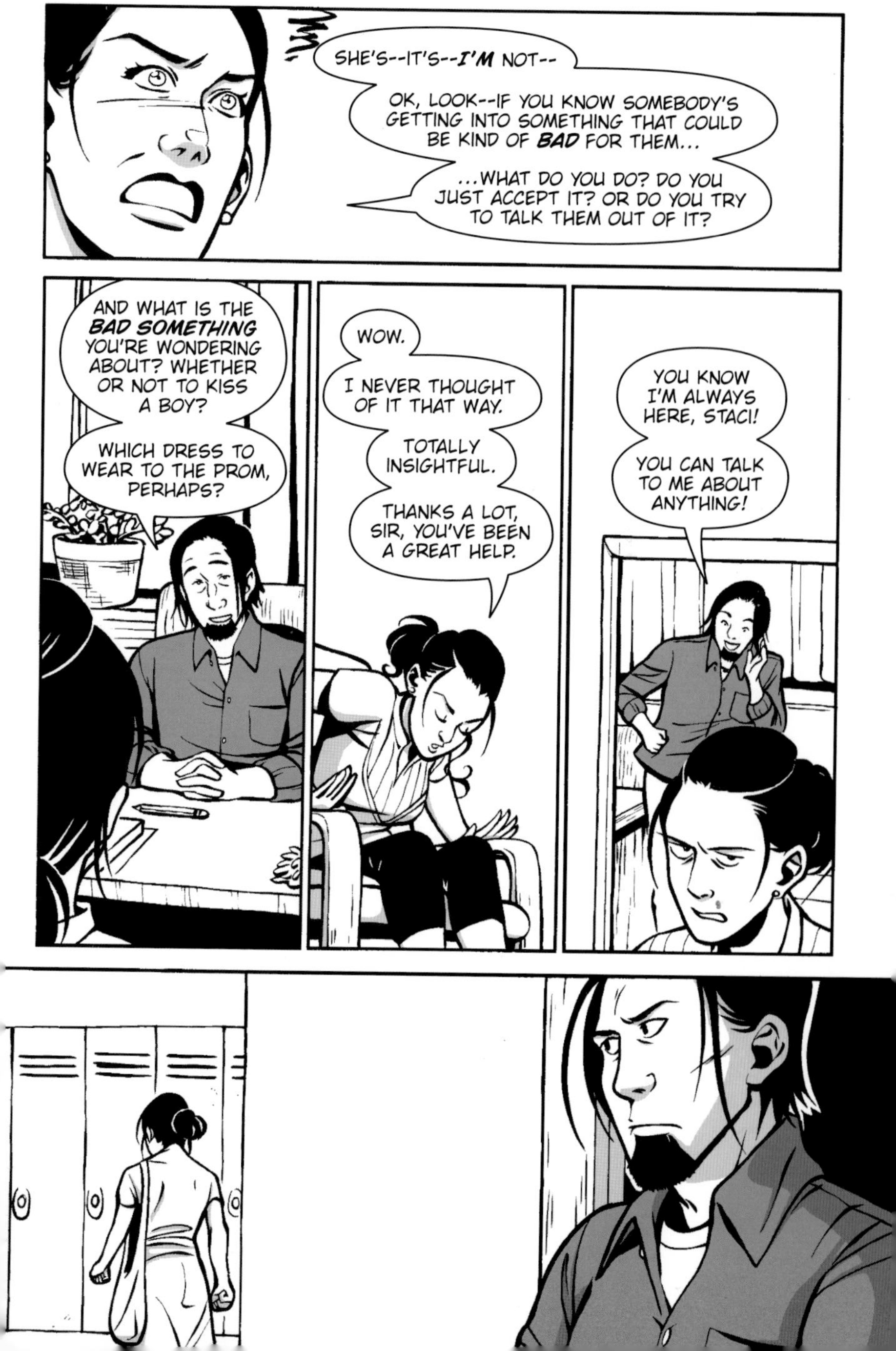
SHE'S--IT'S--*I'M* NOT--
OK, LOOK--IF YOU KNOW SOMEBODY'S GETTING INTO SOMETHING THAT COULD BE KIND OF *BAD* FOR THEM...
...WHAT DO YOU DO? DO YOU JUST ACCEPT IT? OR DO YOU TRY TO TALK THEM OUT OF IT?
AND WHAT IS THE *BAD SOMETHING* YOU'RE WONDERING ABOUT? WHETHER OR NOT TO KISS A BOY?
WHICH DRESS TO WEAR TO THE PROM, PERHAPS?
WOW.
I NEVER THOUGHT OF IT THAT WAY.
TOTALLY INSIGHTFUL.
THANKS A LOT, SIR, YOU'VE BEEN A GREAT HELP.
YOU KNOW I'M ALWAYS HERE, STACI!
YOU CAN TALK TO ME ABOUT ANYTHING!

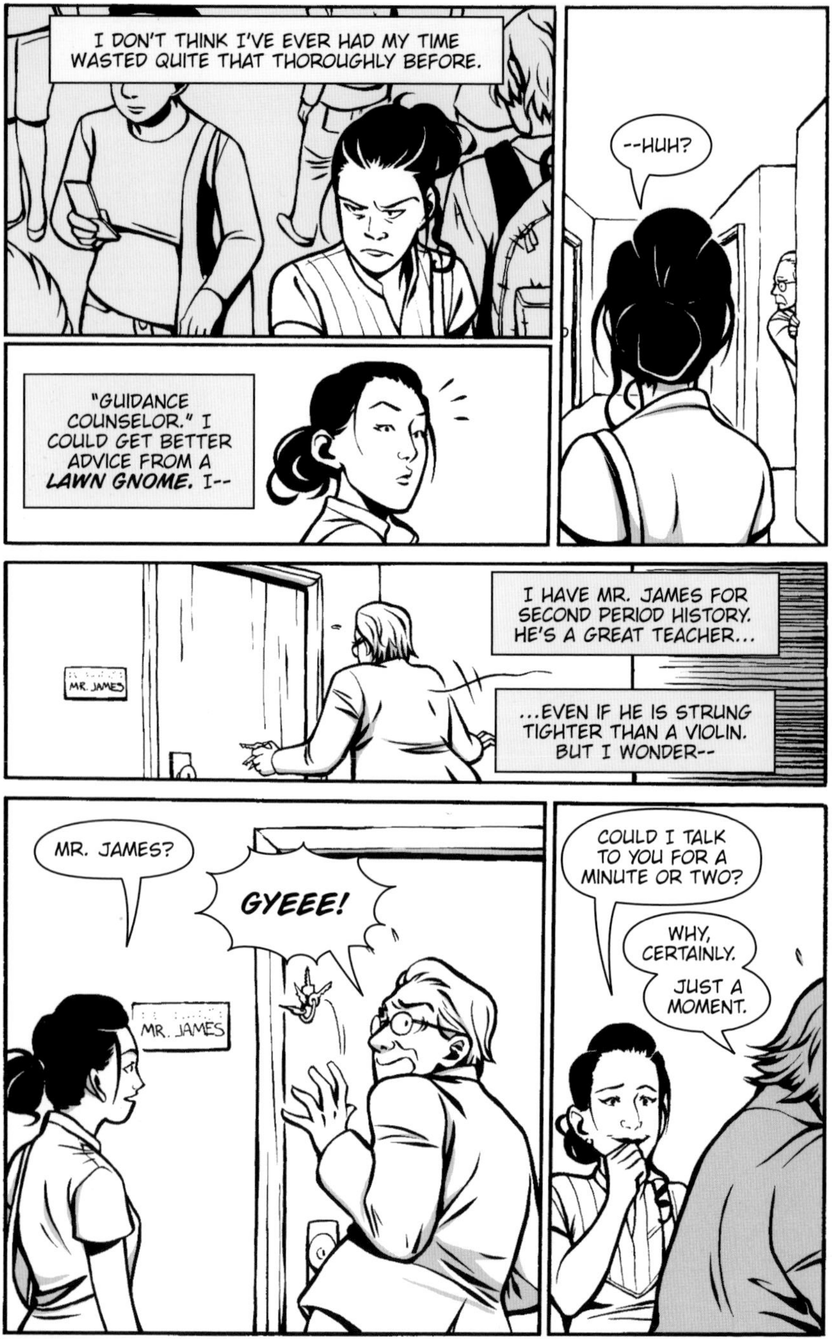
I DON'T THINK I'VE EVER HAD MY TIME WASTED QUITE THAT THOROUGHLY BEFORE.
"GUIDANCE COUNSELOR." I COULD GET BETTER ADVICE FROM A ***LAWN GNOME.*** I--
--HUH?
MR. JAMES
I HAVE MR. JAMES FOR SECOND PERIOD HISTORY. HE'S A GREAT TEACHER...
...EVEN IF HE IS STRUNG TIGHTER THAN A VIOLIN. BUT I WONDER--
MR. JAMES?
GYEEE!
MR. JAMES
COULD I TALK TO YOU FOR A MINUTE OR TWO?
WHY, CERTAINLY.
JUST A MOMENT.

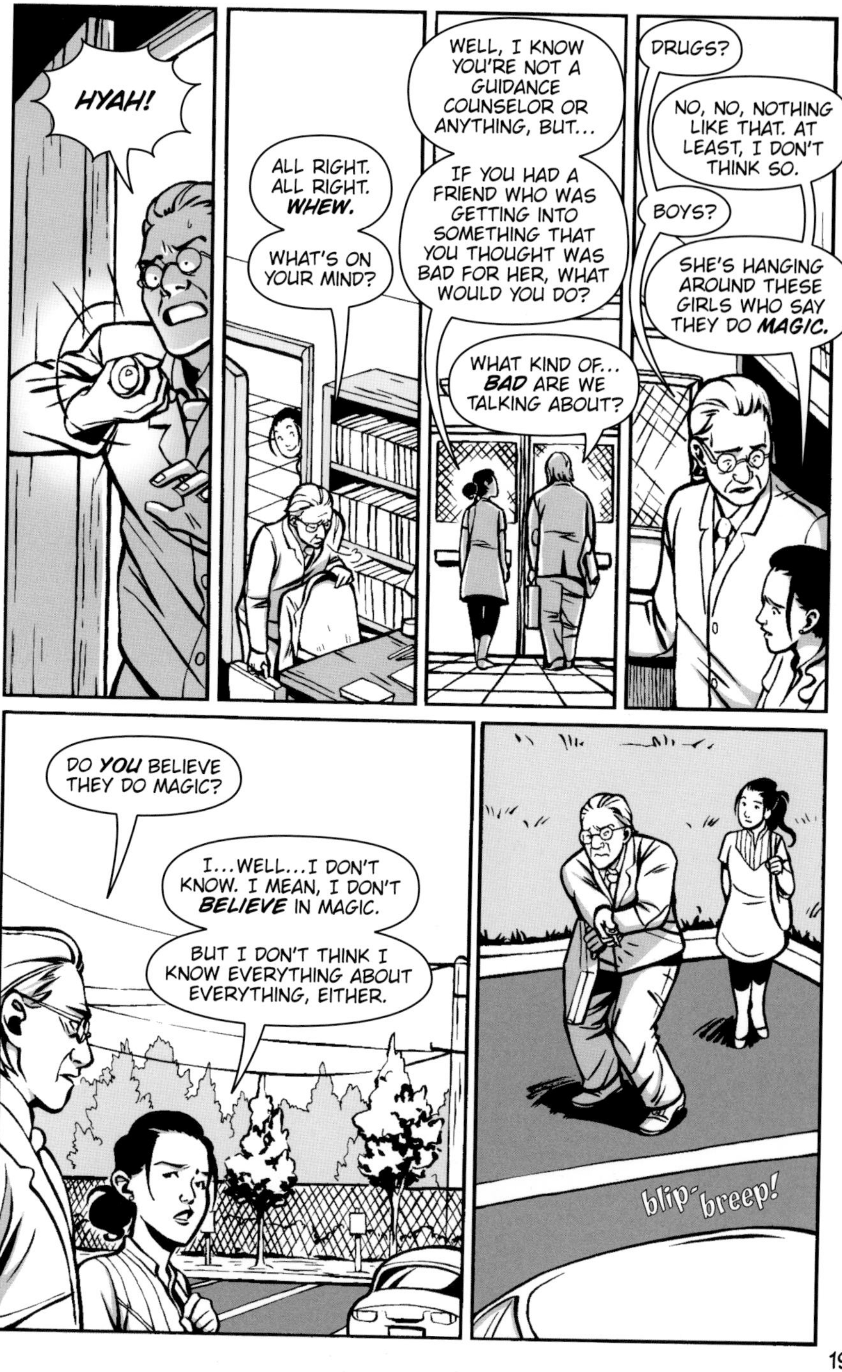
HYAH!
ALL RIGHT. ALL RIGHT. WHEW.
WHAT'S ON YOUR MIND?
WELL, I KNOW YOU'RE NOT A GUIDANCE COUNSELOR OR ANYTHING, BUT...
IF YOU HAD A FRIEND WHO WAS GETTING INTO SOMETHING THAT YOU THOUGHT WAS BAD FOR HER, WHAT WOULD YOU DO?
WHAT KIND OF... BAD ARE WE TALKING ABOUT?
DRUGS?
NO, NO, NOTHING LIKE THAT. AT LEAST, I DON'T THINK SO.
BOYS?
SHE'S HANGING AROUND THESE GIRLS WHO SAY THEY DO MAGIC.
DO YOU BELIEVE THEY DO MAGIC?
I...WELL...I DON'T KNOW. I MEAN, I DON'T BELIEVE IN MAGIC.
BUT I DON'T THINK I KNOW EVERYTHING ABOUT EVERYTHING, EITHER.
blip-breep!

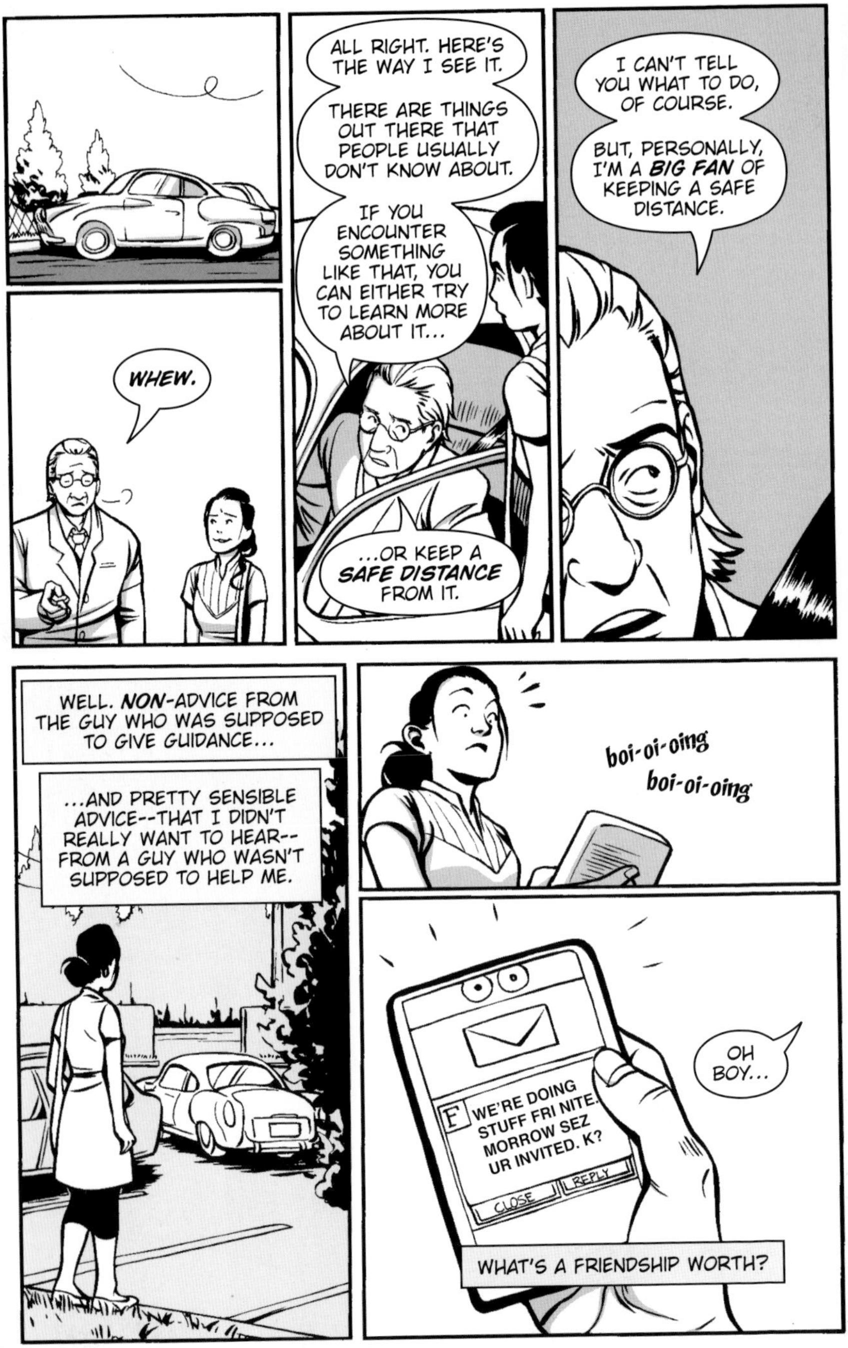
WHEW.
ALL RIGHT. HERE'S THE WAY I SEE IT.
THERE ARE THINGS OUT THERE THAT PEOPLE USUALLY DON'T KNOW ABOUT.
IF YOU ENCOUNTER SOMETHING LIKE THAT, YOU CAN EITHER TRY TO LEARN MORE ABOUT IT...
...OR KEEP A SAFE DISTANCE FROM IT.
I CAN'T TELL YOU WHAT TO DO, OF COURSE.
BUT, PERSONALLY, I'M A BIG FAN OF KEEPING A SAFE DISTANCE.
WELL. NON-ADVICE FROM THE GUY WHO WAS SUPPOSED TO GIVE GUIDANCE...
...AND PRETTY SENSIBLE ADVICE--THAT I DIDN'T REALLY WANT TO HEAR--FROM A GUY WHO WASN'T SUPPOSED TO HELP ME.
boi-oi-oing
boi-oi-oing
F
WE'RE DOING STUFF FRI NITE. MORROW SEZ UR INVITED. K?
CLOSE
REPLY
OH BOY...
WHAT'S A FRIENDSHIP WORTH?

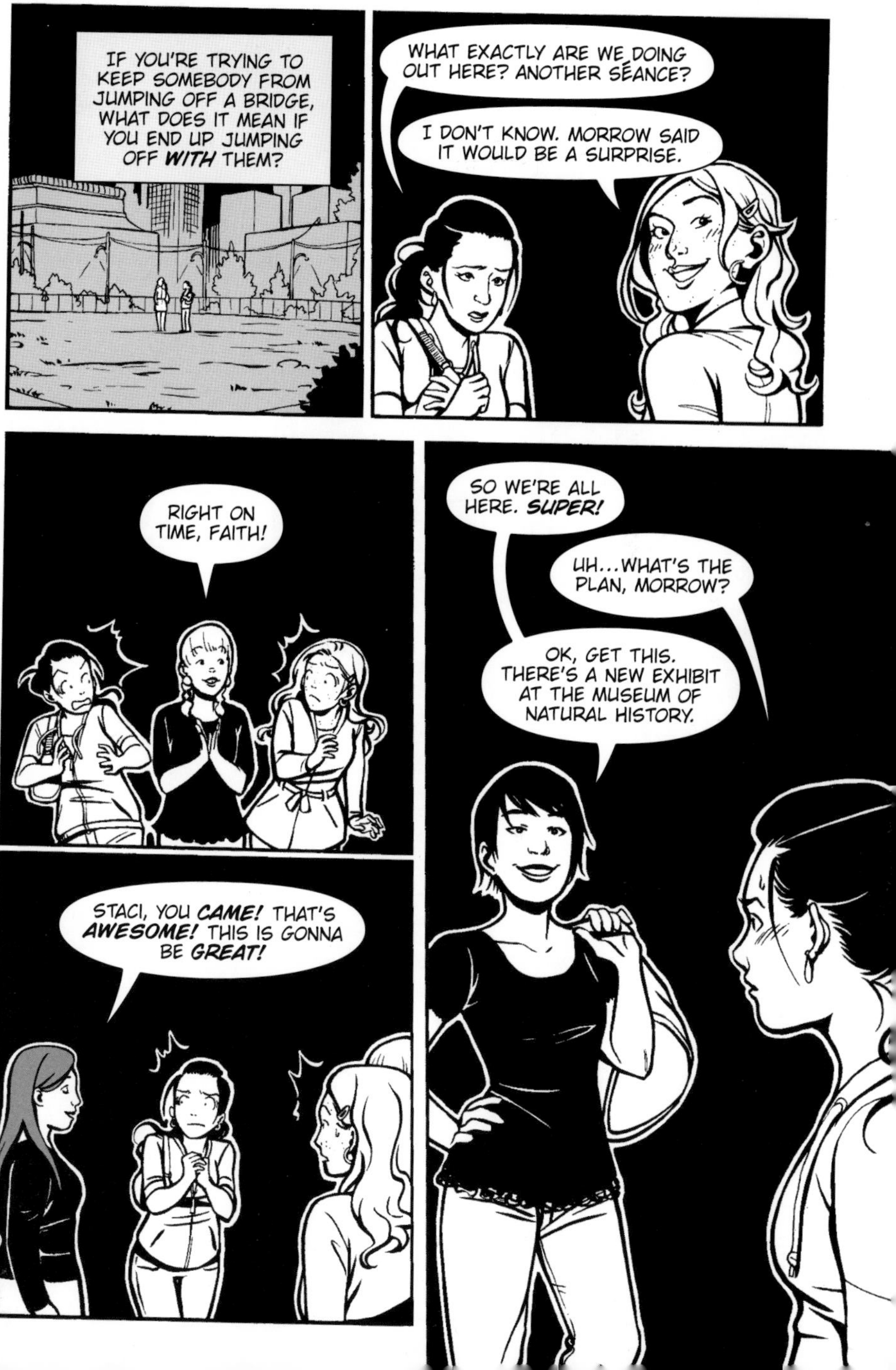
IF YOU'RE TRYING TO KEEP SOMEBODY FROM JUMPING OFF A BRIDGE, WHAT DOES IT MEAN IF YOU END UP JUMPING OFF **WITH** THEM?
WHAT EXACTLY ARE WE DOING OUT HERE? ANOTHER SÉANCE?
I DON'T KNOW. MORROW SAID IT WOULD BE A SURPRISE.
RIGHT ON TIME, FAITH!
STACI, YOU **CAME!** THAT'S **AWESOME!** THIS IS GONNA BE **GREAT!**
SO WE'RE ALL HERE. **SUPER!**
UH...WHAT'S THE PLAN, MORROW?
OK, GET THIS. THERE'S A NEW EXHIBIT AT THE MUSEUM OF NATURAL HISTORY.

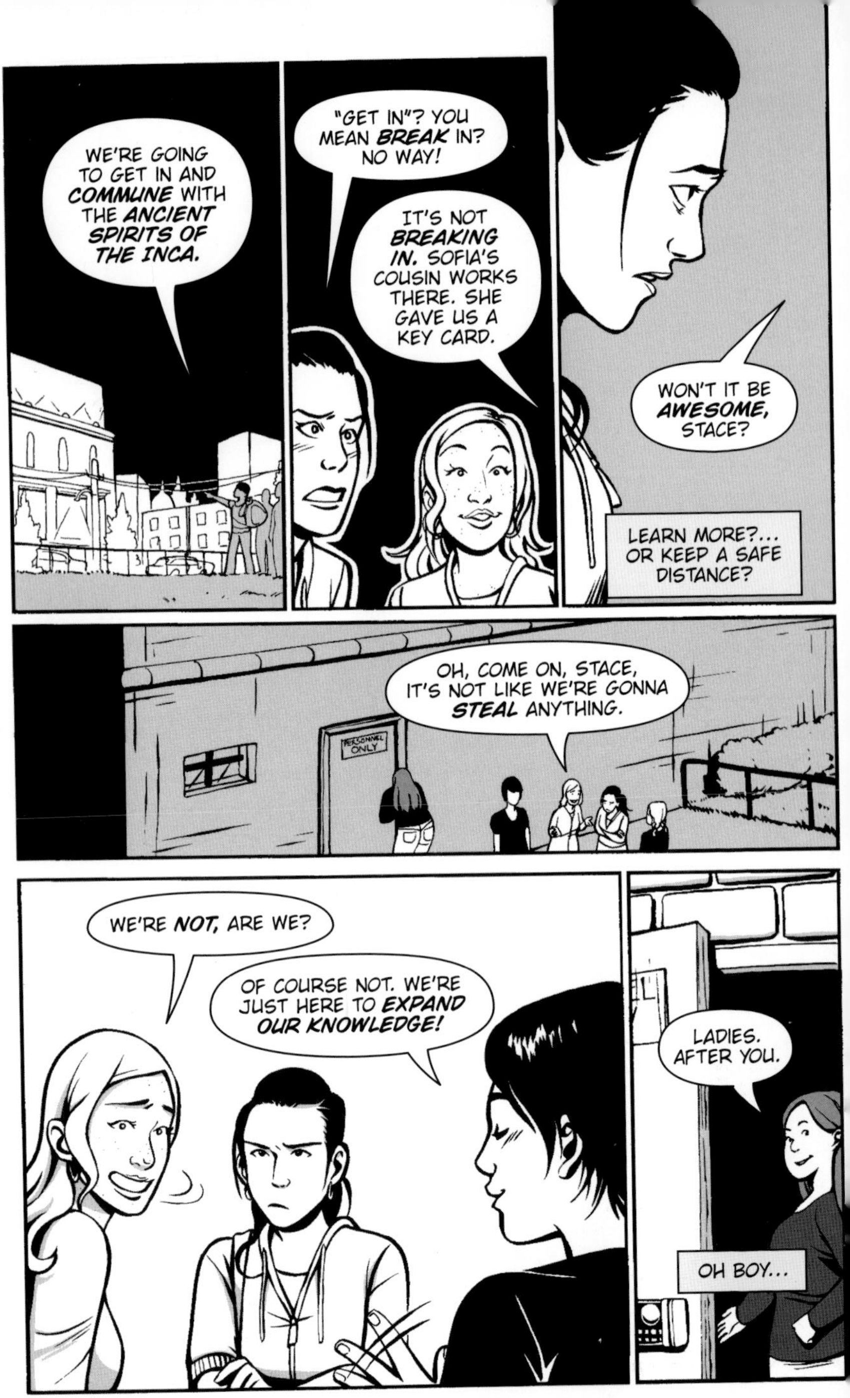
WE'RE GOING TO GET IN AND COMMUNE WITH THE ANCIENT SPIRITS OF THE INCA.
"GET IN"? YOU MEAN BREAK IN? NO WAY!
IT'S NOT BREAKING IN. SOFIA'S COUSIN WORKS THERE. SHE GAVE US A KEY CARD.
WON'T IT BE AWESOME, STACE?
LEARN MORE?... OR KEEP A SAFE DISTANCE?
OH, COME ON, STACE, IT'S NOT LIKE WE'RE GONNA STEAL ANYTHING.
PERSONNEL ONLY
WE'RE NOT, ARE WE?
OF COURSE NOT. WE'RE JUST HERE TO EXPAND OUR KNOWLEDGE!
LADIES. AFTER YOU.
OH BOY...

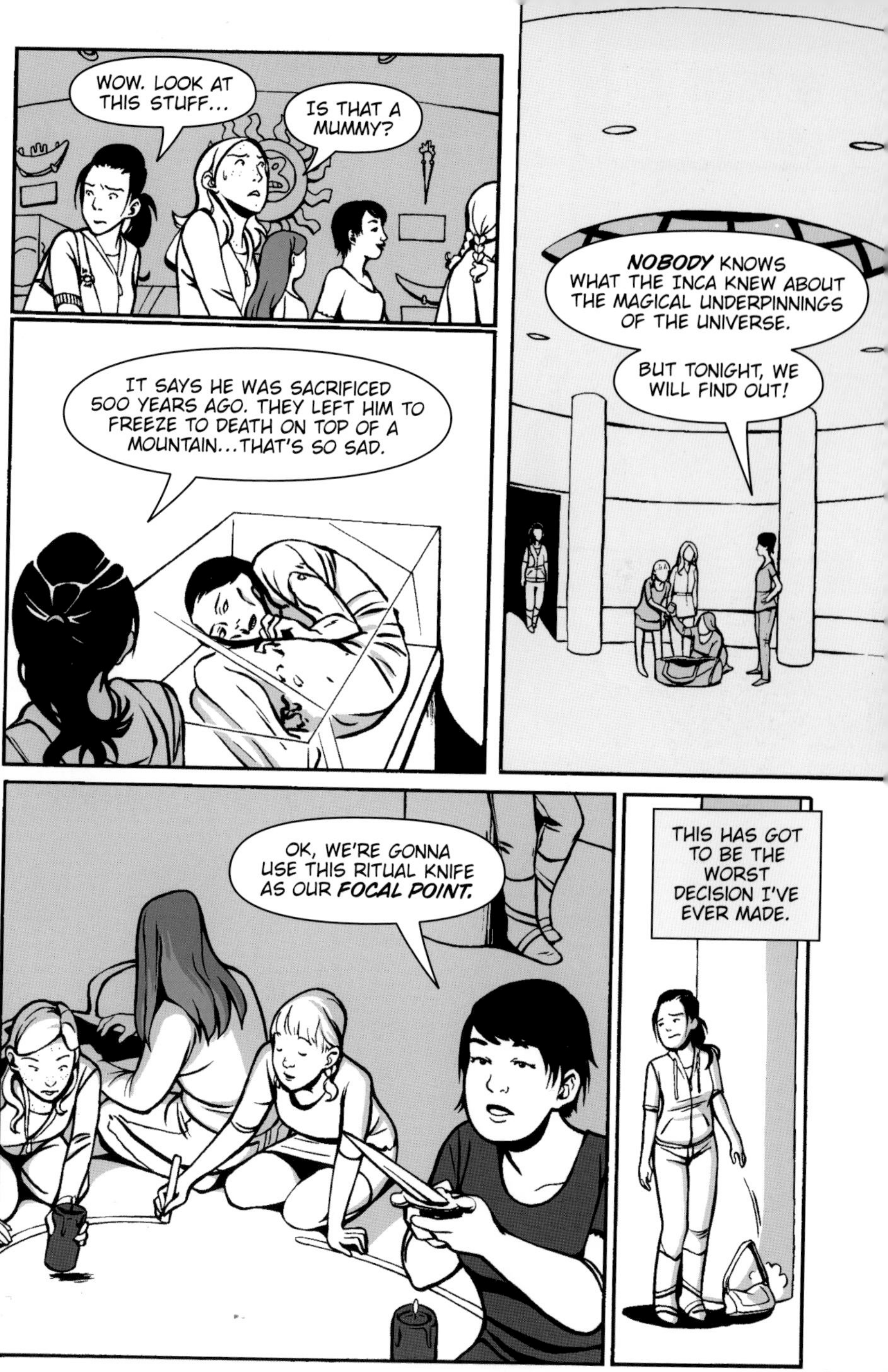
WOW. LOOK AT THIS STUFF...
IS THAT A MUMMY?
IT SAYS HE WAS SACRIFICED 500 YEARS AGO. THEY LEFT HIM TO FREEZE TO DEATH ON TOP OF A MOUNTAIN...THAT'S SO SAD.
NOBODY KNOWS WHAT THE INCA KNEW ABOUT THE MAGICAL UNDERPINNINGS OF THE UNIVERSE.
BUT TONIGHT, WE WILL FIND OUT!
OK, WE'RE GONNA USE THIS RITUAL KNIFE AS OUR ***FOCAL POINT.***
THIS HAS GOT TO BE THE WORST DECISION I'VE EVER MADE.

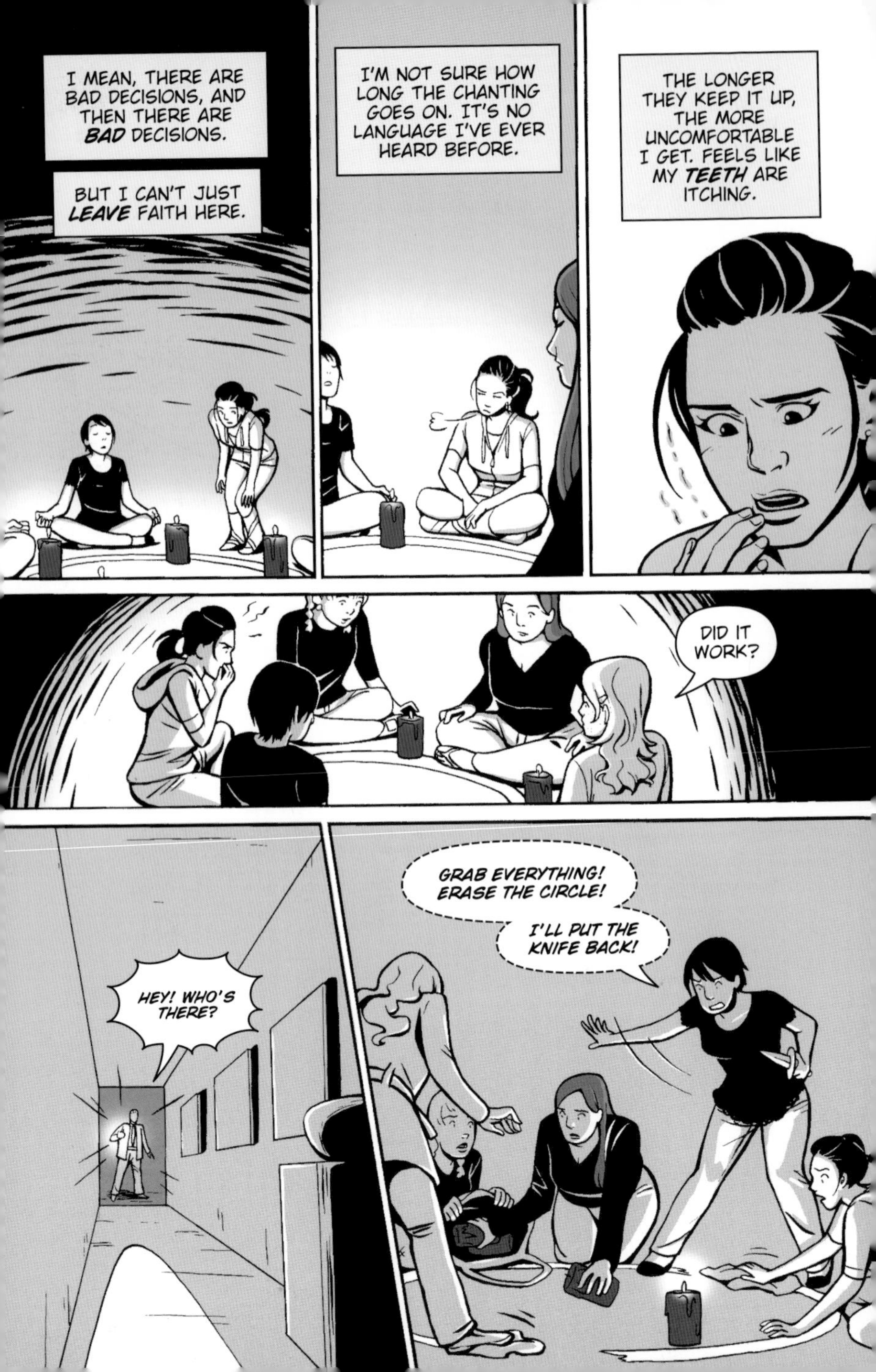
I MEAN, THERE ARE BAD DECISIONS, AND THEN THERE ARE *BAD* DECISIONS.
BUT I CAN'T JUST *LEAVE* FAITH HERE.
I'M NOT SURE HOW LONG THE CHANTING GOES ON. IT'S NO LANGUAGE I'VE EVER HEARD BEFORE.
THE LONGER THEY KEEP IT UP, THE MORE UNCOMFORTABLE I GET. FEELS LIKE MY *TEETH* ARE ITCHING.
DID IT WORK?
HEY! WHO'S THERE?
GRAB EVERYTHING! ERASE THE CIRCLE!
I'LL PUT THE KNIFE BACK!

GO GO GO GO!

OK, SHUT THE DOOR! GET IT SHUT, COME ON!

WOW! THAT WAS *SUPER!*

I DON'T KNOW IF I GAINED ANY *KNOWLEDGE,* BUT WHAT A *RUSH!*

OH NO.

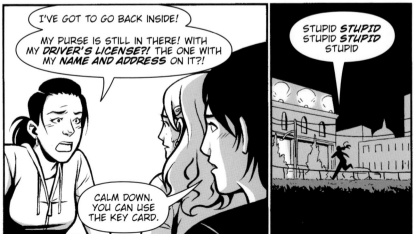

I'VE GOT TO GO BACK INSIDE!

MY PURSE IS STILL IN THERE! WITH MY *DRIVER'S LICENSE?!* THE ONE WITH MY *NAME AND ADDRESS* ON IT?!

CALM DOWN. YOU CAN USE THE KEY CARD.

STUPID *STUPID* STUPID *STUPID* STUPID

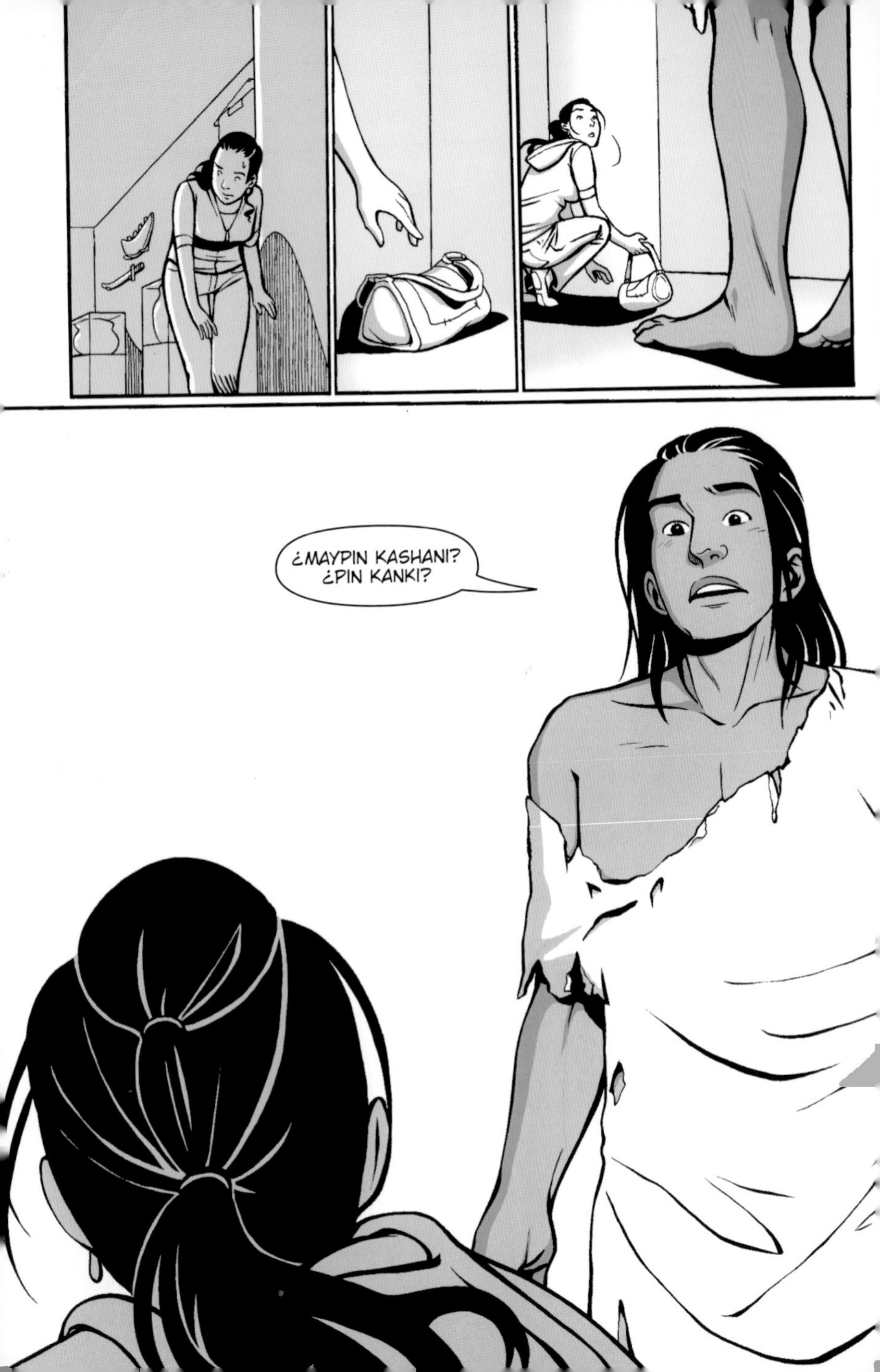
¿MAYPIN KASHANI? ¿PIN KANKI?

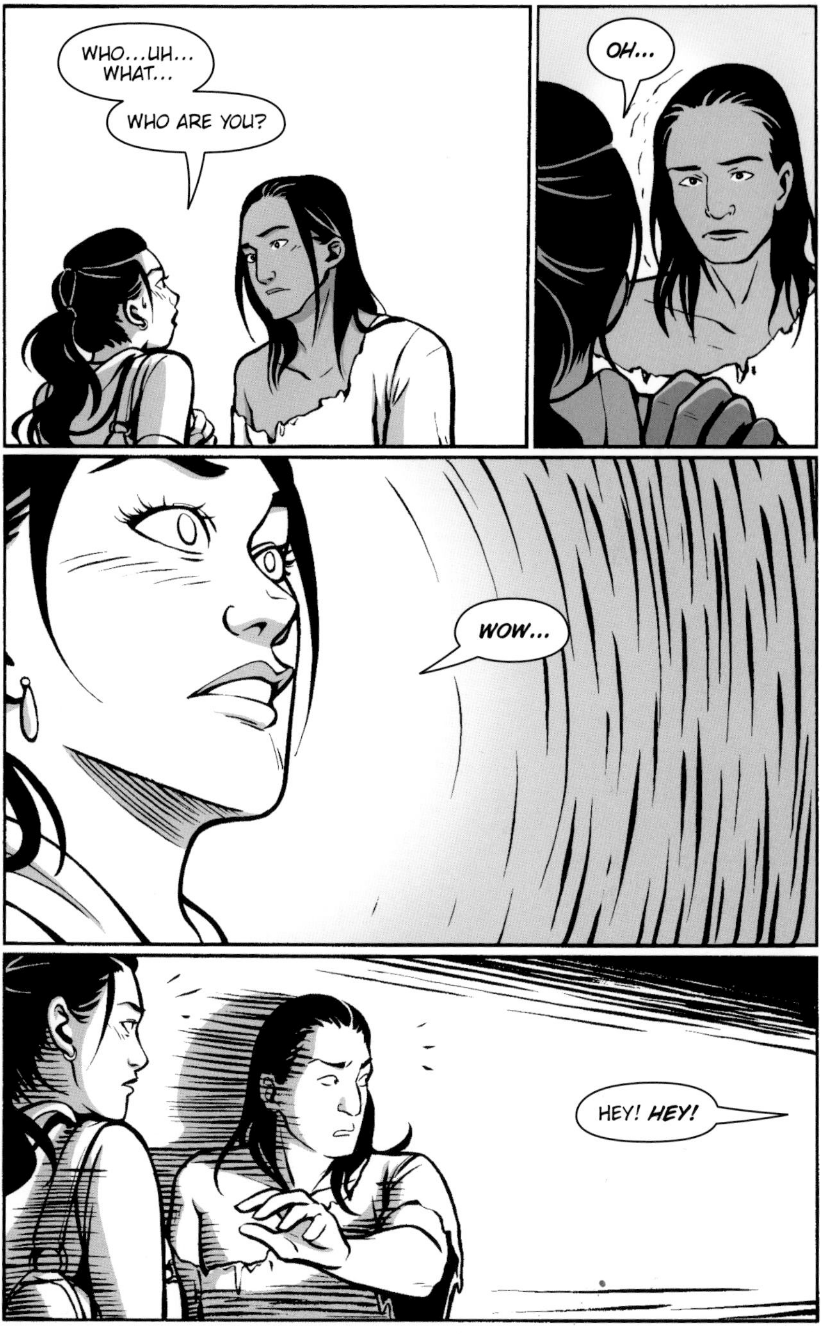
WHO...UH...
WHAT...
WHO ARE YOU?
OH...
WOW...
HEY! HEY!

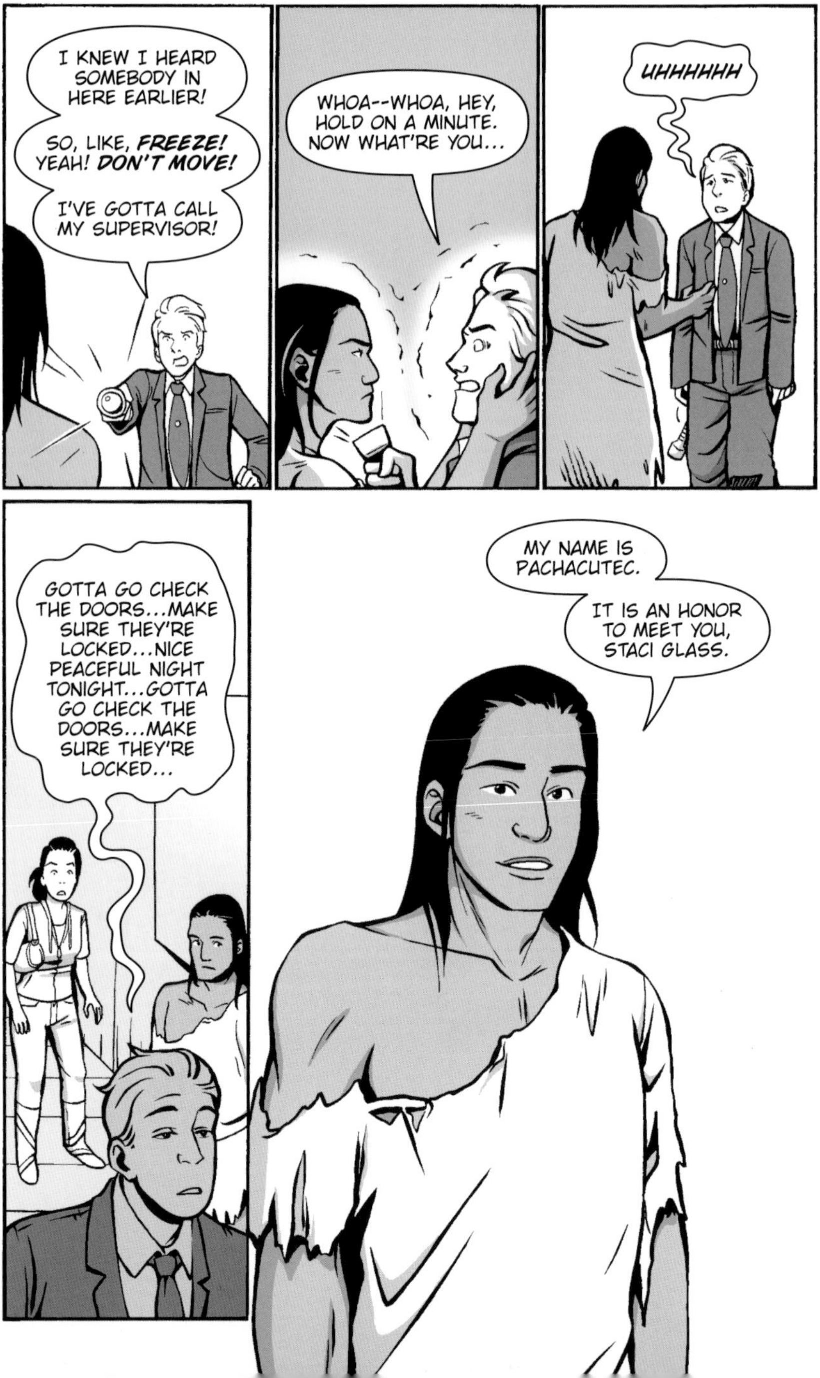
I KNEW I HEARD SOMEBODY IN HERE EARLIER!
SO, LIKE, ***FREEZE!*** YEAH! ***DON'T MOVE!***
I'VE GOTTA CALL MY SUPERVISOR!
WHOA--WHOA, HEY, HOLD ON A MINUTE. NOW WHAT'RE YOU...
UHHHHHH
GOTTA GO CHECK THE DOORS...MAKE SURE THEY'RE LOCKED...NICE PEACEFUL NIGHT TONIGHT...GOTTA GO CHECK THE DOORS...MAKE SURE THEY'RE LOCKED...
MY NAME IS PACHACUTEC.
IT IS AN HONOR TO MEET YOU, STACI GLASS.

CHAPTER TWO

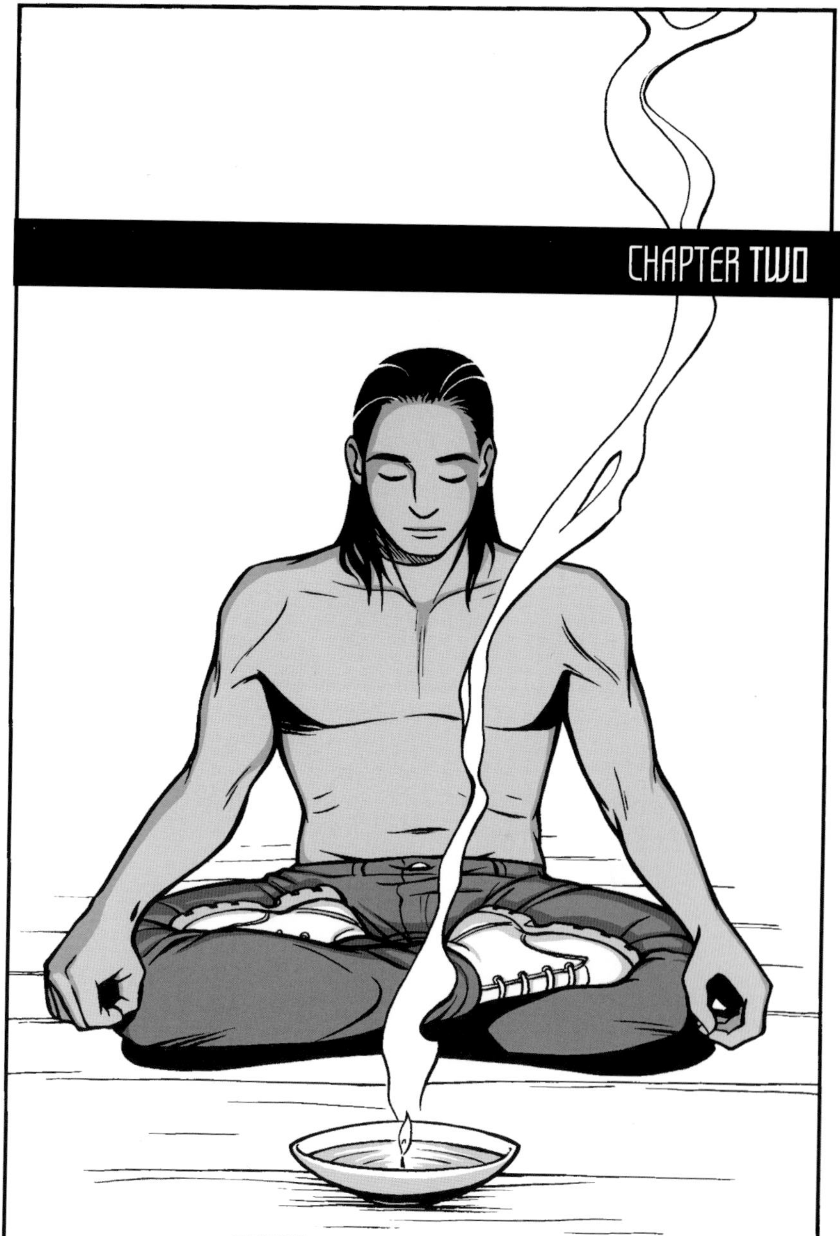

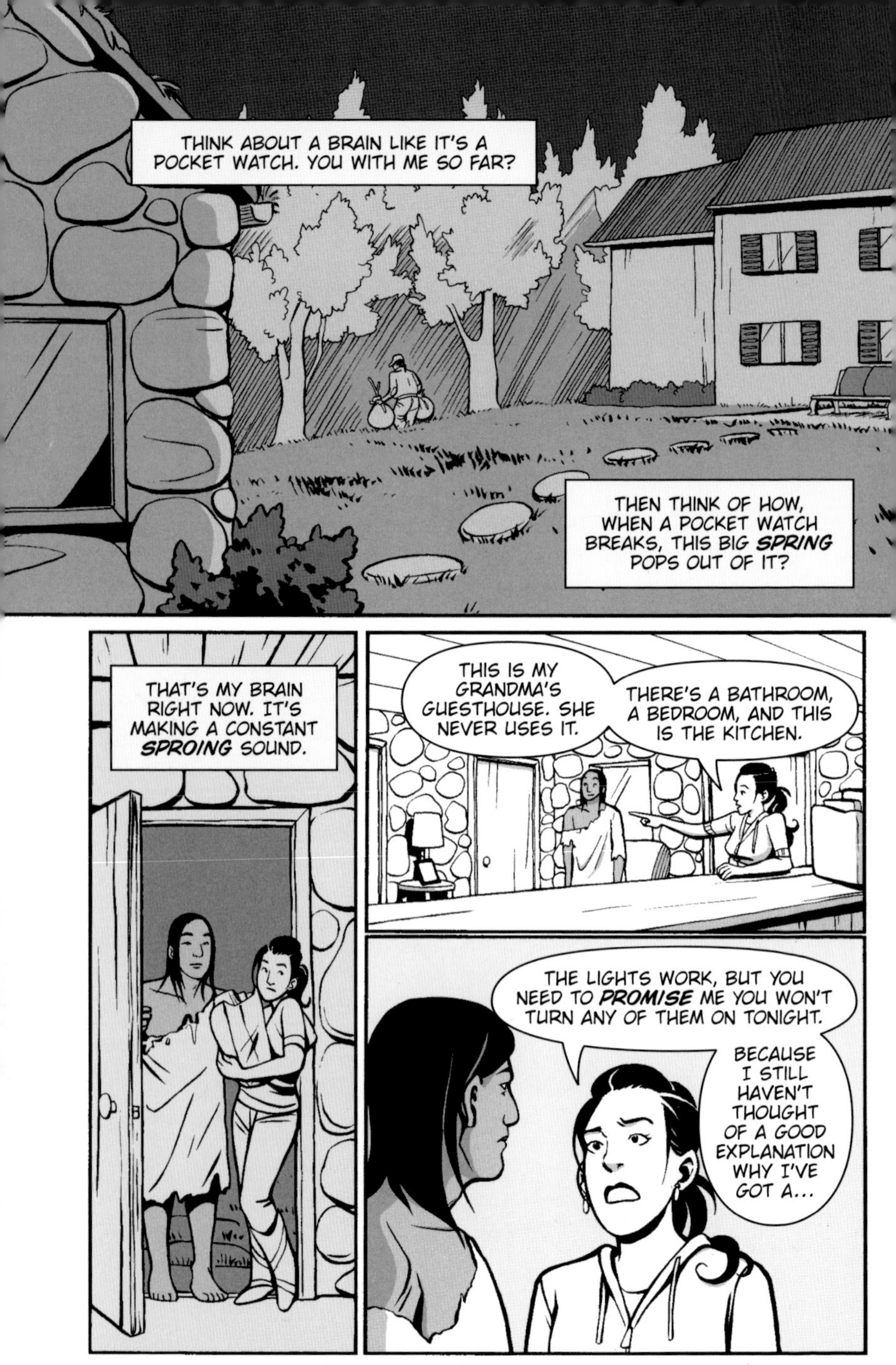
THINK ABOUT A BRAIN LIKE IT'S A POCKET WATCH. YOU WITH ME SO FAR?
THEN THINK OF HOW, WHEN A POCKET WATCH BREAKS, THIS BIG *SPRING* POPS OUT OF IT?
THAT'S MY BRAIN RIGHT NOW. IT'S MAKING A CONSTANT *SPROING* SOUND.
THIS IS MY GRANDMA'S GUESTHOUSE. SHE NEVER USES IT.
THERE'S A BATHROOM, A BEDROOM, AND THIS IS THE KITCHEN.
THE LIGHTS WORK, BUT YOU NEED TO ***PROMISE*** ME YOU WON'T TURN ANY OF THEM ON TONIGHT.
BECAUSE I STILL HAVEN'T THOUGHT OF A GOOD EXPLANATION WHY I'VE GOT A...

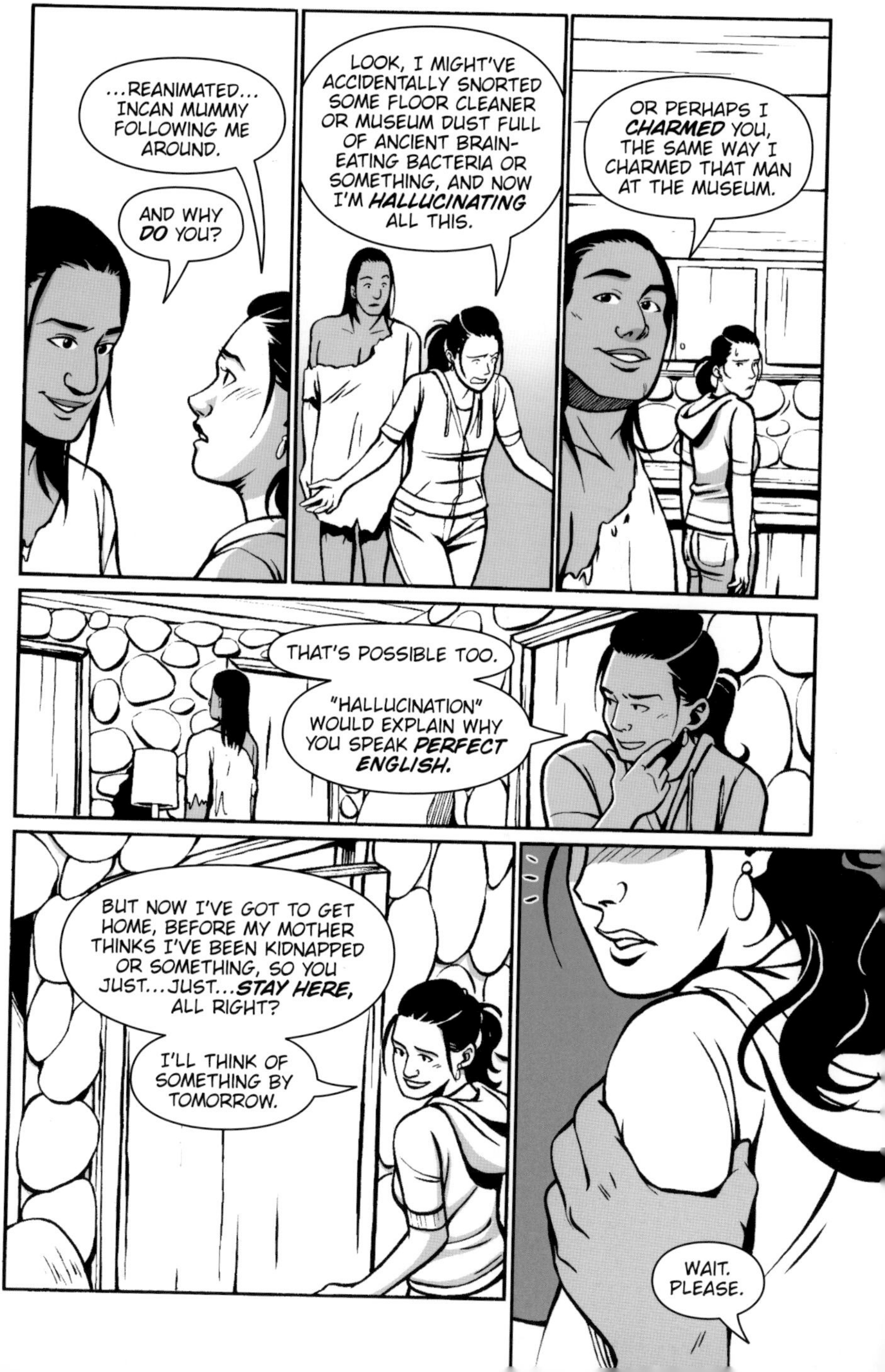
...REANIMATED... INCAN MUMMY FOLLOWING ME AROUND.
AND WHY DO YOU?
LOOK, I MIGHT'VE ACCIDENTALLY SNORTED SOME FLOOR CLEANER OR MUSEUM DUST FULL OF ANCIENT BRAIN-EATING BACTERIA OR SOMETHING, AND NOW I'M HALLUCINATING ALL THIS.
OR PERHAPS I CHARMED YOU, THE SAME WAY I CHARMED THAT MAN AT THE MUSEUM.
THAT'S POSSIBLE TOO.
"HALLUCINATION" WOULD EXPLAIN WHY YOU SPEAK PERFECT ENGLISH.
BUT NOW I'VE GOT TO GET HOME, BEFORE MY MOTHER THINKS I'VE BEEN KIDNAPPED OR SOMETHING, SO YOU JUST...JUST...STAY HERE, ALL RIGHT?
I'LL THINK OF SOMETHING BY TOMORROW.
WAIT. PLEASE.

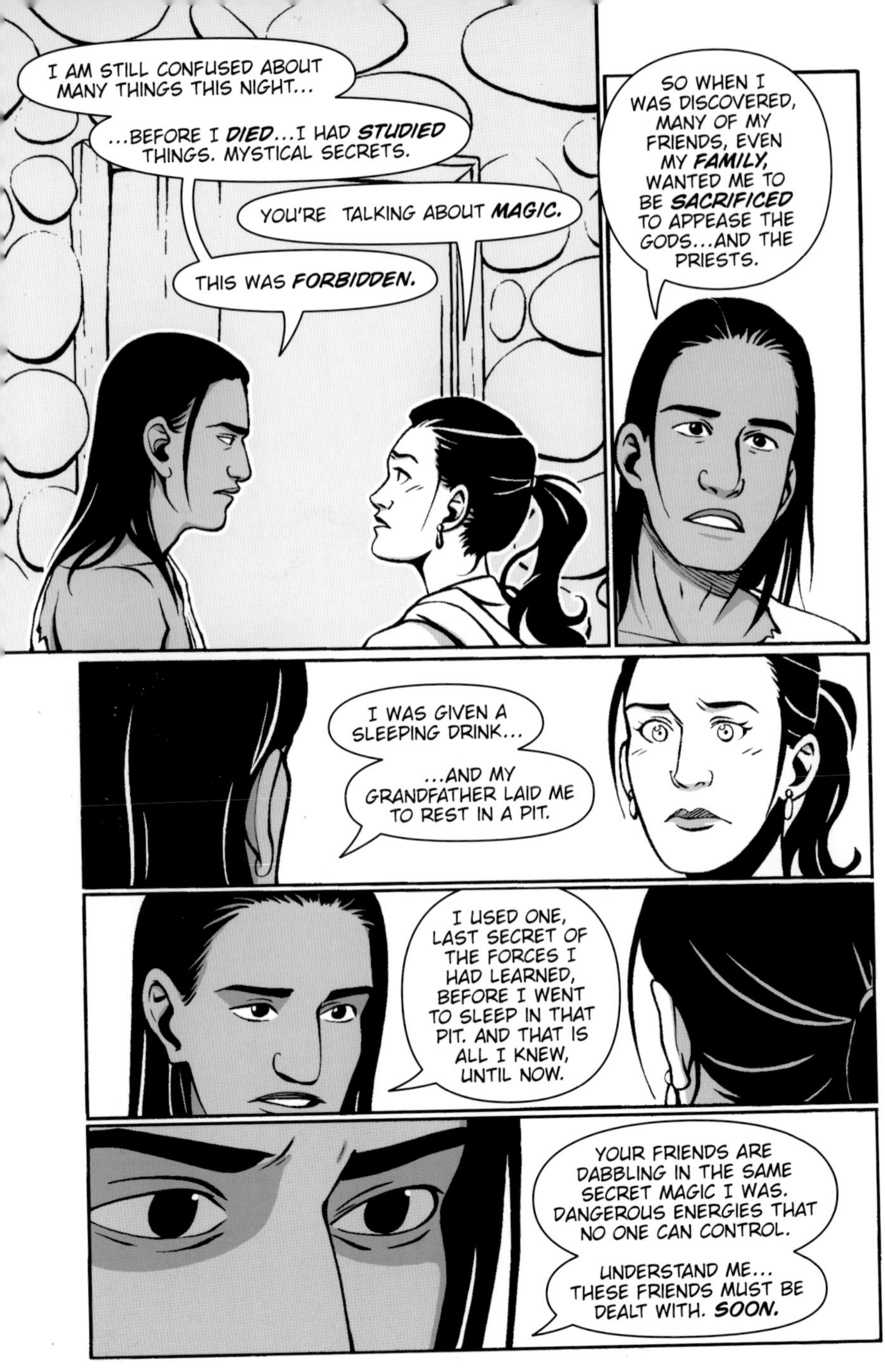
I AM STILL CONFUSED ABOUT MANY THINGS THIS NIGHT...
...BEFORE I **DIED**...I HAD **STUDIED** THINGS. MYSTICAL SECRETS.
YOU'RE TALKING ABOUT **MAGIC.**
THIS WAS **FORBIDDEN.**
SO WHEN I WAS DISCOVERED, MANY OF MY FRIENDS, EVEN MY **FAMILY,** WANTED ME TO BE **SACRIFICED** TO APPEASE THE GODS...AND THE PRIESTS.
I WAS GIVEN A SLEEPING DRINK...
...AND MY GRANDFATHER LAID ME TO REST IN A PIT.
I USED ONE, LAST SECRET OF THE FORCES I HAD LEARNED, BEFORE I WENT TO SLEEP IN THAT PIT. AND THAT IS ALL I KNEW, UNTIL NOW.
YOUR FRIENDS ARE DABBLING IN THE SAME SECRET MAGIC I WAS. DANGEROUS ENERGIES THAT NO ONE CAN CONTROL.
UNDERSTAND ME... THESE FRIENDS MUST BE DEALT WITH. **SOON.**

MAGIC...INCAN MUMMIES...MY HEAD'S GONNA *POP.* LIKE A BIG WATER BALLOON.

MAYBE I DREAMED THE WHOLE THING.

PROBABLY I HAD SOME KIND OF *PSYCHOTIC BREAK.* BUT STILL...

...I KIND OF HOPE I'M *NOT* CRAZY.

HEY! SO I TAKE IT YOU GOT YOUR PURSE BACK OK?

WELL, THERE WEREN'T ANY POLICE REPORTS FILED, I'LL SAY THAT MUCH.

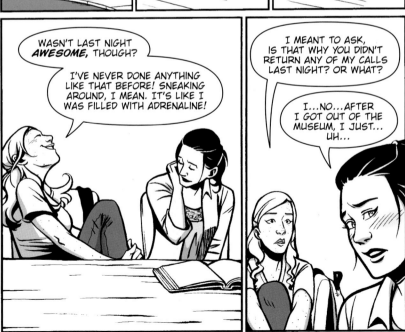

WASN'T LAST NIGHT *AWESOME,* THOUGH?

I'VE NEVER DONE ANYTHING LIKE THAT BEFORE! SNEAKING AROUND, I MEAN. IT'S LIKE I WAS FILLED WITH ADRENALINE!

I MEANT TO ASK, IS THAT WHY YOU DIDN'T RETURN ANY OF MY CALLS LAST NIGHT? OR WHAT?

I...NO...AFTER I GOT OUT OF THE MUSEUM, I JUST... UH...

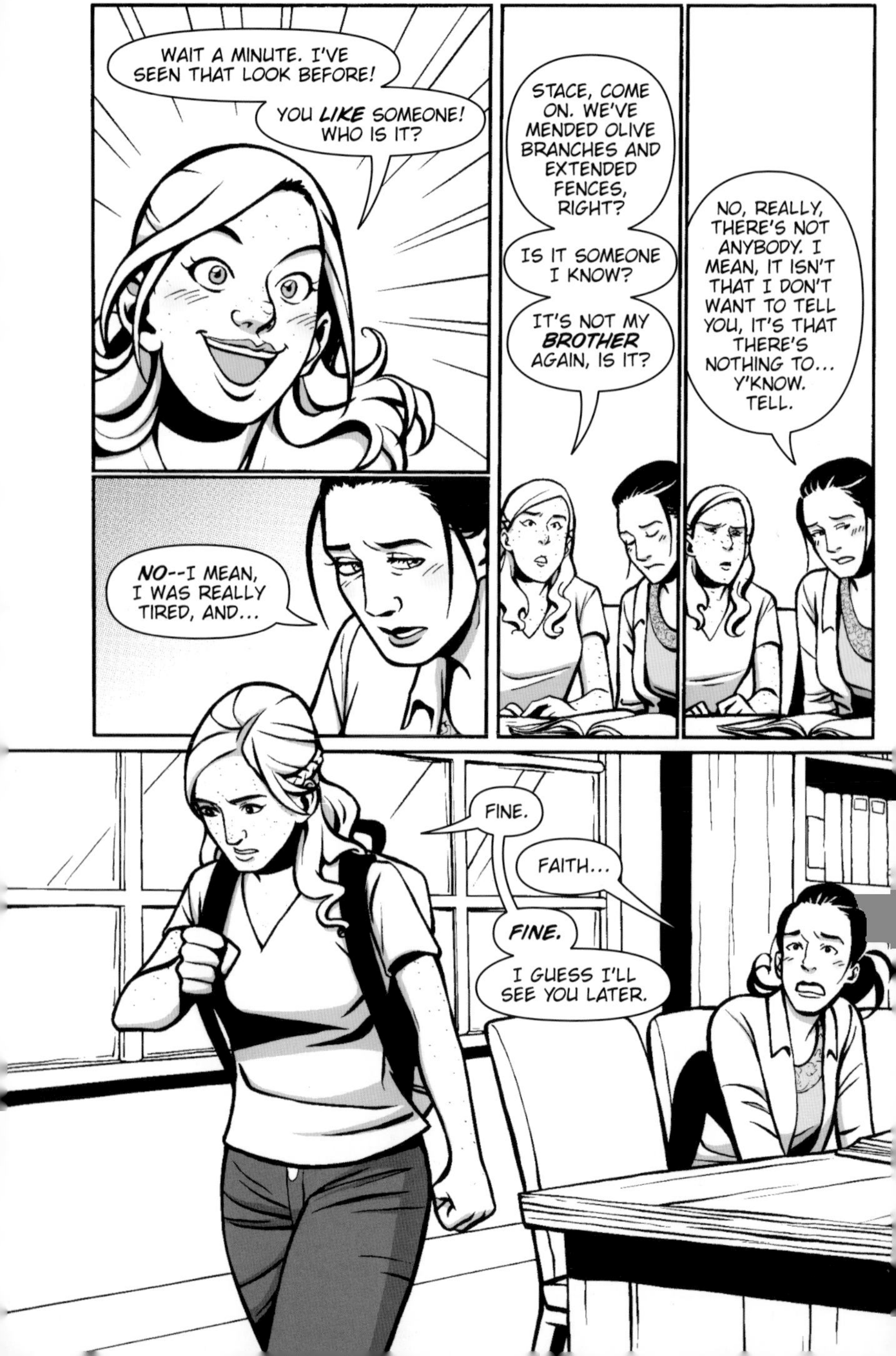
WAIT A MINUTE. I'VE SEEN THAT LOOK BEFORE!
YOU ***LIKE*** SOMEONE! WHO IS IT?
NO--I MEAN, I WAS REALLY TIRED, AND...
STACE, COME ON. WE'VE MENDED OLIVE BRANCHES AND EXTENDED FENCES, RIGHT?
IS IT SOMEONE I KNOW?
IT'S NOT MY ***BROTHER*** AGAIN, IS IT?
NO, REALLY, THERE'S NOT ANYBODY. I MEAN, IT ISN'T THAT I DON'T WANT TO TELL YOU, IT'S THAT THERE'S NOTHING TO... Y'KNOW. TELL.
FINE.
FAITH...
FINE.
I GUESS I'LL SEE YOU LATER.

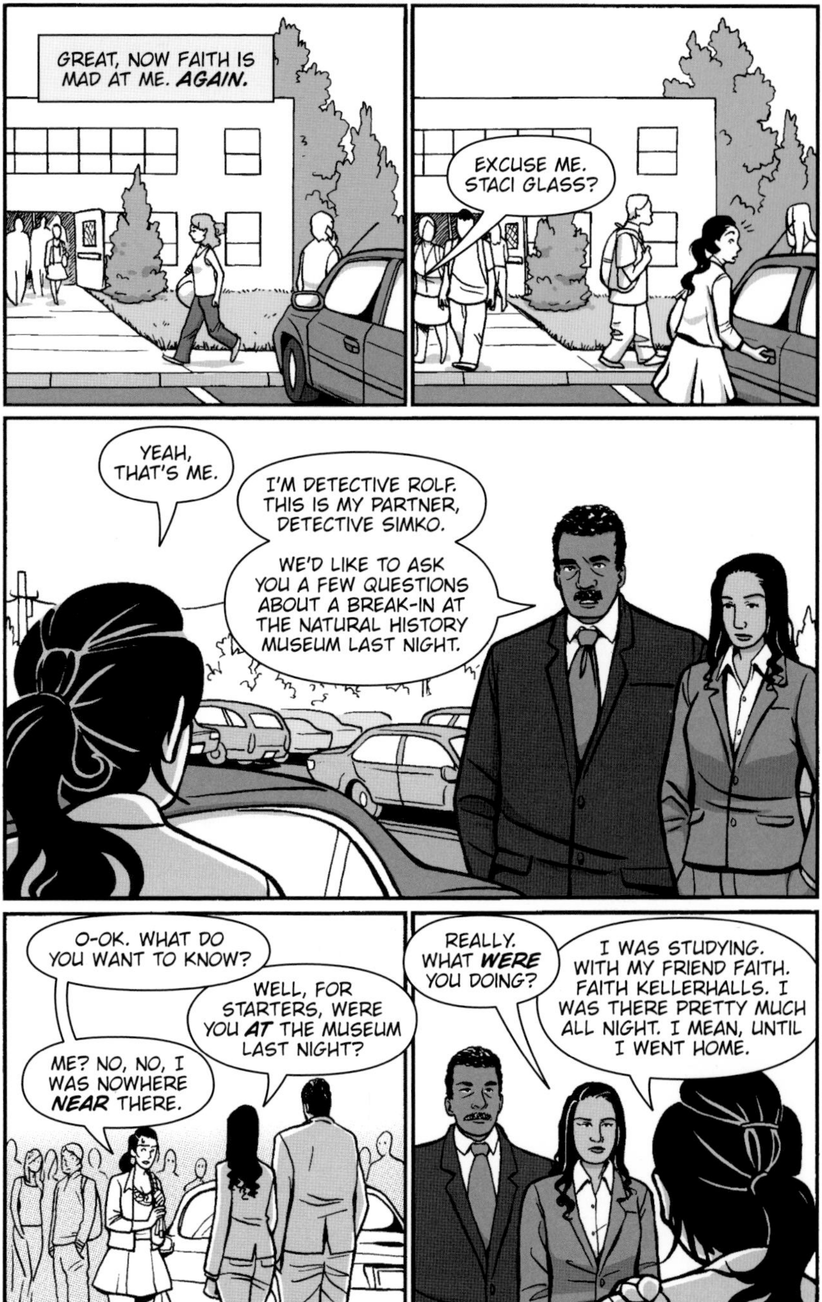
GREAT, NOW FAITH IS MAD AT ME. AGAIN.
EXCUSE ME. STACI GLASS?
YEAH, THAT'S ME.
I'M DETECTIVE ROLF. THIS IS MY PARTNER, DETECTIVE SIMKO.
WE'D LIKE TO ASK YOU A FEW QUESTIONS ABOUT A BREAK-IN AT THE NATURAL HISTORY MUSEUM LAST NIGHT.
O-OK. WHAT DO YOU WANT TO KNOW?
WELL, FOR STARTERS, WERE YOU AT THE MUSEUM LAST NIGHT?
ME? NO, NO, I WAS NOWHERE NEAR THERE.
REALLY. WHAT WERE YOU DOING?
I WAS STUDYING. WITH MY FRIEND FAITH. FAITH KELLERHALLS. I WAS THERE PRETTY MUCH ALL NIGHT. I MEAN, UNTIL I WENT HOME.

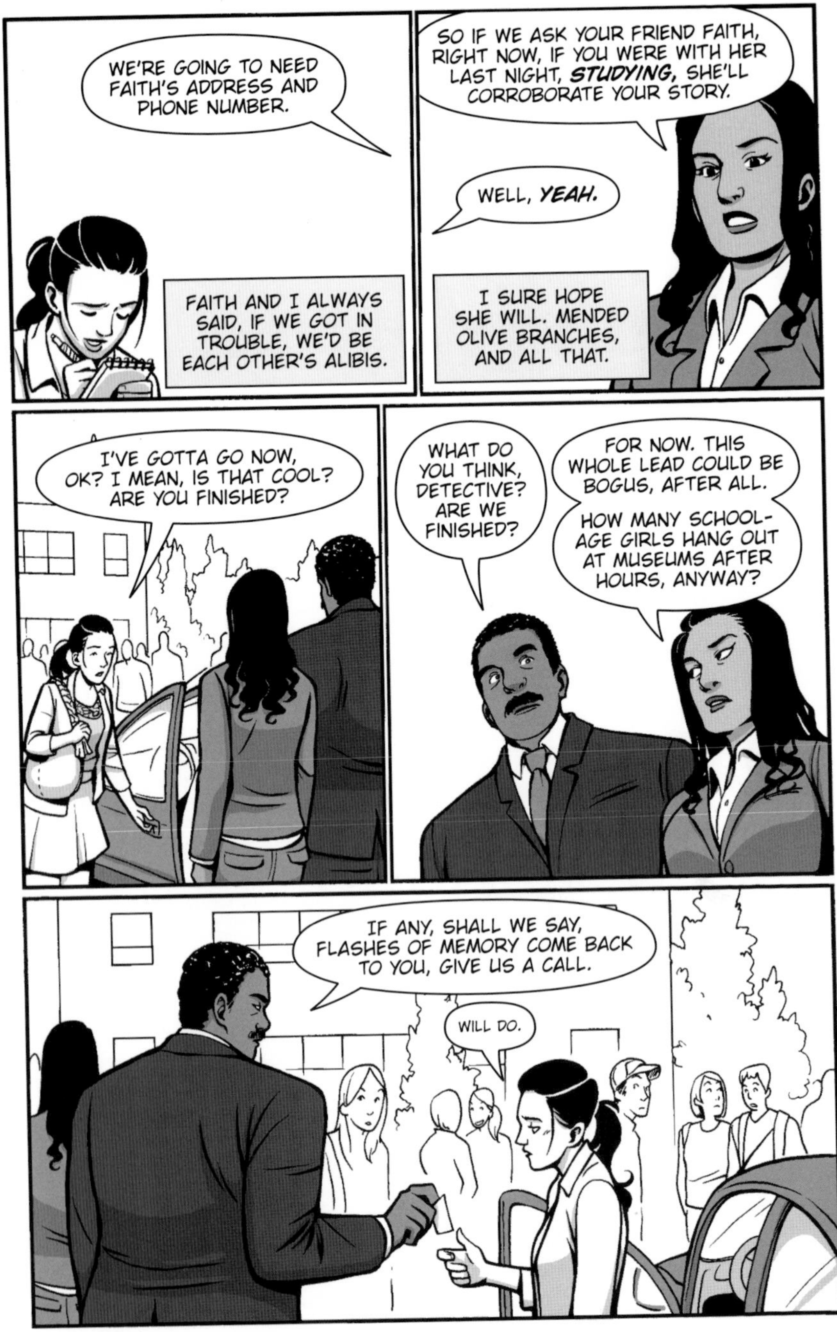
WE'RE GOING TO NEED FAITH'S ADDRESS AND PHONE NUMBER.
FAITH AND I ALWAYS SAID, IF WE GOT IN TROUBLE, WE'D BE EACH OTHER'S ALIBIS.
SO IF WE ASK YOUR FRIEND FAITH, RIGHT NOW, IF YOU WERE WITH HER LAST NIGHT, *STUDYING,* SHE'LL CORROBORATE YOUR STORY.
WELL, *YEAH.*
I SURE HOPE SHE WILL. MENDED OLIVE BRANCHES, AND ALL THAT.
I'VE GOTTA GO NOW, OK? I MEAN, IS THAT COOL? ARE YOU FINISHED?
WHAT DO YOU THINK, DETECTIVE? ARE WE FINISHED?
FOR NOW. THIS WHOLE LEAD COULD BE BOGUS, AFTER ALL.
HOW MANY SCHOOL-AGE GIRLS HANG OUT AT MUSEUMS AFTER HOURS, ANYWAY?
IF ANY, SHALL WE SAY, FLASHES OF MEMORY COME BACK TO YOU, GIVE US A CALL.
WILL DO.

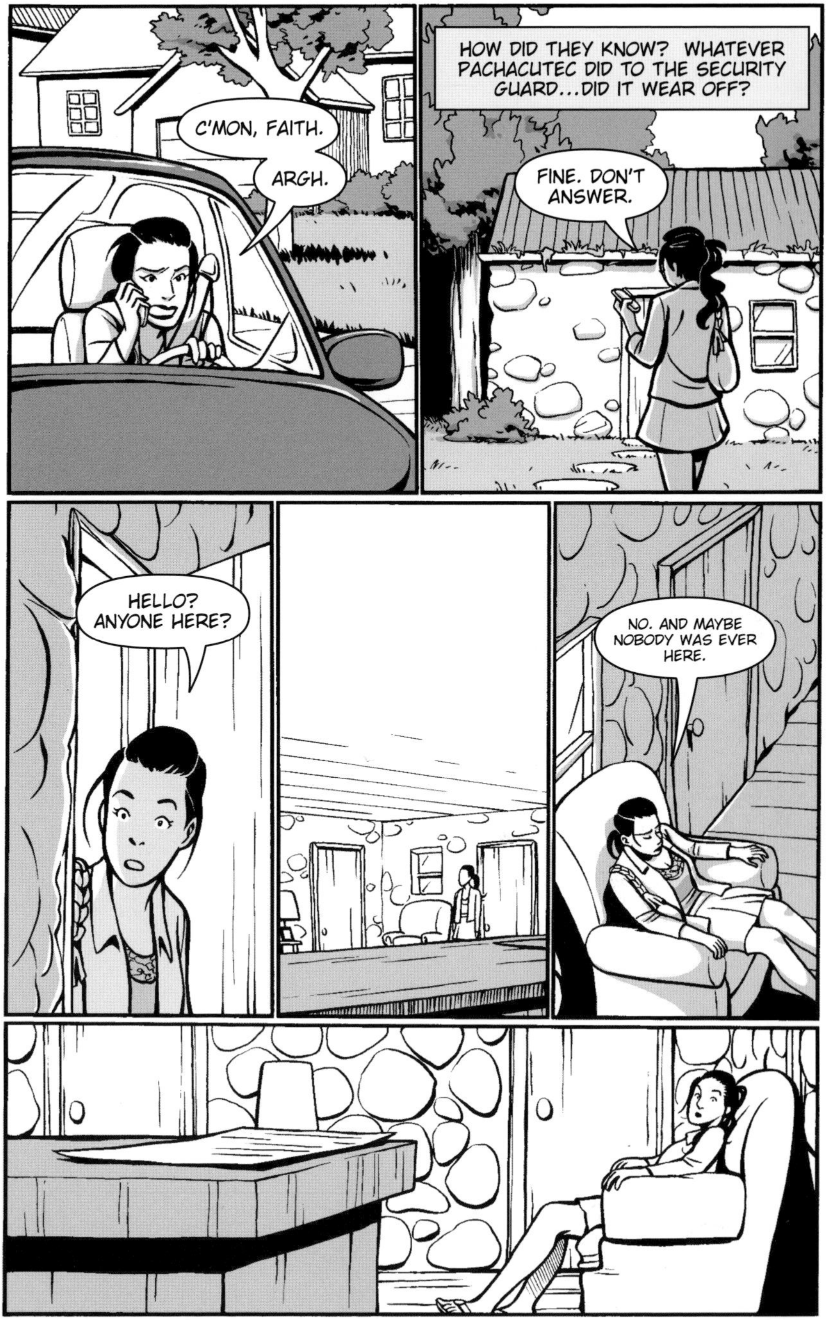
C'MON, FAITH.
ARGH.
HOW DID THEY KNOW? WHATEVER PACHACUTEC DID TO THE SECURITY GUARD...DID IT WEAR OFF?
FINE. DON'T ANSWER.
HELLO? ANYONE HERE?
NO. AND MAYBE NOBODY WAS EVER HERE.

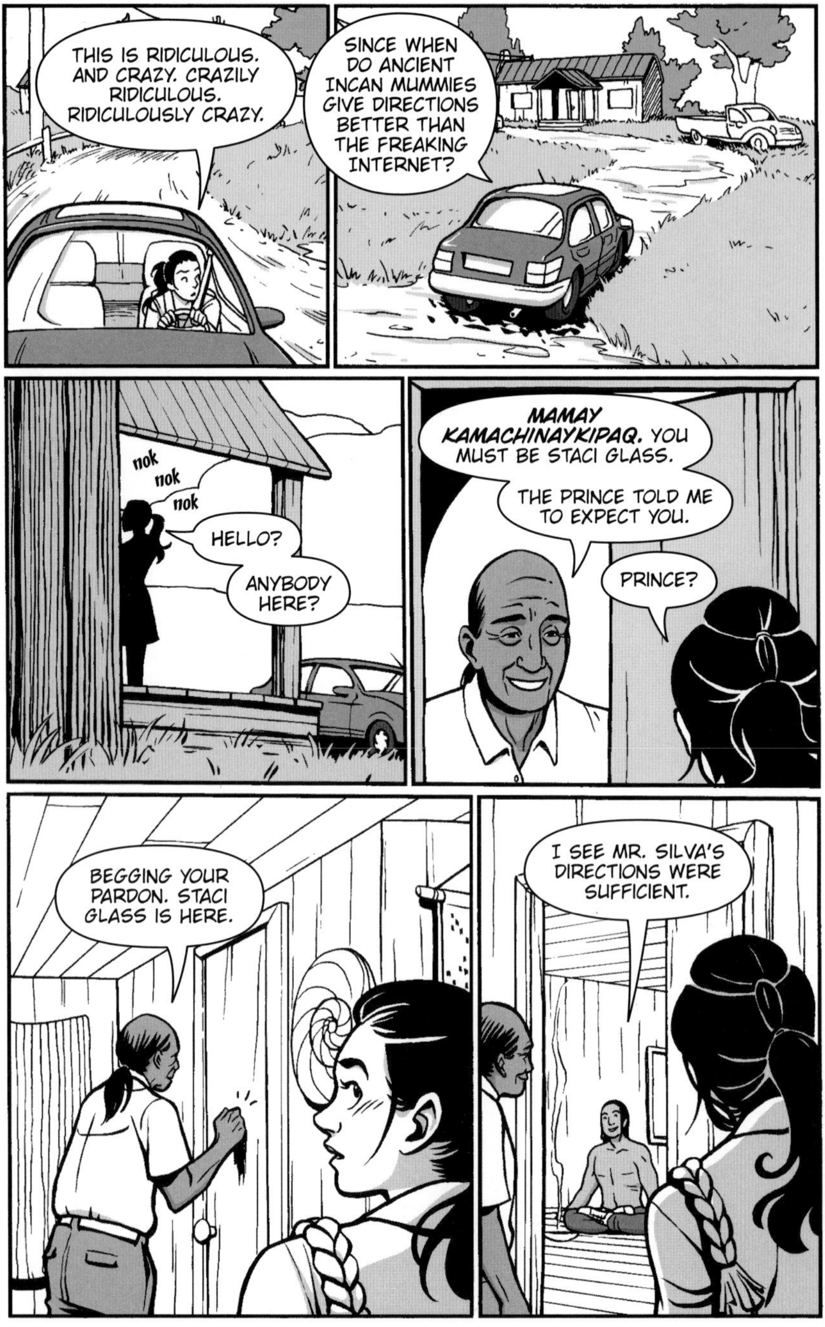
THIS IS RIDICULOUS. AND CRAZY. CRAZILY RIDICULOUS. RIDICULOUSLY CRAZY.
SINCE WHEN DO ANCIENT INCAN MUMMIES GIVE DIRECTIONS BETTER THAN THE FREAKING INTERNET?
nok nok nok
HELLO?
ANYBODY HERE?
MAMAY KAMACHINAYKIPAQ. YOU MUST BE STACI GLASS.
THE PRINCE TOLD ME TO EXPECT YOU.
PRINCE?
BEGGING YOUR PARDON. STACI GLASS IS HERE.
I SEE MR. SILVA'S DIRECTIONS WERE SUFFICIENT.

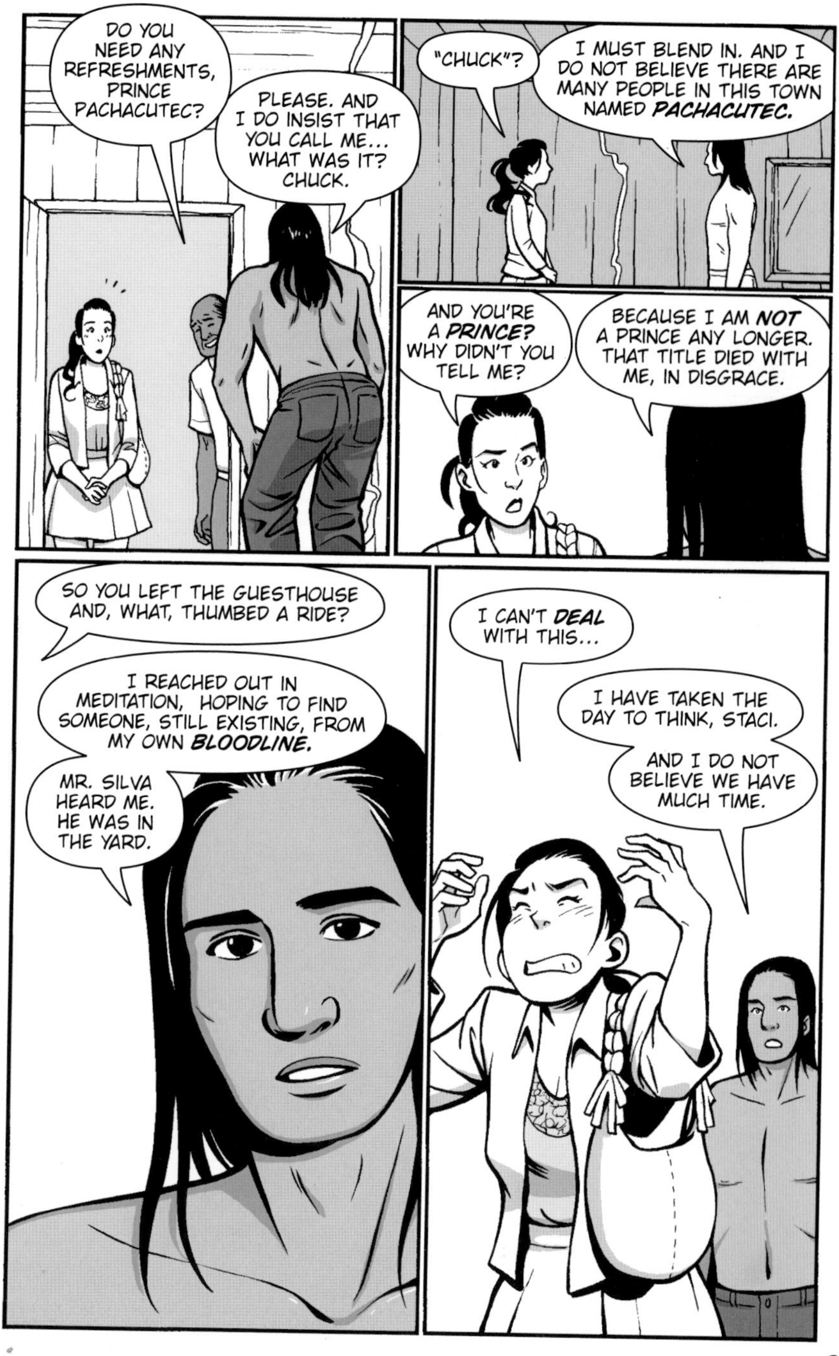
DO YOU NEED ANY REFRESHMENTS, PRINCE PACHACUTEC?
PLEASE. AND I DO INSIST THAT YOU CALL ME... WHAT WAS IT? CHUCK.
"CHUCK"?
I MUST BLEND IN. AND I DO NOT BELIEVE THERE ARE MANY PEOPLE IN THIS TOWN NAMED PACHACUTEC.
AND YOU'RE A PRINCE? WHY DIDN'T YOU TELL ME?
BECAUSE I AM NOT A PRINCE ANY LONGER. THAT TITLE DIED WITH ME, IN DISGRACE.
SO YOU LEFT THE GUESTHOUSE AND, WHAT, THUMBED A RIDE?
I REACHED OUT IN MEDITATION, HOPING TO FIND SOMEONE, STILL EXISTING, FROM MY OWN BLOODLINE.
MR. SILVA HEARD ME. HE WAS IN THE YARD.
I CAN'T DEAL WITH THIS...
I HAVE TAKEN THE DAY TO THINK, STACI.
AND I DO NOT BELIEVE WE HAVE MUCH TIME.

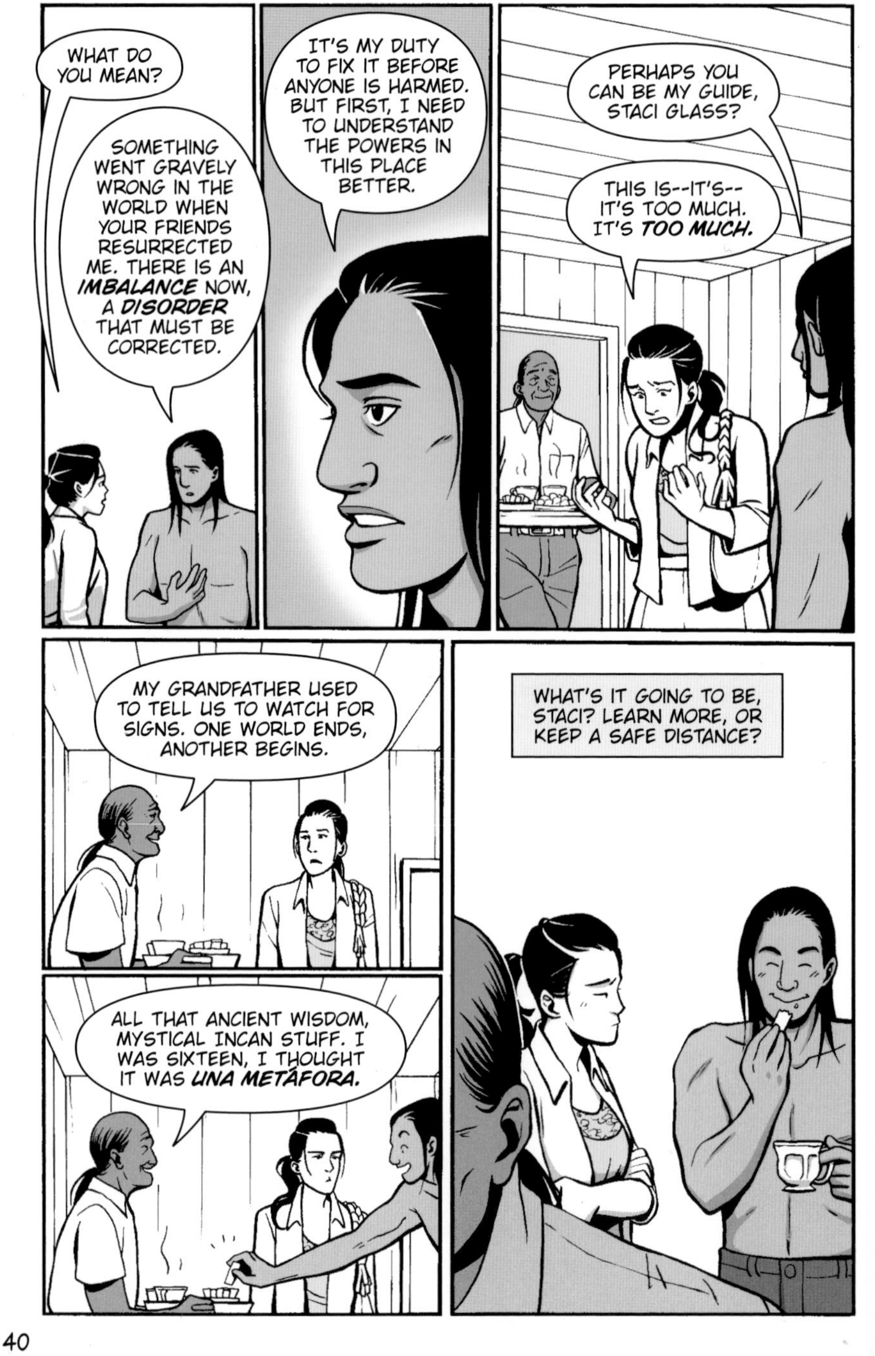
WHAT DO YOU MEAN?
SOMETHING WENT GRAVELY WRONG IN THE WORLD WHEN YOUR FRIENDS RESURRECTED ME. THERE IS AN IMBALANCE NOW, A DISORDER THAT MUST BE CORRECTED.
IT'S MY DUTY TO FIX IT BEFORE ANYONE IS HARMED. BUT FIRST, I NEED TO UNDERSTAND THE POWERS IN THIS PLACE BETTER.
PERHAPS YOU CAN BE MY GUIDE, STACI GLASS?
THIS IS--IT'S--IT'S TOO MUCH. IT'S TOO MUCH.
MY GRANDFATHER USED TO TELL US TO WATCH FOR SIGNS. ONE WORLD ENDS, ANOTHER BEGINS.
ALL THAT ANCIENT WISDOM, MYSTICAL INCAN STUFF. I WAS SIXTEEN, I THOUGHT IT WAS UNA METÁFORA.
WHAT'S IT GOING TO BE, STACI? LEARN MORE, OR KEEP A SAFE DISTANCE?

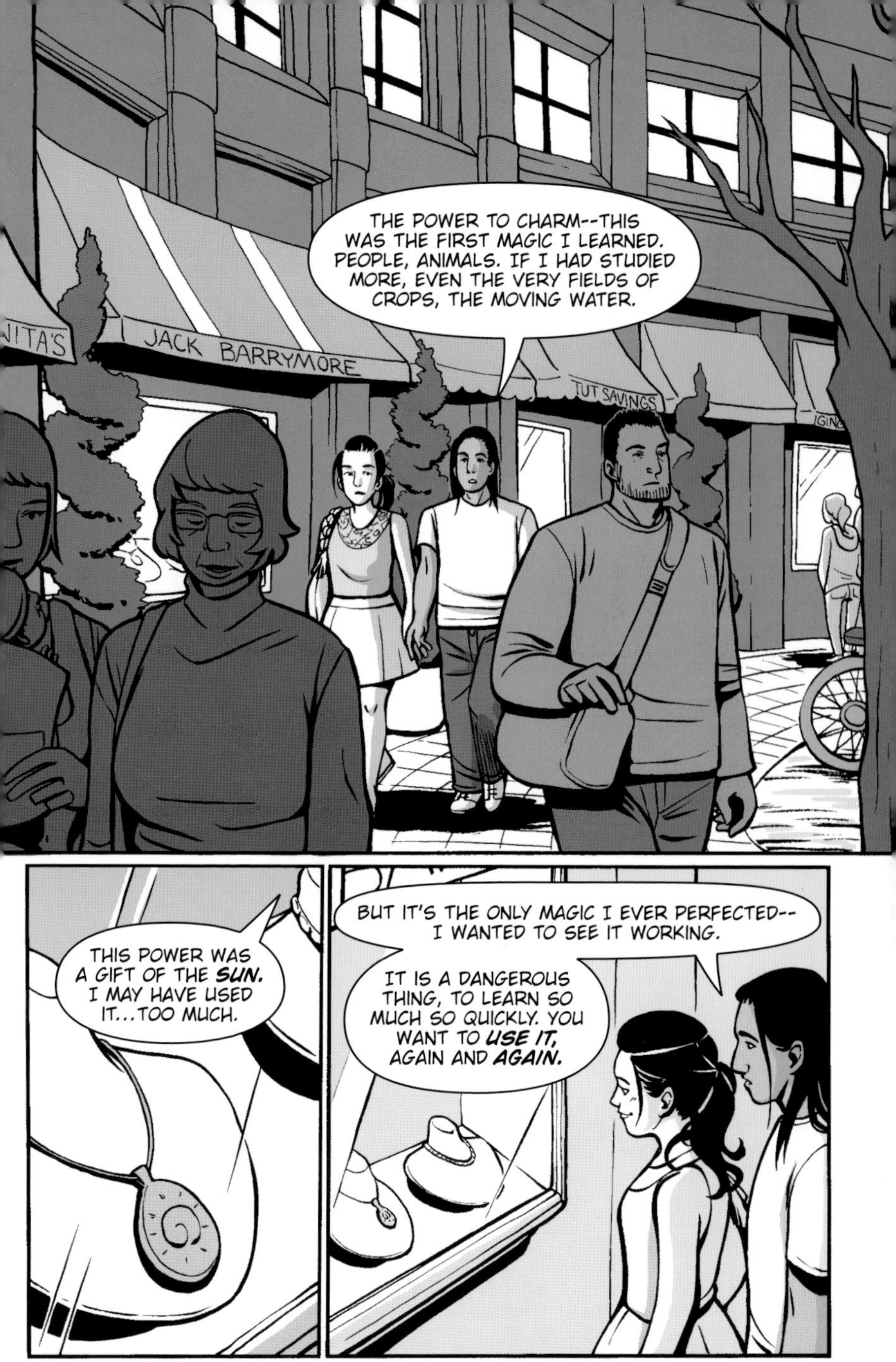
THE POWER TO CHARM--THIS WAS THE FIRST MAGIC I LEARNED. PEOPLE, ANIMALS. IF I HAD STUDIED MORE, EVEN THE VERY FIELDS OF CROPS, THE MOVING WATER.
JITA'S
JACK BARRYMORE
TUT SAVINGS
THIS POWER WAS A GIFT OF THE SUN. I MAY HAVE USED IT...TOO MUCH.
BUT IT'S THE ONLY MAGIC I EVER PERFECTED-- I WANTED TO SEE IT WORKING.
IT IS A DANGEROUS THING, TO LEARN SO MUCH SO QUICKLY. YOU WANT TO USE IT, AGAIN AND AGAIN.

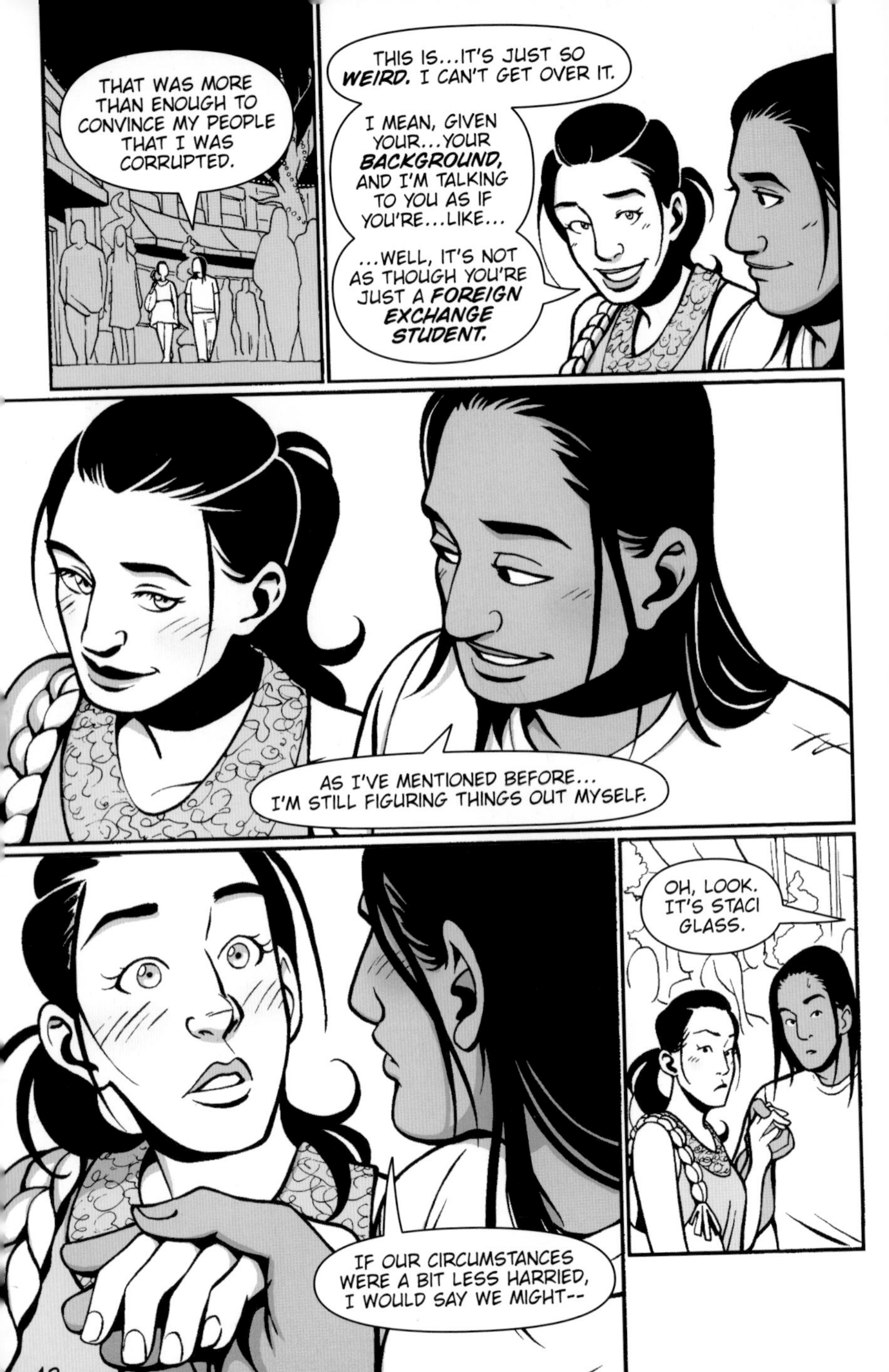
THAT WAS MORE THAN ENOUGH TO CONVINCE MY PEOPLE THAT I WAS CORRUPTED.
THIS IS...IT'S JUST SO *WEIRD.* I CAN'T GET OVER IT.
I MEAN, GIVEN YOUR...YOUR *BACKGROUND,* AND I'M TALKING TO YOU AS IF YOU'RE...LIKE...
...WELL, IT'S NOT AS THOUGH YOU'RE JUST A *FOREIGN EXCHANGE STUDENT.*
AS I'VE MENTIONED BEFORE... I'M STILL FIGURING THINGS OUT MYSELF.
IF OUR CIRCUMSTANCES WERE A BIT LESS HARRIED, I WOULD SAY WE MIGHT--
OH, LOOK. IT'S STACI GLASS.

WHAT A PURELY COINCIDENTAL MEETING THIS IS.

WHO'S YOUR FRIEND, STACI?

CHUCK SILVA. I'M FROM PERU.

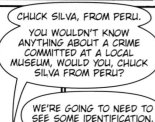

CHUCK SILVA, FROM PERU.

YOU WOULDN'T KNOW ANYTHING ABOUT A CRIME COMMITTED AT A LOCAL MUSEUM, WOULD YOU, CHUCK SILVA FROM PERU?

WE'RE GOING TO NEED TO SEE SOME IDENTIFICATION, CHUCK.

MY IDENTIFICATION IS PERFECTLY IN ORDER.

THERE IS NOTHING SUSPICIOUS ABOUT ME WHATSOEVER.

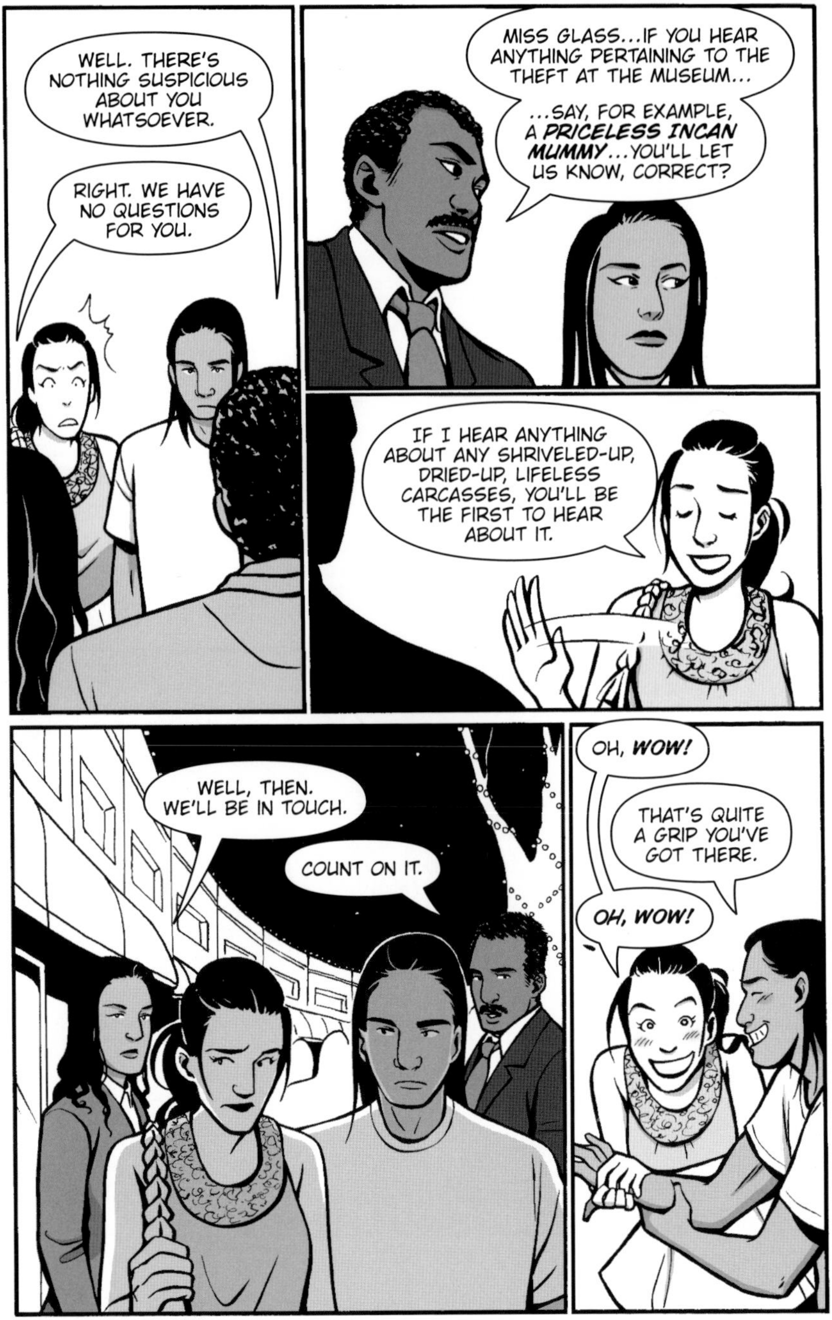
WELL. THERE'S NOTHING SUSPICIOUS ABOUT YOU WHATSOEVER.
RIGHT. WE HAVE NO QUESTIONS FOR YOU.
MISS GLASS...IF YOU HEAR ANYTHING PERTAINING TO THE THEFT AT THE MUSEUM...
...SAY, FOR EXAMPLE, A *PRICELESS INCAN MUMMY*...YOU'LL LET US KNOW, CORRECT?
IF I HEAR ANYTHING ABOUT ANY SHRIVELED-UP, DRIED-UP, LIFELESS CARCASSES, YOU'LL BE THE FIRST TO HEAR ABOUT IT.
WELL, THEN. WE'LL BE IN TOUCH.
COUNT ON IT.
OH, *WOW!*
THAT'S QUITE A GRIP YOU'VE GOT THERE.
OH, WOW!

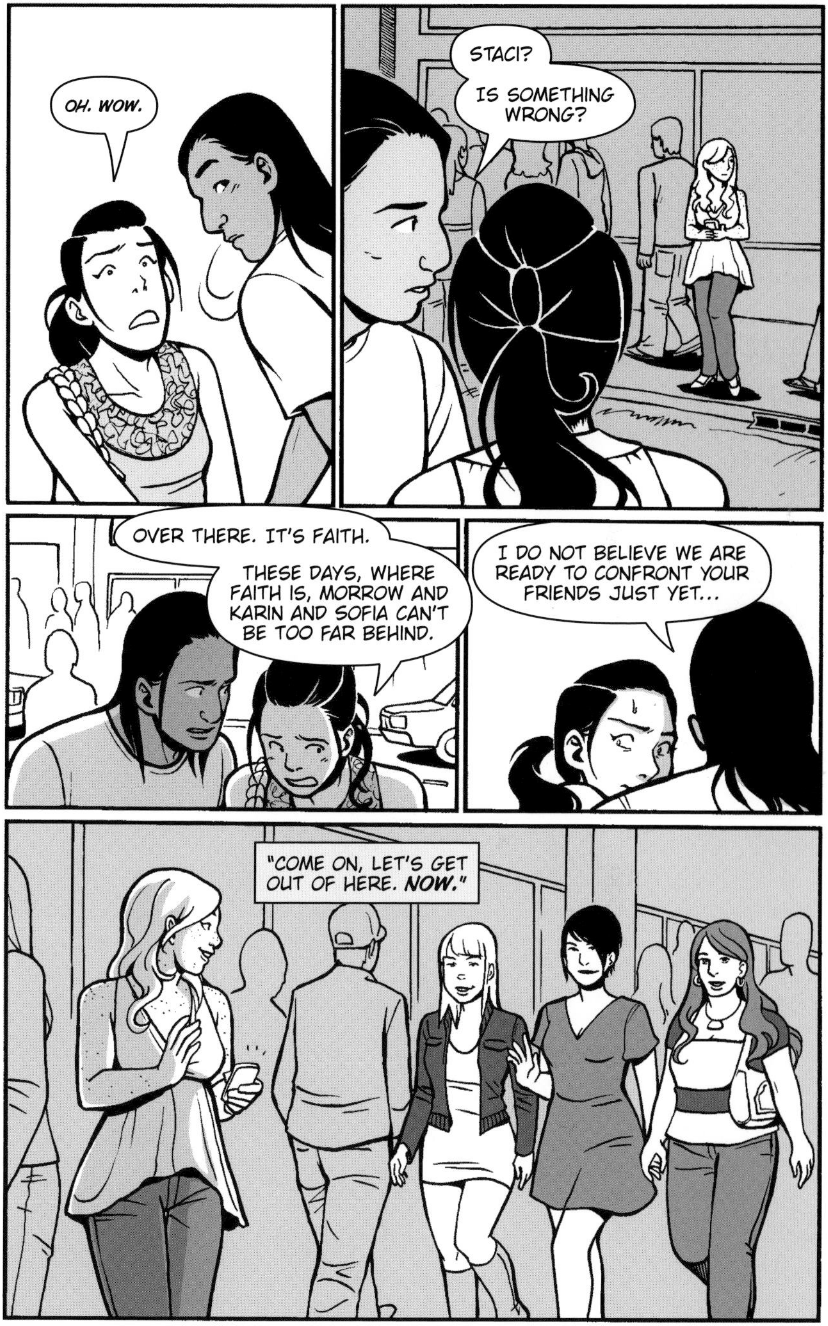
OH. WOW.
STACI?
IS SOMETHING WRONG?
OVER THERE. IT'S FAITH.
THESE DAYS, WHERE FAITH IS, MORROW AND KARIN AND SOFIA CAN'T BE TOO FAR BEHIND.
I DO NOT BELIEVE WE ARE READY TO CONFRONT YOUR FRIENDS JUST YET...
"COME ON, LET'S GET OUT OF HERE. NOW."

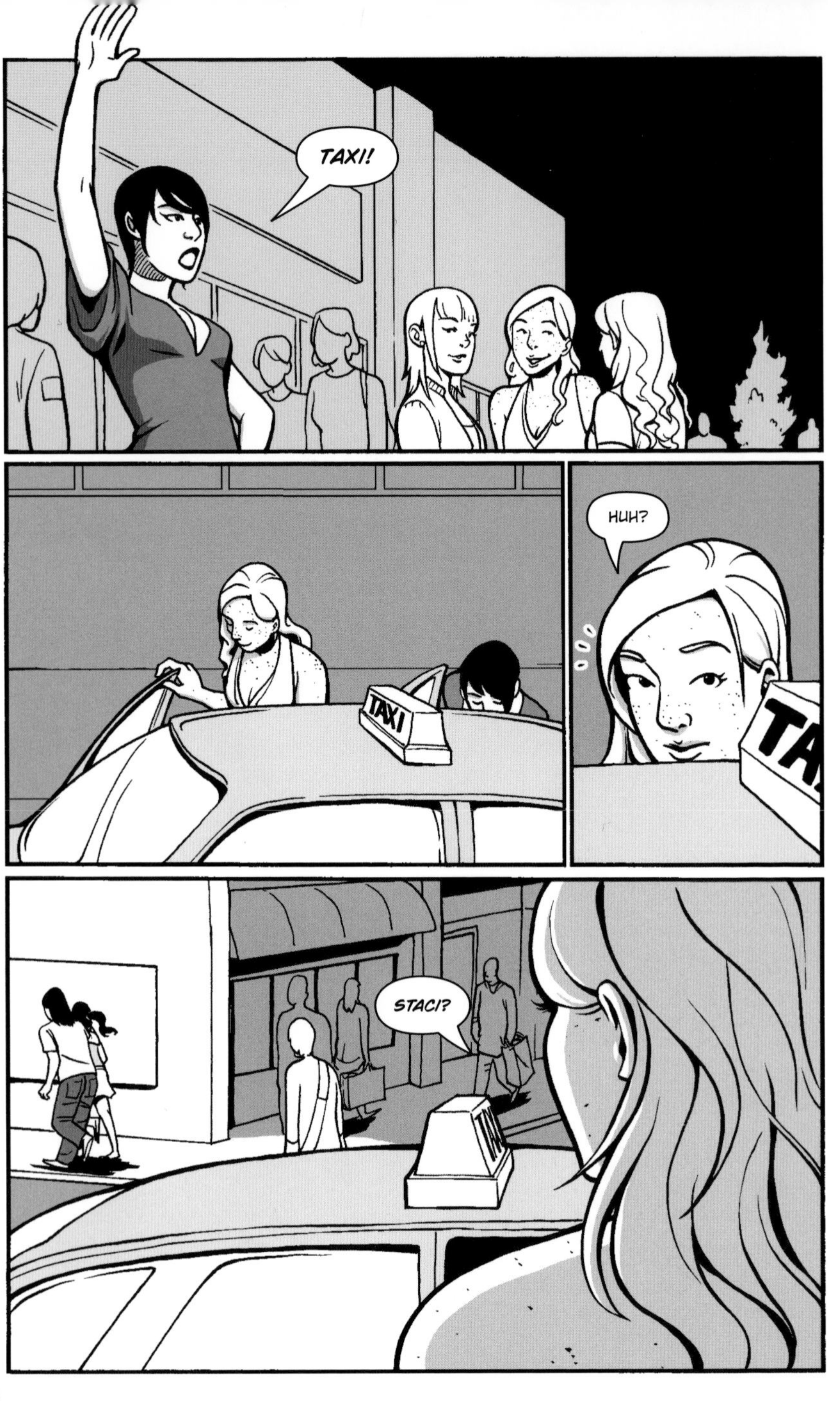
TAXI!
TAXI
HUH?
TAXI
STACI?

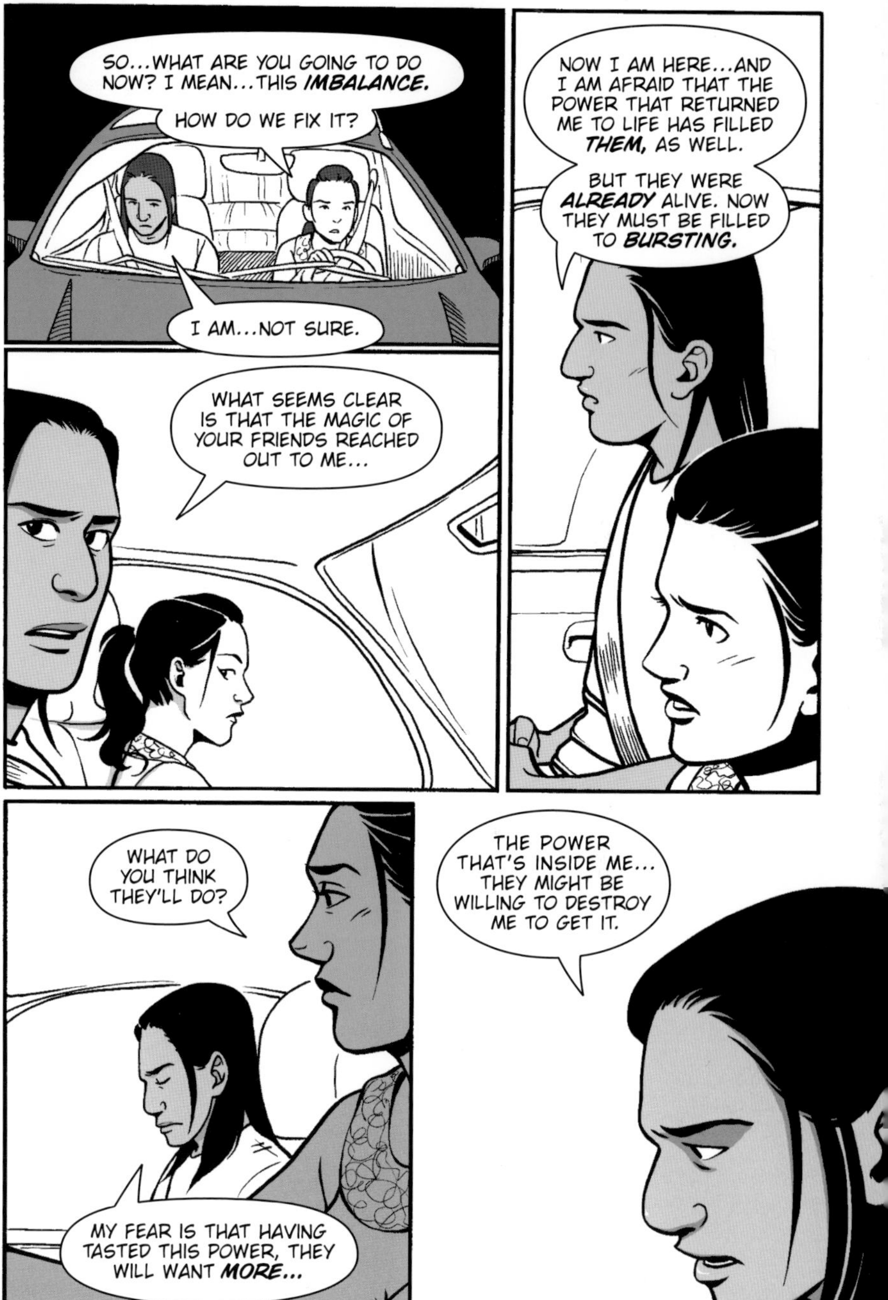
SO...WHAT ARE YOU GOING TO DO NOW? I MEAN...THIS *IMBALANCE.*
HOW DO WE FIX IT?
I AM...NOT SURE.
WHAT SEEMS CLEAR IS THAT THE MAGIC OF YOUR FRIENDS REACHED OUT TO ME...
NOW I AM HERE...AND I AM AFRAID THAT THE POWER THAT RETURNED ME TO LIFE HAS FILLED *THEM,* AS WELL.
BUT THEY WERE *ALREADY* ALIVE. NOW THEY MUST BE FILLED TO *BURSTING.*
WHAT DO YOU THINK THEY'LL DO?
MY FEAR IS THAT HAVING TASTED THIS POWER, THEY WILL WANT *MORE...*
THE POWER THAT'S INSIDE ME... THEY MIGHT BE WILLING TO DESTROY ME TO GET IT.

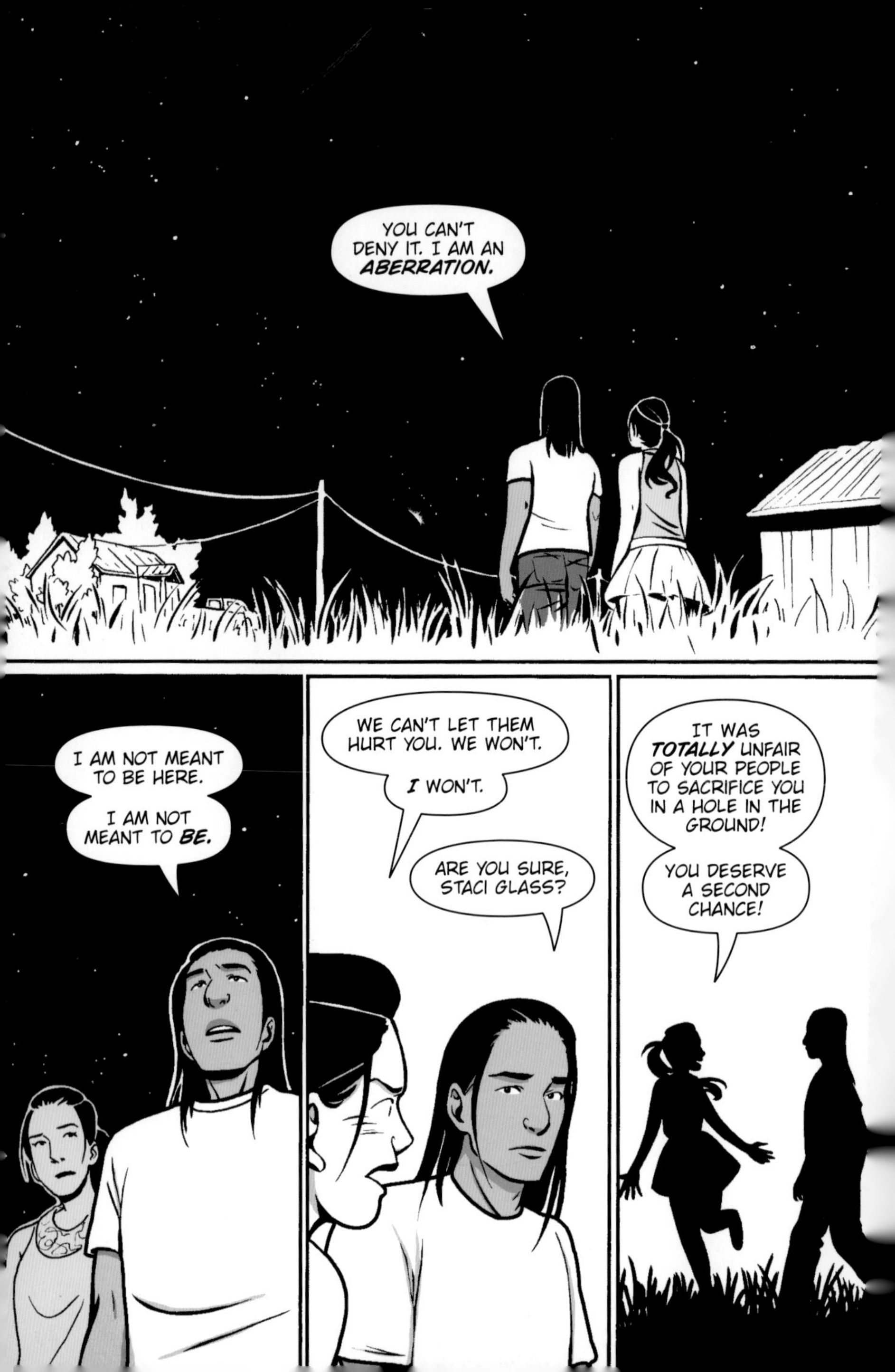
YOU CAN'T DENY IT. I AM AN *ABERRATION.*
I AM NOT MEANT TO BE HERE.
I AM NOT MEANT TO *BE.*
WE CAN'T LET THEM HURT YOU. WE WON'T.
I WON'T.
ARE YOU SURE, STACI GLASS?
IT WAS *TOTALLY* UNFAIR OF YOUR PEOPLE TO SACRIFICE YOU IN A HOLE IN THE GROUND!
YOU DESERVE A SECOND CHANCE!

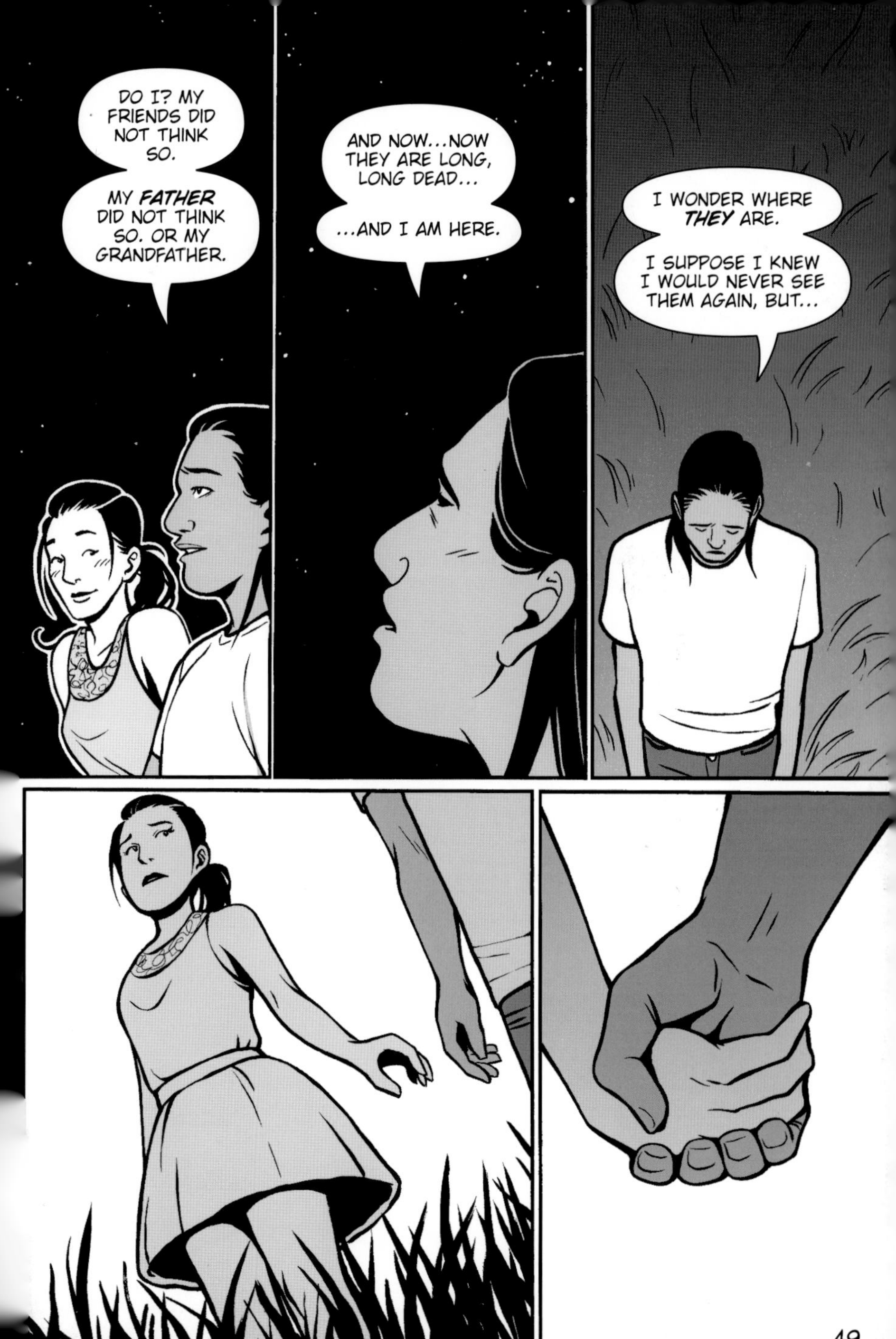
DO I? MY FRIENDS DID NOT THINK SO.
MY FATHER DID NOT THINK SO. OR MY GRANDFATHER.
AND NOW...NOW THEY ARE LONG, LONG DEAD...
...AND I AM HERE.
I WONDER WHERE THEY ARE.
I SUPPOSE I KNEW I WOULD NEVER SEE THEM AGAIN, BUT...

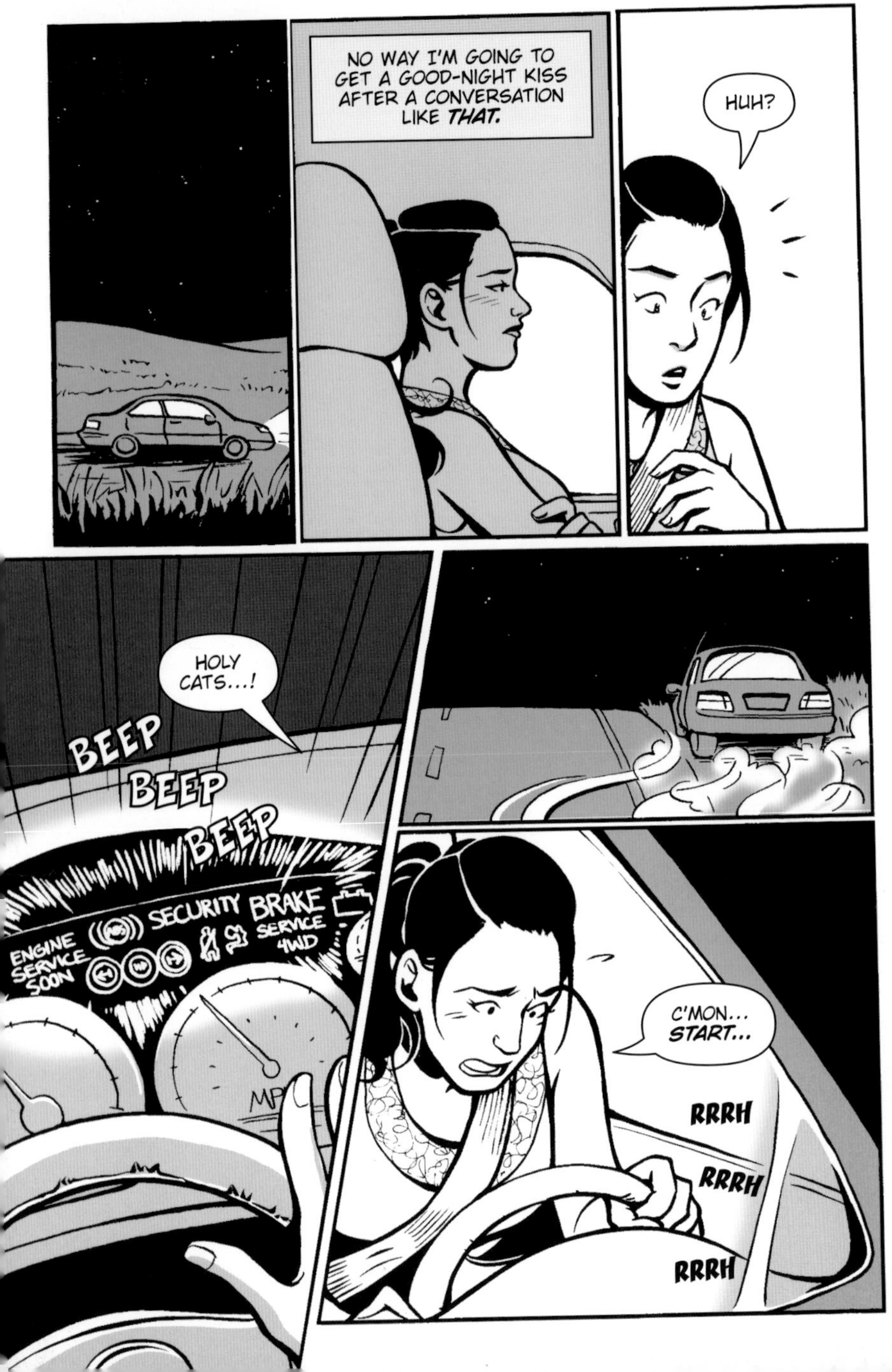
NO WAY I'M GOING TO GET A GOOD-NIGHT KISS AFTER A CONVERSATION LIKE *THAT.*
HUH?
HOLY CATS...!
BEEP
BEEP
BEEP
ENGINE SERVICE SOON
SECURITY
BRAKE
SERVICE 4WD
MPH
C'MON... *START...*
RRRH
RRRH
RRRH

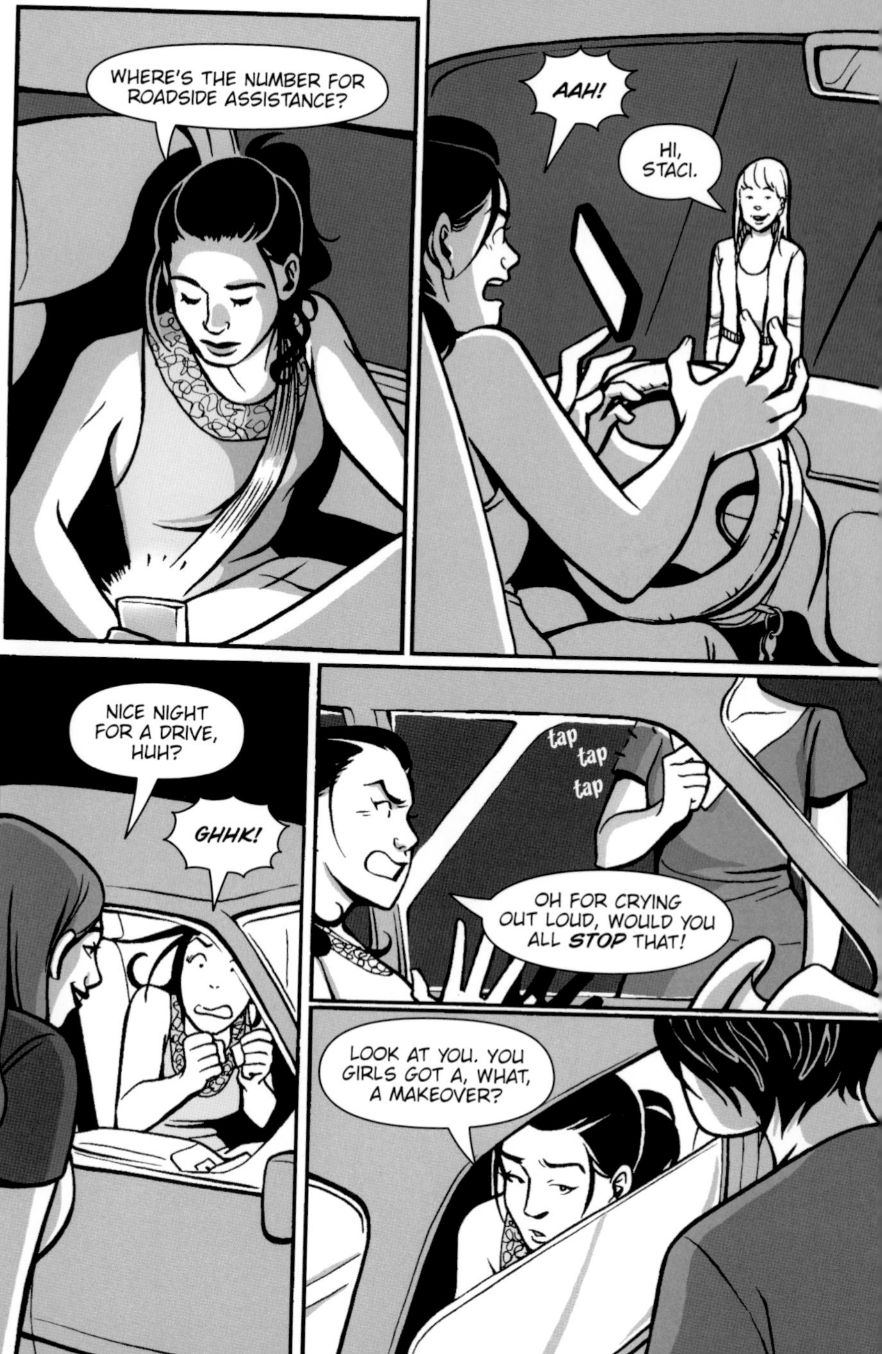
WHERE'S THE NUMBER FOR ROADSIDE ASSISTANCE?
AAH!
HI, STACI.
NICE NIGHT FOR A DRIVE, HUH?
GHHK!
tap tap tap
OH FOR CRYING OUT LOUD, WOULD YOU ALL STOP THAT!
LOOK AT YOU. YOU GIRLS GOT A, WHAT, A MAKEOVER?

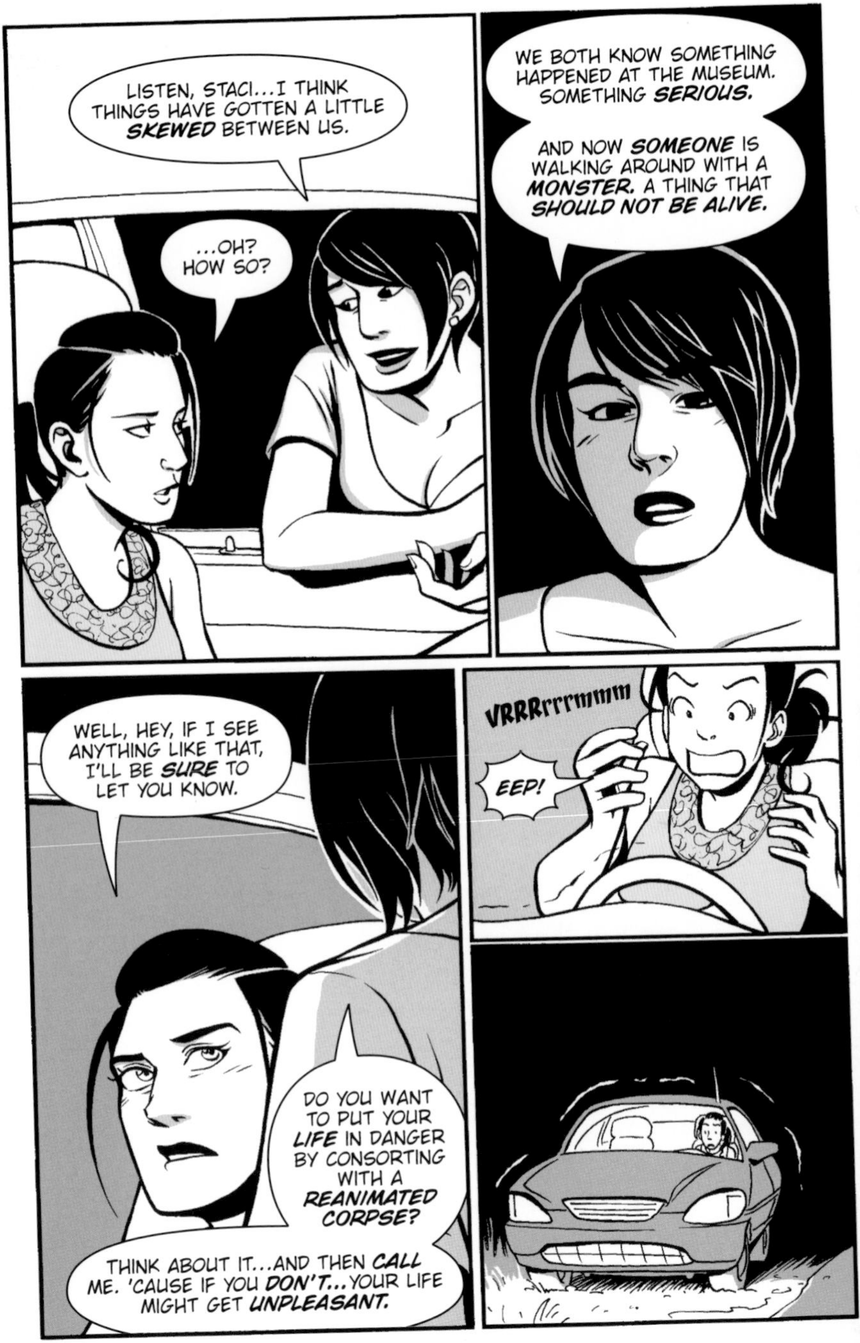
LISTEN, STACI...I THINK THINGS HAVE GOTTEN A LITTLE **SKEWED** BETWEEN US.
...OH? HOW SO?
WE BOTH KNOW SOMETHING HAPPENED AT THE MUSEUM. SOMETHING **SERIOUS.**
AND NOW **SOMEONE** IS WALKING AROUND WITH A **MONSTER.** A THING THAT **SHOULD NOT BE ALIVE.**
WELL, HEY, IF I SEE ANYTHING LIKE THAT, I'LL BE **SURE** TO LET YOU KNOW.
DO YOU WANT TO PUT YOUR **LIFE** IN DANGER BY CONSORTING WITH A **REANIMATED CORPSE?**
THINK ABOUT IT...AND THEN **CALL** ME. 'CAUSE IF YOU **DON'T...** YOUR LIFE MIGHT GET **UNPLEASANT.**
VRRRrrrmmm
EEP!

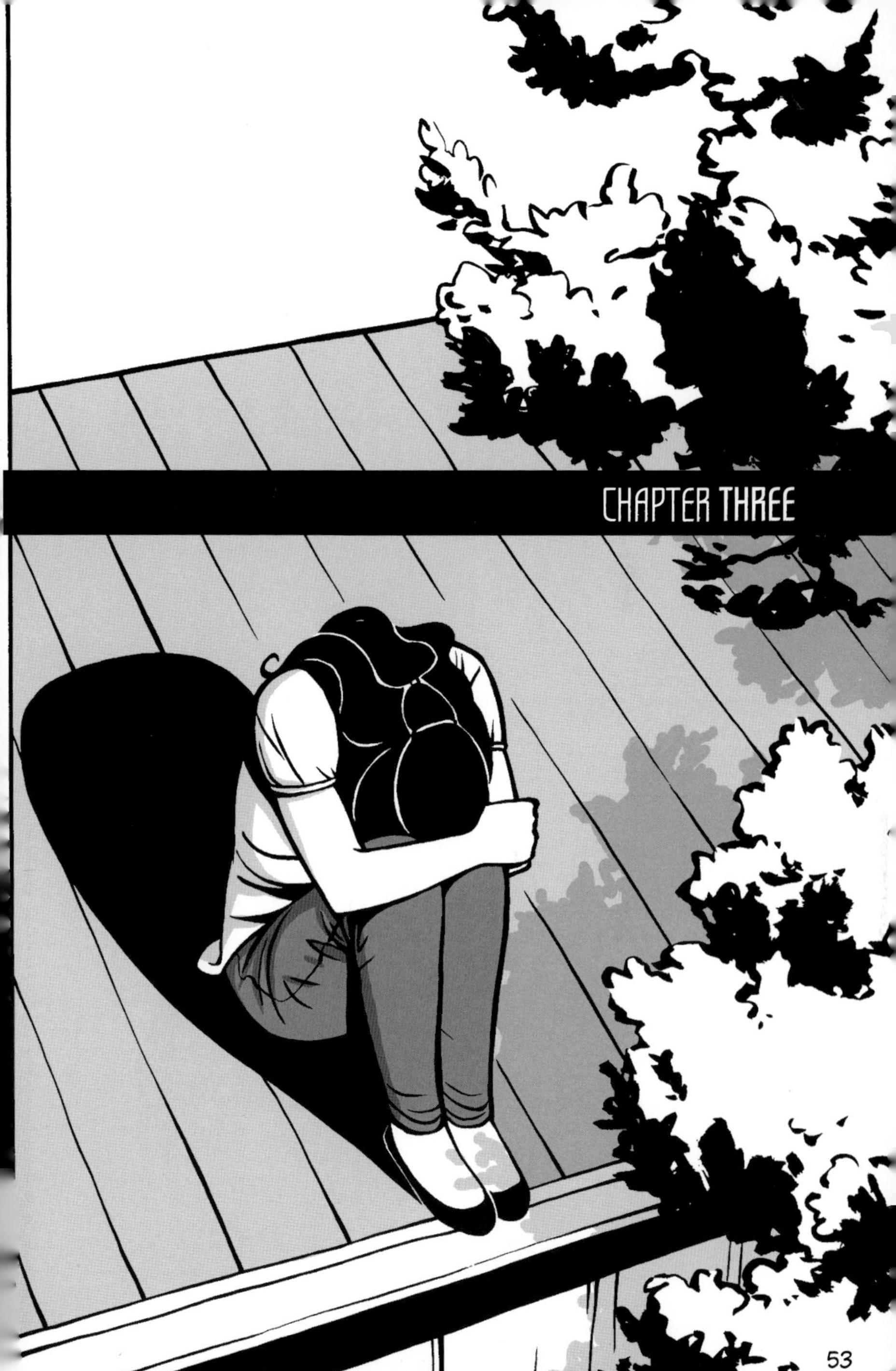
CHAPTER THREE

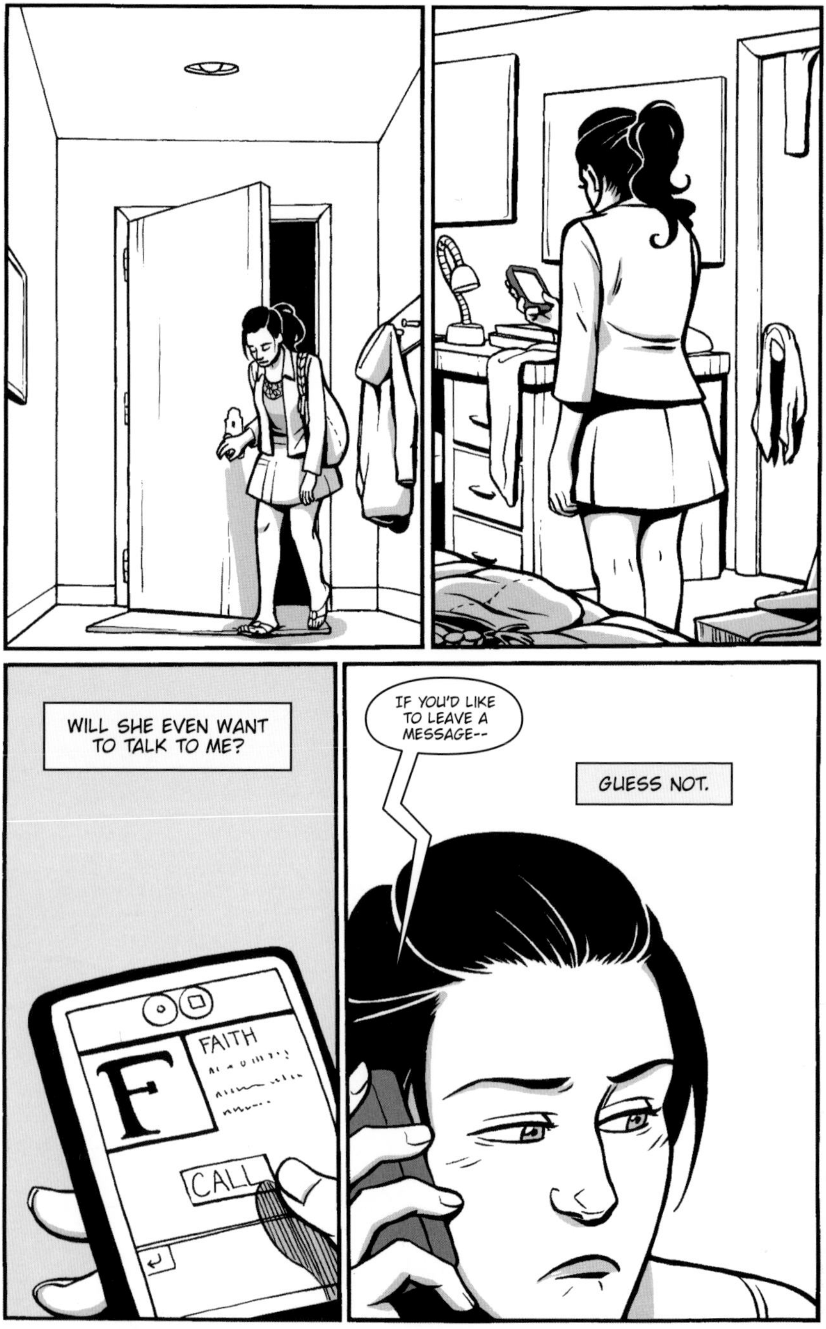
WILL SHE EVEN WANT TO TALK TO ME?
FAITH
CALL
IF YOU'D LIKE TO LEAVE A MESSAGE--
GUESS NOT.

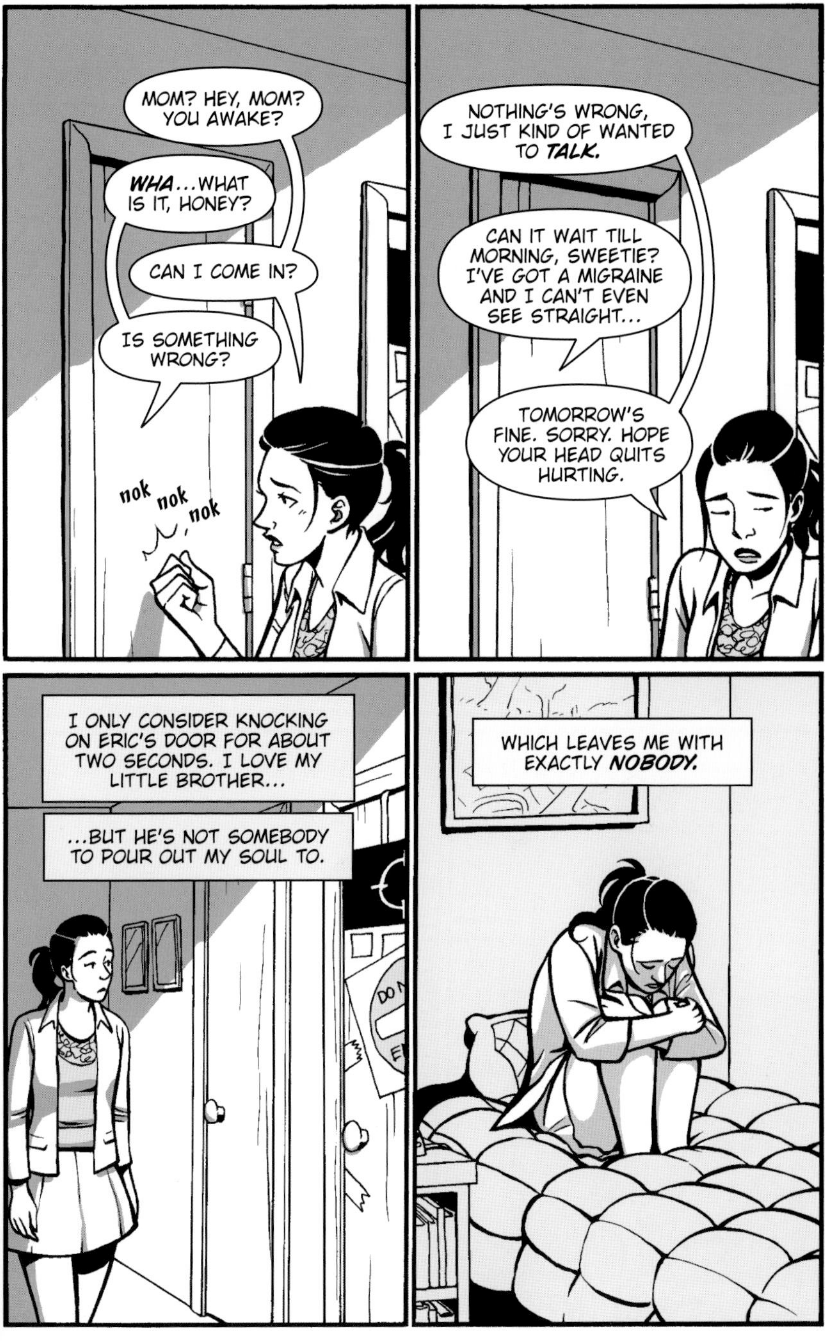
MOM? HEY, MOM? YOU AWAKE?
WHA...WHAT IS IT, HONEY?
CAN I COME IN?
IS SOMETHING WRONG?
nok nok nok
NOTHING'S WRONG, I JUST KIND OF WANTED TO TALK.
CAN IT WAIT TILL MORNING, SWEETIE? I'VE GOT A MIGRAINE AND I CAN'T EVEN SEE STRAIGHT...
TOMORROW'S FINE. SORRY. HOPE YOUR HEAD QUITS HURTING.
I ONLY CONSIDER KNOCKING ON ERIC'S DOOR FOR ABOUT TWO SECONDS. I LOVE MY LITTLE BROTHER...
...BUT HE'S NOT SOMEBODY TO POUR OUT MY SOUL TO.
WHICH LEAVES ME WITH EXACTLY NOBODY.

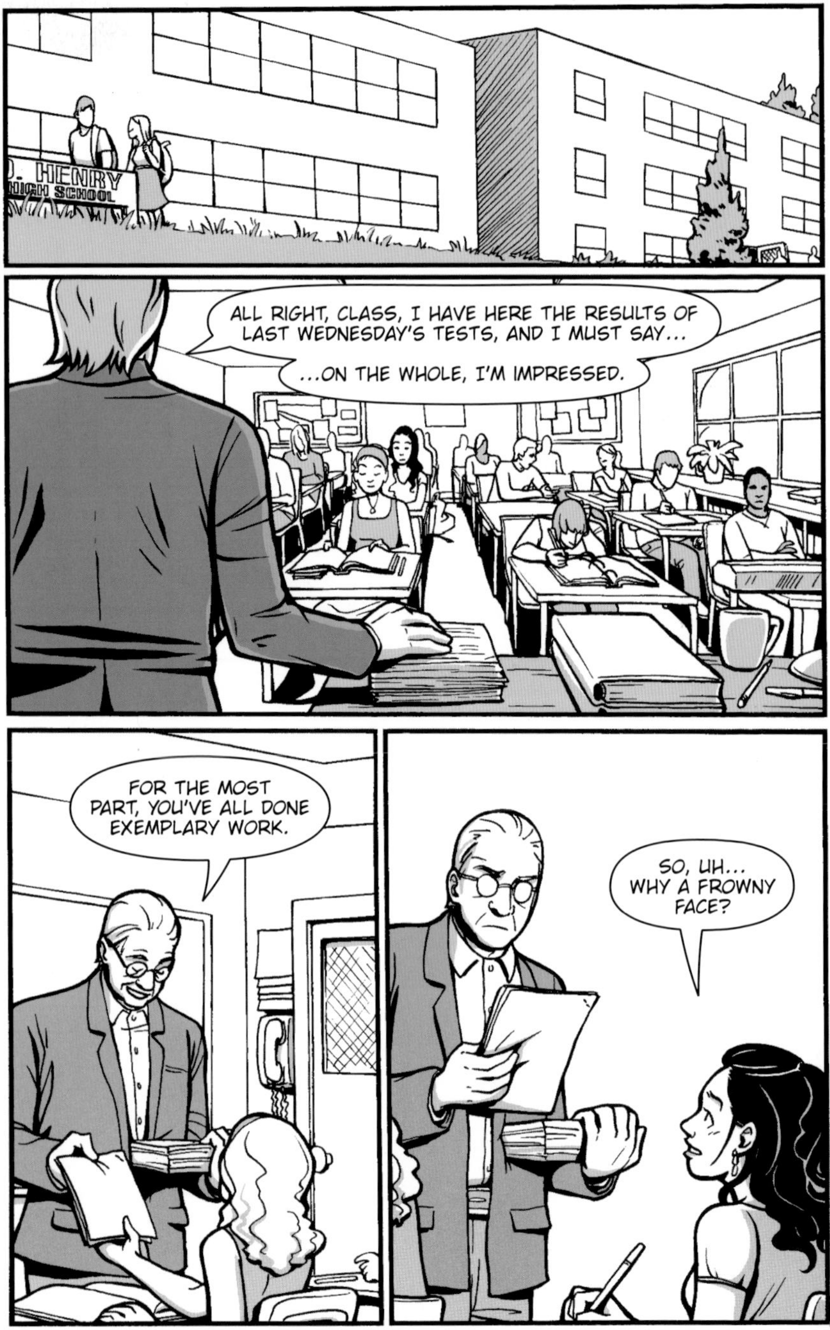
HENRY
SCHOOL
ALL RIGHT, CLASS, I HAVE HERE THE RESULTS OF LAST WEDNESDAY'S TESTS, AND I MUST SAY...
...ON THE WHOLE, I'M IMPRESSED.
FOR THE MOST PART, YOU'VE ALL DONE EXEMPLARY WORK.
SO, UH... WHY A FROWNY FACE?

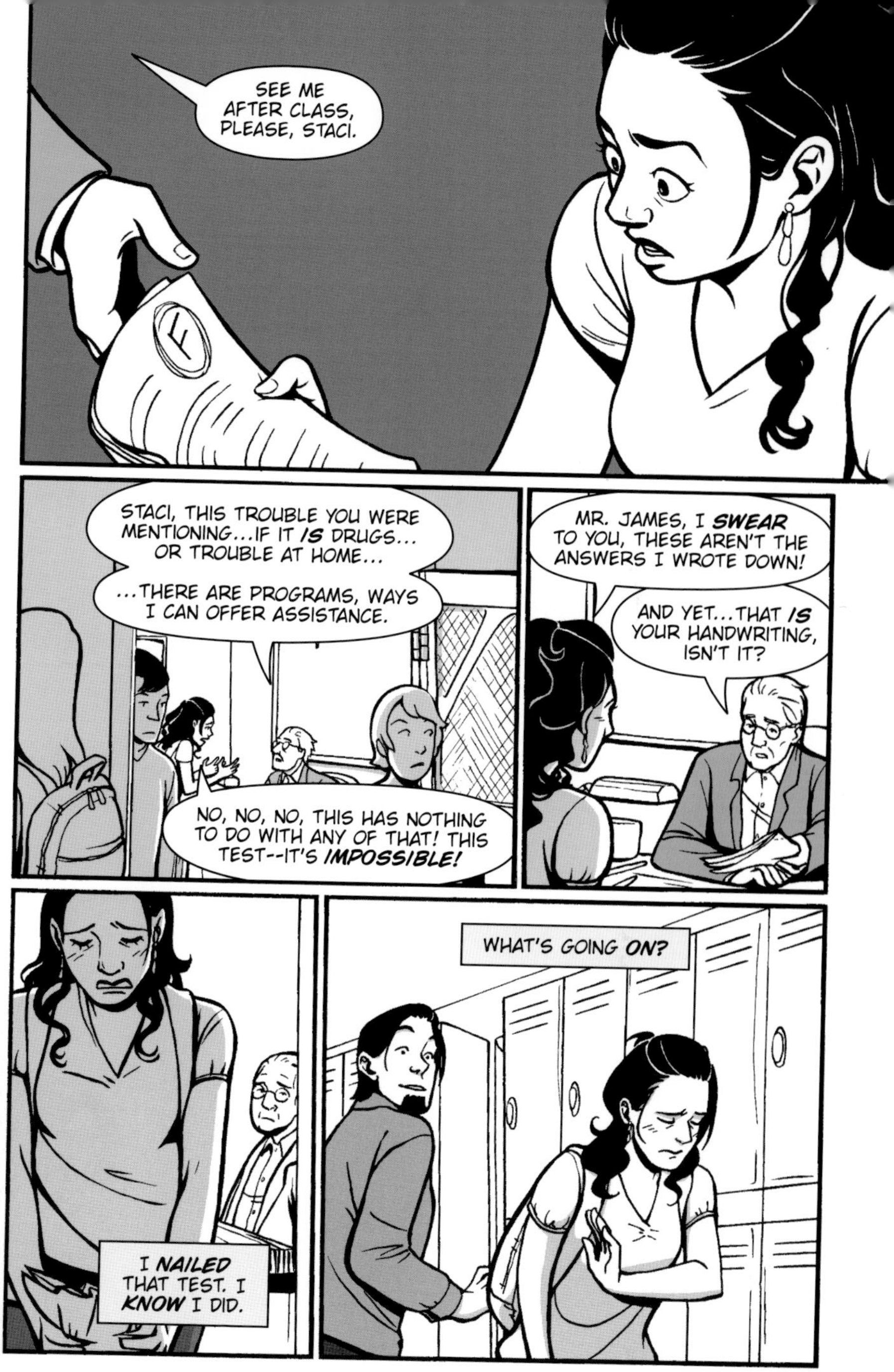
SEE ME AFTER CLASS, PLEASE, STACI.
F
STACI, THIS TROUBLE YOU WERE MENTIONING...IF IT *IS* DRUGS... OR TROUBLE AT HOME...
...THERE ARE PROGRAMS, WAYS I CAN OFFER ASSISTANCE.
NO, NO, NO, THIS HAS NOTHING TO DO WITH ANY OF THAT! THIS TEST--IT'S *IMPOSSIBLE!*
MR. JAMES, I *SWEAR* TO YOU, THESE AREN'T THE ANSWERS I WROTE DOWN!
AND YET...THAT *IS* YOUR HANDWRITING, ISN'T IT?
I *NAILED* THAT TEST. I *KNOW* I DID.
WHAT'S GOING *ON?*

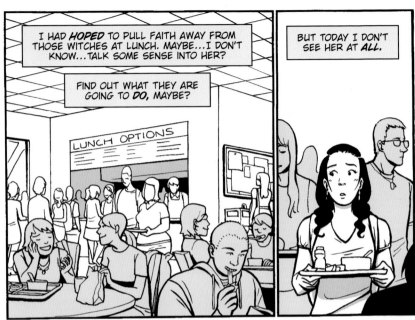

I HAD *HOPED* TO PULL FAITH AWAY FROM THOSE WITCHES AT LUNCH. MAYBE...I DON'T KNOW...TALK SOME SENSE INTO HER?

FIND OUT WHAT THEY ARE GOING TO *DO*, MAYBE?

BUT TODAY I DON'T SEE HER AT *ALL*.

HEY--MIND IF I JOIN YOU GUYS?

WELL...AT LEAST BRAD AND JEANNIE STILL LIKE ME. IF I DON'T HAVE A *NORMAL CONVERSATION* SOON, I'M GOING TO GO *NUTS*.

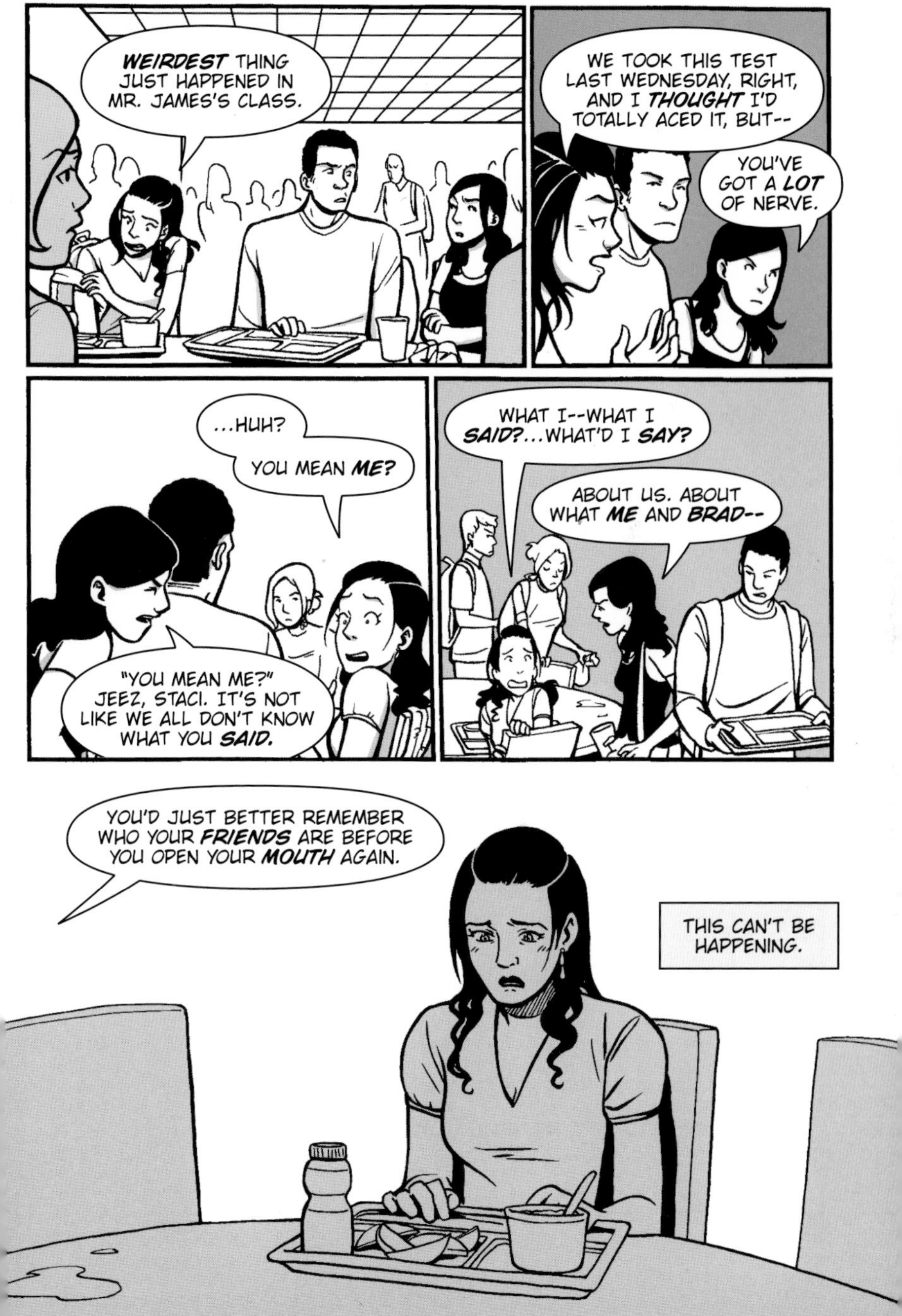
WEIRDEST THING JUST HAPPENED IN MR. JAMES'S CLASS.
WE TOOK THIS TEST LAST WEDNESDAY, RIGHT, AND I THOUGHT I'D TOTALLY ACED IT, BUT--
YOU'VE GOT A LOT OF NERVE.
...HUH?
YOU MEAN ME?
"YOU MEAN ME?" JEEZ, STACI. IT'S NOT LIKE WE ALL DON'T KNOW WHAT YOU SAID.
WHAT I--WHAT I SAID?...WHAT'D I SAY?
ABOUT US. ABOUT WHAT ME AND BRAD--
YOU'D JUST BETTER REMEMBER WHO YOUR FRIENDS ARE BEFORE YOU OPEN YOUR MOUTH AGAIN.
THIS CAN'T BE HAPPENING.

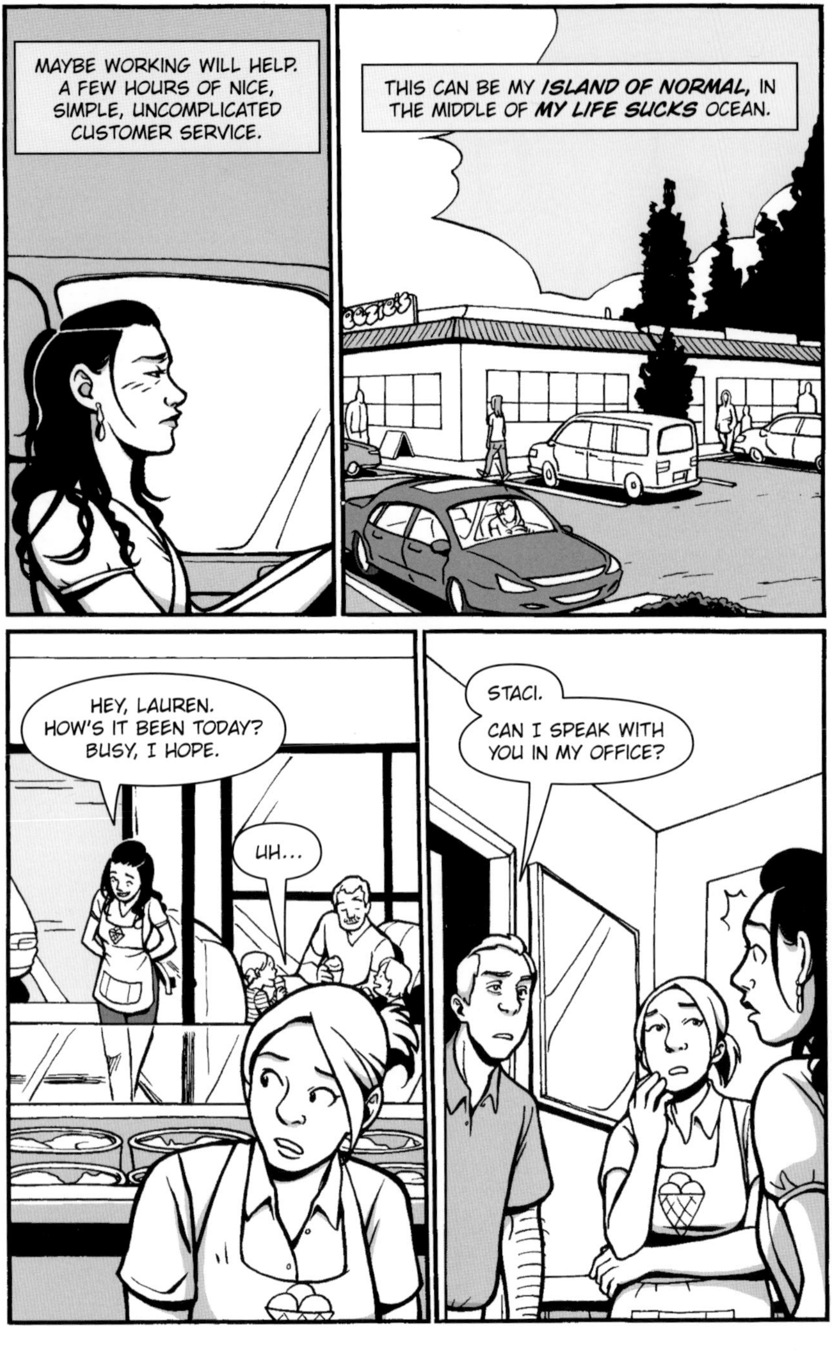
MAYBE WORKING WILL HELP. A FEW HOURS OF NICE, SIMPLE, UNCOMPLICATED CUSTOMER SERVICE.
THIS CAN BE MY ISLAND OF NORMAL, IN THE MIDDLE OF MY LIFE SUCKS OCEAN.
HEY, LAUREN. HOW'S IT BEEN TODAY? BUSY, I HOPE.
UH...
STACI.
CAN I SPEAK WITH YOU IN MY OFFICE?

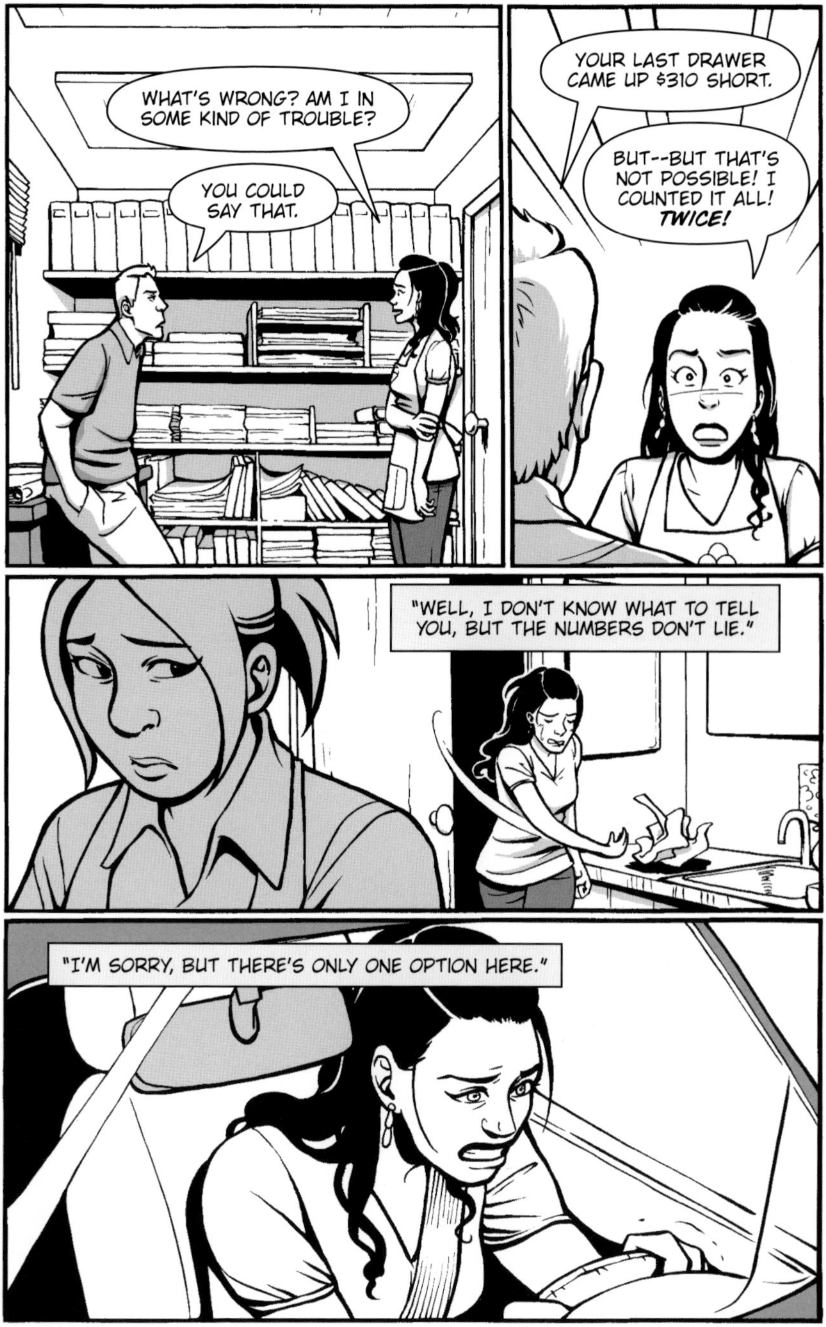
WHAT'S WRONG? AM I IN SOME KIND OF TROUBLE?
YOU COULD SAY THAT.
YOUR LAST DRAWER CAME UP $310 SHORT.
BUT--BUT THAT'S NOT POSSIBLE! I COUNTED IT ALL! ***TWICE!***
"WELL, I DON'T KNOW WHAT TO TELL YOU, BUT THE NUMBERS DON'T LIE."
"I'M SORRY, BUT THERE'S ONLY ONE OPTION HERE."

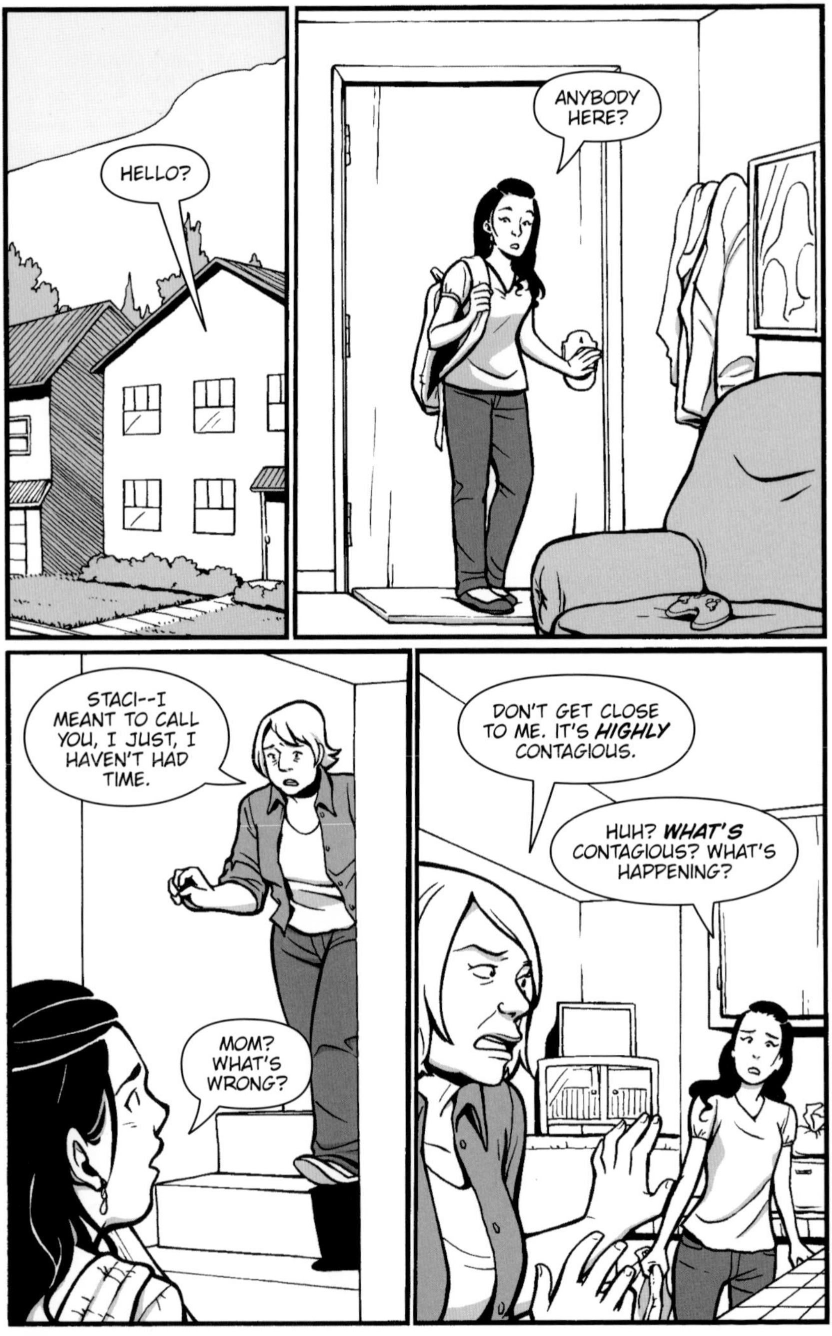
HELLO?
ANYBODY HERE?
STACI--I MEANT TO CALL YOU, I JUST, I HAVEN'T HAD TIME.
MOM? WHAT'S WRONG?
DON'T GET CLOSE TO ME. IT'S ***HIGHLY*** CONTAGIOUS.
HUH? ***WHAT'S*** CONTAGIOUS? WHAT'S HAPPENING?

IT'S YOUR **BROTHER.** HE'S GOT **CHICKEN POX.** THE DOCTOR SAID IT WAS THE MOST VIRULENT STRAIN HE'D EVER SEEN.

WOKE UP WITH IT THIS MORNING. SPOTS ALL OVER HIS BODY.

OH--OH **CRAP.** I'VE NEVER **HAD** CHICKEN POX!

EXACTLY. SO KEEP YOUR DISTANCE FROM ME, AND FOR GOD'S SAKE, DON'T GO NEAR YOUR BROTHER.

WELL...WHAT CAN I **DO?** HOW CAN I **HELP?**

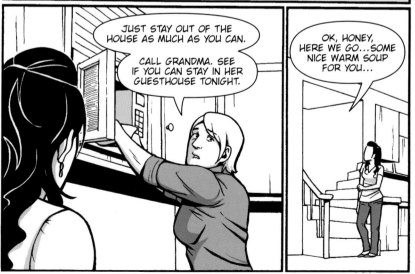

JUST STAY OUT OF THE HOUSE AS MUCH AS YOU CAN.

CALL GRANDMA. SEE IF YOU CAN STAY IN HER GUESTHOUSE TONIGHT.

OK, HONEY, HERE WE GO...SOME NICE WARM SOUP FOR YOU...

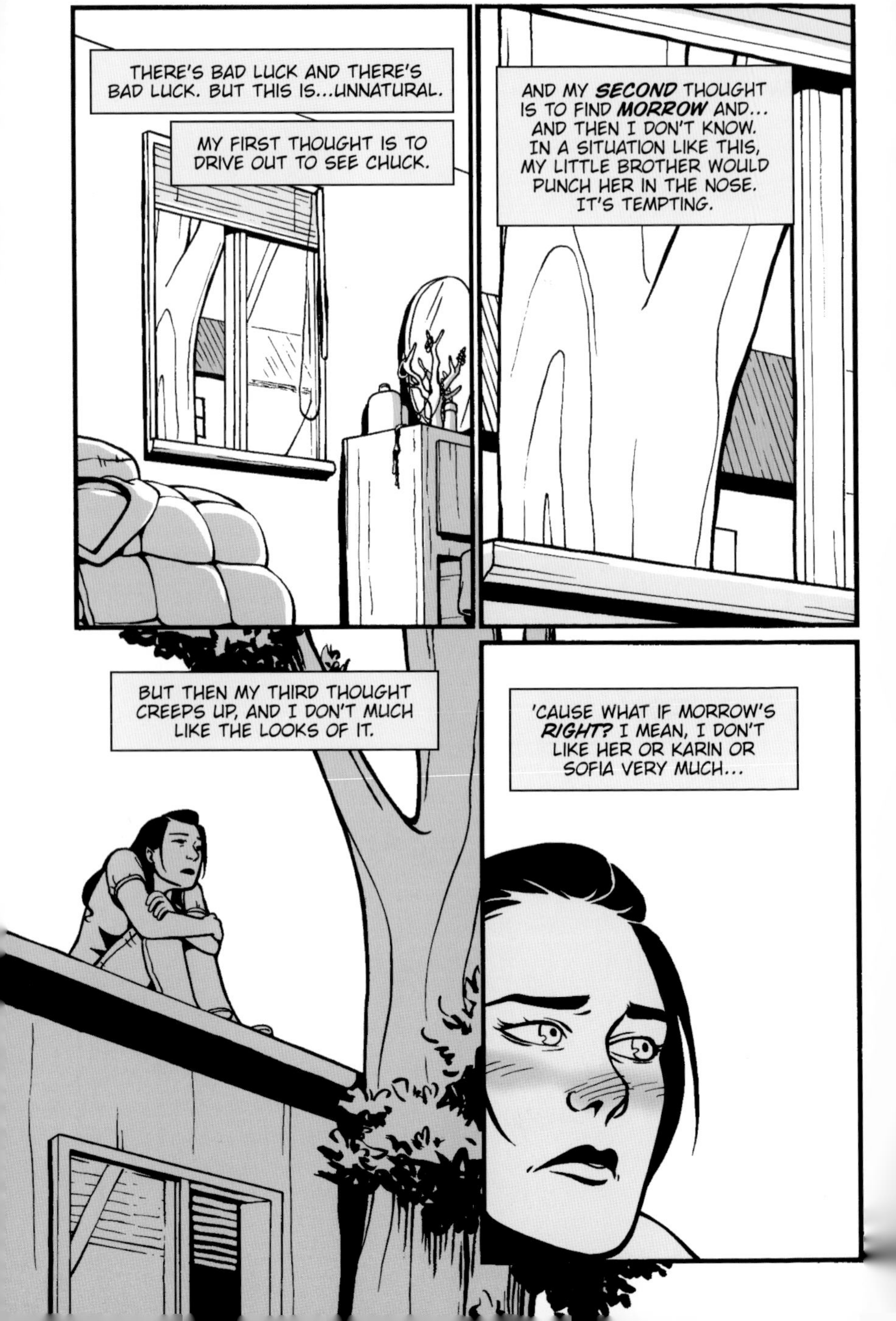
THERE'S BAD LUCK AND THERE'S BAD LUCK. BUT THIS IS...UNNATURAL.
MY FIRST THOUGHT IS TO DRIVE OUT TO SEE CHUCK.
AND MY SECOND THOUGHT IS TO FIND MORROW AND... AND THEN I DON'T KNOW. IN A SITUATION LIKE THIS, MY LITTLE BROTHER WOULD PUNCH HER IN THE NOSE. IT'S TEMPTING.
BUT THEN MY THIRD THOUGHT CREEPS UP, AND I DON'T MUCH LIKE THE LOOKS OF IT.
'CAUSE WHAT IF MORROW'S RIGHT? I MEAN, I DON'T LIKE HER OR KARIN OR SOFIA VERY MUCH...

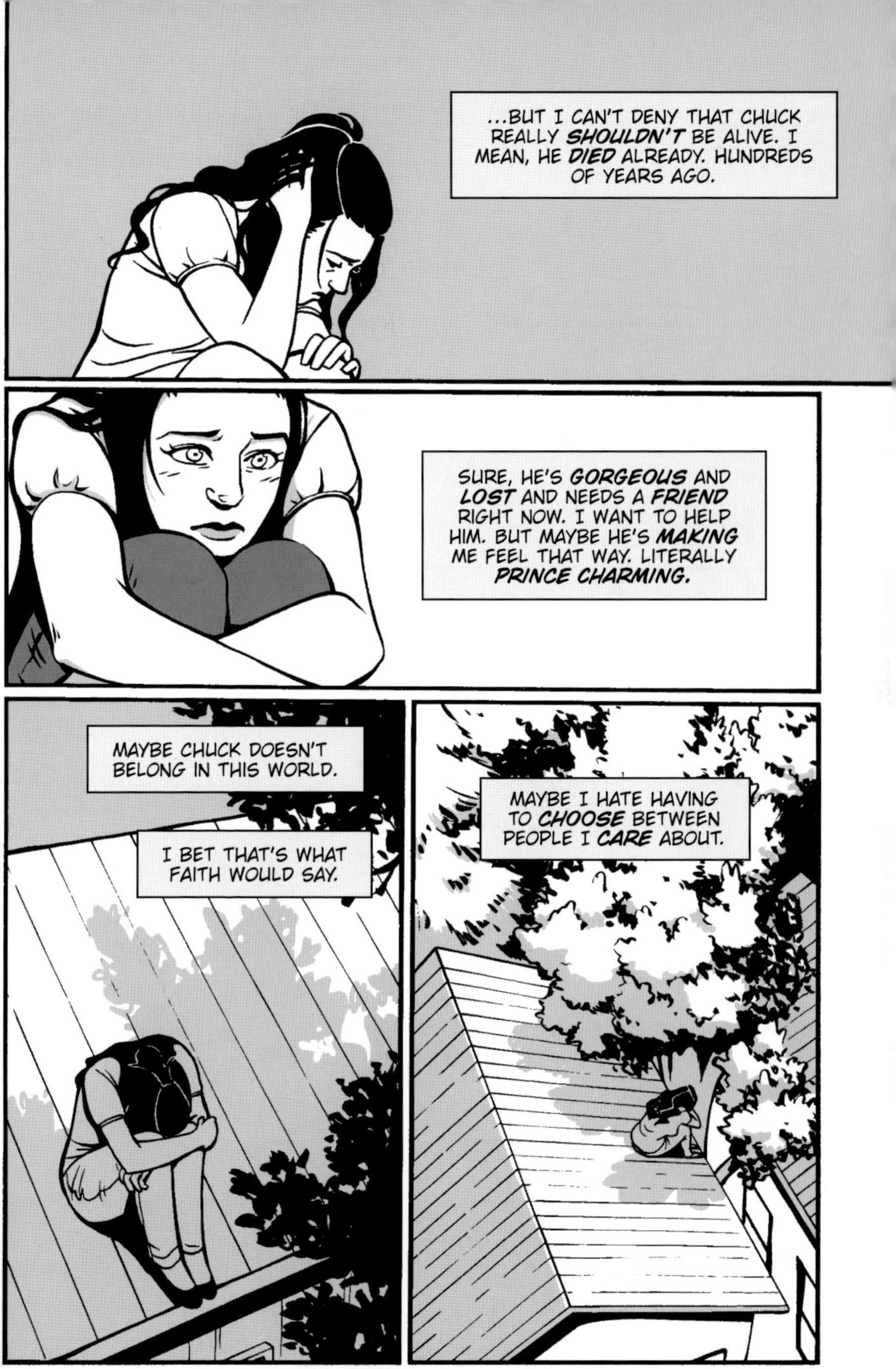
...BUT I CAN'T DENY THAT CHUCK REALLY SHOULDN'T BE ALIVE. I MEAN, HE DIED ALREADY. HUNDREDS OF YEARS AGO.
SURE, HE'S GORGEOUS AND LOST AND NEEDS A FRIEND RIGHT NOW. I WANT TO HELP HIM. BUT MAYBE HE'S MAKING ME FEEL THAT WAY. LITERALLY PRINCE CHARMING.
MAYBE CHUCK DOESN'T BELONG IN THIS WORLD.
I BET THAT'S WHAT FAITH WOULD SAY.
MAYBE I HATE HAVING TO CHOOSE BETWEEN PEOPLE I CARE ABOUT.

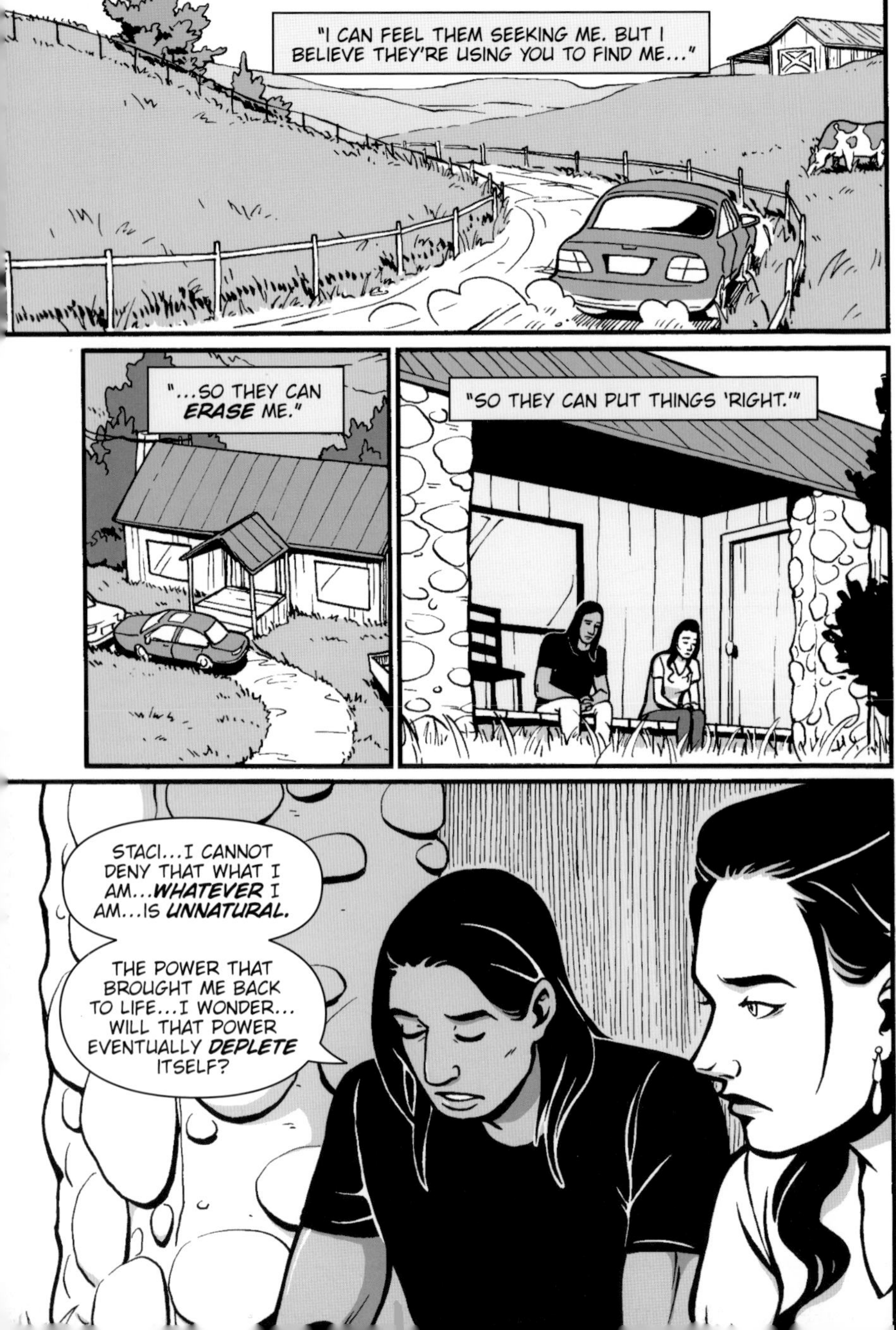
"I CAN FEEL THEM SEEKING ME. BUT I BELIEVE THEY'RE USING YOU TO FIND ME..."
"...SO THEY CAN ERASE ME."
"SO THEY CAN PUT THINGS 'RIGHT.'"
STACI...I CANNOT DENY THAT WHAT I AM...WHATEVER I AM...IS UNNATURAL.
THE POWER THAT BROUGHT ME BACK TO LIFE...I WONDER... WILL THAT POWER EVENTUALLY DEPLETE ITSELF?

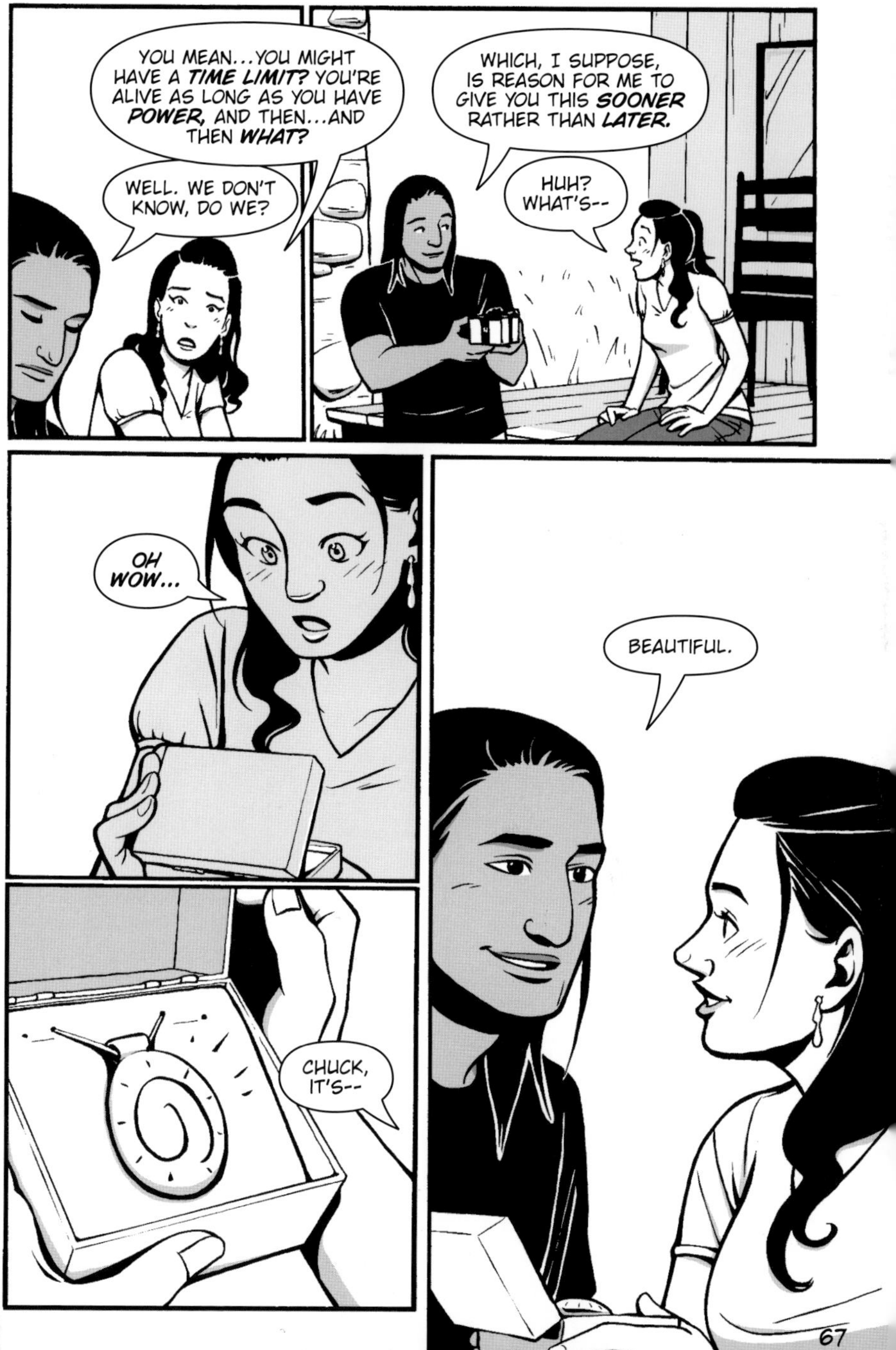
YOU MEAN...YOU MIGHT HAVE A TIME LIMIT? YOU'RE ALIVE AS LONG AS YOU HAVE POWER, AND THEN...AND THEN WHAT?
WELL. WE DON'T KNOW, DO WE?
WHICH, I SUPPOSE, IS REASON FOR ME TO GIVE YOU THIS SOONER RATHER THAN LATER.
HUH? WHAT'S--
OH WOW...
CHUCK, IT'S--
BEAUTIFUL.

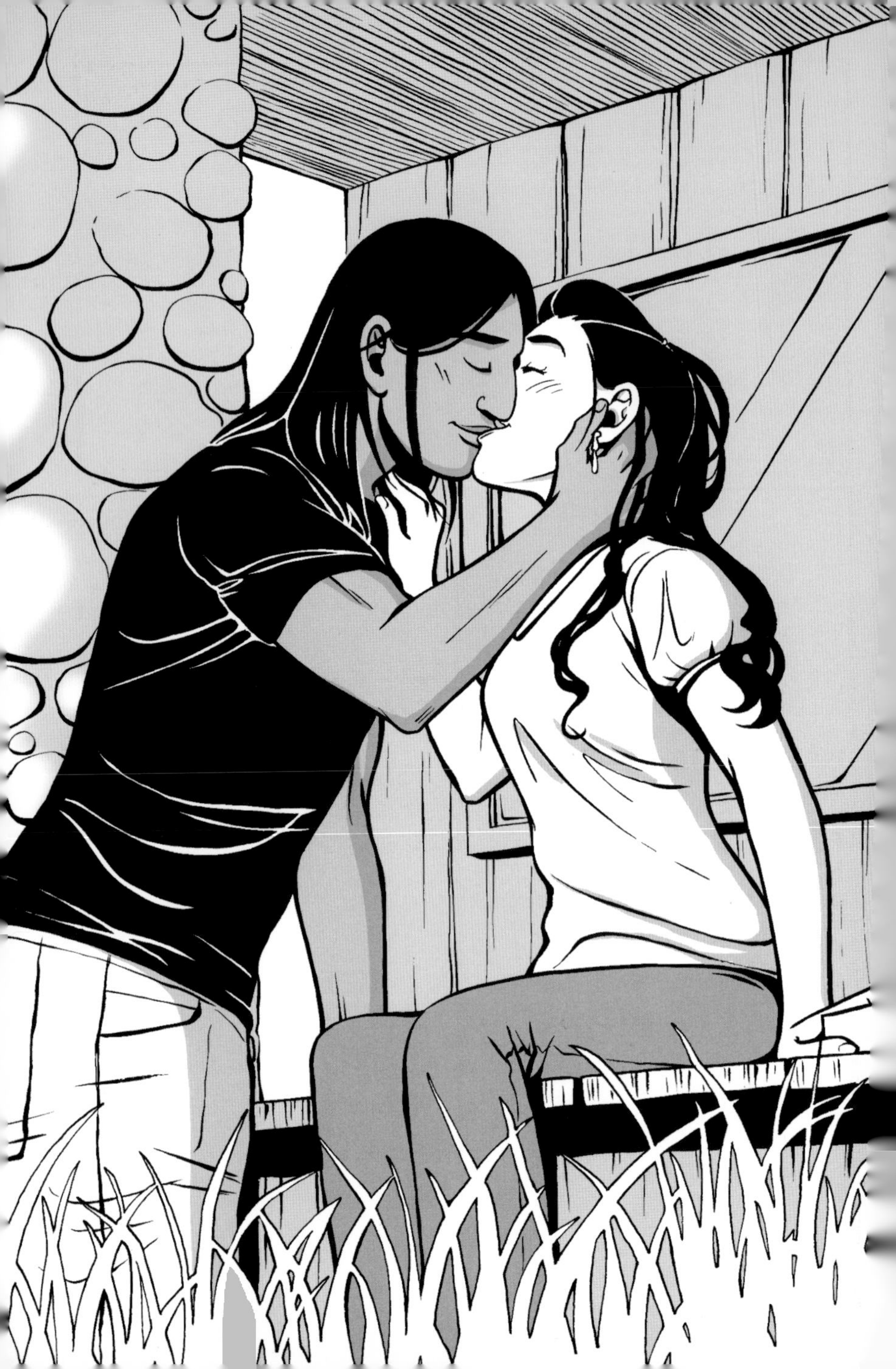

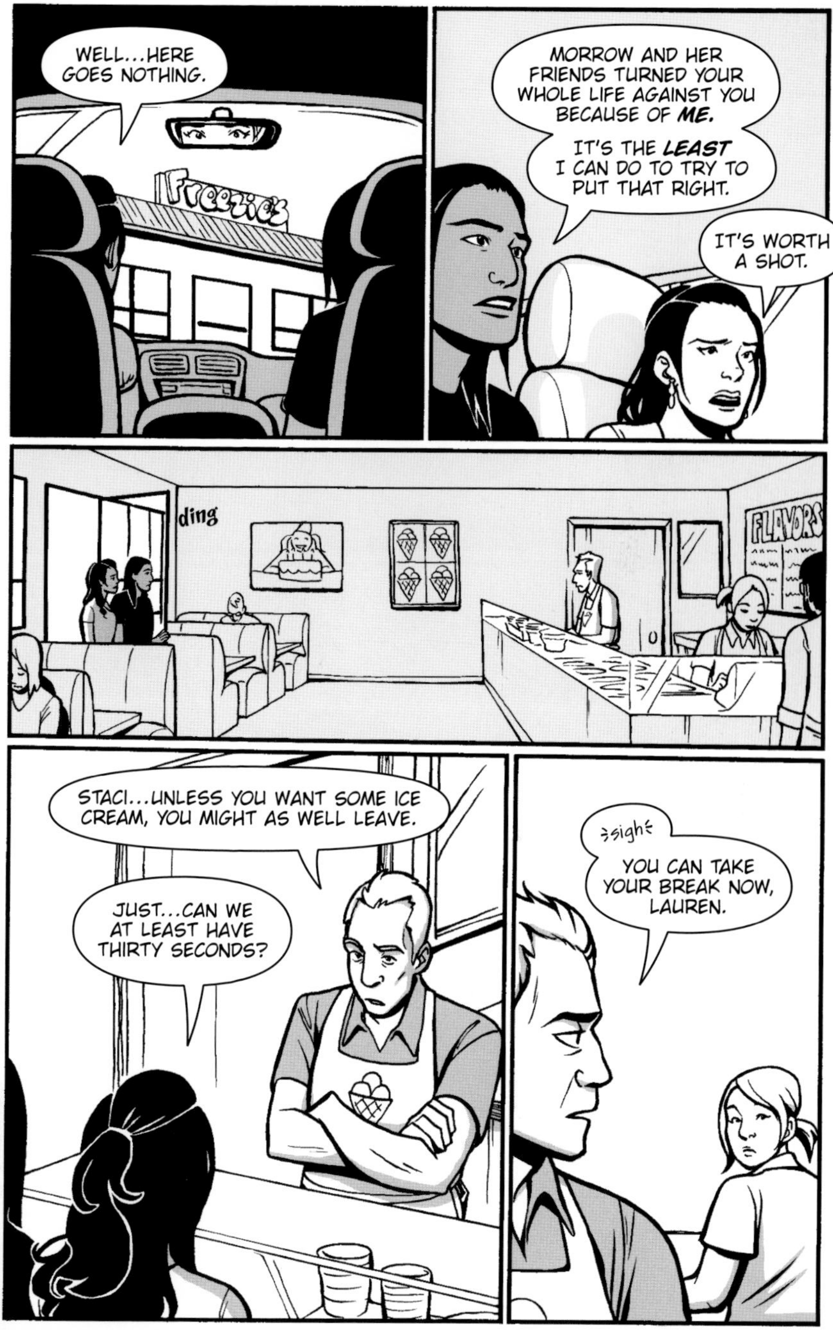
WELL...HERE GOES NOTHING.
Freezie's
MORROW AND HER FRIENDS TURNED YOUR WHOLE LIFE AGAINST YOU BECAUSE OF ME.
IT'S THE LEAST I CAN DO TO TRY TO PUT THAT RIGHT.
IT'S WORTH A SHOT.
ding
FLAVORS
STACI...UNLESS YOU WANT SOME ICE CREAM, YOU MIGHT AS WELL LEAVE.
JUST...CAN WE AT LEAST HAVE THIRTY SECONDS?
sigh
YOU CAN TAKE YOUR BREAK NOW, LAUREN.

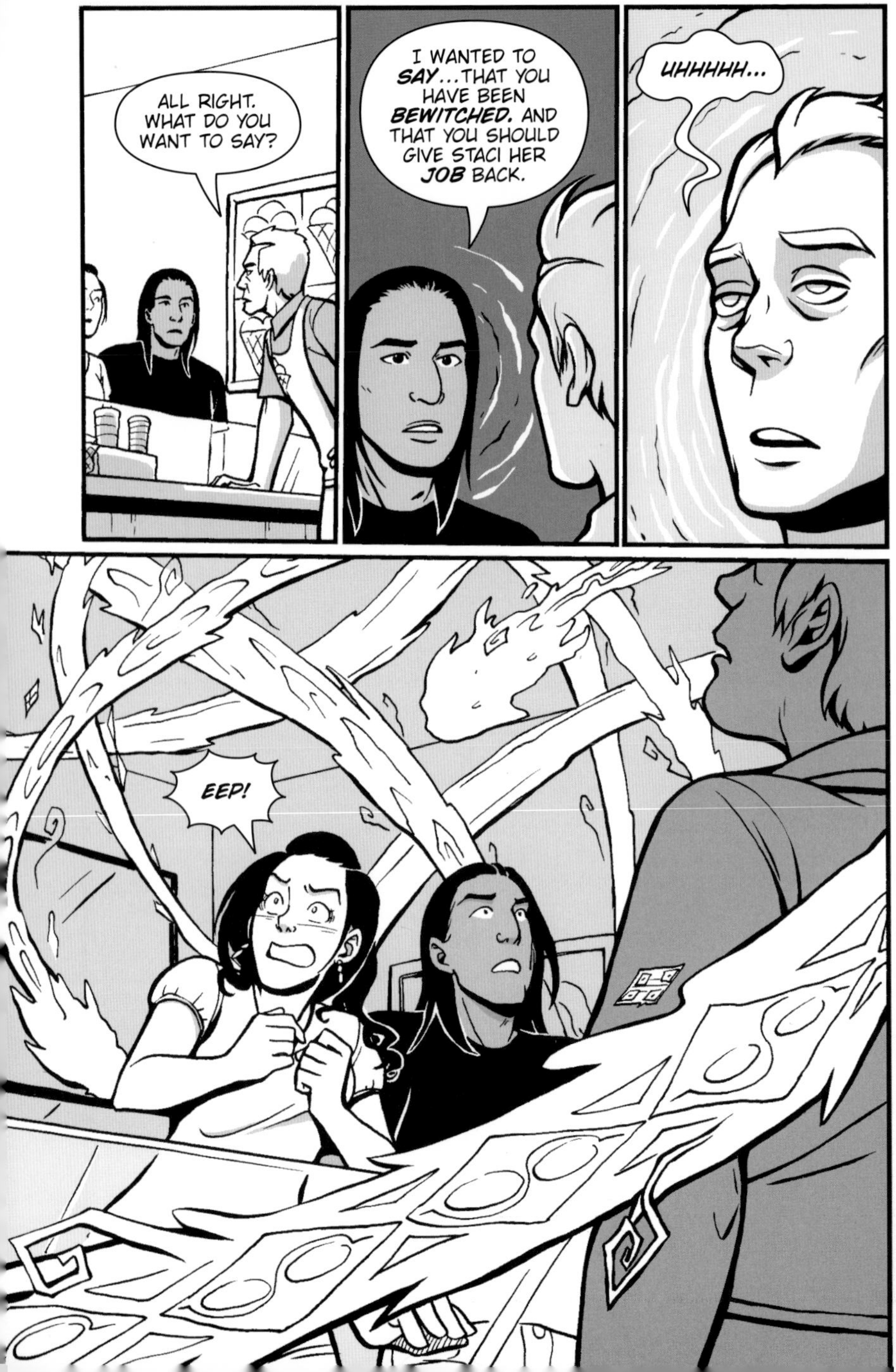
ALL RIGHT. WHAT DO YOU WANT TO SAY?
I WANTED TO *SAY*...THAT YOU HAVE BEEN *BEWITCHED.* AND THAT YOU SHOULD GIVE STACI HER *JOB* BACK.
UHHHHH...
EEP!

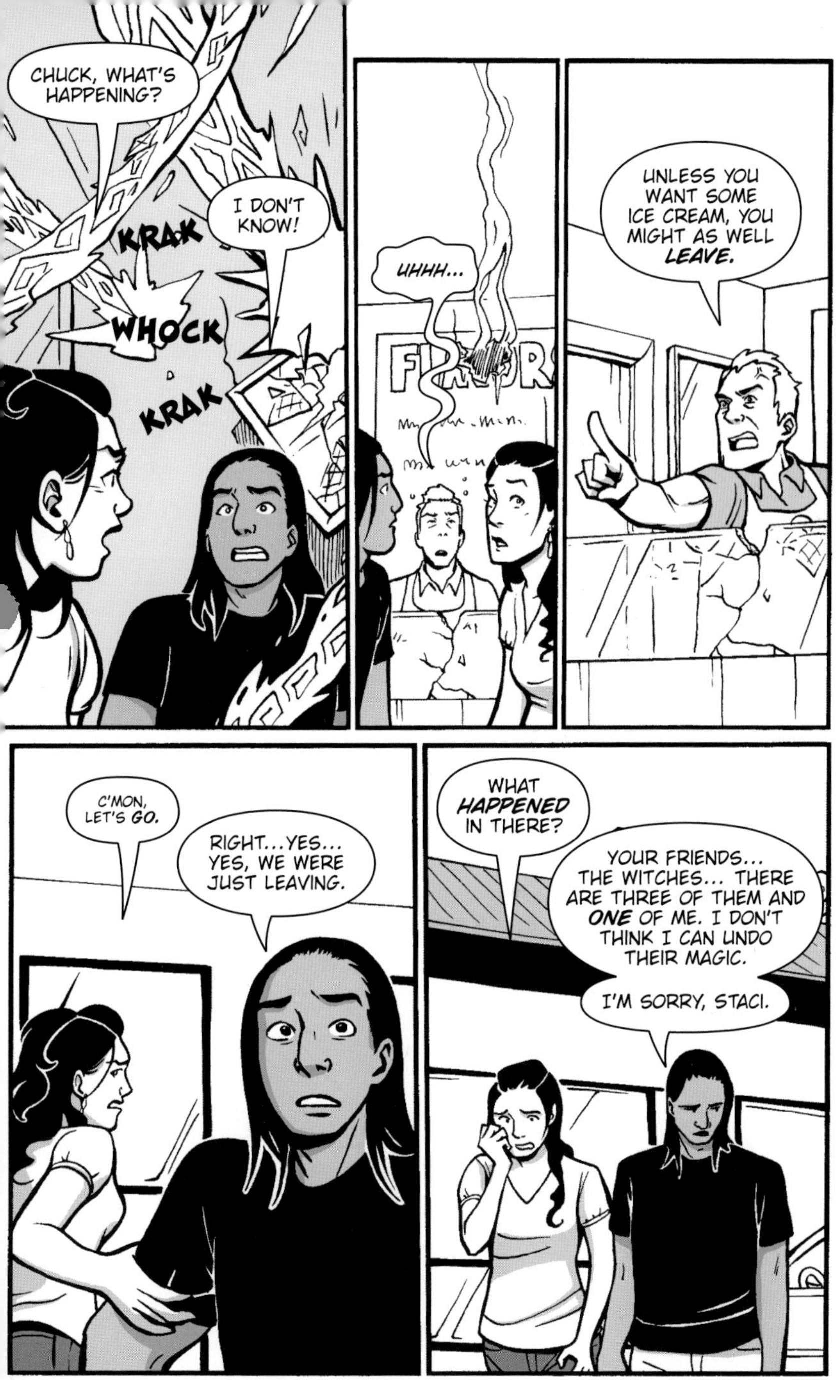
CHUCK, WHAT'S HAPPENING?
I DON'T KNOW!
KRAK
WHOCK
KRAK
UHHH...
UNLESS YOU WANT SOME ICE CREAM, YOU MIGHT AS WELL LEAVE.
C'MON, LET'S GO.
RIGHT... YES... YES, WE WERE JUST LEAVING.
WHAT HAPPENED IN THERE?
YOUR FRIENDS... THE WITCHES... THERE ARE THREE OF THEM AND ONE OF ME. I DON'T THINK I CAN UNDO THEIR MAGIC.
I'M SORRY, STACI.

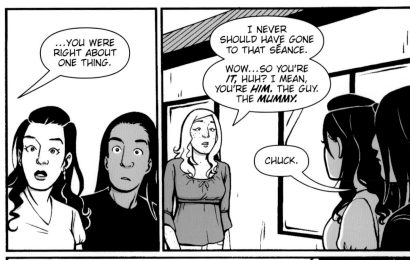

...YOU WERE RIGHT ABOUT ONE THING.

I NEVER SHOULD HAVE GONE TO THAT SÉANCE.

WOW...SO YOU'RE *IT*, HUH? I MEAN, YOU'RE *HIM*. THE GUY. THE *MUMMY*.

CHUCK.

SERIOUSLY-- "CHUCK"?

FAITH...WHAT DO YOU WANT?

I WANT TO TALK TO YOU. BOTH OF YOU.

AND IF I CAN, I WANT TO *HELP.*

CAN WE GO SOMEWHERE ELSE?

OK. THIS SHOULD BE PRIVATE ENOUGH. SO SPILL. WHY THE SUDDEN CHANGE OF HEART?

WELL...I FOUND OUT WHAT THEY DID TO YOU.

YOU MEAN THE *HEX*?

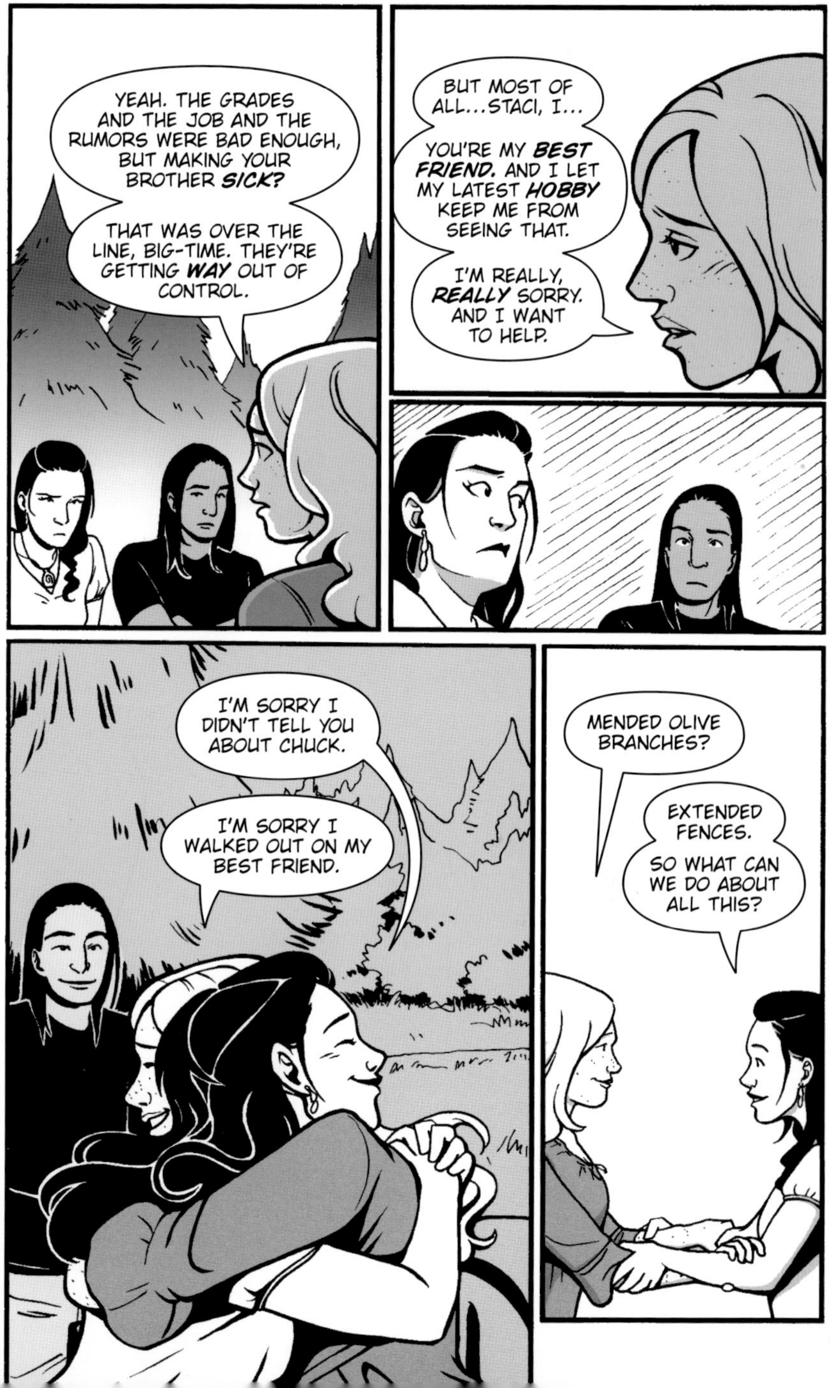
YEAH. THE GRADES AND THE JOB AND THE RUMORS WERE BAD ENOUGH, BUT MAKING YOUR BROTHER *SICK?*
THAT WAS OVER THE LINE, BIG-TIME. THEY'RE GETTING *WAY* OUT OF CONTROL.
BUT MOST OF ALL...STACI, I...
YOU'RE MY *BEST FRIEND.* AND I LET MY LATEST *HOBBY* KEEP ME FROM SEEING THAT.
I'M REALLY, *REALLY* SORRY. AND I WANT TO HELP.
I'M SORRY I DIDN'T TELL YOU ABOUT CHUCK.
I'M SORRY I WALKED OUT ON MY BEST FRIEND.
MENDED OLIVE BRANCHES?
EXTENDED FENCES.
SO WHAT CAN WE DO ABOUT ALL THIS?

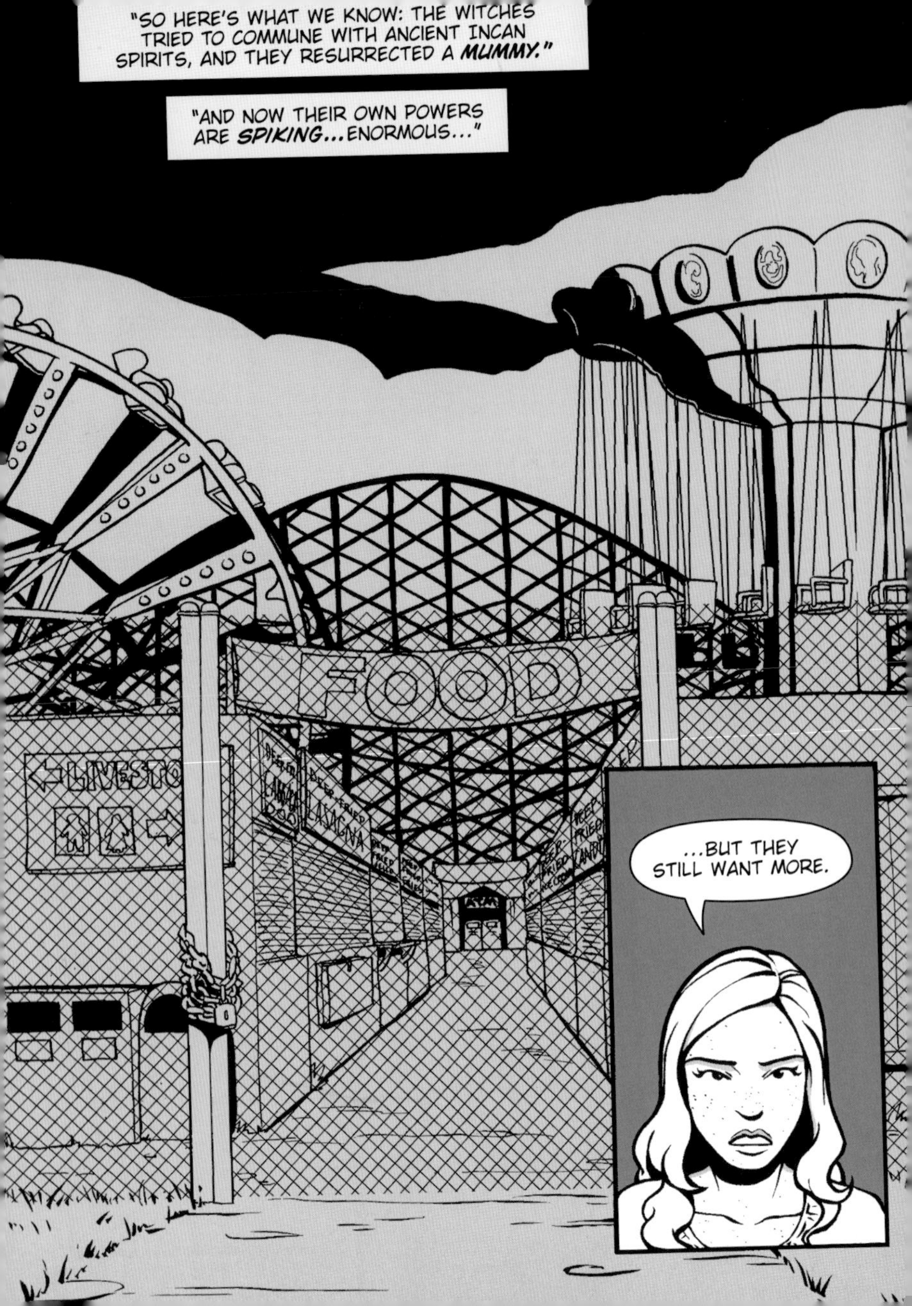
"SO HERE'S WHAT WE KNOW: THE WITCHES TRIED TO COMMUNE WITH ANCIENT INCAN SPIRITS, AND THEY RESURRECTED A ***MUMMY.***"
"AND NOW THEIR OWN POWERS ARE ***SPIKING...*** ENORMOUS..."
FOOD
DEEP-FRIED LASAGNA
...BUT THEY STILL WANT MORE.

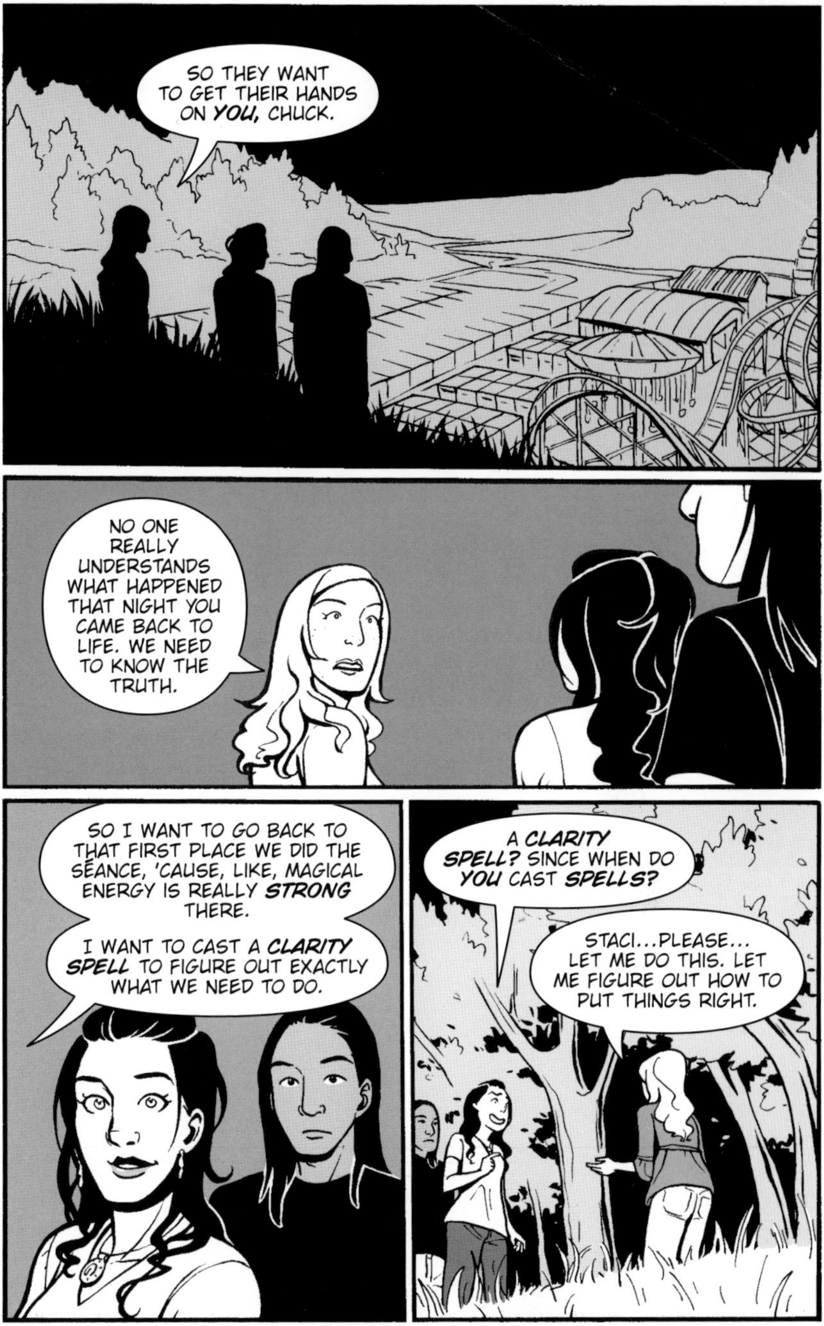
SO THEY WANT TO GET THEIR HANDS ON YOU, CHUCK.
NO ONE REALLY UNDERSTANDS WHAT HAPPENED THAT NIGHT YOU CAME BACK TO LIFE. WE NEED TO KNOW THE TRUTH.
SO I WANT TO GO BACK TO THAT FIRST PLACE WE DID THE SÉANCE, 'CAUSE, LIKE, MAGICAL ENERGY IS REALLY STRONG THERE.
I WANT TO CAST A CLARITY SPELL TO FIGURE OUT EXACTLY WHAT WE NEED TO DO.
A CLARITY SPELL? SINCE WHEN DO YOU CAST SPELLS?
STACI...PLEASE... LET ME DO THIS. LET ME FIGURE OUT HOW TO PUT THINGS RIGHT.

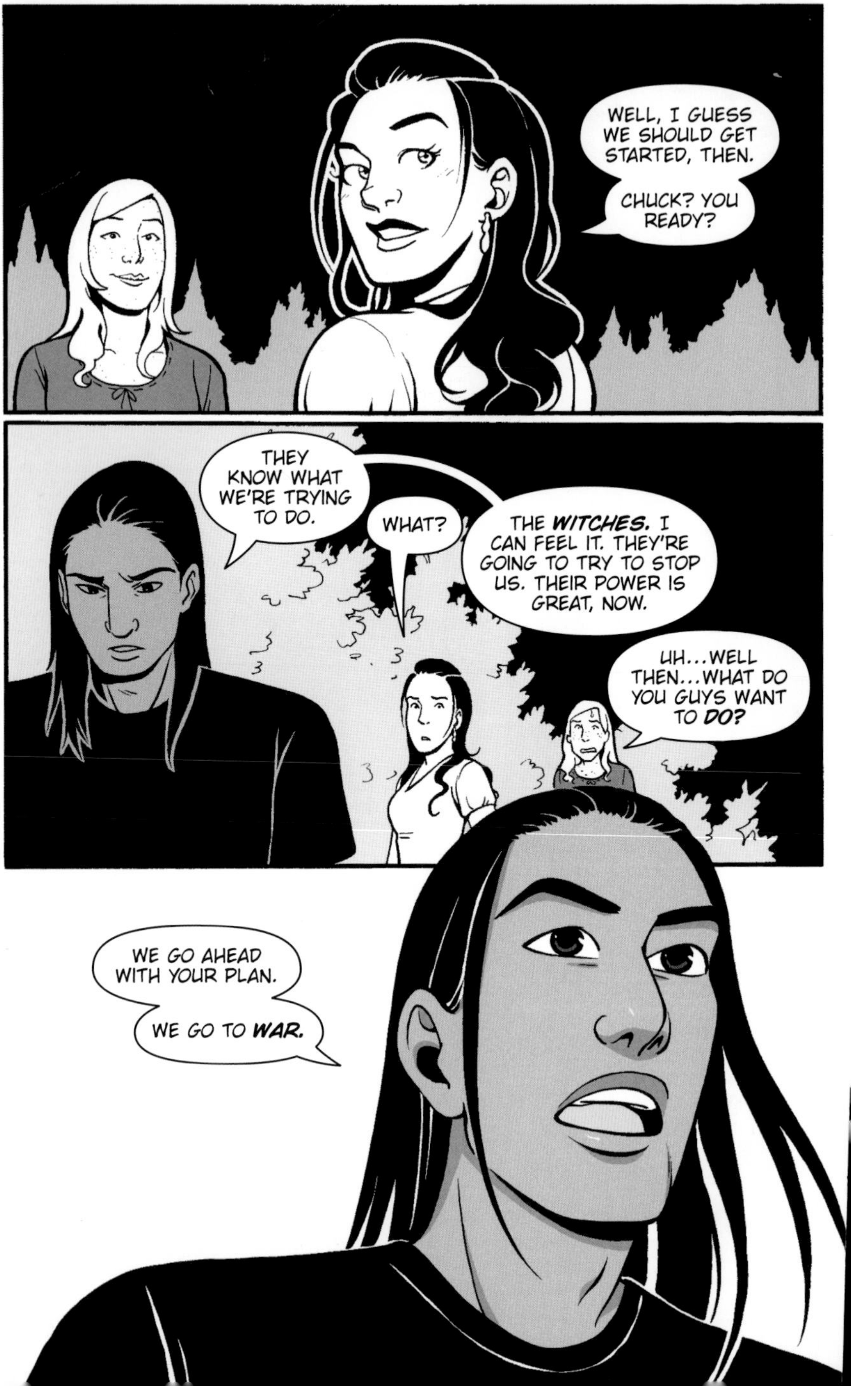

WELL, I GUESS WE SHOULD GET STARTED, THEN.
CHUCK? YOU READY?
THEY KNOW WHAT WE'RE TRYING TO DO.
WHAT?
THE *WITCHES.* I CAN FEEL IT. THEY'RE GOING TO TRY TO STOP US. THEIR POWER IS GREAT, NOW.
UH...WELL THEN...WHAT DO YOU GUYS WANT TO *DO?*
WE GO AHEAD WITH YOUR PLAN.
WE GO TO *WAR.*

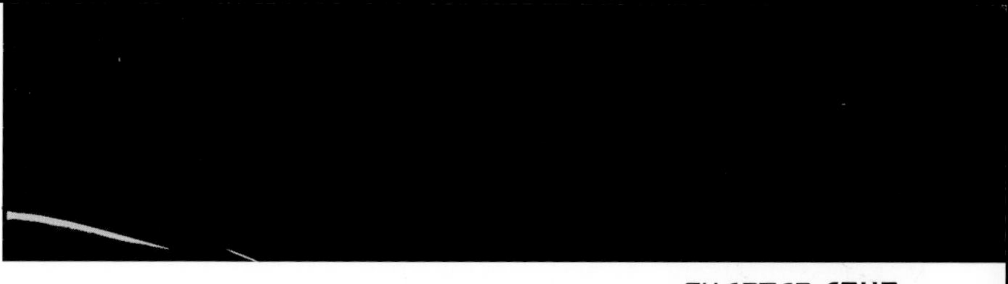

CHAPTER FOUR

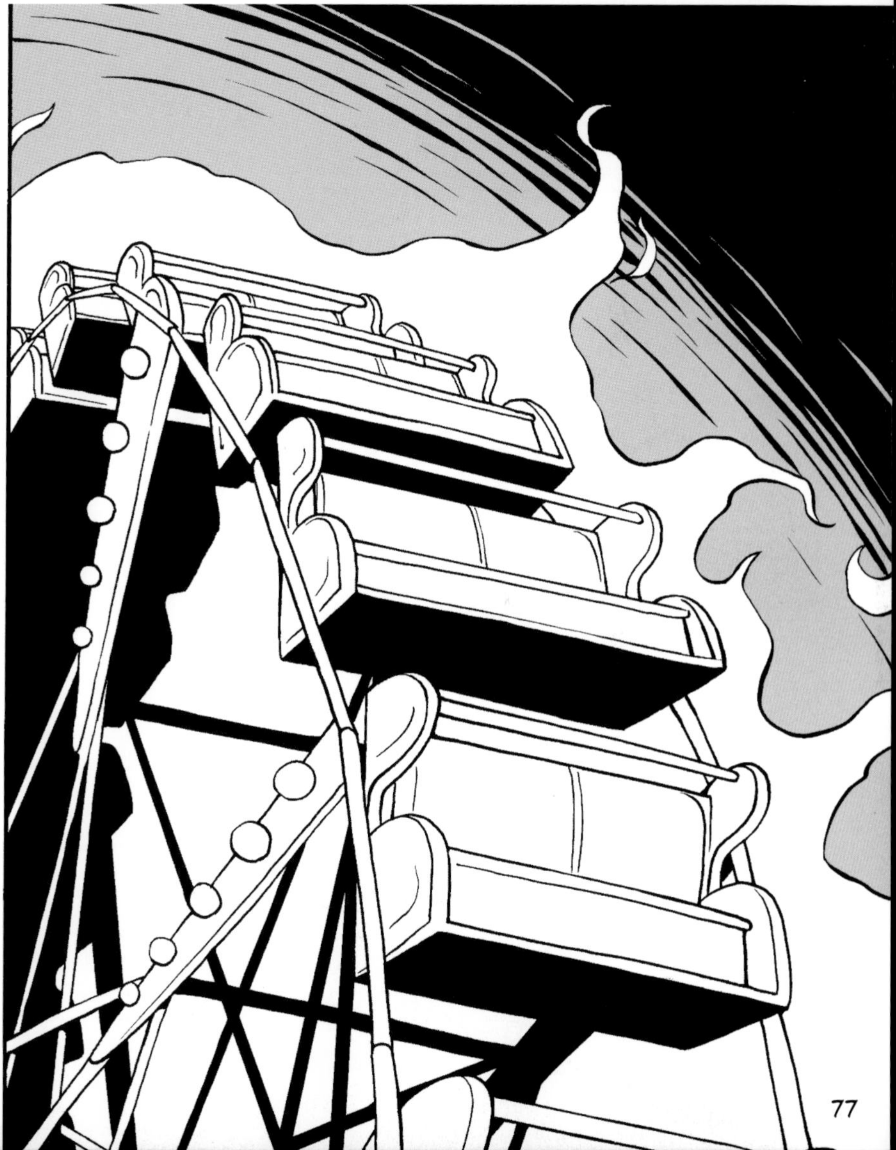

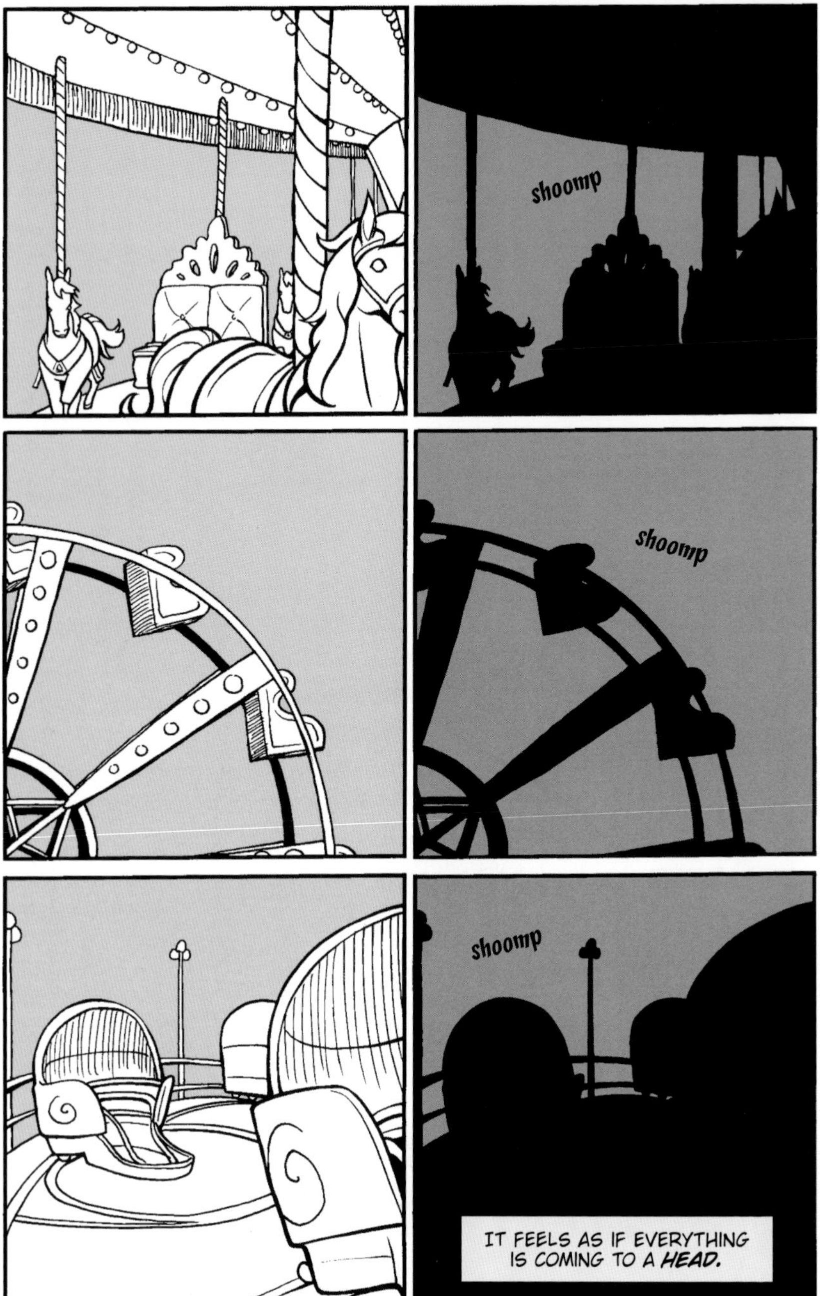
shoomp
shoomp
shoomp
IT FEELS AS IF EVERYTHING IS COMING TO A *HEAD.*

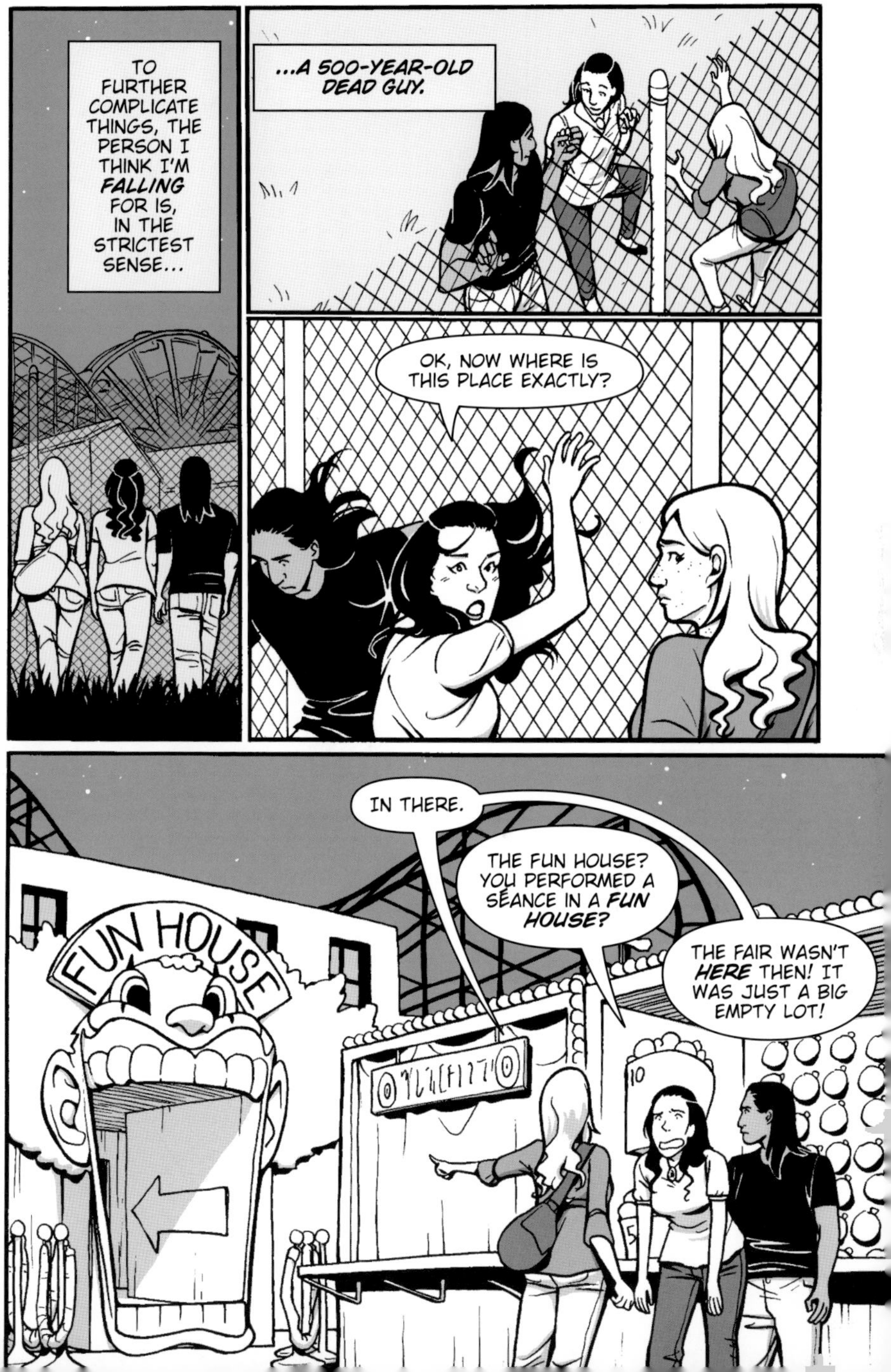
TO FURTHER COMPLICATE THINGS, THE PERSON I THINK I'M *FALLING* FOR IS, IN THE STRICTEST SENSE...
...A 500-YEAR-OLD DEAD GUY.
OK, NOW WHERE IS THIS PLACE EXACTLY?
IN THERE.
THE FUN HOUSE? YOU PERFORMED A SÉANCE IN A *FUN HOUSE?*
THE FAIR WASN'T *HERE* THEN! IT WAS JUST A BIG EMPTY LOT!
FUN HOUSE
10

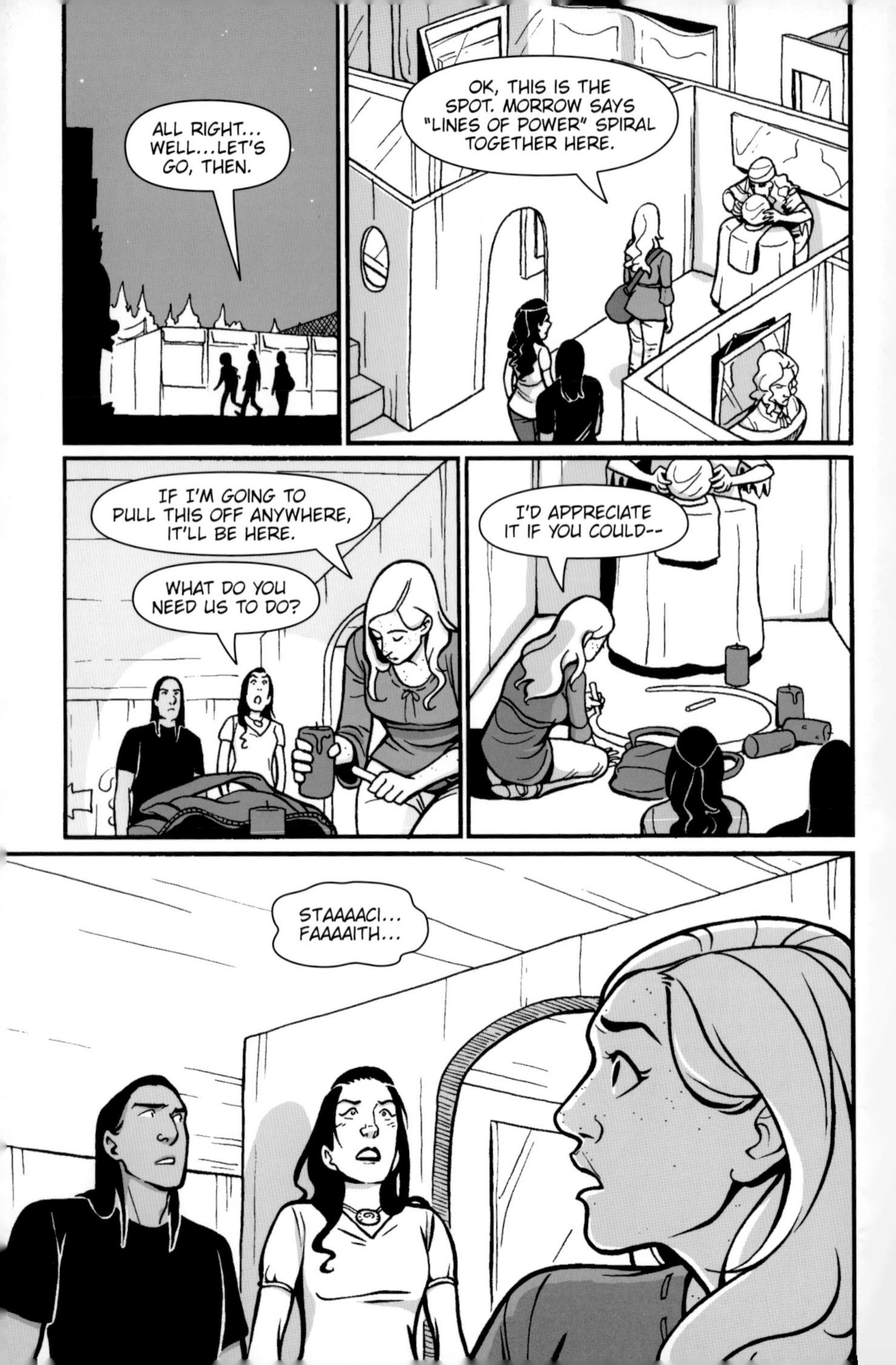
ALL RIGHT... WELL...LET'S GO, THEN.
OK, THIS IS THE SPOT. MORROW SAYS "LINES OF POWER" SPIRAL TOGETHER HERE.
IF I'M GOING TO PULL THIS OFF ANYWHERE, IT'LL BE HERE.
WHAT DO YOU NEED US TO DO?
I'D APPRECIATE IT IF YOU COULD--
STAAAACI... FAAAAITH...

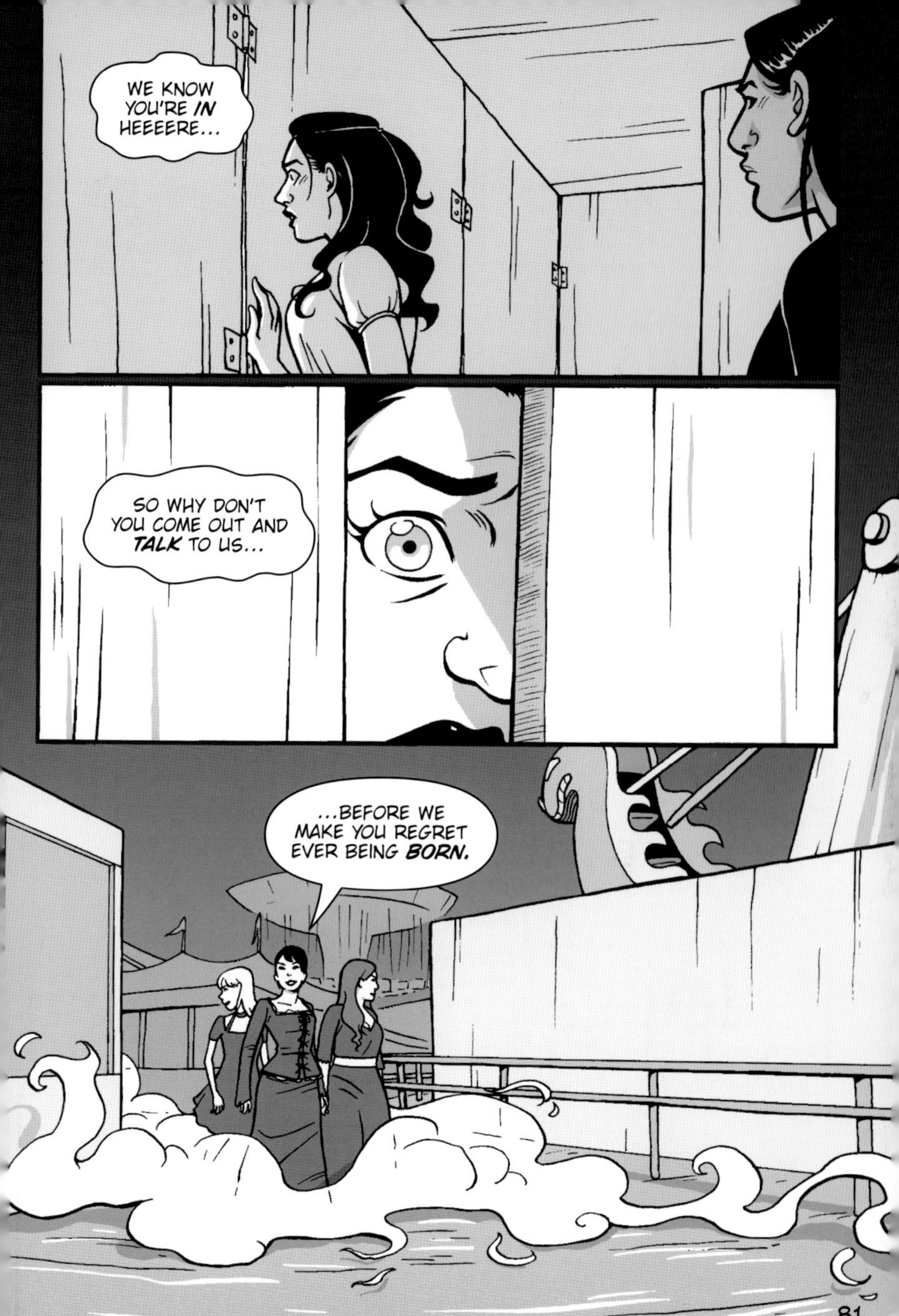
WE KNOW YOU'RE *IN* HEEEERE...
SO WHY DON'T YOU COME OUT AND *TALK* TO US...
...BEFORE WE MAKE YOU REGRET EVER BEING *BORN.*

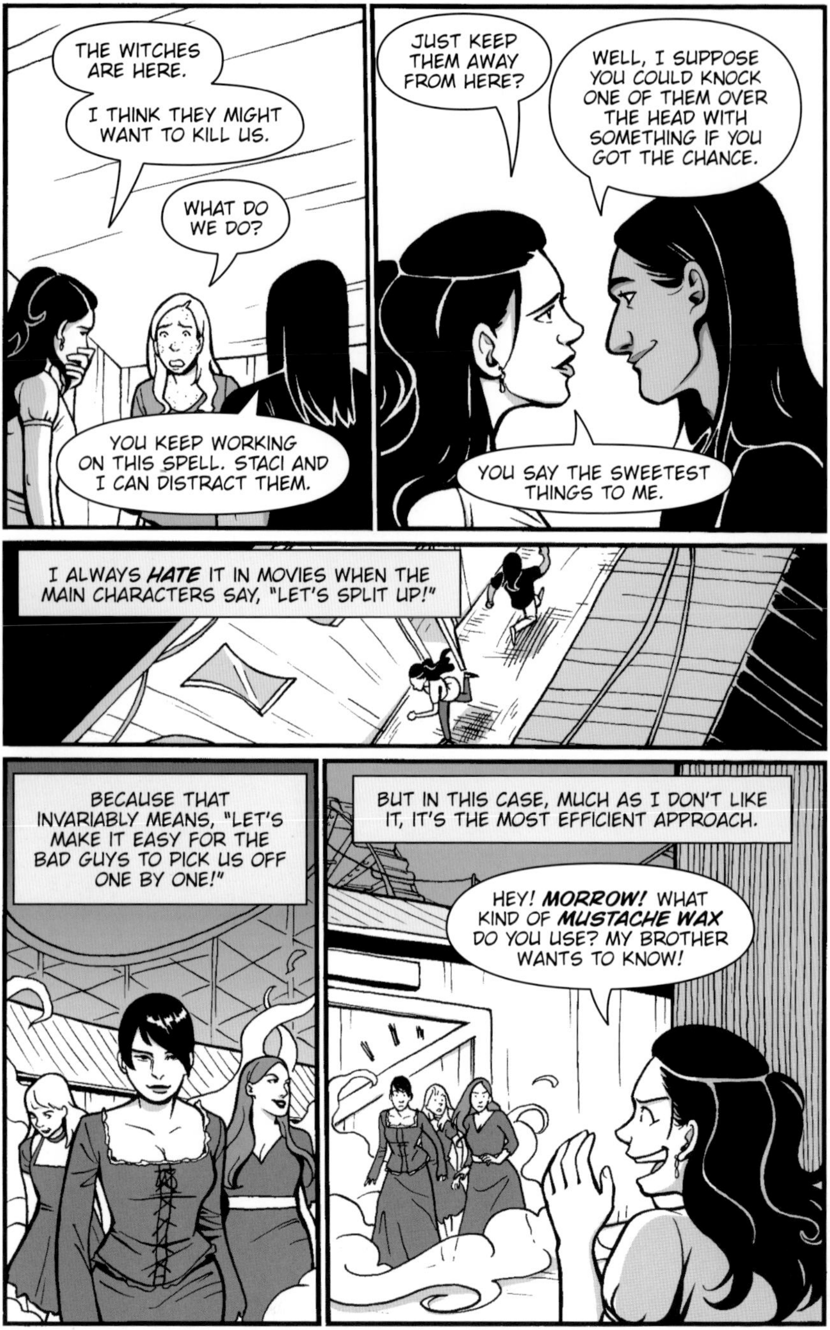
THE WITCHES ARE HERE.
I THINK THEY MIGHT WANT TO KILL US.
WHAT DO WE DO?
YOU KEEP WORKING ON THIS SPELL. STACI AND I CAN DISTRACT THEM.
JUST KEEP THEM AWAY FROM HERE?
WELL, I SUPPOSE YOU COULD KNOCK ONE OF THEM OVER THE HEAD WITH SOMETHING IF YOU GOT THE CHANCE.
YOU SAY THE SWEETEST THINGS TO ME.
I ALWAYS ***HATE*** IT IN MOVIES WHEN THE MAIN CHARACTERS SAY, "LET'S SPLIT UP!"
BECAUSE THAT INVARIABLY MEANS, "LET'S MAKE IT EASY FOR THE BAD GUYS TO PICK US OFF ONE BY ONE!"
BUT IN THIS CASE, MUCH AS I DON'T LIKE IT, IT'S THE MOST EFFICIENT APPROACH.
HEY! ***MORROW!*** WHAT KIND OF ***MUSTACHE WAX*** DO YOU USE? MY BROTHER WANTS TO KNOW!

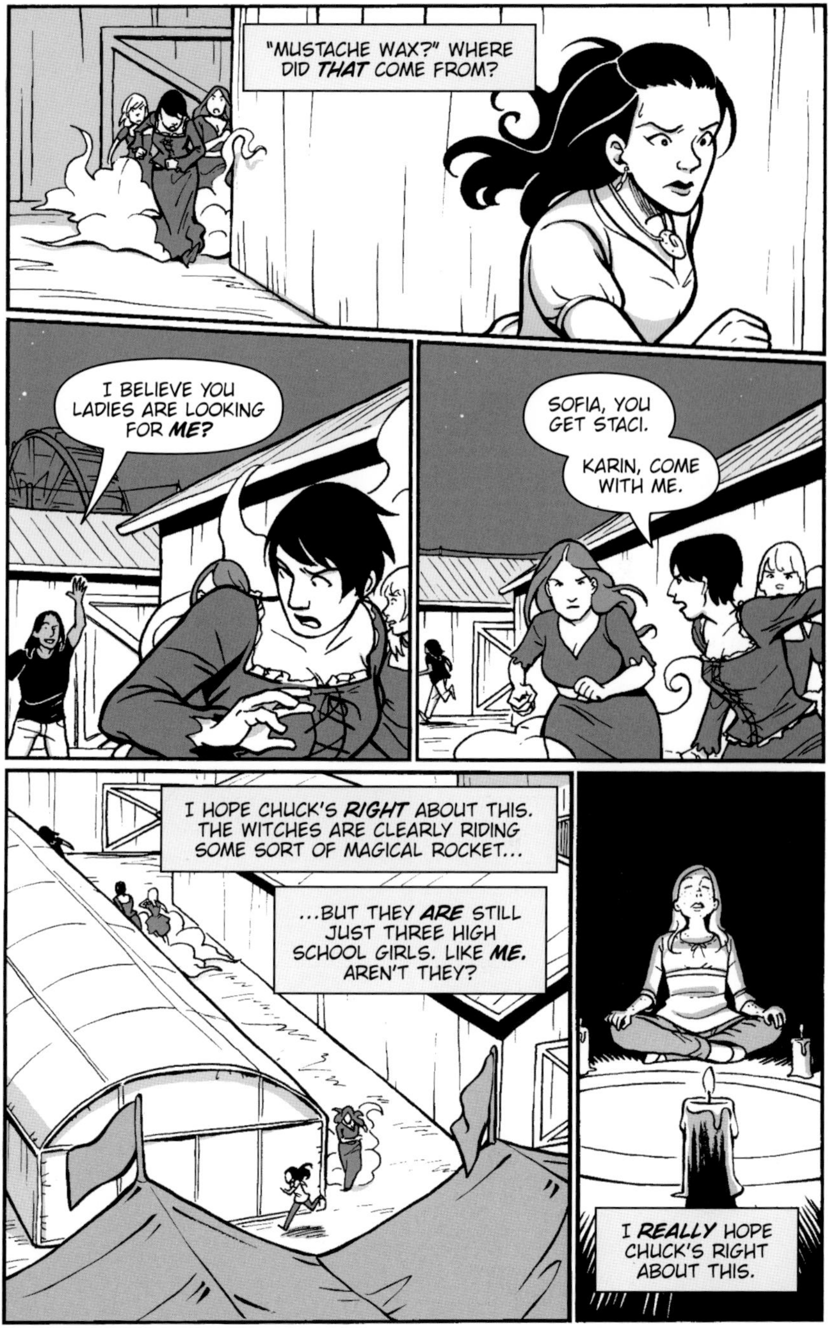
"MUSTACHE WAX?" WHERE DID THAT COME FROM?
I BELIEVE YOU LADIES ARE LOOKING FOR ME?
SOFIA, YOU GET STACI.
KARIN, COME WITH ME.
I HOPE CHUCK'S RIGHT ABOUT THIS. THE WITCHES ARE CLEARLY RIDING SOME SORT OF MAGICAL ROCKET...
...BUT THEY ARE STILL JUST THREE HIGH SCHOOL GIRLS. LIKE ME. AREN'T THEY?
I REALLY HOPE CHUCK'S RIGHT ABOUT THIS.

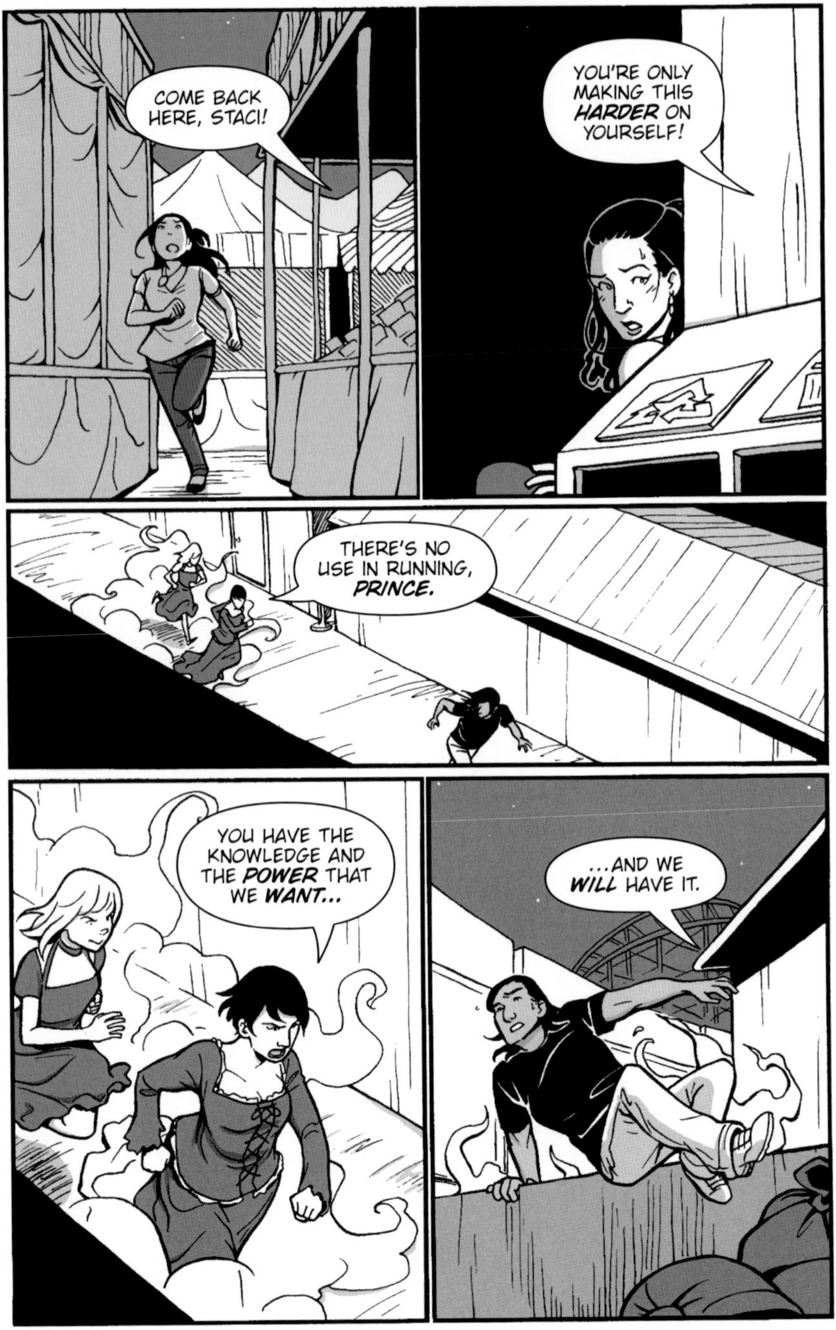
COME BACK HERE, STACI!
YOU'RE ONLY MAKING THIS **HARDER** ON YOURSELF!
THERE'S NO USE IN RUNNING, ***PRINCE.***
YOU HAVE THE KNOWLEDGE AND THE ***POWER*** THAT WE ***WANT...***
...AND WE ***WILL*** HAVE IT.

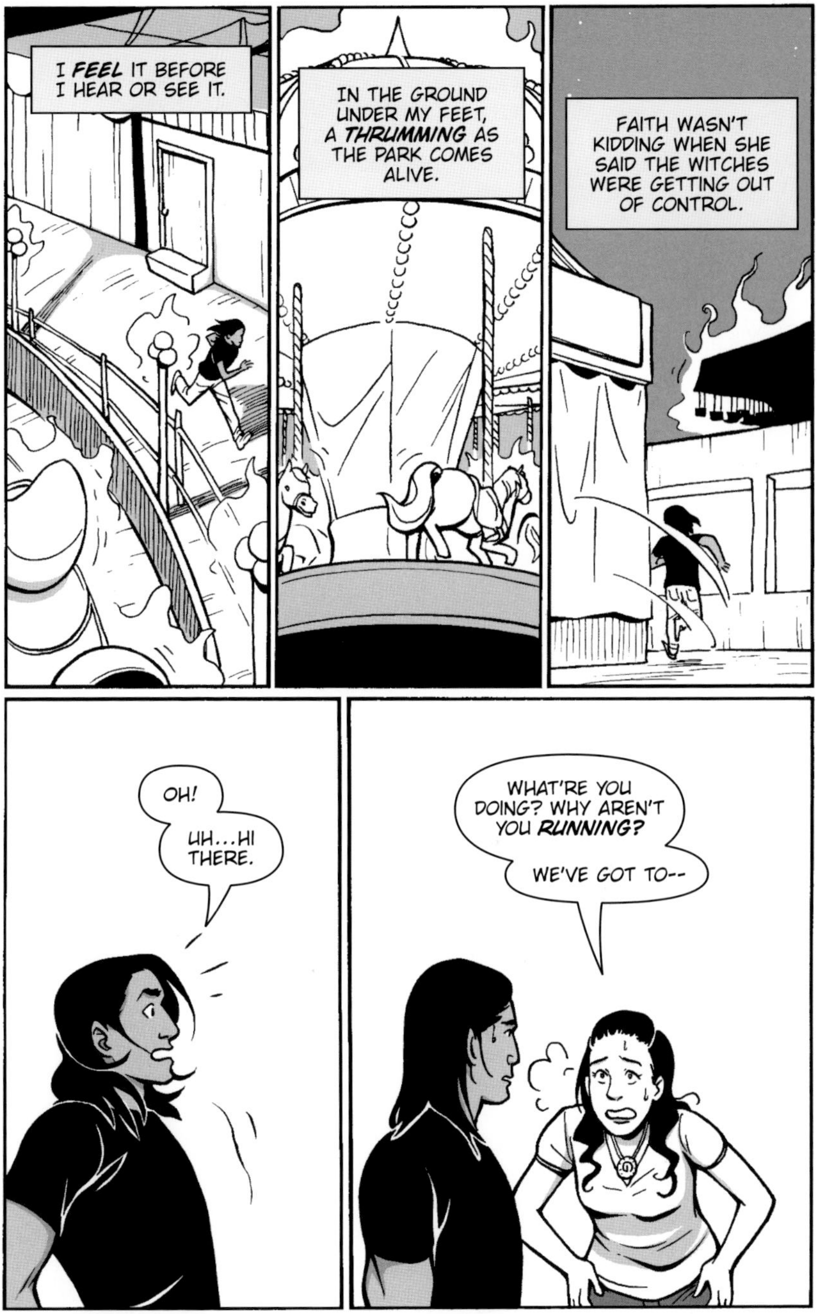
I FEEL IT BEFORE I HEAR OR SEE IT.
IN THE GROUND UNDER MY FEET, A THRUMMING AS THE PARK COMES ALIVE.
FAITH WASN'T KIDDING WHEN SHE SAID THE WITCHES WERE GETTING OUT OF CONTROL.
OH!
UH...HI THERE.
WHAT'RE YOU DOING? WHY AREN'T YOU RUNNING?
WE'VE GOT TO--

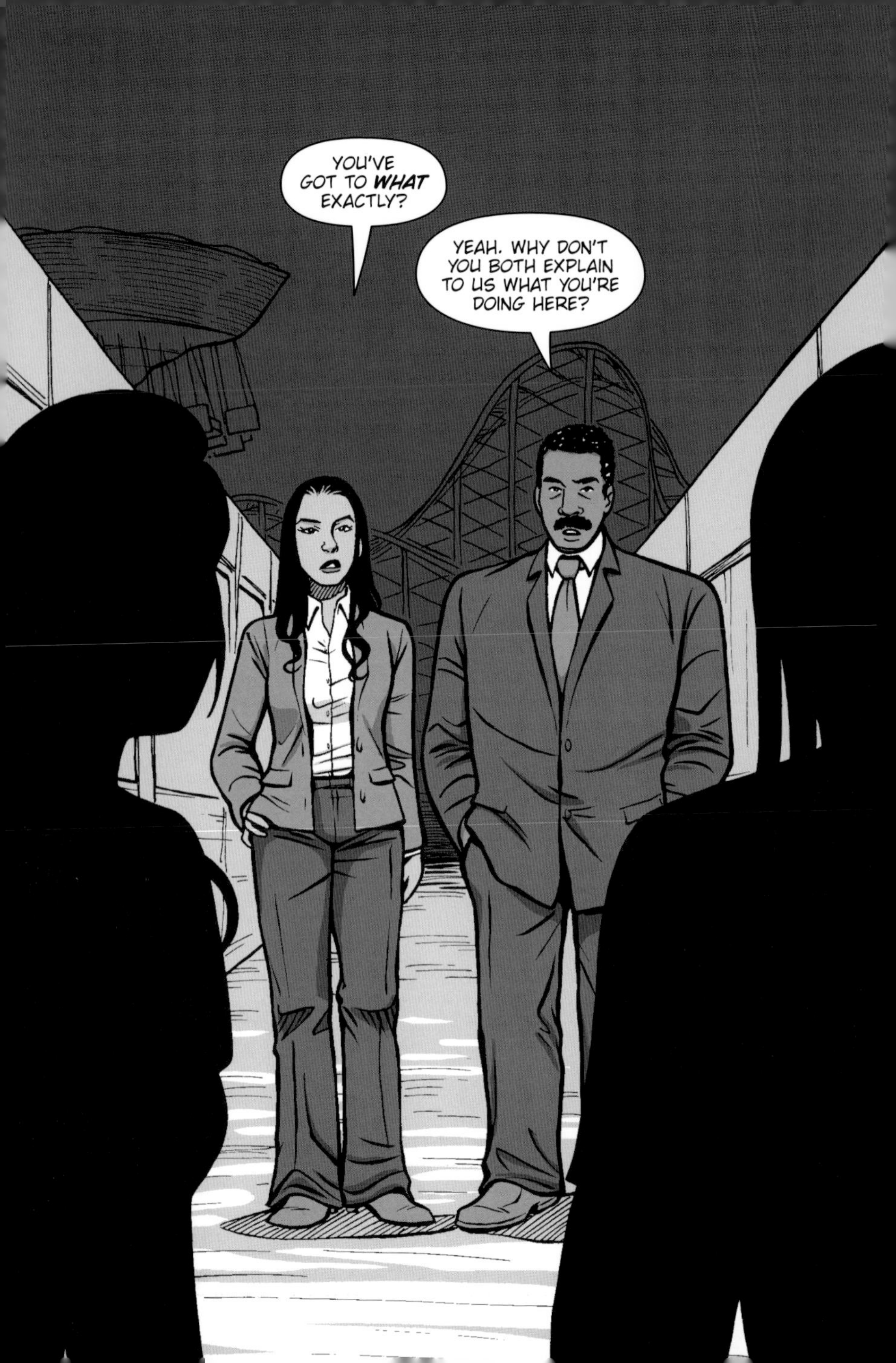
YOU'VE GOT TO WHAT EXACTLY?
YEAH. WHY DON'T YOU BOTH EXPLAIN TO US WHAT YOU'RE DOING HERE?

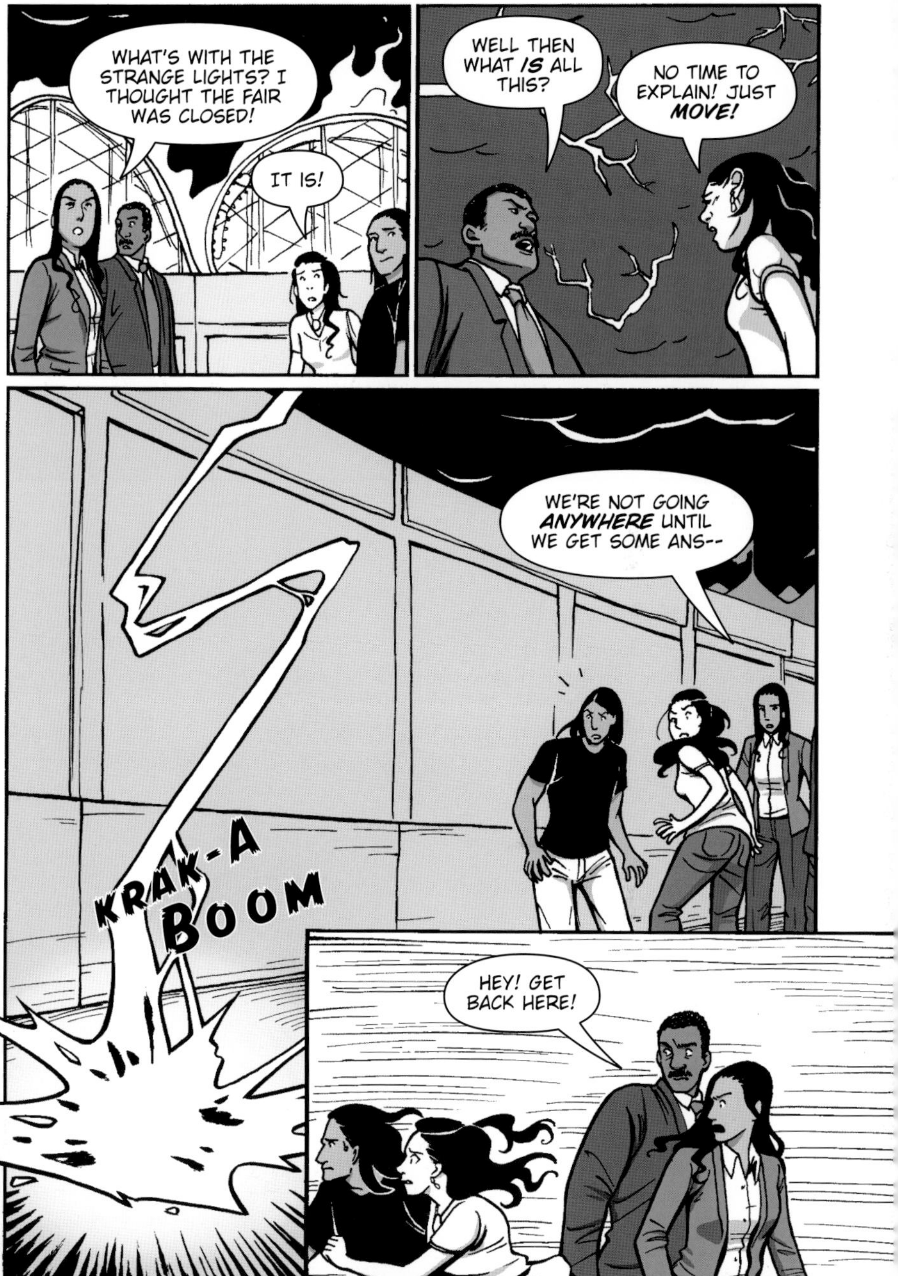
WHAT'S WITH THE STRANGE LIGHTS? I THOUGHT THE FAIR WAS CLOSED!
IT IS!
WELL THEN WHAT IS ALL THIS?
NO TIME TO EXPLAIN! JUST MOVE!
WE'RE NOT GOING ANYWHERE UNTIL WE GET SOME ANS--
KRAK-A BOOM
HEY! GET BACK HERE!

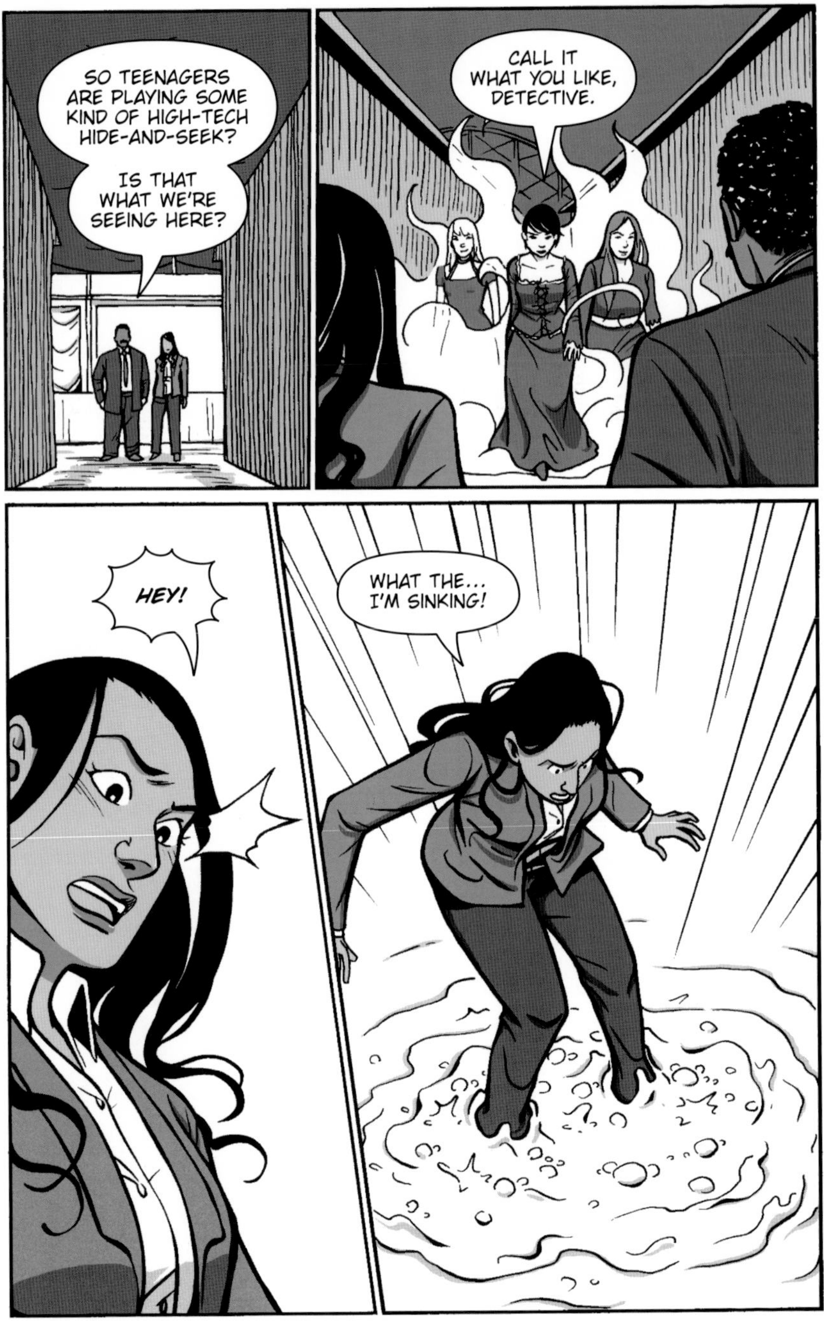
SO TEENAGERS ARE PLAYING SOME KIND OF HIGH-TECH HIDE-AND-SEEK?
IS THAT WHAT WE'RE SEEING HERE?
CALL IT WHAT YOU LIKE, DETECTIVE.
HEY!
WHAT THE... I'M SINKING!

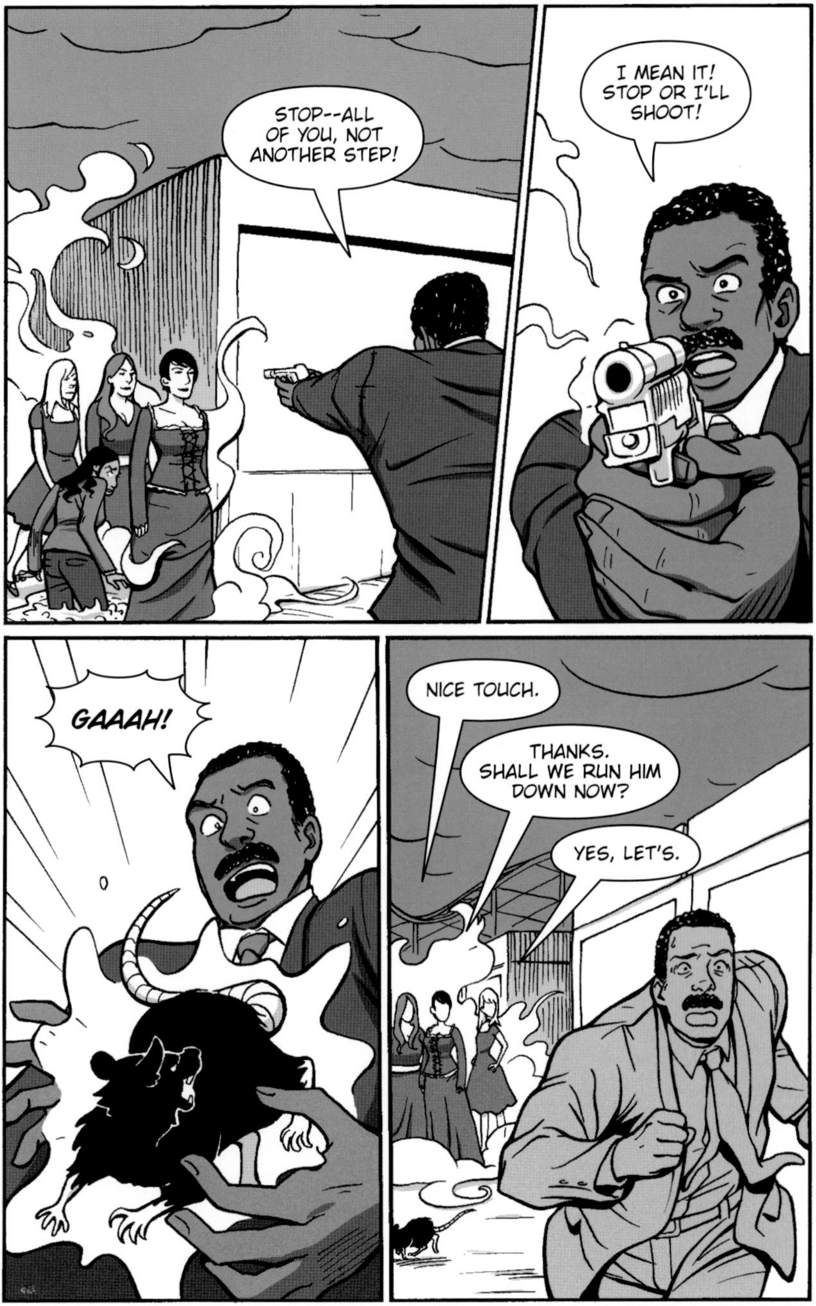
STOP--ALL OF YOU, NOT ANOTHER STEP!
I MEAN IT! STOP OR I'LL SHOOT!
GAAAH!
NICE TOUCH.
THANKS. SHALL WE RUN HIM DOWN NOW?
YES, LET'S.

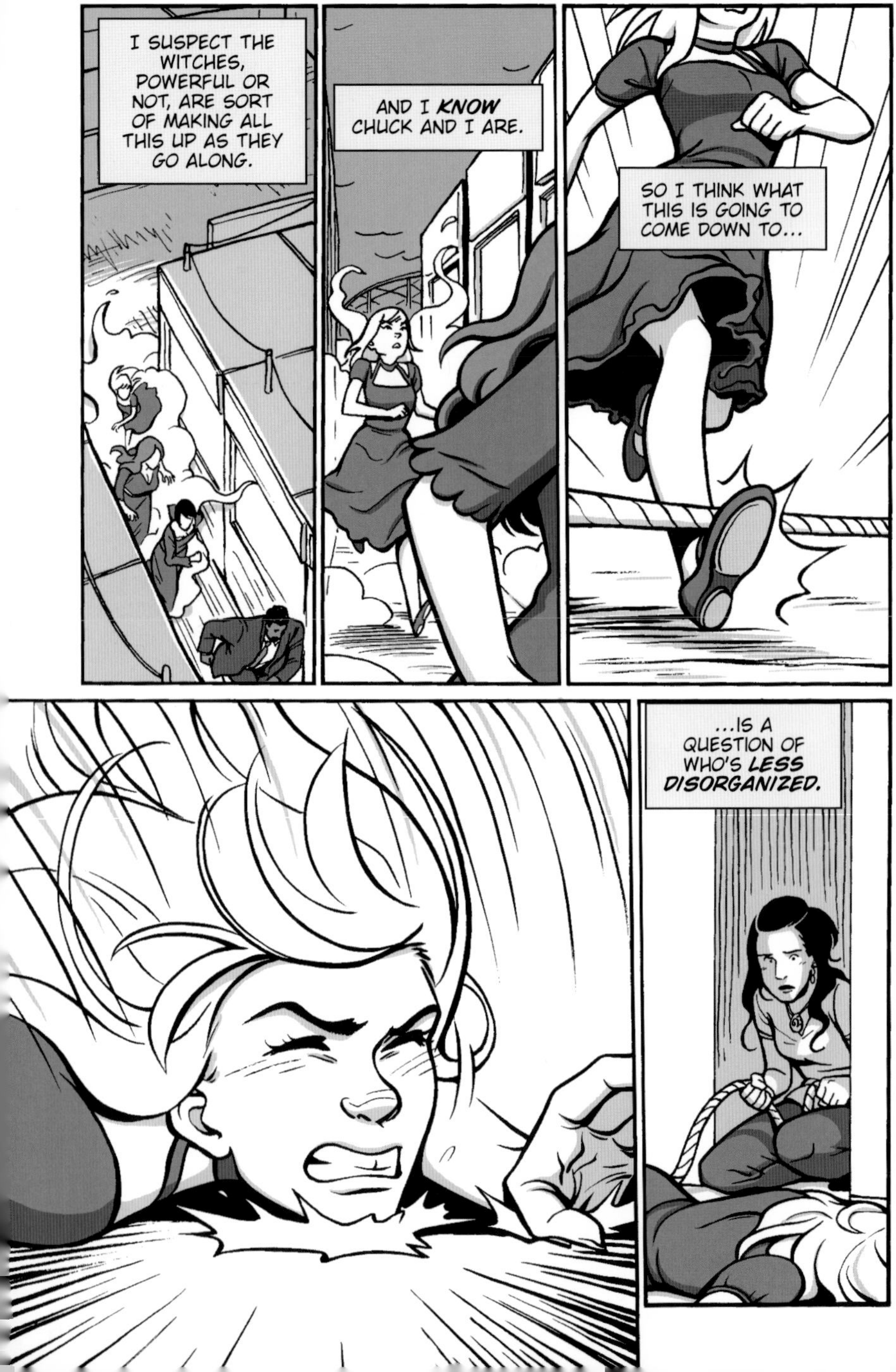
I SUSPECT THE WITCHES, POWERFUL OR NOT, ARE SORT OF MAKING ALL THIS UP AS THEY GO ALONG.
AND I *KNOW* CHUCK AND I ARE.
SO I THINK WHAT THIS IS GOING TO COME DOWN TO...
...IS A QUESTION OF WHO'S *LESS DISORGANIZED.*

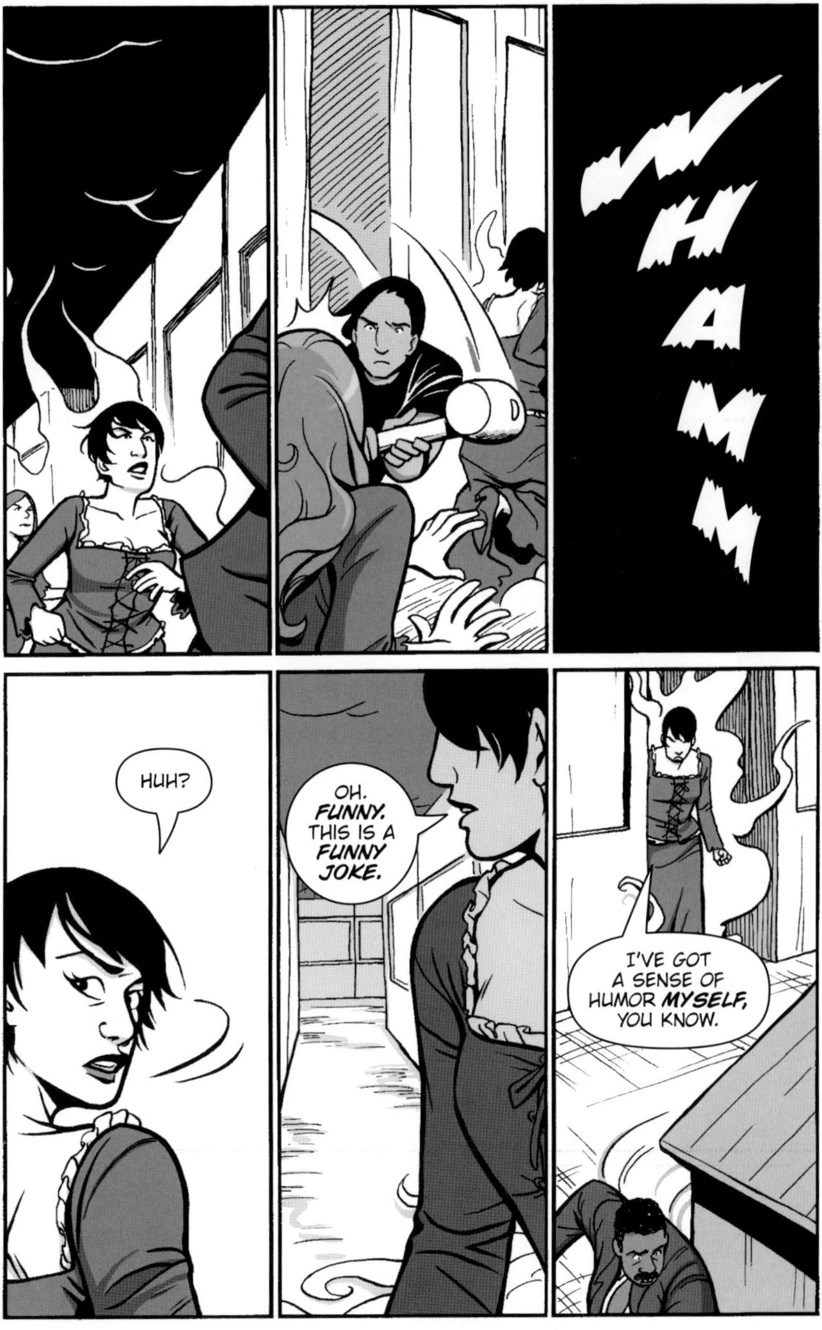
WHAM
HUH?
OH. FUNNY. THIS IS A FUNNY JOKE.
I'VE GOT A SENSE OF HUMOR MYSELF, YOU KNOW.

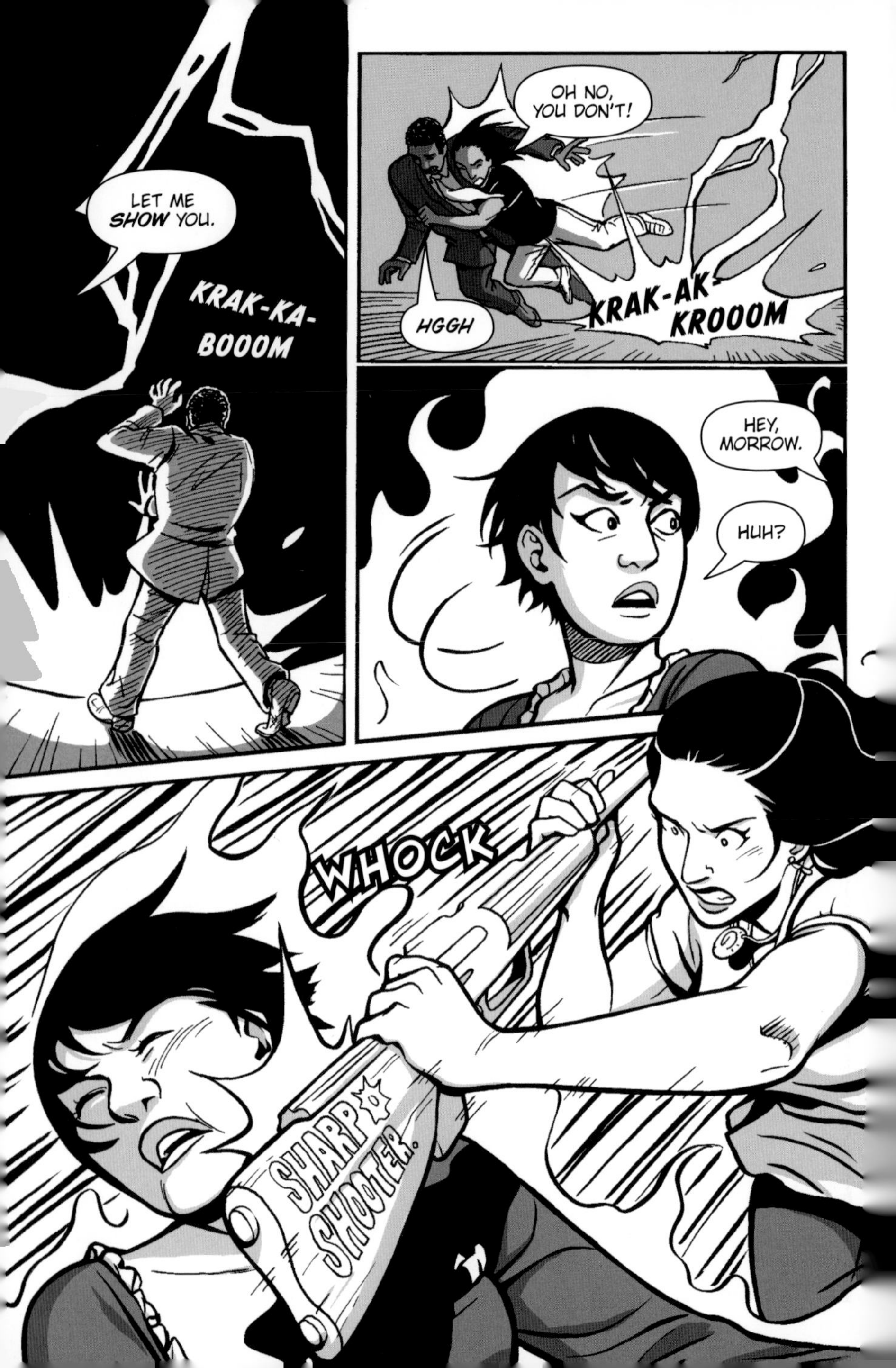
LET ME SHOW YOU.
KRAK-KA-BOOOM
OH NO, YOU DON'T!
HGGH
KRAK-AK-KROOOM
HEY, MORROW.
HUH?
WHOCK
SHARP SHOOTER

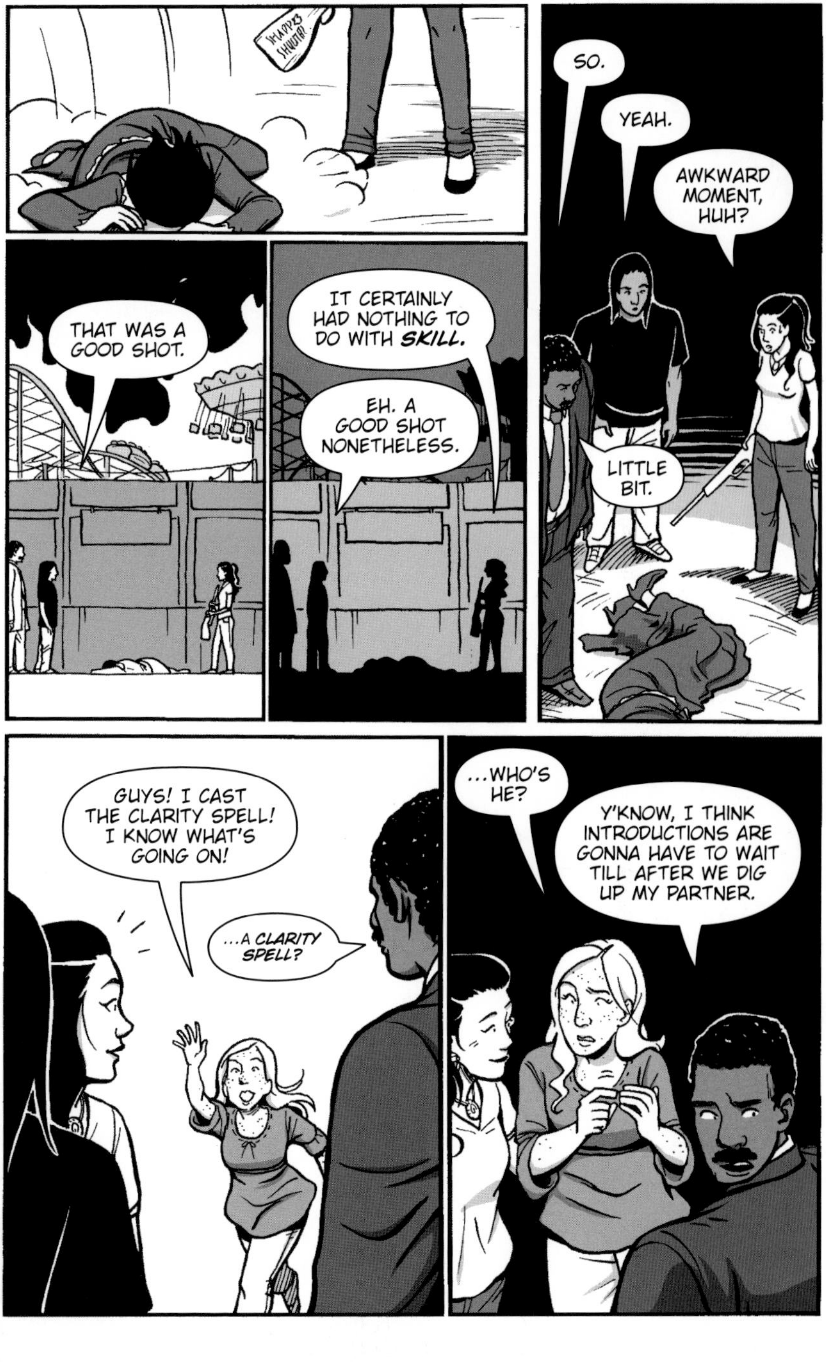
THAT WAS A GOOD SHOT.
IT CERTAINLY HAD NOTHING TO DO WITH *SKILL.*
EH. A GOOD SHOT NONETHELESS.
SO.
YEAH.
AWKWARD MOMENT, HUH?
LITTLE BIT.
GUYS! I CAST THE CLARITY SPELL! I KNOW WHAT'S GOING ON!
...A *CLARITY SPELL?*
...WHO'S HE?
Y'KNOW, I THINK INTRODUCTIONS ARE GONNA HAVE TO WAIT TILL AFTER WE DIG UP MY PARTNER.

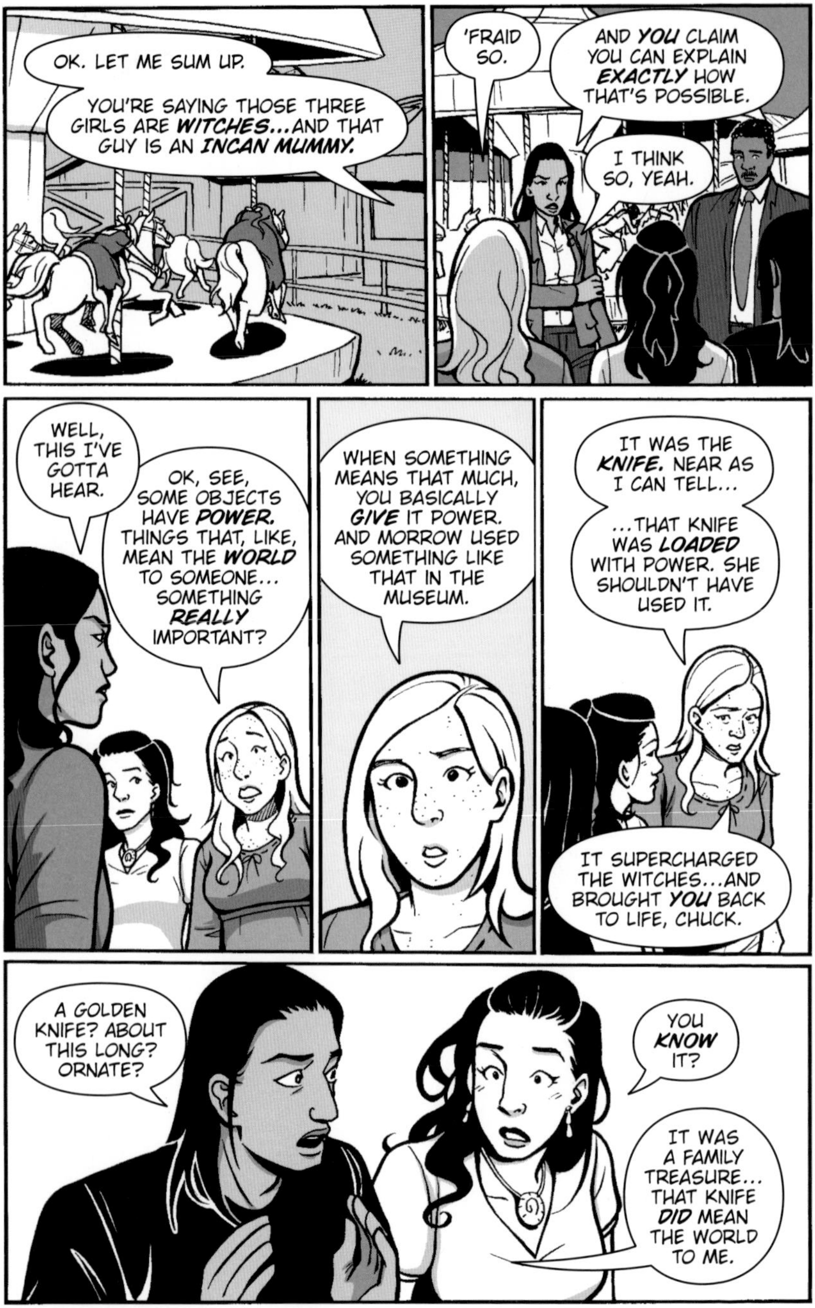

OK. LET ME SUM UP.
YOU'RE SAYING THOSE THREE GIRLS ARE WITCHES...AND THAT GUY IS AN INCAN MUMMY.
'FRAID SO.
AND YOU CLAIM YOU CAN EXPLAIN EXACTLY HOW THAT'S POSSIBLE.
I THINK SO, YEAH.
WELL, THIS I'VE GOTTA HEAR.
OK, SEE, SOME OBJECTS HAVE POWER. THINGS THAT, LIKE, MEAN THE WORLD TO SOMEONE... SOMETHING REALLY IMPORTANT?
WHEN SOMETHING MEANS THAT MUCH, YOU BASICALLY GIVE IT POWER. AND MORROW USED SOMETHING LIKE THAT IN THE MUSEUM.
IT WAS THE KNIFE. NEAR AS I CAN TELL...
...THAT KNIFE WAS LOADED WITH POWER. SHE SHOULDN'T HAVE USED IT.
IT SUPERCHARGED THE WITCHES...AND BROUGHT YOU BACK TO LIFE, CHUCK.
A GOLDEN KNIFE? ABOUT THIS LONG? ORNATE?
YOU KNOW IT?
IT WAS A FAMILY TREASURE... THAT KNIFE DID MEAN THE WORLD TO ME.

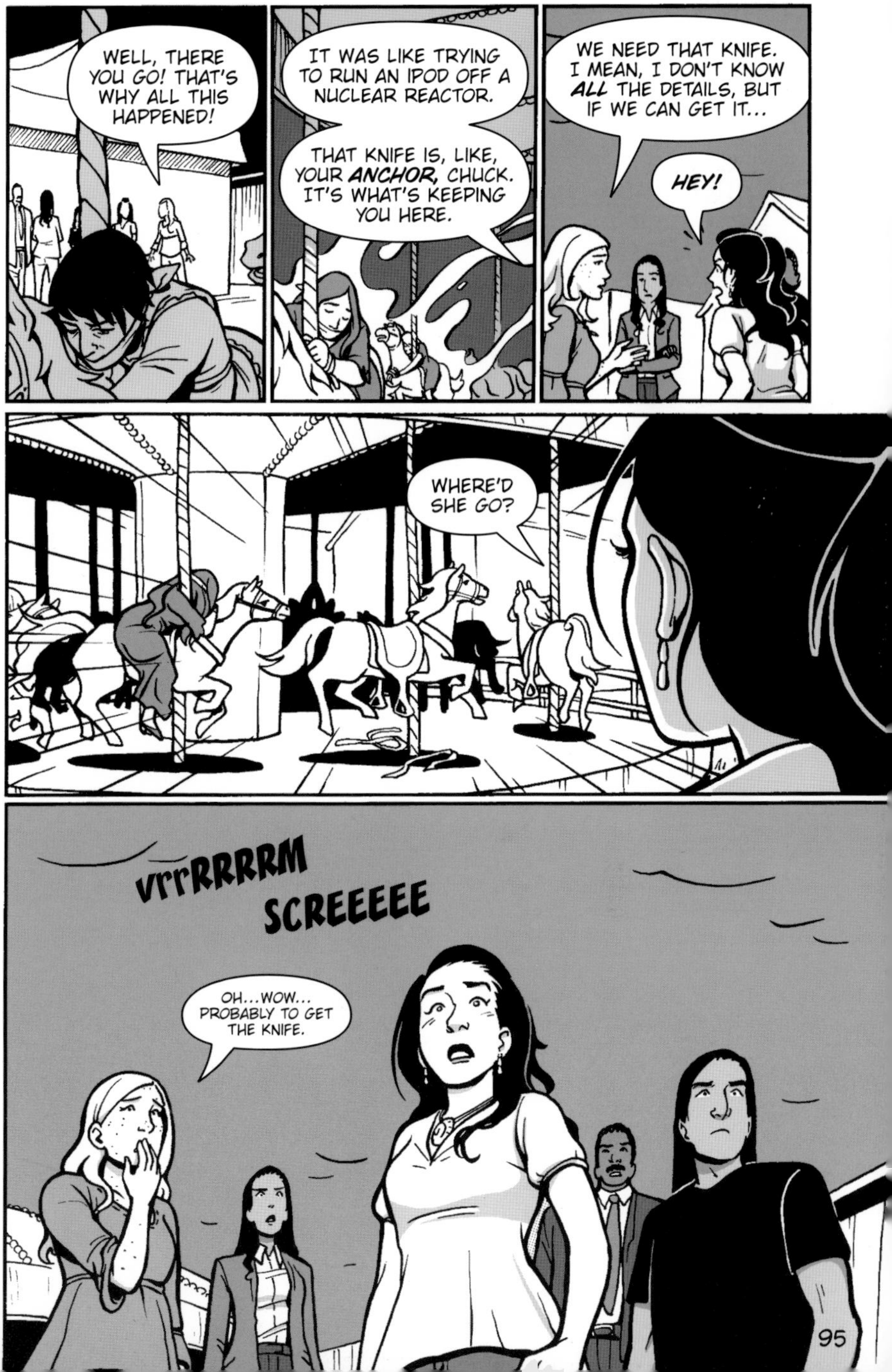
WELL, THERE YOU GO! THAT'S WHY ALL THIS HAPPENED!
IT WAS LIKE TRYING TO RUN AN IPOD OFF A NUCLEAR REACTOR.
THAT KNIFE IS, LIKE, YOUR ANCHOR, CHUCK. IT'S WHAT'S KEEPING YOU HERE.
WE NEED THAT KNIFE. I MEAN, I DON'T KNOW ALL THE DETAILS, BUT IF WE CAN GET IT...
HEY!
WHERE'D SHE GO?
VrrRRRRM
SCREEEEE
OH...WOW... PROBABLY TO GET THE KNIFE.

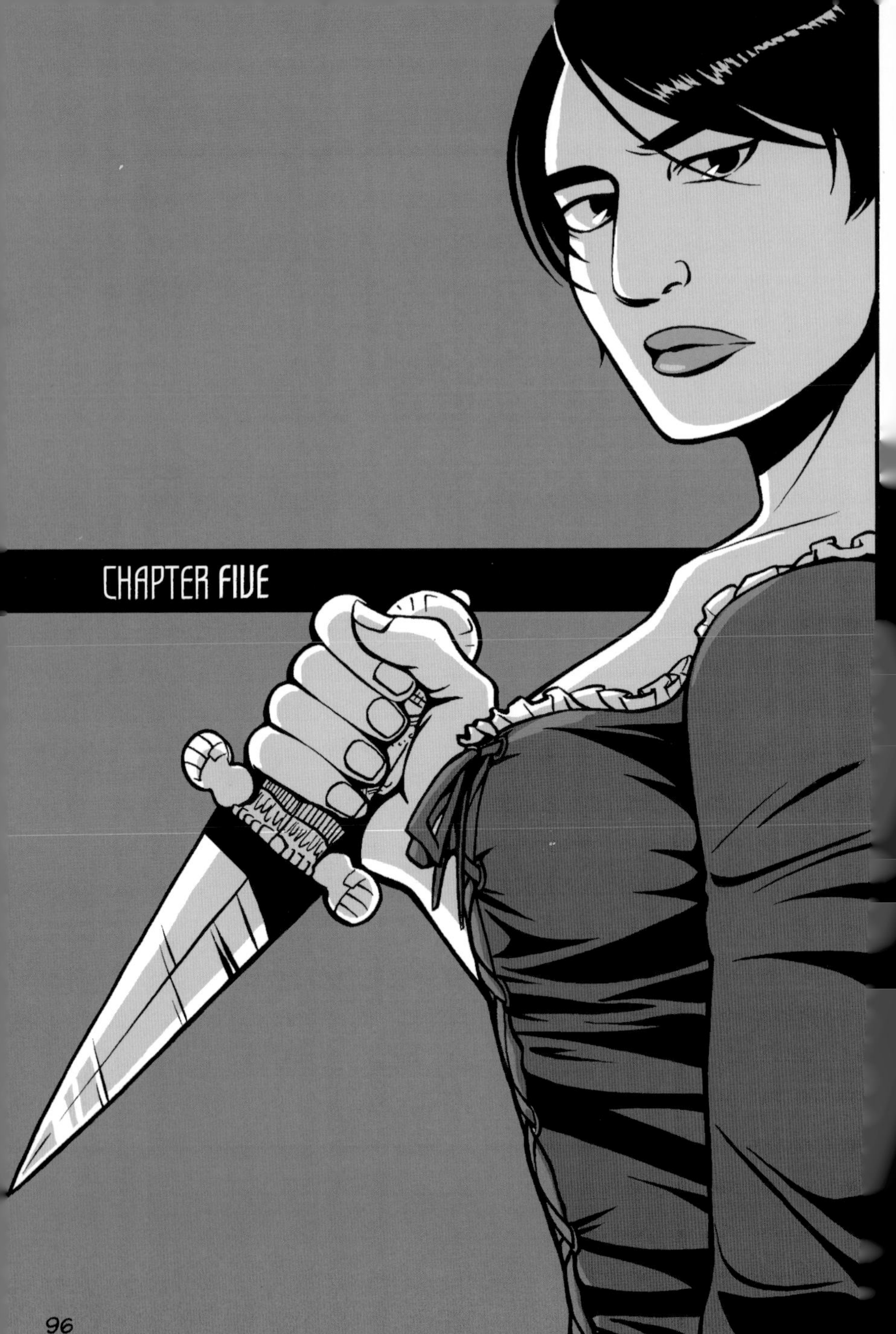
CHAPTER FIVE

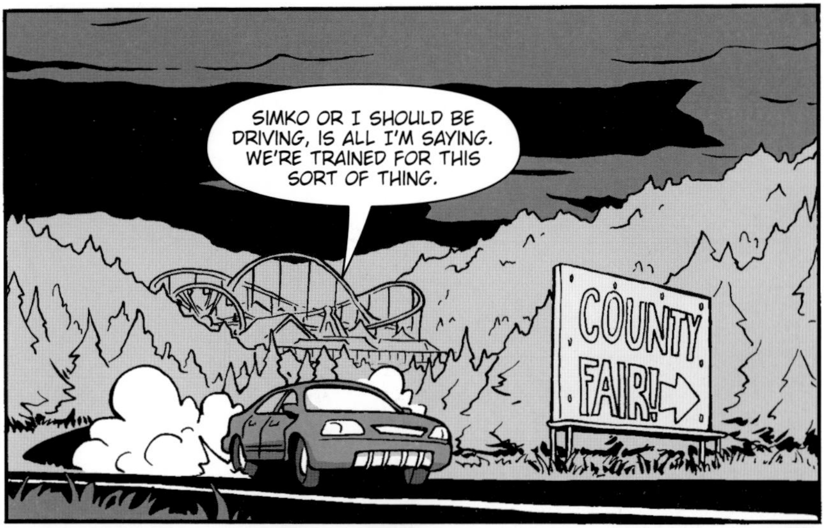
SIMKO OR I SHOULD BE DRIVING, IS ALL I'M SAYING. WE'RE TRAINED FOR THIS SORT OF THING.
COUNTY FAIR!

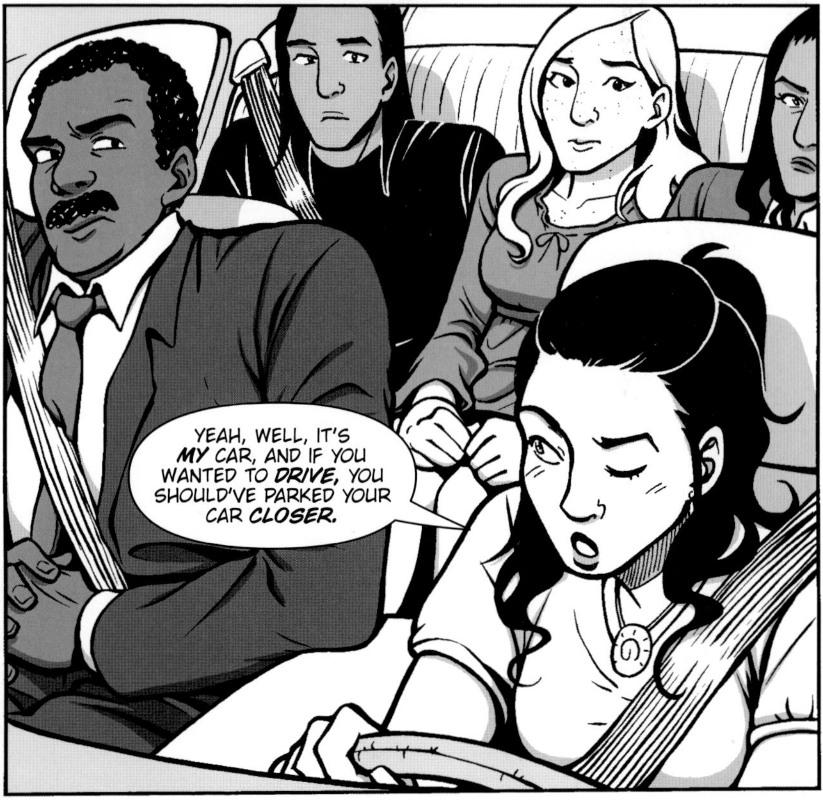
YEAH, WELL, IT'S **MY** CAR, AND IF YOU WANTED TO **DRIVE,** YOU SHOULD'VE PARKED YOUR CAR **CLOSER.**

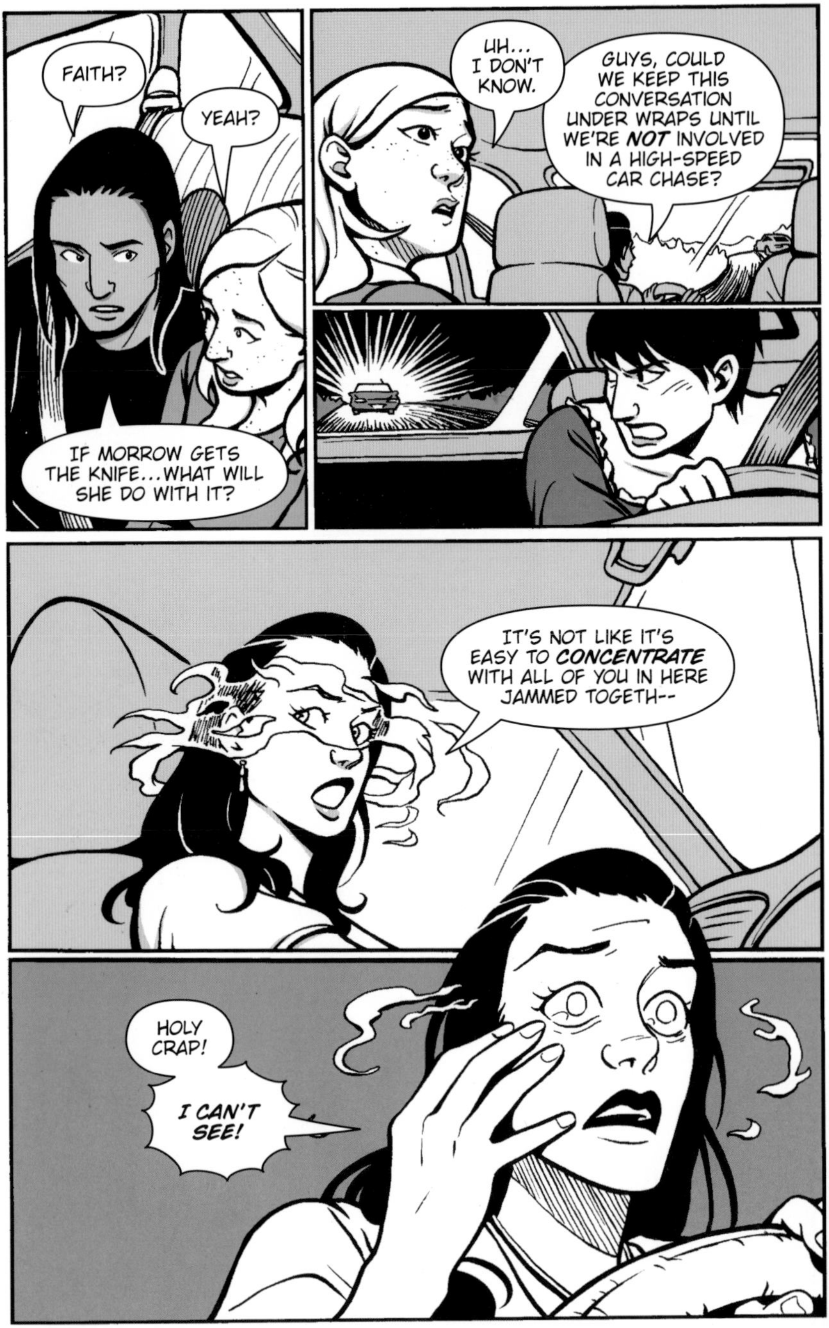
FAITH?
YEAH?
IF MORROW GETS THE KNIFE...WHAT WILL SHE DO WITH IT?
UH... I DON'T KNOW.
GUYS, COULD WE KEEP THIS CONVERSATION UNDER WRAPS UNTIL WE'RE NOT INVOLVED IN A HIGH-SPEED CAR CHASE?
IT'S NOT LIKE IT'S EASY TO CONCENTRATE WITH ALL OF YOU IN HERE JAMMED TOGETH--
HOLY CRAP!
I CAN'T SEE!

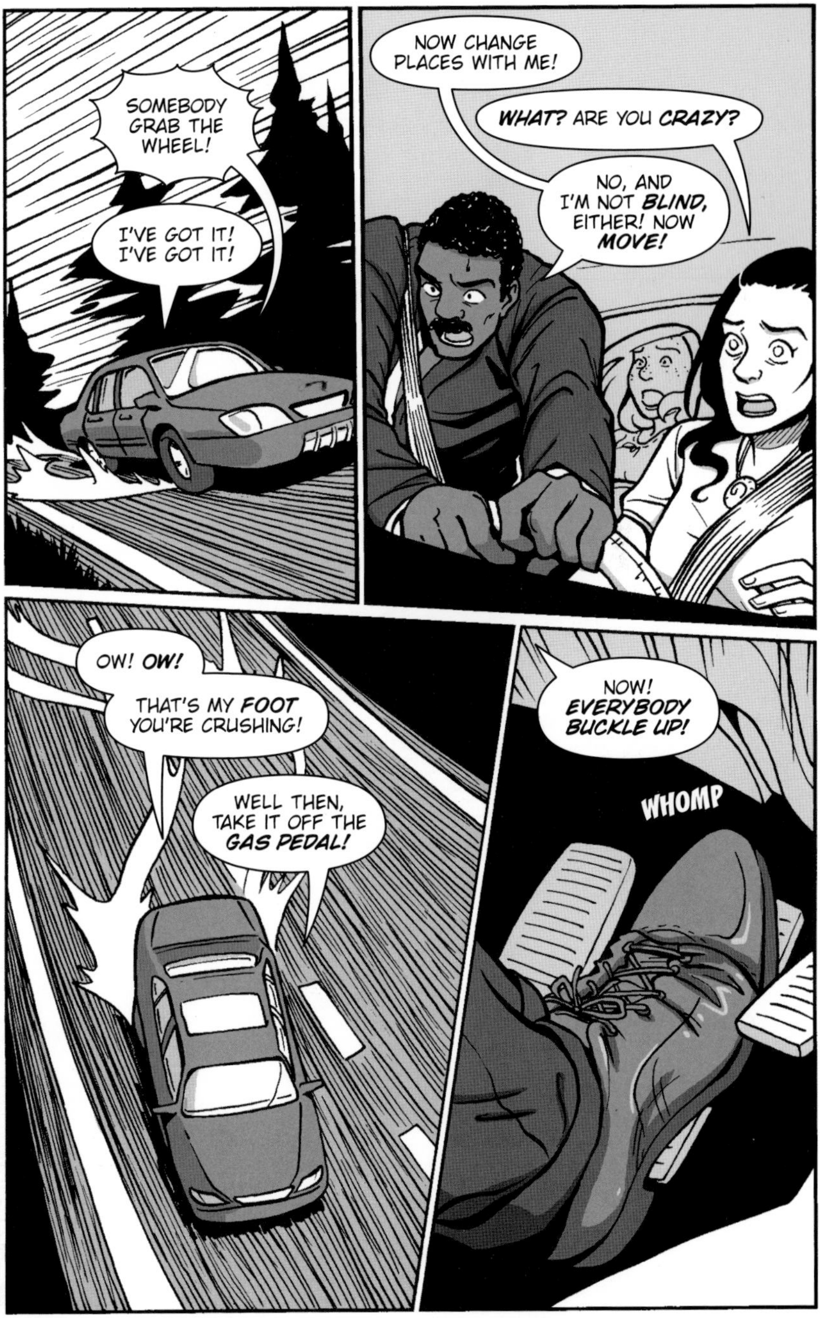
SOMEBODY GRAB THE WHEEL!
I'VE GOT IT! I'VE GOT IT!
NOW CHANGE PLACES WITH ME!
WHAT? ARE YOU CRAZY?
NO, AND I'M NOT BLIND, EITHER! NOW MOVE!
OW! OW!
THAT'S MY FOOT YOU'RE CRUSHING!
WELL THEN, TAKE IT OFF THE GAS PEDAL!
NOW! EVERYBODY BUCKLE UP!
WHOMP

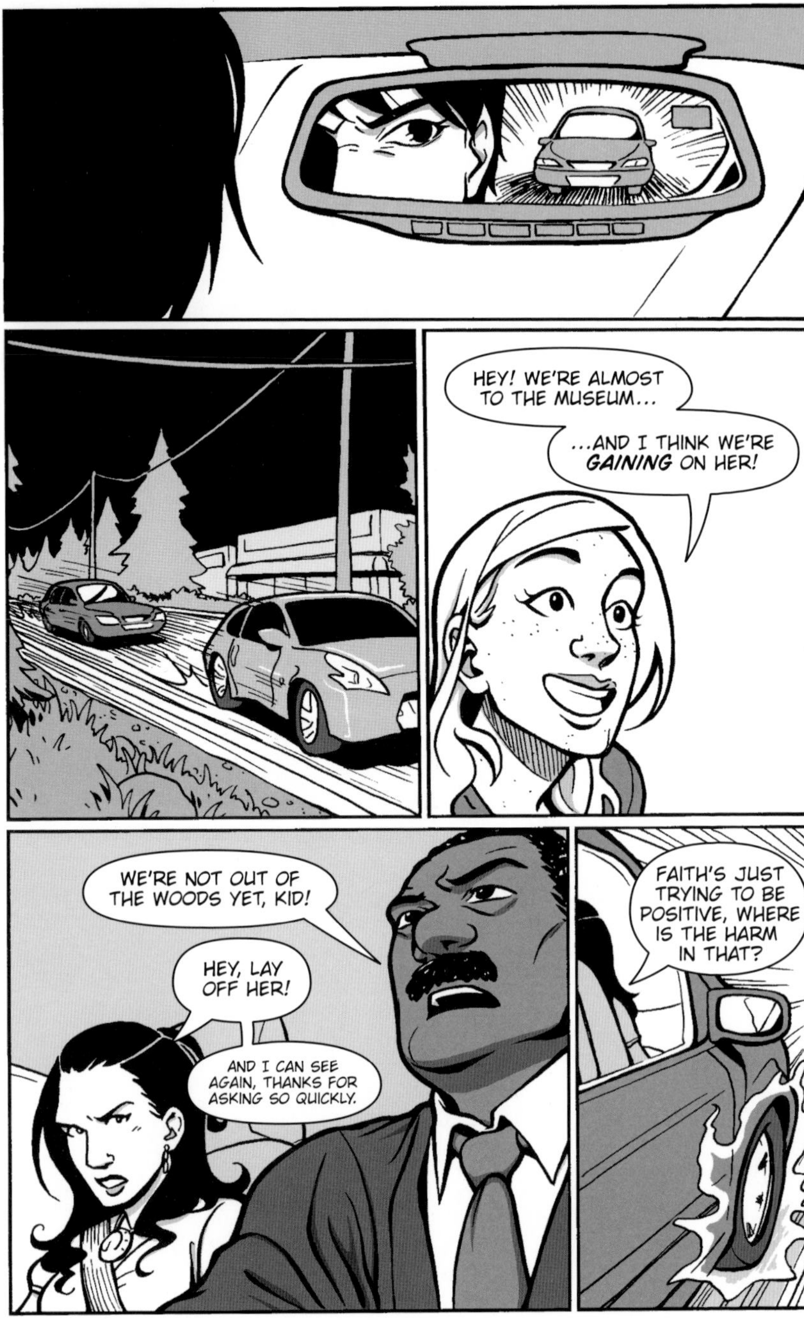
HEY! WE'RE ALMOST TO THE MUSEUM...
...AND I THINK WE'RE *GAINING* ON HER!
WE'RE NOT OUT OF THE WOODS YET, KID!
HEY, LAY OFF HER!
AND I CAN SEE AGAIN, THANKS FOR ASKING SO QUICKLY.
FAITH'S JUST TRYING TO BE POSITIVE, WHERE IS THE HARM IN THAT?

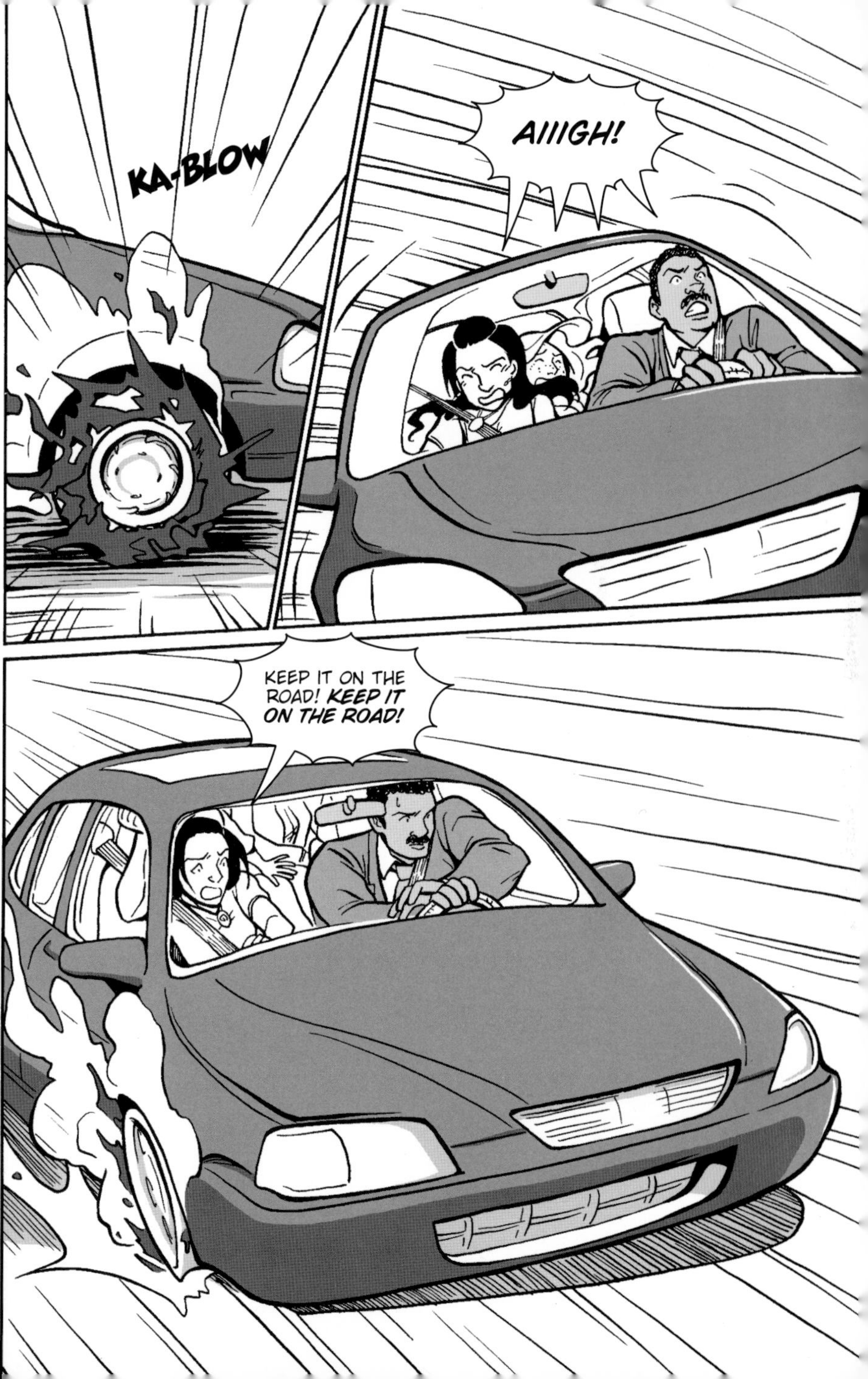
KA-BLOW
AIIIGH!
KEEP IT ON THE ROAD! KEEP IT ON THE ROAD!

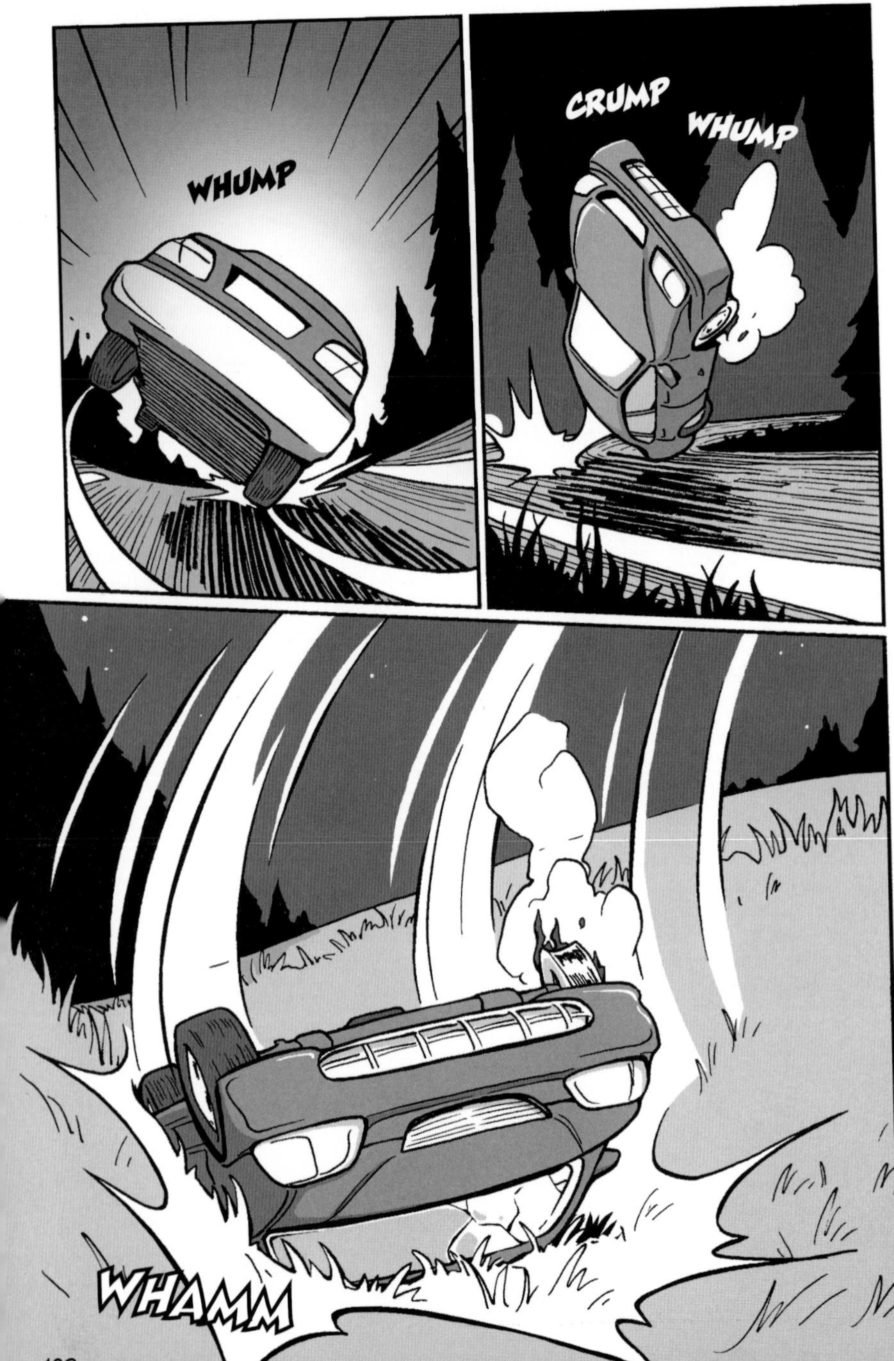
WHUMP
CRUMP
WHUMP
WHAMM

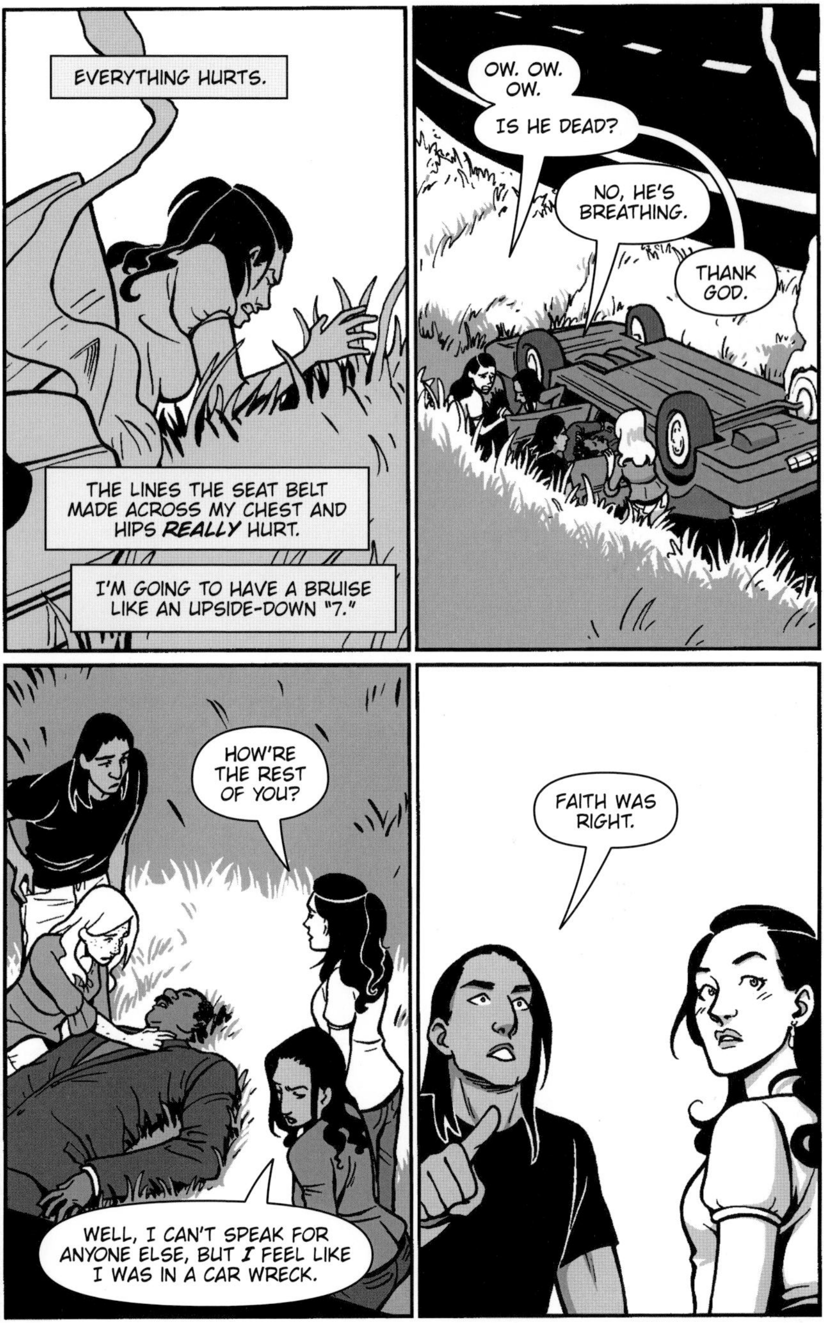
EVERYTHING HURTS.
THE LINES THE SEAT BELT MADE ACROSS MY CHEST AND HIPS *REALLY* HURT.
I'M GOING TO HAVE A BRUISE LIKE AN UPSIDE-DOWN "7."
OW. OW. OW.
IS HE DEAD?
NO, HE'S BREATHING.
THANK GOD.
HOW'RE THE REST OF YOU?
WELL, I CAN'T SPEAK FOR ANYONE ELSE, BUT *I* FEEL LIKE I WAS IN A CAR WRECK.
FAITH WAS RIGHT.

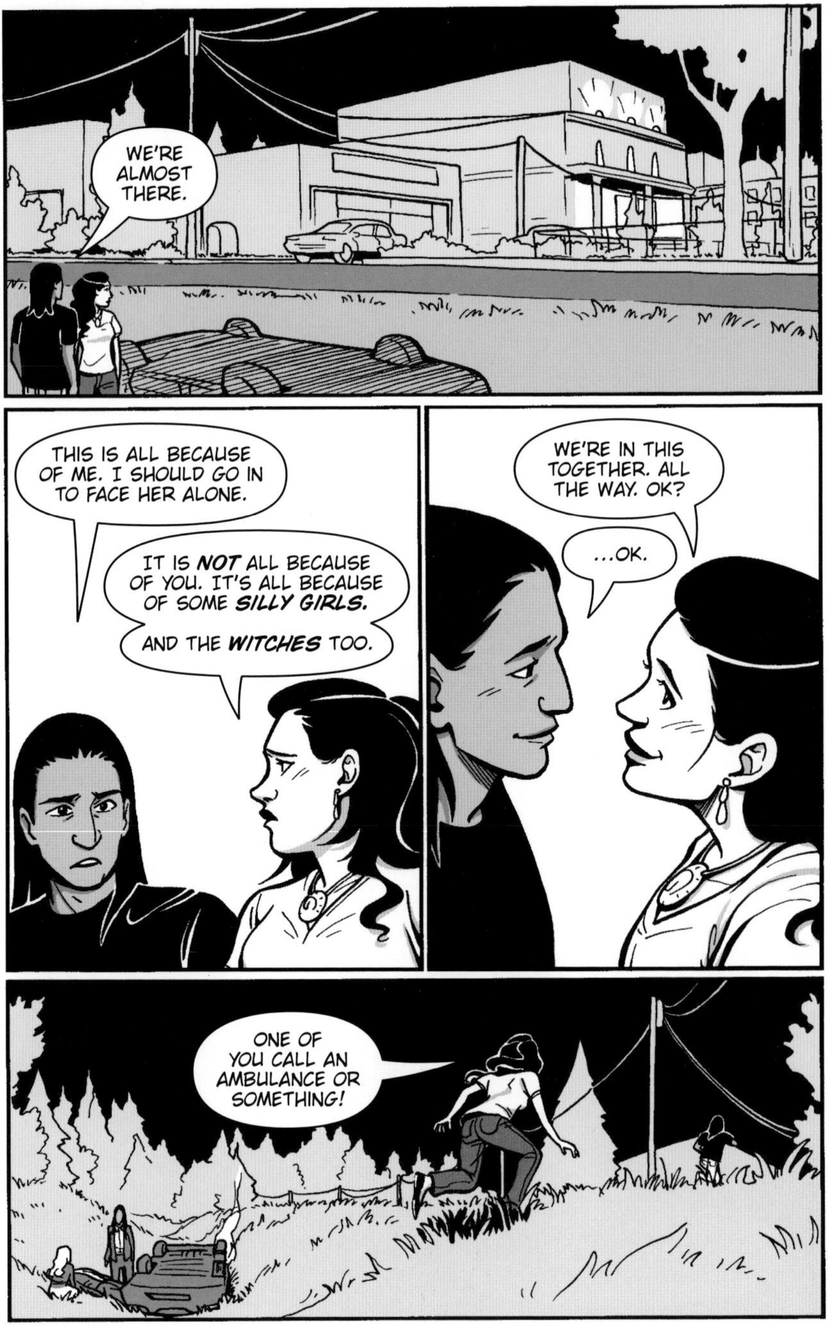
WE'RE ALMOST THERE.
THIS IS ALL BECAUSE OF ME. I SHOULD GO IN TO FACE HER ALONE.
IT IS NOT ALL BECAUSE OF YOU. IT'S ALL BECAUSE OF SOME SILLY GIRLS.
AND THE WITCHES TOO.
WE'RE IN THIS TOGETHER. ALL THE WAY. OK?
...OK.
ONE OF YOU CALL AN AMBULANCE OR SOMETHING!

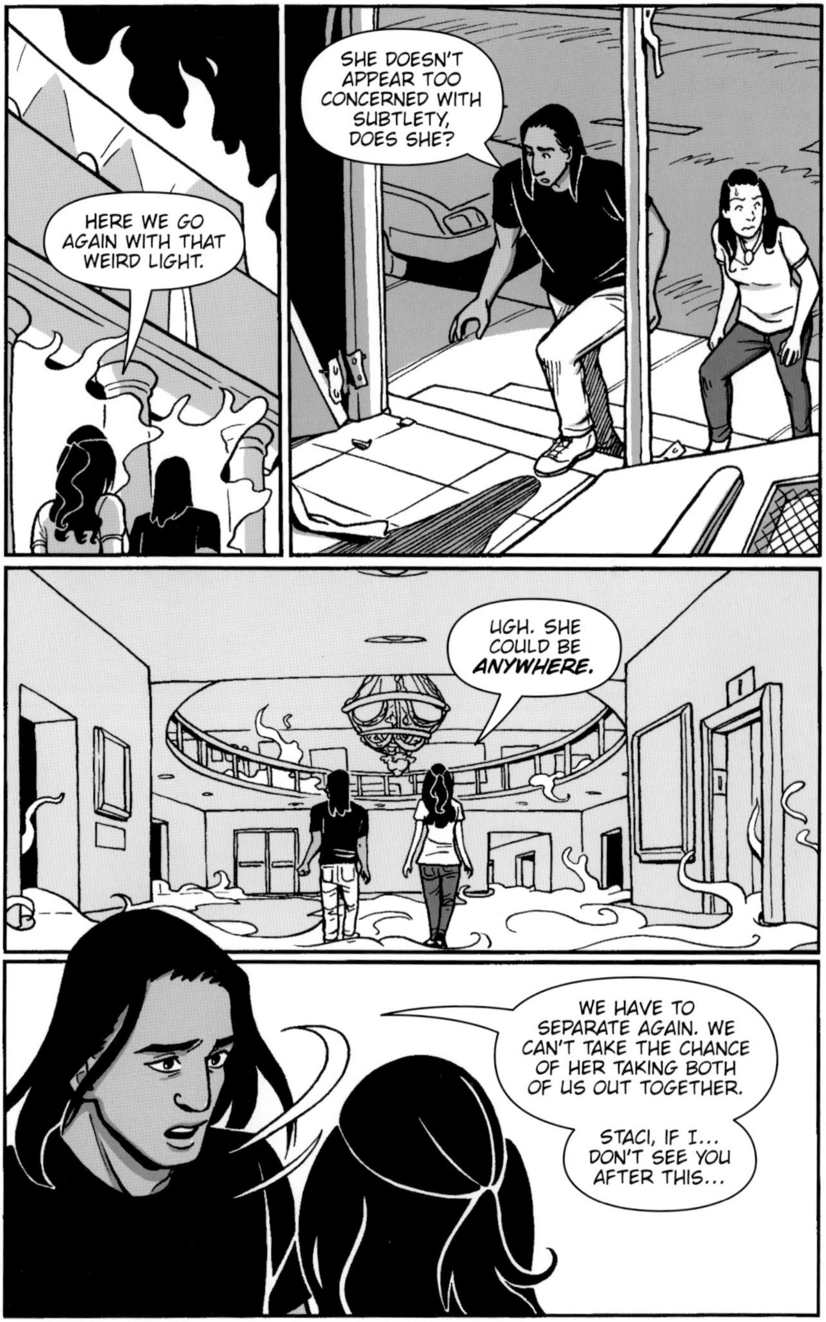
HERE WE GO AGAIN WITH THAT WEIRD LIGHT.
SHE DOESN'T APPEAR TOO CONCERNED WITH SUBTLETY, DOES SHE?
UGH. SHE COULD BE *ANYWHERE.*
WE HAVE TO SEPARATE AGAIN. WE CAN'T TAKE THE CHANCE OF HER TAKING BOTH OF US OUT TOGETHER.
STACI, IF I... DON'T SEE YOU AFTER THIS...

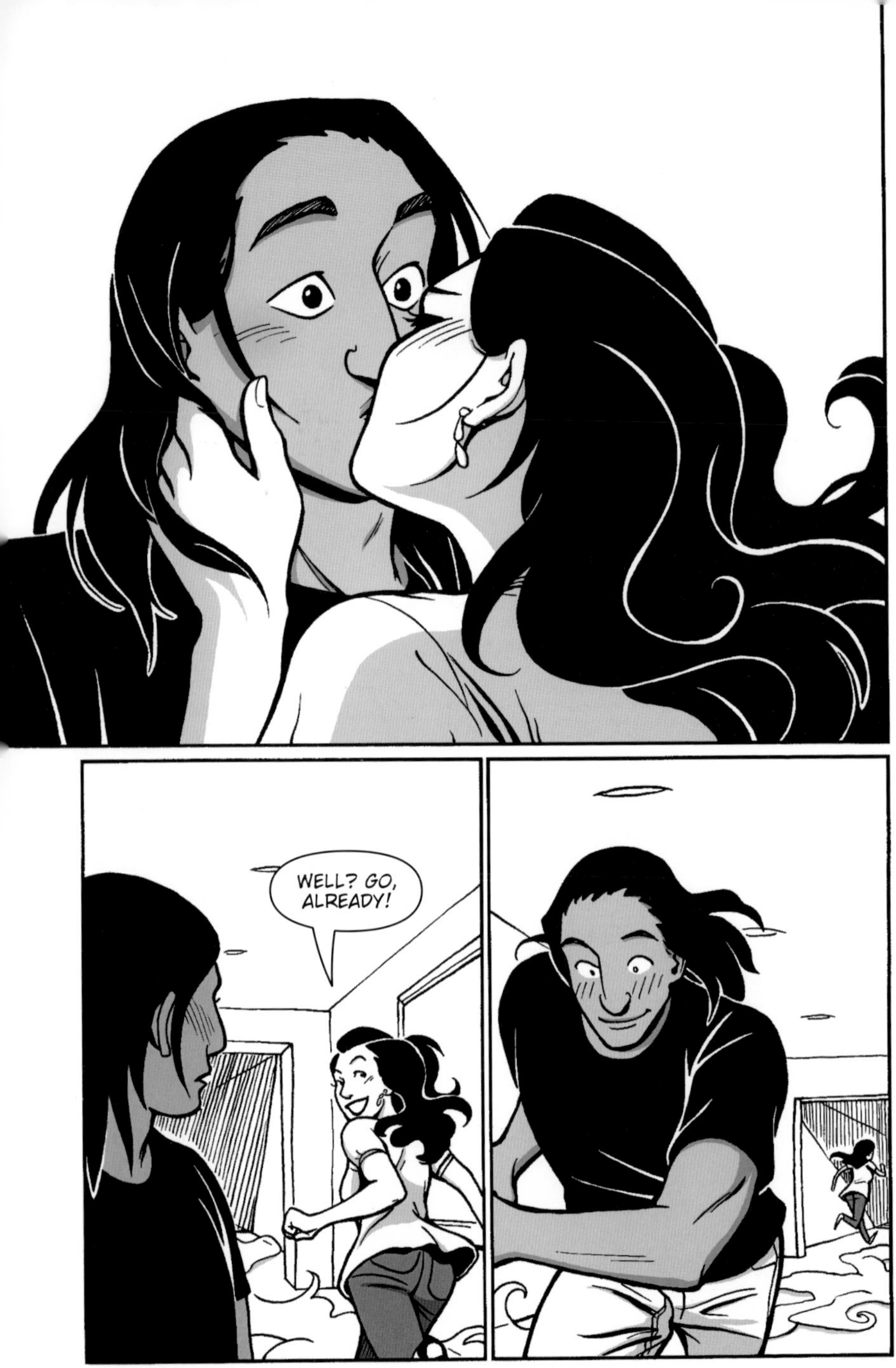
WELL? GO,
ALREADY!

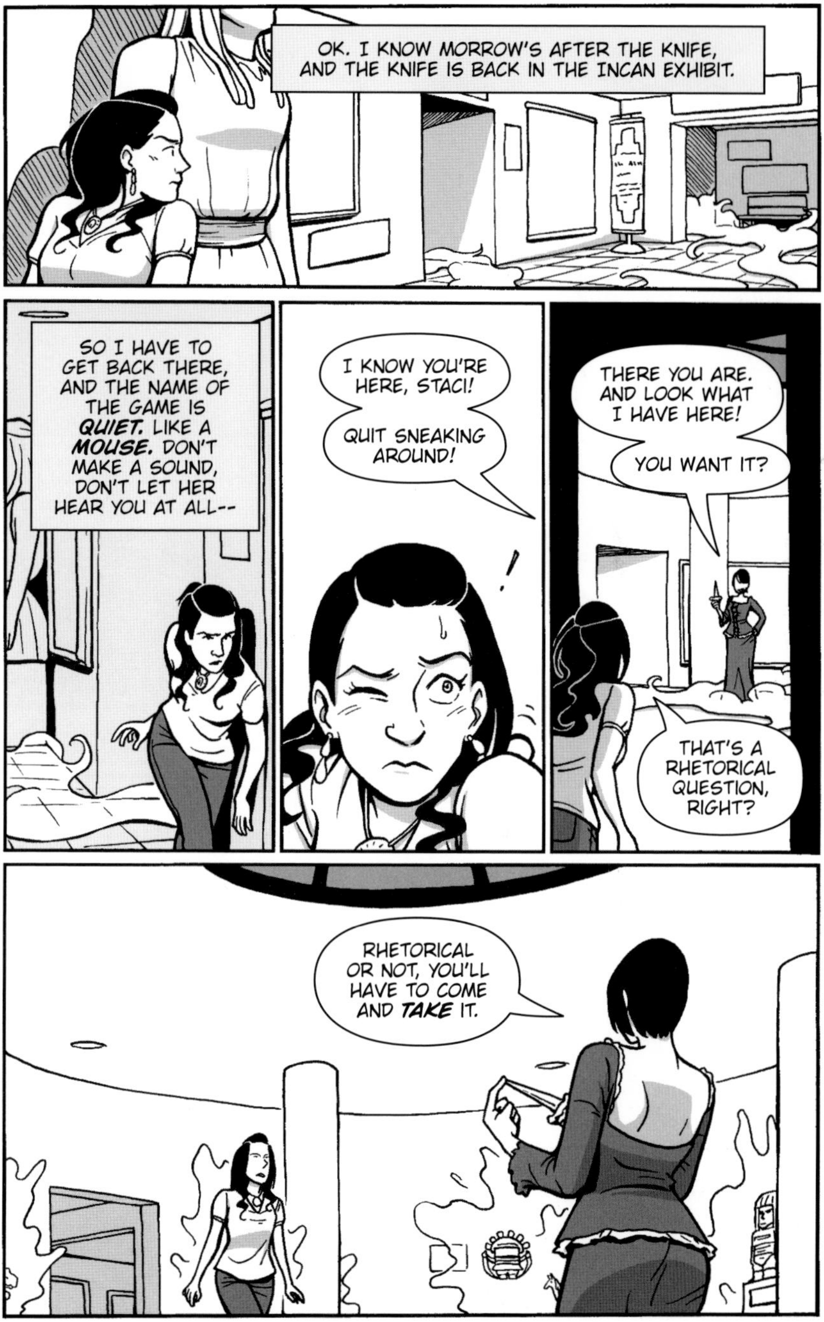
OK. I KNOW MORROW'S AFTER THE KNIFE, AND THE KNIFE IS BACK IN THE INCAN EXHIBIT.
SO I HAVE TO GET BACK THERE, AND THE NAME OF THE GAME IS **QUIET.** LIKE A **MOUSE.** DON'T MAKE A SOUND, DON'T LET HER HEAR YOU AT ALL--
I KNOW YOU'RE HERE, STACI!
QUIT SNEAKING AROUND!
!
THERE YOU ARE. AND LOOK WHAT I HAVE HERE!
YOU WANT IT?
THAT'S A RHETORICAL QUESTION, RIGHT?
RHETORICAL OR NOT, YOU'LL HAVE TO COME AND **TAKE** IT.

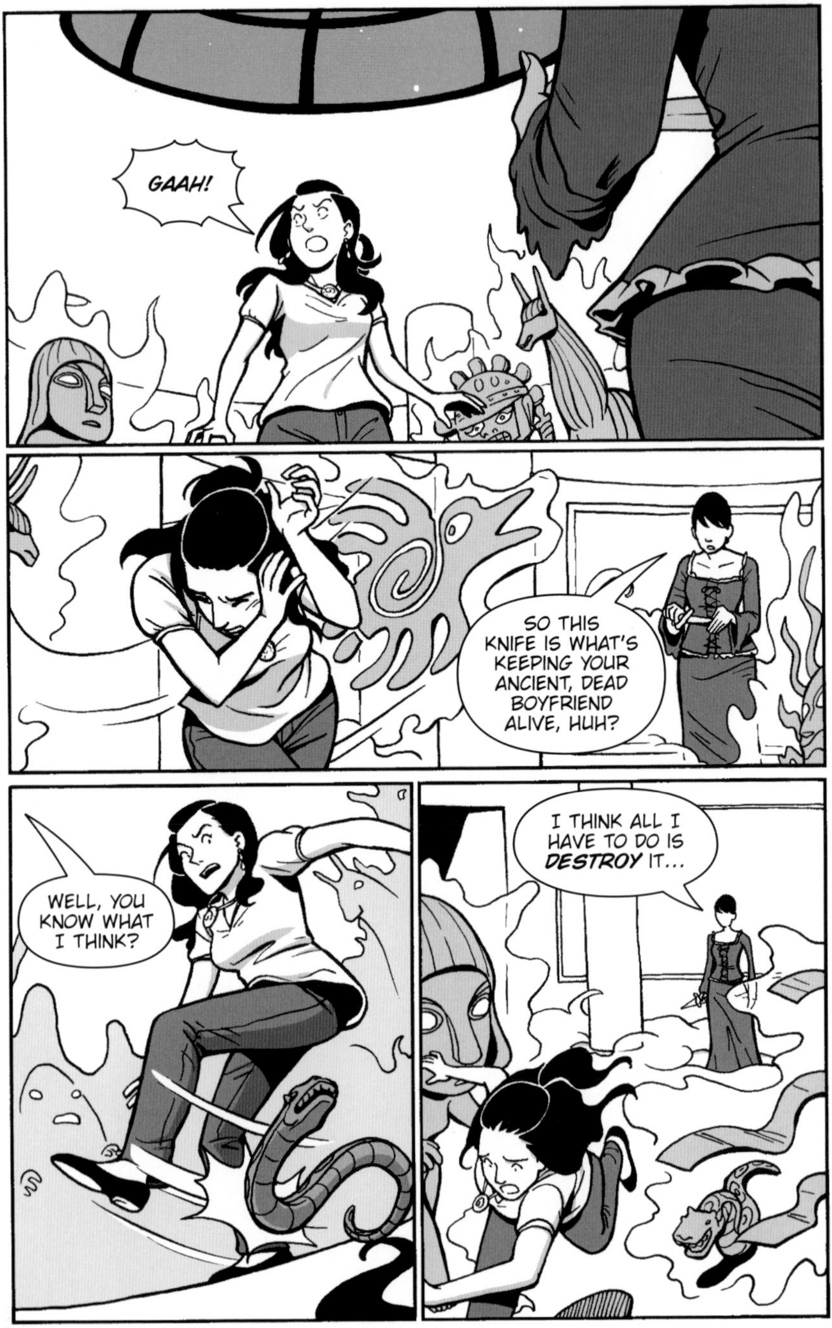
GAAH!
SO THIS KNIFE IS WHAT'S KEEPING YOUR ANCIENT, DEAD BOYFRIEND ALIVE, HUH?
WELL, YOU KNOW WHAT I THINK?
I THINK ALL I HAVE TO DO IS *DESTROY* IT...

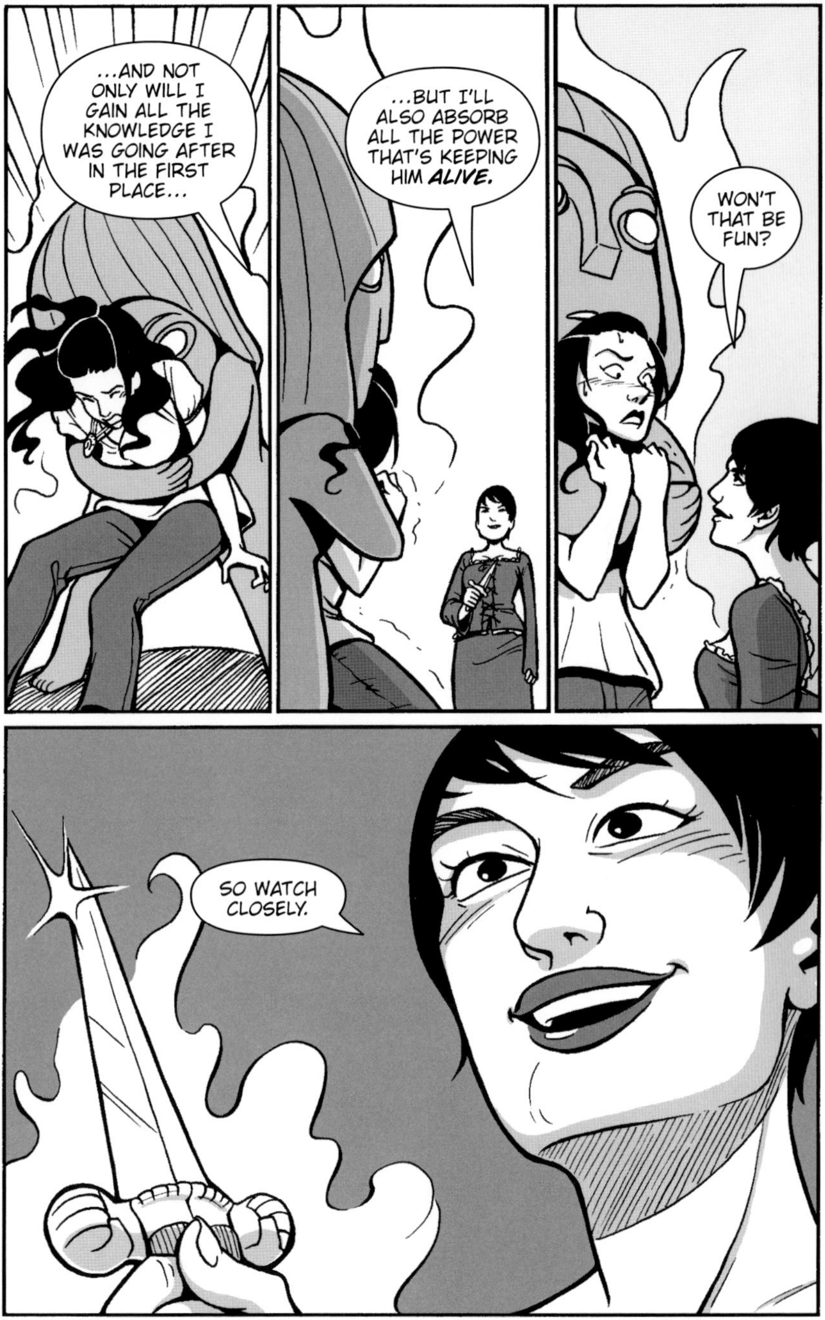
...AND NOT ONLY WILL I GAIN ALL THE KNOWLEDGE I WAS GOING AFTER IN THE FIRST PLACE...
...BUT I'LL ALSO ABSORB ALL THE POWER THAT'S KEEPING HIM ALIVE.
WON'T THAT BE FUN?
SO WATCH CLOSELY.

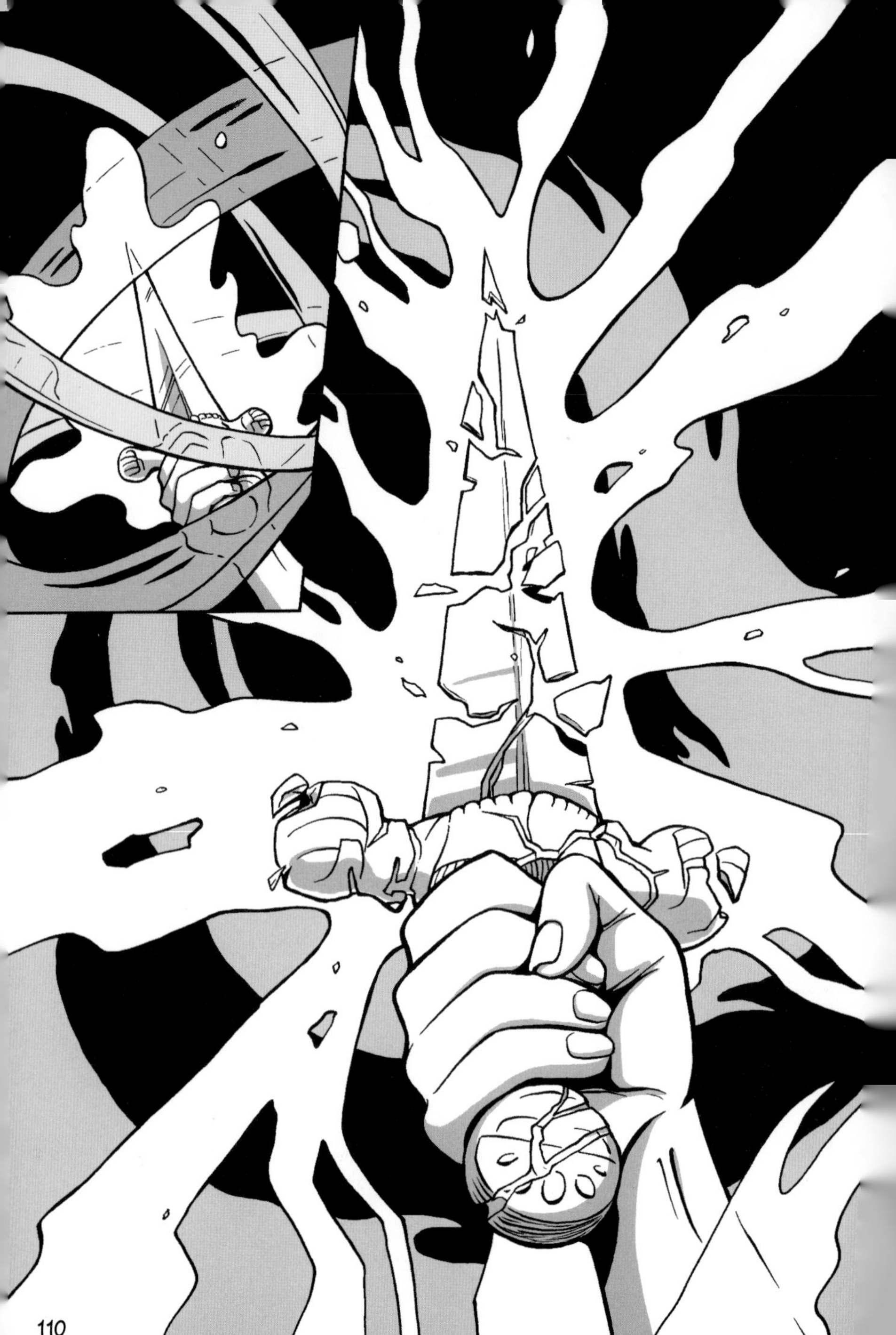

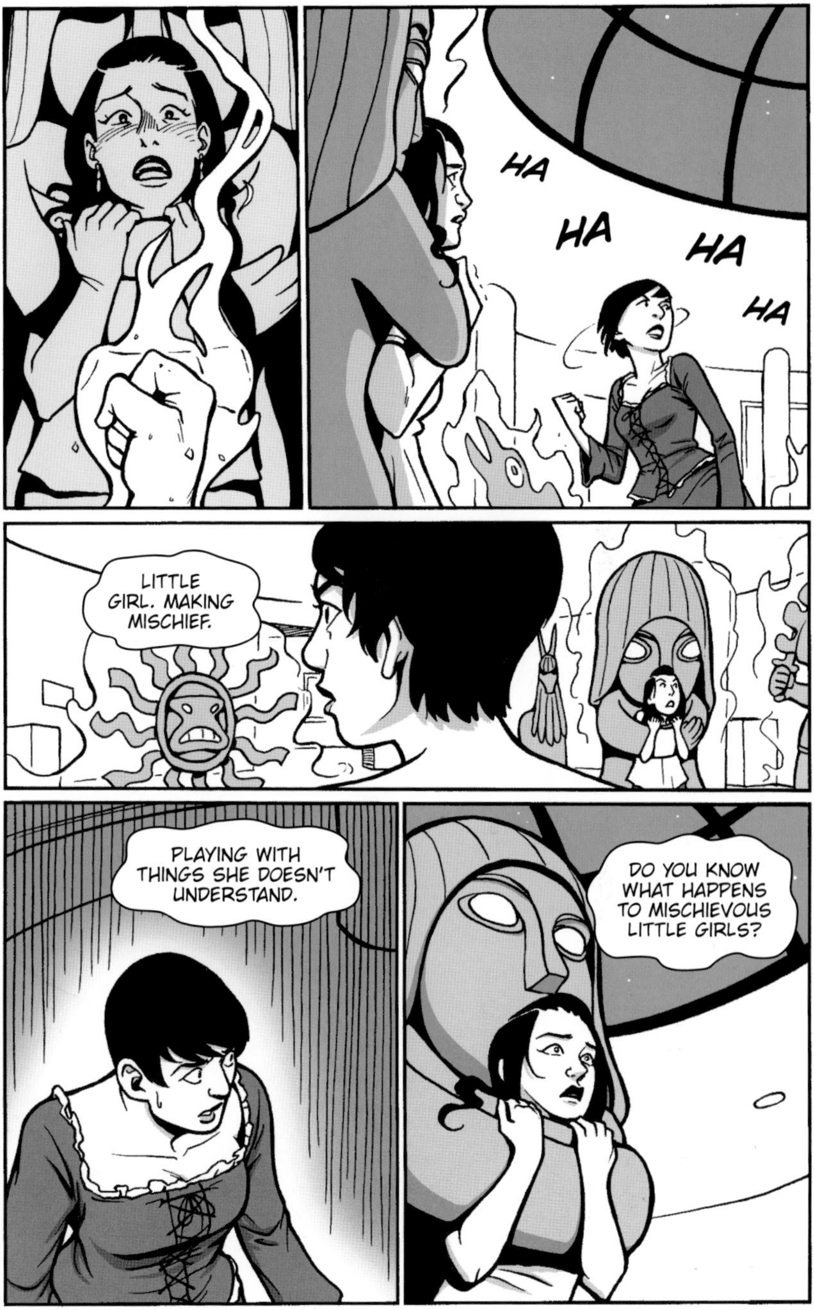
HA
HA
HA
HA
LITTLE GIRL. MAKING MISCHIEF.
PLAYING WITH THINGS SHE DOESN'T UNDERSTAND.
DO YOU KNOW WHAT HAPPENS TO MISCHIEVOUS LITTLE GIRLS?

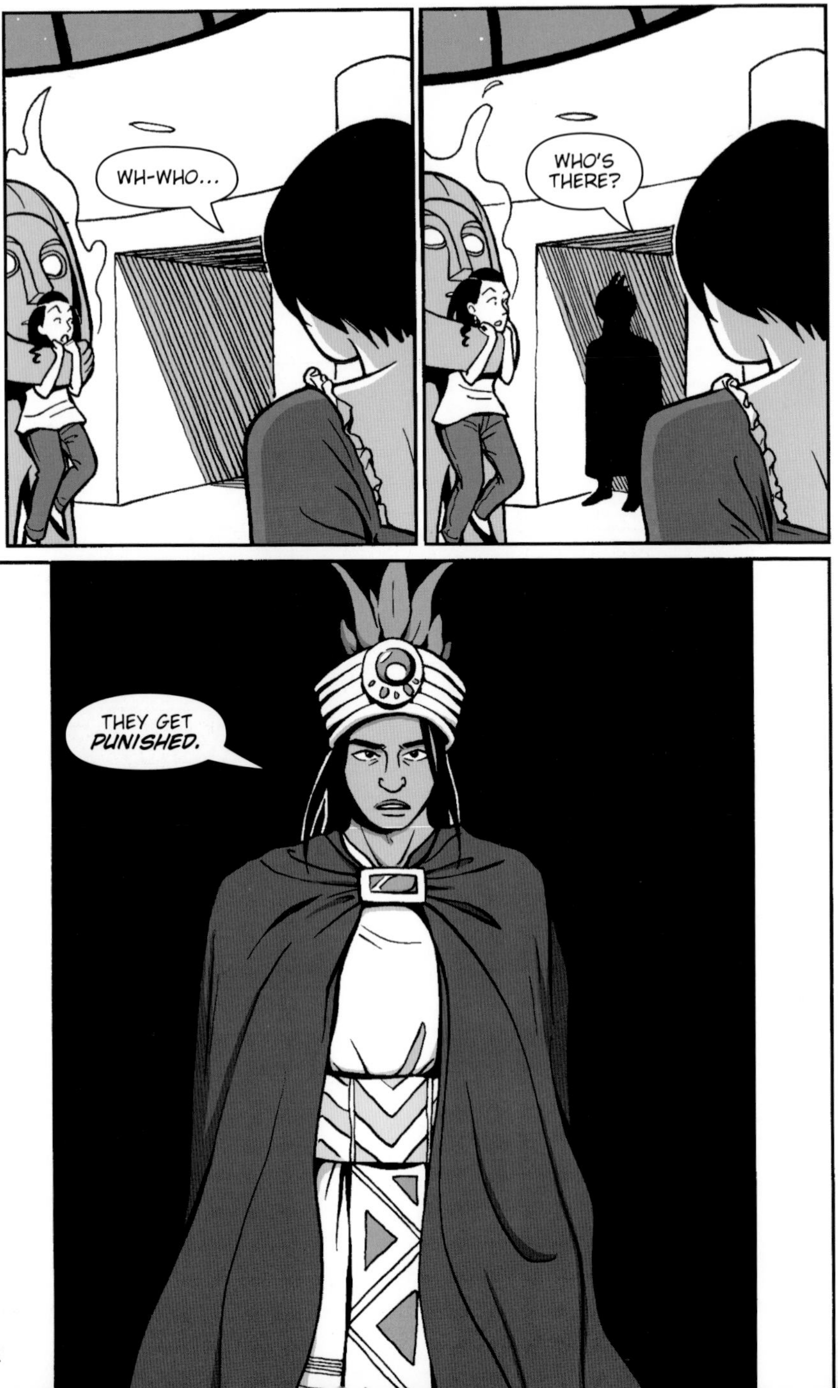
WH-WHO...
WHO'S THERE?
THEY GET PUNISHED.

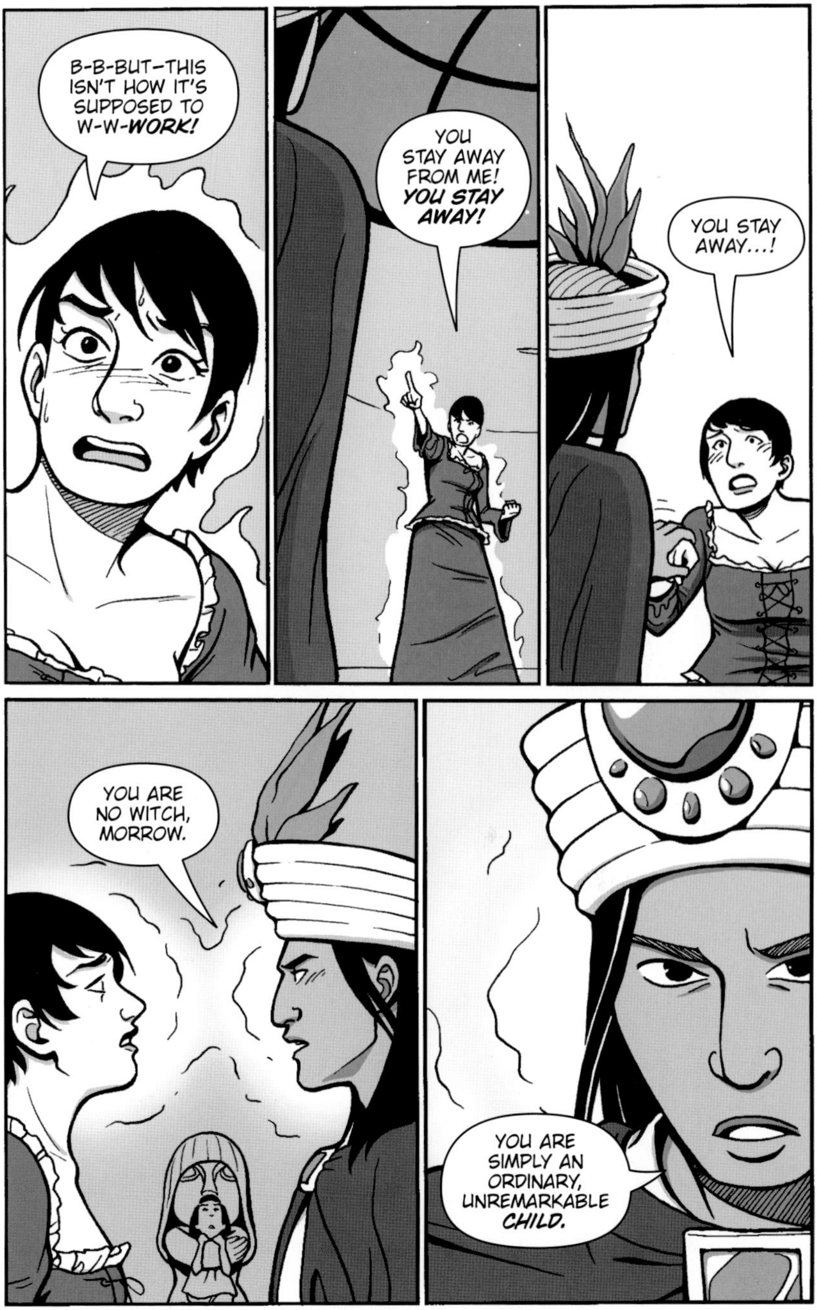
B-B-BUT—THIS ISN'T HOW IT'S SUPPOSED TO W-W-**WORK!**
YOU STAY AWAY FROM ME! ***YOU STAY AWAY!***
YOU STAY AWAY...!
YOU ARE NO WITCH, MORROW.
YOU ARE SIMPLY AN ORDINARY, UNREMARKABLE ***CHILD.***

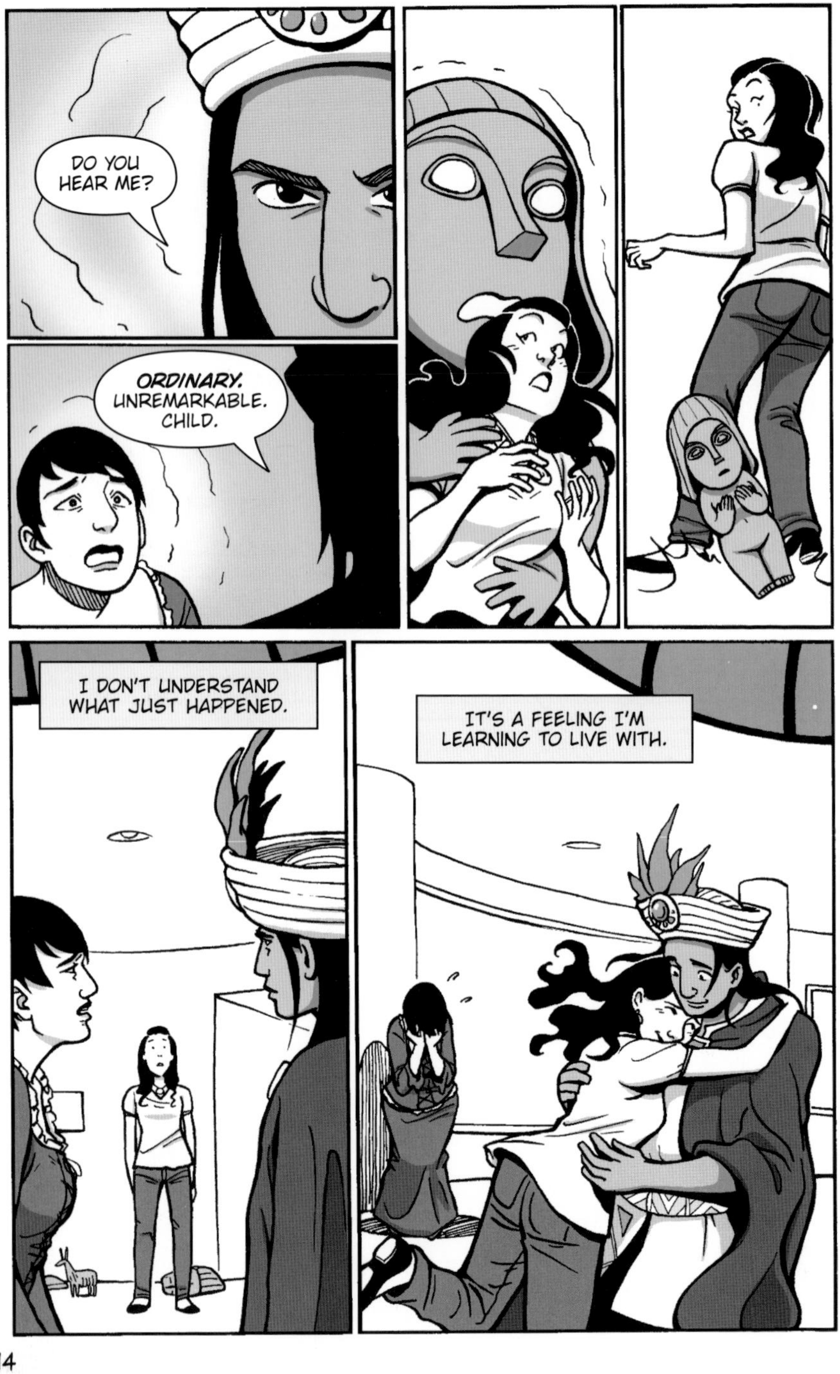
DO YOU HEAR ME?
ORDINARY. UNREMARKABLE. CHILD.
I DON'T UNDERSTAND WHAT JUST HAPPENED.
IT'S A FEELING I'M LEARNING TO LIVE WITH.

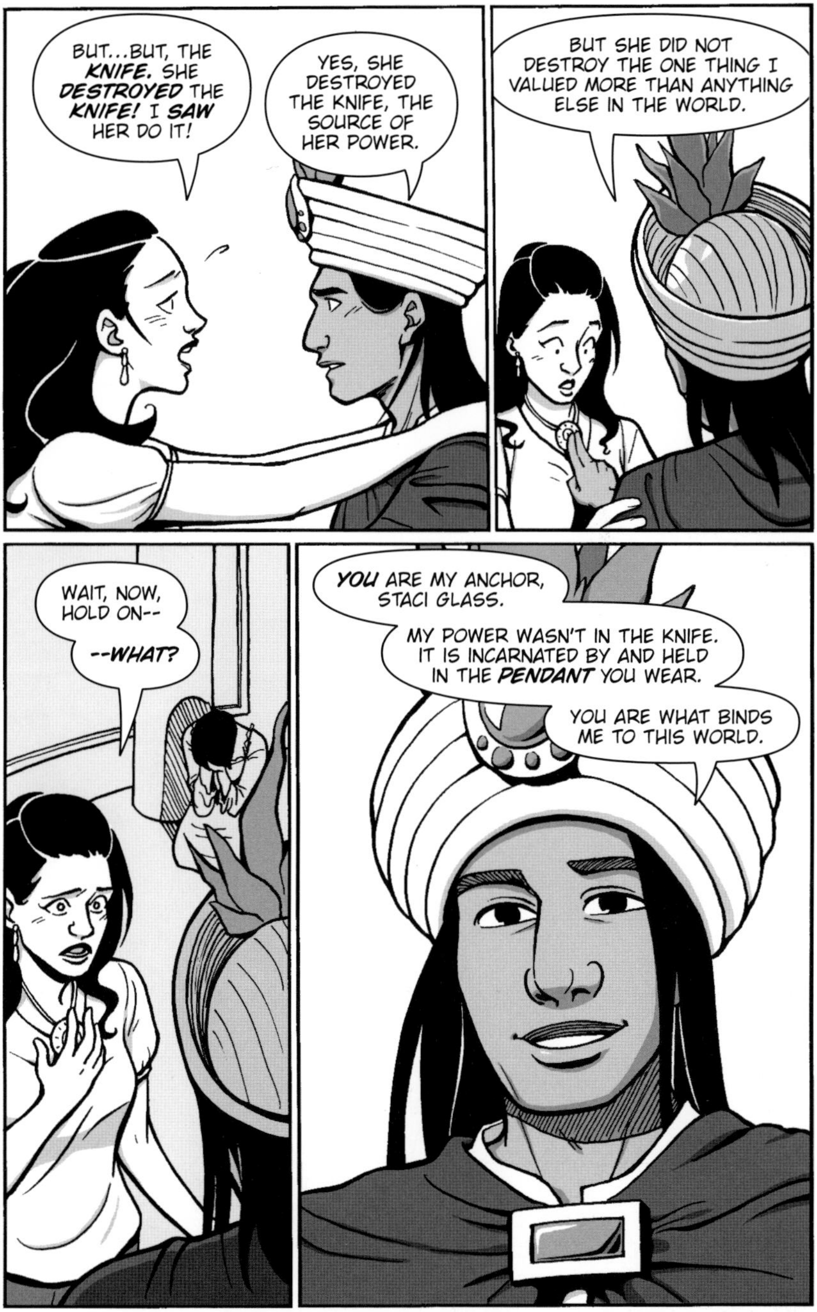

BUT...BUT, THE KNIFE. SHE DESTROYED THE KNIFE! I SAW HER DO IT!
YES, SHE DESTROYED THE KNIFE, THE SOURCE OF HER POWER.
BUT SHE DID NOT DESTROY THE ONE THING I VALUED MORE THAN ANYTHING ELSE IN THE WORLD.
WAIT, NOW, HOLD ON--
--WHAT?
YOU ARE MY ANCHOR, STACI GLASS.
MY POWER WASN'T IN THE KNIFE. IT IS INCARNATED BY AND HELD IN THE PENDANT YOU WEAR.
YOU ARE WHAT BINDS ME TO THIS WORLD.

OH, WOW.

BUT...I DON'T...I MEAN, IF YOU...

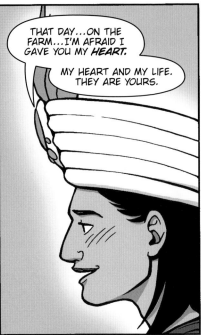

THAT DAY...ON THE FARM...I'M AFRAID I GAVE YOU MY *HEART*.

MY HEART AND MY LIFE. THEY ARE YOURS.

THIS WHOLE THING...MY WHOLE *LIFE*... I'VE ALWAYS HAD TROUBLE FIGURING OUT WHO TO BE *LOYAL* TO.

AND NOW THAT I'M LITERALLY HOLDING SOMEONE'S *LIFE* IN MY HANDS...

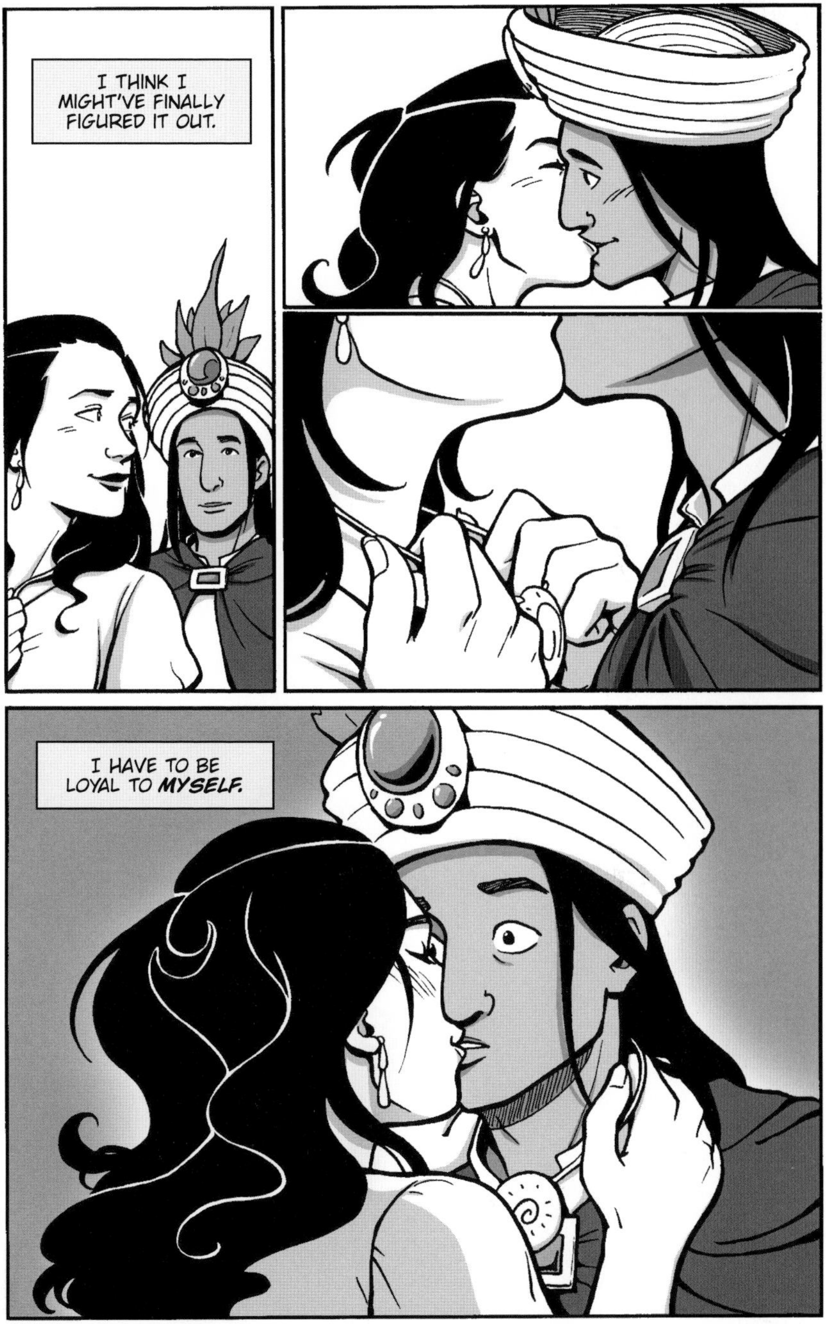
I THINK I MIGHT'VE FINALLY FIGURED IT OUT.
I HAVE TO BE LOYAL TO ***MYSELF.***

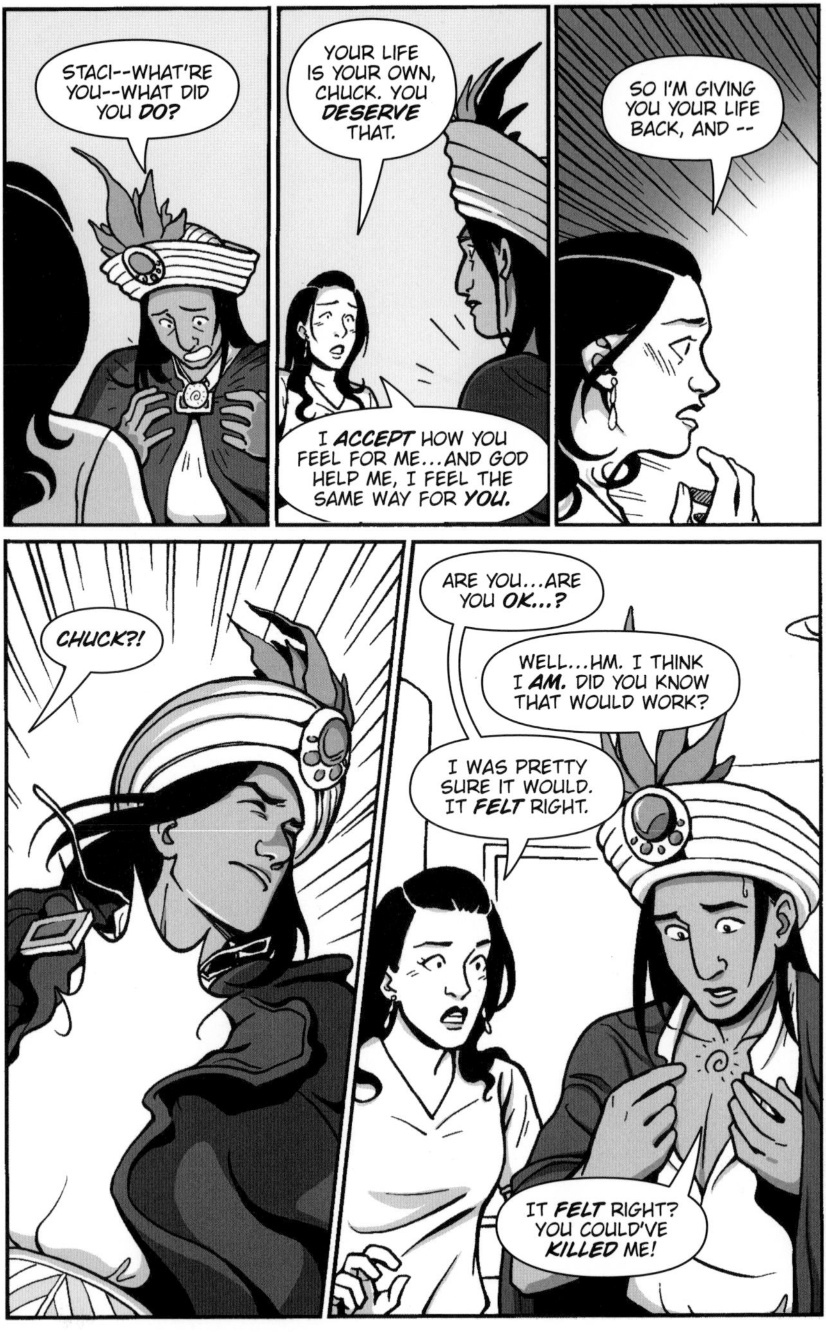
STACI--WHAT'RE YOU--WHAT DID YOU **DO?**
YOUR LIFE IS YOUR OWN, CHUCK. YOU **DESERVE** THAT.
I **ACCEPT** HOW YOU FEEL FOR ME...AND GOD HELP ME, I FEEL THE SAME WAY FOR **YOU.**
SO I'M GIVING YOU YOUR LIFE BACK, AND --
CHUCK?!
ARE YOU...ARE YOU **OK...?**
WELL...HM. I THINK I **AM.** DID YOU KNOW THAT WOULD WORK?
I WAS PRETTY SURE IT WOULD. IT **FELT** RIGHT.
IT **FELT** RIGHT? YOU COULD'VE **KILLED** ME!

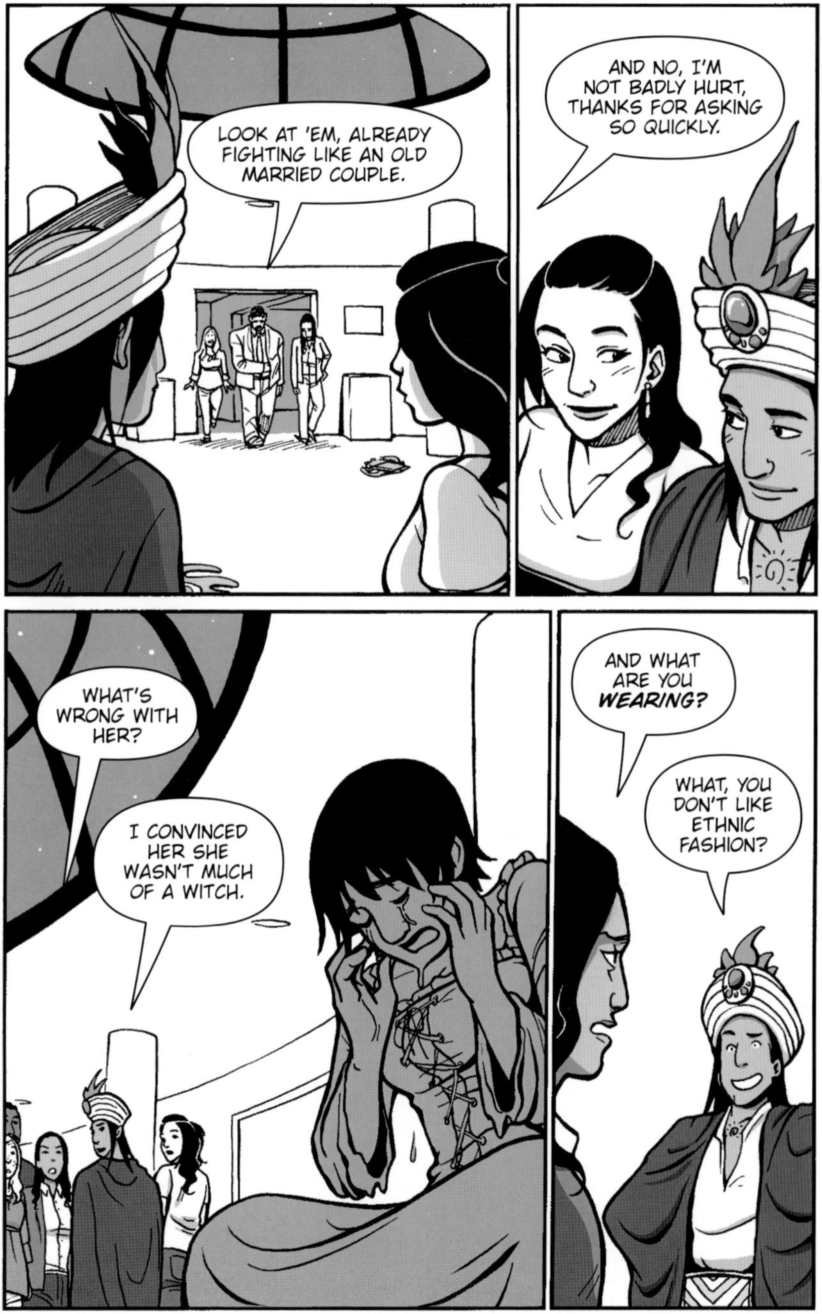
LOOK AT 'EM, ALREADY FIGHTING LIKE AN OLD MARRIED COUPLE.
AND NO, I'M NOT BADLY HURT, THANKS FOR ASKING SO QUICKLY.
WHAT'S WRONG WITH HER?
I CONVINCED HER SHE WASN'T MUCH OF A WITCH.
AND WHAT ARE YOU *WEARING?*
WHAT, YOU DON'T LIKE ETHNIC FASHION?

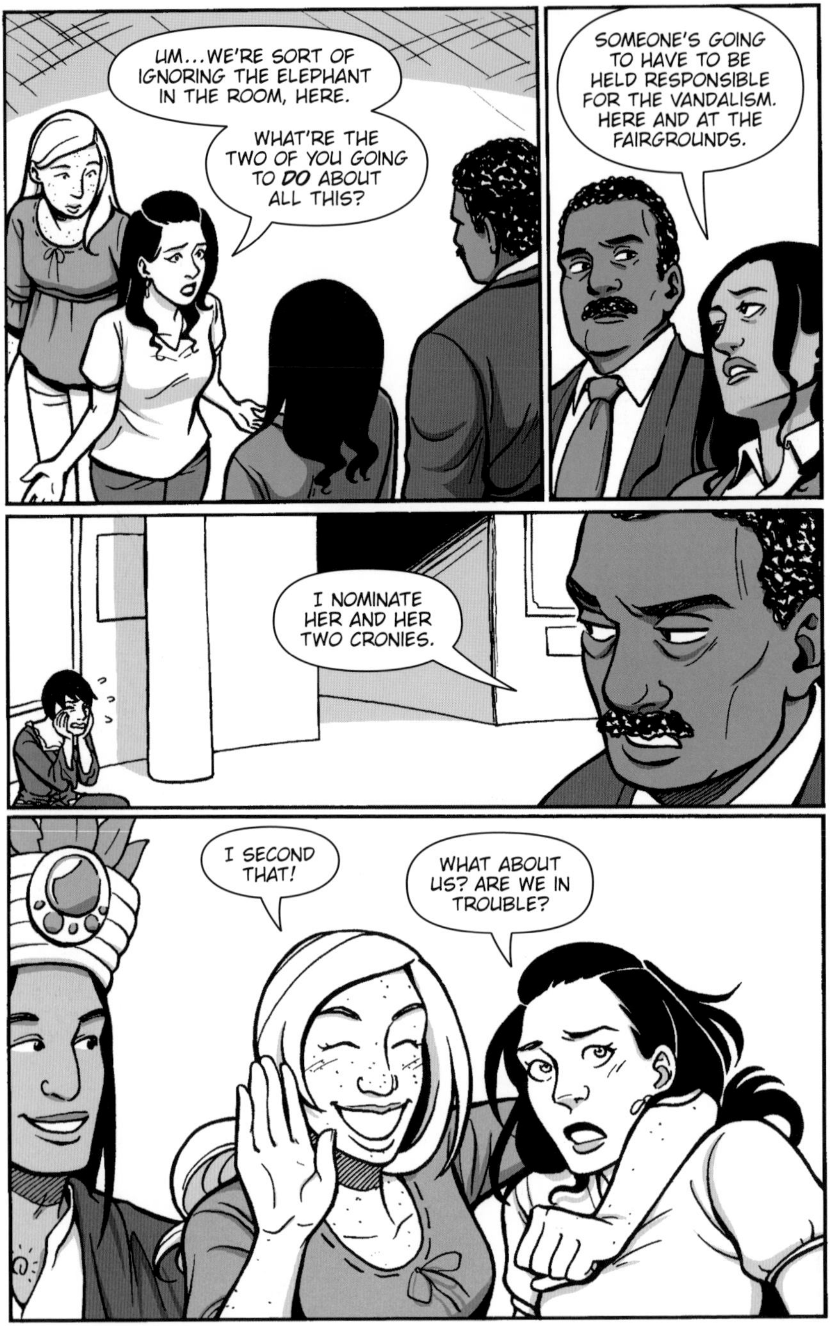
UM...WE'RE SORT OF IGNORING THE ELEPHANT IN THE ROOM, HERE.
WHAT'RE THE TWO OF YOU GOING TO **DO** ABOUT ALL THIS?
SOMEONE'S GOING TO HAVE TO BE HELD RESPONSIBLE FOR THE VANDALISM. HERE AND AT THE FAIRGROUNDS.
I NOMINATE HER AND HER TWO CRONIES.
I SECOND THAT!
WHAT ABOUT US? ARE WE IN TROUBLE?

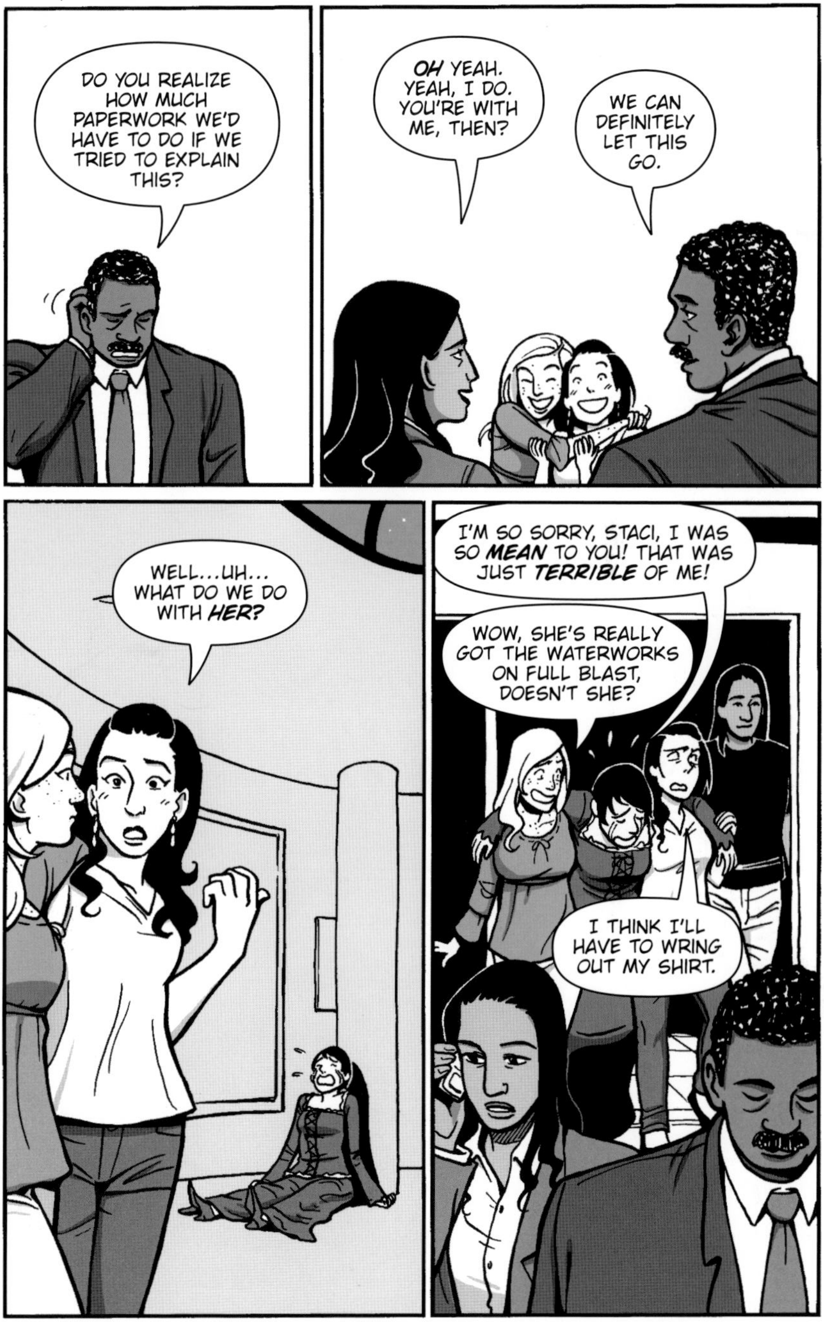
DO YOU REALIZE HOW MUCH PAPERWORK WE'D HAVE TO DO IF WE TRIED TO EXPLAIN THIS?
OH YEAH. YEAH, I DO. YOU'RE WITH ME, THEN?
WE CAN DEFINITELY LET THIS GO.
WELL...UH... WHAT DO WE DO WITH HER?
I'M SO SORRY, STACI, I WAS SO MEAN TO YOU! THAT WAS JUST TERRIBLE OF ME!
WOW, SHE'S REALLY GOT THE WATERWORKS ON FULL BLAST, DOESN'T SHE?
I THINK I'LL HAVE TO WRING OUT MY SHIRT.

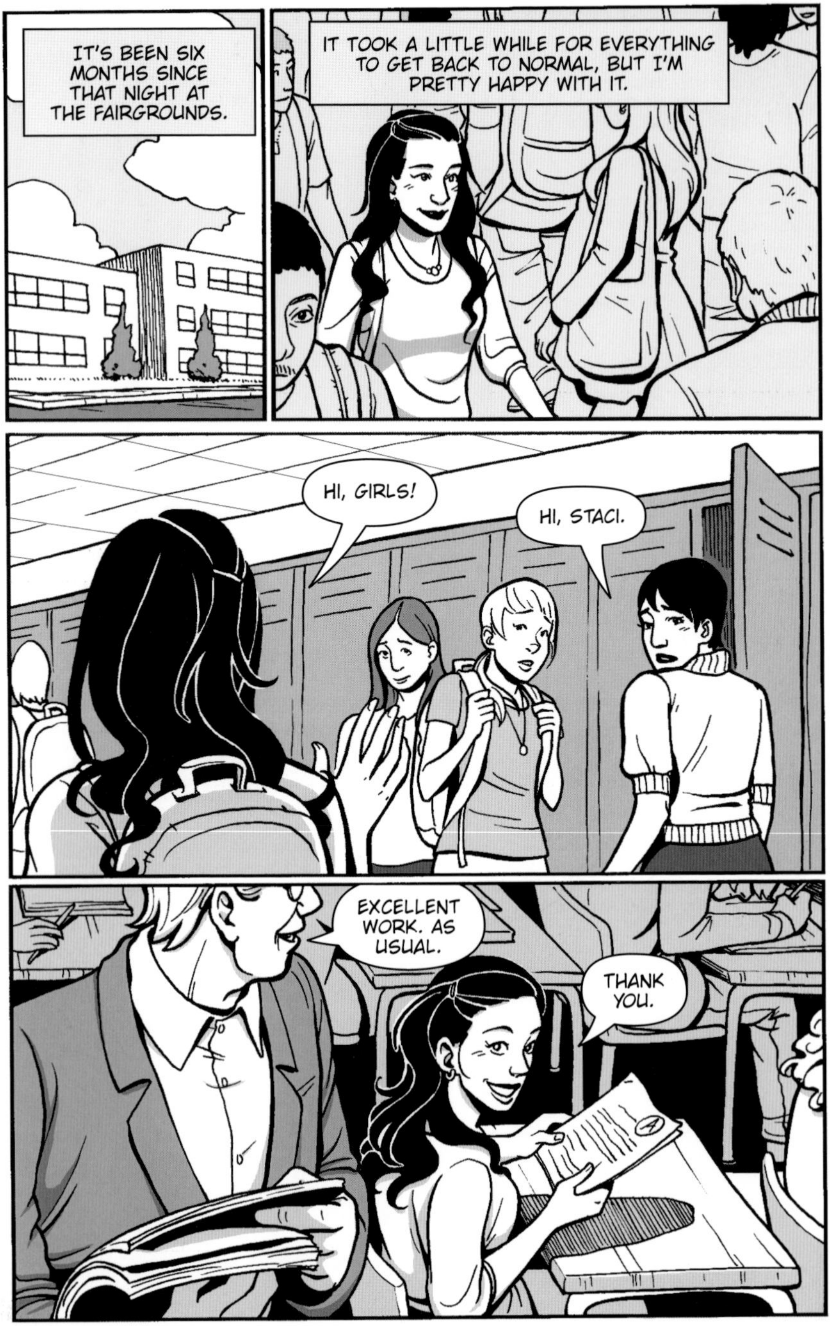
IT'S BEEN SIX MONTHS SINCE THAT NIGHT AT THE FAIRGROUNDS.
IT TOOK A LITTLE WHILE FOR EVERYTHING TO GET BACK TO NORMAL, BUT I'M PRETTY HAPPY WITH IT.
HI, GIRLS!
HI, STACI.
EXCELLENT WORK. AS USUAL.
THANK YOU.

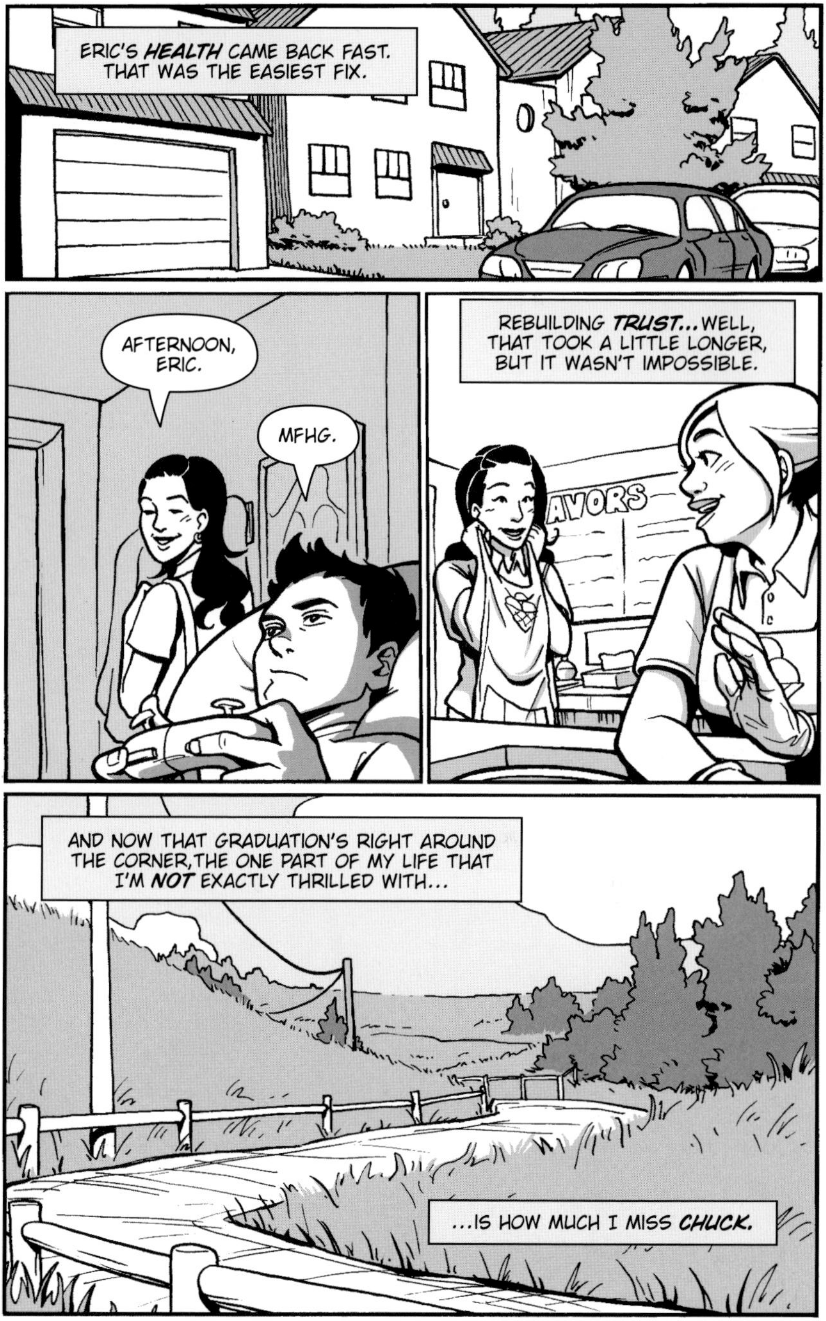
ERIC'S **HEALTH** CAME BACK FAST. THAT WAS THE EASIEST FIX.
AFTERNOON, ERIC.
MFHG.
REBUILDING **TRUST...** WELL, THAT TOOK A LITTLE LONGER, BUT IT WASN'T IMPOSSIBLE.
AVORS
AND NOW THAT GRADUATION'S RIGHT AROUND THE CORNER, THE ONE PART OF MY LIFE THAT I'M **NOT** EXACTLY THRILLED WITH...
...IS HOW MUCH I MISS **CHUCK.**

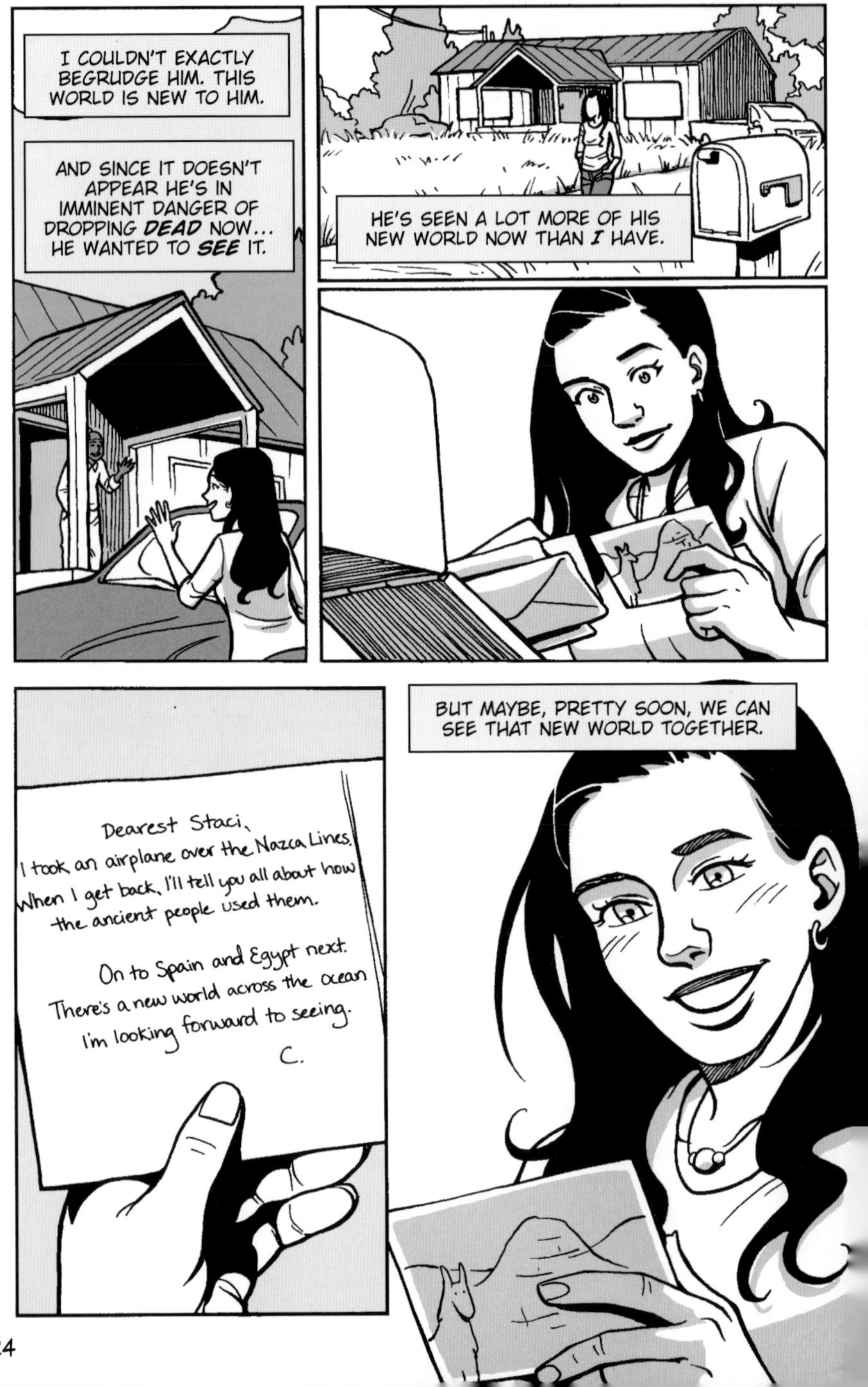

I COULDN'T EXACTLY BEGRUDGE HIM. THIS WORLD IS NEW TO HIM.
AND SINCE IT DOESN'T APPEAR HE'S IN IMMINENT DANGER OF DROPPING DEAD NOW... HE WANTED TO SEE IT.
HE'S SEEN A LOT MORE OF HIS NEW WORLD NOW THAN I HAVE.
Dearest Staci,
I took an airplane over the Nazca Lines.
When I get back, I'll tell you all about how the ancient people used them.
On to Spain and Egypt next.
There's a new world across the ocean I'm looking forward to seeing.
C.
BUT MAYBE, PRETTY SOON, WE CAN SEE THAT NEW WORLD TOGETHER.

Q & A WITH
PACHACUTEC (AKA CHUCK)

You're from Peru?
I thought mummies came from Egypt!

Most people think that, but since I began my travels, I've learned that mummification has been practiced all over the world. Ancient Egyptians started preserving their dead 5,000 years ago, but they weren't alone. The world's oldest mummies came from my ancient ancestors, the Chinchorros, who lived in southern Peru 7,000 years ago. The Chinchorros did not reserve mummification for the privileged. Everyone, young or old, rich or poor, was mummified. Mummies have also been discovered in Siberia, China, Italy, Australia, Mexico, and many other places. Perhaps the only place mummification hasn't been practiced is Antarctica—which is unfortunate, because preserving the dead would be very simple there!

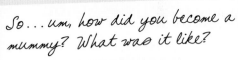

So . . . um, how did you become a mummy? What was it like?

There are two types of mummies: those that are intentionally preserved, like the Egyptian ones you are probably familiar with, and those that were naturally created in environments that are very cold, very dry, or have low oxygen content.

125

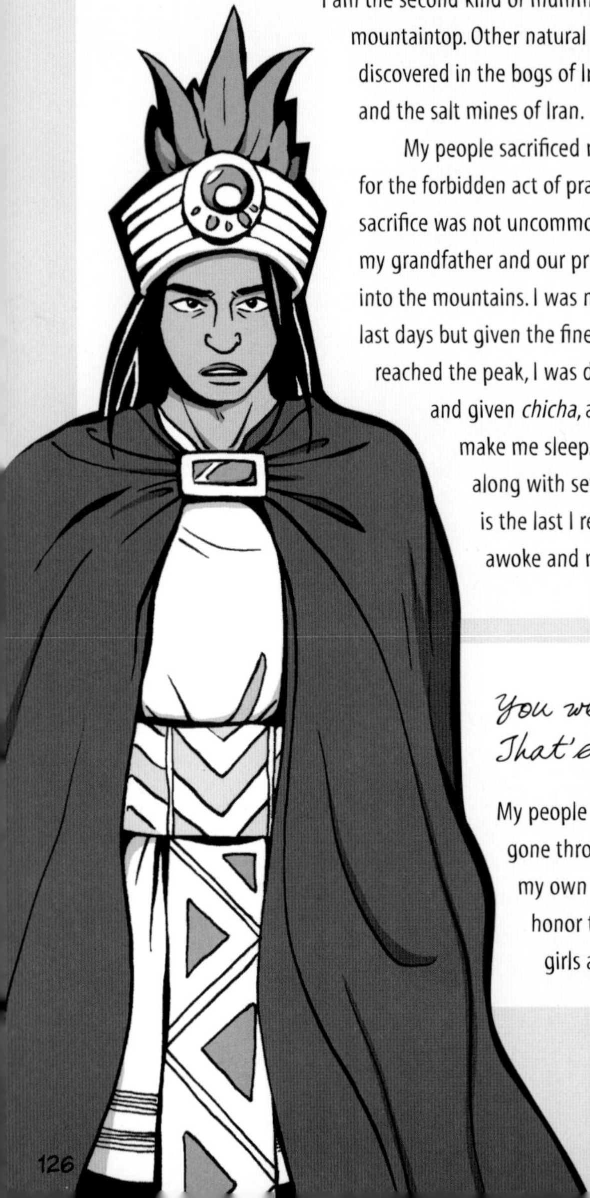

I am the second kind of mummy. I met my end on a frozen mountaintop. Other natural mummies have been discovered in the bogs of Ireland, the deserts of China, and the salt mines of Iran.

My people sacrificed me to the gods, punishment for the forbidden act of practicing magic. Human sacrifice was not uncommon for the Incas. Along with my grandfather and our priests, I made the long trek into the mountains. I was not treated cruelly in those last days but given the finest food to eat. When we reached the peak, I was dressed in my royal clothes and given *chicha*, a fermented corn drink, to make me sleep. I was lowered into a pit along with several precious items. This is the last I remember before the day I awoke and met Staci Glass.

You were sacrificed? That's so sad.

My people did not think so . . . having gone through the experience, I have my own opinion. It was considered an honor to be given to the gods. Young girls and boys were selected for their beauty and purity—only a prefect specimen would honor the gods. The chosen girls lived a life of comfort and ease in a special temple. They were even escorted to the capital to meet the emperor. Unwilling parents could simply arrange a marriage for their child at an early age, making him or her ineligible for sacrifice.

Were you really a prince?

I was a prince and a warrior, but those honors were taken from me when I used my powers in the heat of battle. An invading army had attacked the capital—I fought while my brother and father fled to the mountains. The day would have been lost had I not used my magic. I transformed the nearby stones into mighty warriors who fended off the intruders. It was my highest moment and perhaps my lowest. My family was displeased, so they made a gift of me to the gods and secretly crowned my brother in my place.

Look in your history book. You'll find the story there (but not the whole story, of course).

ABOUT THE AUTHOR
AND THE ARTIST

Comic book author and video game writer DAN JOLLEY has created work for Marvel, DC, Dark Horse, and TokyoPop and for game developers including Activision and Ubisoft. He is also the author of several Graphic Myths and Legends titles including *Odysseus: Escaping Poseidon's Curse*, *Pigling: A Cinderella Story*, and *The Hero Twins: Against the Lords of Death*. Among his Twisted Journeys® titles are *Vampire Hunt*, *Escape from Pyramid X*, and *Agent Mongoose and the Hypno-Beam Scheme*. He wrote *My Boyfriend Bites*, the third book in the My Boyfriend is a Monster series, and also scripts story lines and dialogue for video games such as *Transformers: War for Cybertron* and *Prototype 2*. He lives in Georgia with his wife Tracy and four cats.

NATALIE "TALLY" NOURIGAT is a sequential artist living in Portland, Oregon. She is a member of Periscope Studio and has the pleasure of making comics for a living. Her other comic work includes *Between Gears* (from Image Comics) and *A Boy and a Girl* (from Oni Press).